They descended upon her, pinning her flailing arms back against the wheel so she couldn't resist. She screamed like an animal, thrashing wildly, determined to break free. But it was to no avail.

Weakened to the point of pain, she felt herself sinking into darkness, so at first the imperceptible shift didn't register. Then she felt it. The men's slavering madness had turned to alert respect.

They moved from her like a parting sea as a figure stepped through the smoke. Gabrielle's heart stopped. Standing before her, with a fierce scowl on his face, was the one man who could tame these brutes—the pirate lord Rodrigo.

*"Ella â minga,"* he snarled. **She's mine.**

*Books by Katherine O'Neal*

MASTER OF PARADISE

THE LAST HIGHWAYMAN

PRINCESS OF THIEVES

# Master
## of
# Paradise

# Katherine
# O'Neal

BANTAM BOOKS
New York   Toronto   London   Sydney   Auckland

Master of Paradise
A Bantam Book / December 1995

Maps by Ron Toelke.

ISBN 0-553-56956-2

Published simultaneously in the United States and Canada

Bantam Books are published by Bantam Books, a division of Bantam
Doubleday Dell Publishing Group, Inc. Its trademark, consisting of the
words "Bantam Books" and the portrayal of a rooster, is Registered in
U.S. Patent and Trademark Office and in other countries. Marca
Registrada. Bantam Books, 1540 Broadway, New York, New York 10036.

PRINTED IN THE UNITED STATES OF AMERICA

OPM    0  9  8  7  6  5  4  3  2  1

*For my own*

*Master*

*of*

*Paradise . . .*

*with everlasting devotion*

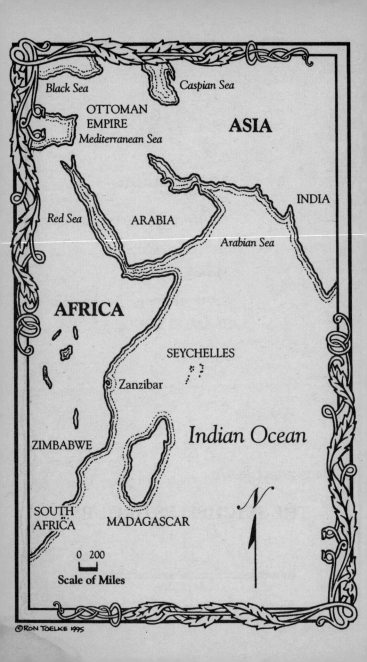

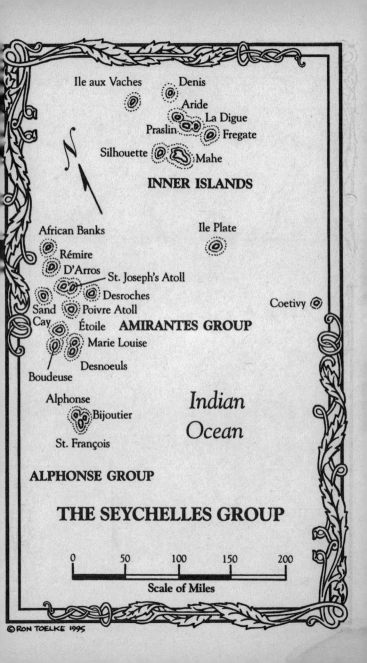

Ile aux Vaches · Denis

Aride
La Digue
Praslin ·· Fregate

Silhouette Mahe

**INNER ISLANDS**

N

African Banks

Ile Plate

Rémire

D'Arros
St. Joseph's Atoll
Desroches
Sand Poivre Atoll
Cay Étoile **AMIRANTES GROUP**

Coetivy

Marie Louise

Desnoeuls

Boudeuse

Alphonse
Bijoutier

St. François

*Indian*

*Ocean*

**ALPHONSE GROUP**

# THE SEYCHELLES GROUP

| 0 | 50 | 100 | 150 | 200 |

**Scale of Miles**

© RON TOELKE 1995

# Prologue

*Gabrielle raced along* the sprawling grounds of Westbury Grange, dressed in the starched black maid's gown with its pristine apron tied to her waist and the hated white cap upon her head. Behind her, she could hear the sounds of the party drifting out from doors opened to the summer night—music, laughter, the clink of fine crystal. She should be there, serving champagne to guests from a heavy silver tray, smiling vacantly at the gentlemen as their ladies inspected her with curiosity and disdain.

But she was free from all that now. As she sped along, the sense of liberty was delicious. In only moments, she would finally be with Rodrigo.

*Rodrigo!*

All evening, they'd carried out the charade, pretending they were nothing to each other. He'd stood there with his elbow resting coolly against the mantel, swirling his drink—a tall, golden Portuguese god with dark blond hair that occasionally rebelled and tumbled over his wide forehead. He hadn't glanced at her even once. Until the moment when he suddenly looked her way, giving her the signal—his lion's eyes smoldering with a brazenness that sucked the air from her lungs. Then he quietly slipped away.

She couldn't abandon her post for some time. The delay had been agony, knowing he was out there, waiting for her. It was the last time she would see him for perhaps as much as two years. He'd just graduated first in his class from Haileybury, the exclusive training academy of the British East India Company, and was shipping out the next day to India—his first assignment as an officer of the Company. This was his farewell celebration.

She remembered the first time she'd seen him. He'd been brought to Westbury Grange at the age of thirteen —a strange boy with dead eyes, snatched from his home in the Indian Ocean, the son of a notorious pirate who'd been hanged before his eyes. To be taken in by the duke in a grand gesture of magnanimity, educated in the finest schools, and molded into a perfect Company man. There was now little of that boy in his appearance. He looked very much the English gentleman, his features as classic as those of any aristocrat, with his handsome chiseled face, Roman nose, tapered jaw, and full, sensual mouth.

They'd been drawn to each other from the start. Their family roots were each deep in the colonies of the Indian Ocean, though she, the duke's bastard daughter, had never been there herself. They recognized in each other a yearning for that distant lost paradise. As children, on the occasions when he was living at the Grange, they'd sneak off together and play games that made them both forget the hell of their existence. She saw him less after he left for school; but when she did, the bond was immediate and electric. She only had to look at him to feel the exuberance of joy bubbling inside, to envision the freedom of escape his presence would provide. They'd grown up playmates, but in the last year their friendship had followed its natural course and blossomed into a deep and passionate secret love.

Now she ran to him through the sultry night, over gently rolling hills, through a thicket of apple trees, to the sloping bank of the river beyond. He was there, with his jacket open, his cravat tugged low, the top stud of his shirt undone. He was so exquisite, standing in the moonlight with his face angled upward, sniffing the sea air. Everything she'd ever longed for in a man—exciting, romantic, the spawn of an adventurer. A man who could sweep her away from this life of misery.

She stopped a few yards from him, content to watch him, to feel the unspeakable jubilation of knowing this time was theirs, that no one could take it away. He sensed her presence and turned. His eyes were heavy, hooded, scorching her from afar. Soundlessly, he stalked forward, giving her the impression she was being dominated by the very maleness of his presence. She felt small before him as he grasped the sides of her face and crushed her mouth to his, conquering her with a sizzling open-mouthed kiss.

His mouth moved like a cyclone, leaving her parted lips, skimming her cheek, dipping to burrow into the hollows of her throat. As if by magic, her starched blouse melted beneath his fingers, and his hands were shoving it down, his lips traveling in a delectable trail to her shoulders, her collarbone. He jerked her uniform down, baring her breasts to the night air. At once his hands were on them, kneading skillfully, lifting a globe to better accommodate the eagerness of his mouth. He teased a nipple with his restlessly flicking tongue, then sucked until she felt her knees buckle beneath her.

Catching her in a swift motion, he hoisted her into his arms, greedily tasting of the sweet summons of her breast as he strode toward the waiting boat. The only sounds they heard were the lapping of the river and her rapid breathing. He stepped into the flatboat like a man born to the sea, unmindful of the rocking jolt beneath their weight. Bending, he settled her on the hard seat with a final lingering taste of her breast. As he tried to straighten, she grabbed his broad shoulders and pulled him back.

"Rodrigo," she panted in a husky voice, "don't leave me now."

"Do you want me to take you right here, in this boat?" he asked in a deep voice that still carried traces of a Portuguese accent.

She was grateful for the darkness, so he couldn't see the sudden flush of her cheeks. The realization that this was their final night together crackled between them like a covenant of things to come. She felt wild with anticipation.

Her heart fluttering, she said, "No, darling. I can wait to reach our island of love." Their own private island, that magical place where the only happy moments of her life had been spent.

He read the promise in her eyes and gave her an ardent gaze. She was breathing rashly now, her body tingling with an awareness of his intentions—and her own. She couldn't wait to give herself to the only man she'd ever loved. Here, in the moonlight, one last time. A lovely memory to take with him on the lonely voyage across the seas.

"Hurry," she breathed.

His lips curved in a rare smile. "Usually it's I who am impatient."

Her toes tingled at the implications. That this wonderful man was impatient for her gave her a warm feeling of well-being. It was what he'd always given her, even as a boy: the knowledge of what it was to be wanted for the first time in her life. . . .

He took up the long pole and, submerging it in the river, gave a mighty shove. They surged into the water. Even in the fragile light, she could see his shoulders bunch and strain beneath the confines of his jacket. She loved to watch him work the pole as they floated gracefully through the current. They'd started meeting here in the first place because he never wanted to be far from water. He seemed at home on a boat, at ease with himself, sure of his actions, master of all he surveyed. She felt a thrill race through her. Watching him, she thought of his pirate father and was certain there were hidden dimensions to Rodrigo that even *she* couldn't guess.

It wasn't a long trip. The island glistened halfway to the opposite bank, a small reef less than fifty yards across. They called it Willow Island because of the protrusion of willows that adorned the perimeter, draping their lacy leaves poetically to the soft, moist banks. As children they'd played here with her younger brother, Cullen, tagging along behind. They used to swim to the island, pretending it was a smuggler's cove, and she a titled lady captured by his brigand and imprisoned on an island far from the reaches of the law. Here they'd laughed and howled at the tops of their lungs, trudging through the muddy banks of the river with feet bare and heads hatless against the summer suns—blithe spirits away from the austerity of the duke's household. Here, they'd dreamed their dreams. They were the only happy times of Gabrielle's life. Rodrigo would spin fanciful tales of how he'd grow up to be a pirate like his father and carry her away from her dreary life. She'd known the stories for what they were; but a part of her, even now, still believed.

He anchored the boat onshore with efficient motions, then came to carry her from the boat and set her feet on the ground. There, in the luminescence of the moon, beneath the shelter of dangling leaves, she finished what he'd begun, removing her cap, stripping off the uniform she so despised, and dropping each piece to the ground. Slowly, as he'd taught her. Everything slow. Like a cat stretching in the sun. Rodrigo watched with sweltering eyes as he, too, shed his clothing to reveal a body of tempered steel.

Gabrielle preened before him, glorying in her autonomy, in the liberation of her real and naked self. She reached up and unbound the curls of her chocolate hair, allowing it to tumble free. At seventeen, she was soft and curvy, voluptuous in the way he preferred. Her breasts just filled his large hands. Her rounded buttocks spanned the breadth of his palms. As she heard the intake of his breath, she felt a familiar heat.

She sauntered toward him with a seductive air. Caressing the muscles of his shoulders with light fingers, she brought her lips to the sculpted power of his chest. Nibbling him, she worked her way down the taut flesh, dropping slowly, as she progressed, to her knees. There, she took him in hand, stroking him, willing herself to breathe. She leaned over and kissed him with moist lips, heard his gasp as she felt him grow and swell beneath her hand. He was tremendous, always larger than she remembered, alive and throbbing beneath her lips.

"You're magnificent. I never dreamed a man could be as beautiful as you."

Dropping to her level, his hairy legs bending fluidly so they caught the shimmer of the moon, he kissed her deeply as he stroked her with practiced hands. She felt wicked, a woman of forbidden delights, kissing him in the moonlight with nothing between them to protect her from his assault. As he kissed her, her head began to spin, as if she were drowning in his heat.

Trailing his lips to her cheek, her ear, the back of her neck, he turned her so her back was to him. She felt his hot tongue on her shoulder blades, moving down her spine. At the same time his hand found her between her legs. She whimpered with a need so intense, she thought she'd faint. As he followed the path of her spine he bent her slowly, so that by the time he was nibbling at the back of her waist, she'd shifted forward on her knees, supporting herself with outthrust hands.

Then, all at once she felt him behind her, hard as a shaft of steel against the soft, dewy moisture his fingers had aroused. He lifted her hips in a single savage move, preparing to enter from behind. Suddenly the tutored gentleman was gone. In his place was a being as dark and fierce as any pirate vision she'd ever had. Gone was any pretense of deportment. He seemed suddenly barbaric, relentless and unmercifully resolute.

Yet, her loins screamed out for him. His fist in her hair, tugging back her head, made her pant a sultry breath. It thrilled her so, she couldn't wait to meet the ravages of his desires. She wanted him now, in their final rendezvous, more than she ever had.

Tightening his grip on her hair, he put his mouth to her ear, whispering feverishly to her in Portuguese.

"What are you saying?" she panted. "Tell me so I'll understand."

He'd taught her Portuguese as a child, of course. She knew exactly what he was saying. But she wanted to hear it again. It was one of the games they played—her making believe she understood less than she did.

She heard his playful laugh, so deep in his throat that it came out in a sexual growl. "You vixen, you know damned well what I said."

"Tell me again," she teased, "so I can be sure."

"What is it you want to hear?" he said against her ear. "That I've never wanted any woman the way I've wanted you? That when I'm with you, I wonder that my heart can long for anything else? That I'm a fool to leave you? Fool I may be, *carícia*. Yet leave, I must."

She turned and wound her arms around his neck, playfully nipping at the column of his throat. "You could always fulfill your promise to me and spirit me away. I should fancy playing stowaway, with no one but you knowing I'm aboard."

She heard the sadness in his voice as he said, "Would that I could."

Trying not to think of the endless nights without him, trying only to envision their happiness on his return, she hugged him close. "Never mind, darling. It will only be for two years. We must remember that and be brave. And when you return . . . when we're married . . ."

She felt him stiffen, felt the emotional withdrawal she hadn't felt since he'd first arrived. With resolute hands, he loosened her arms from his neck and, his ardor cooled, got to his feet, then stepped aside.

The silence between them was tense, strained. She felt as if he'd thrown ice water in her face. Since he said nothing, refusing to break the stillness, she took the initiative.

"Rodrigo, what is it? What have I said?"

"I'm not coming back." He bent and reached for his pants.

She was silent for a moment, watching him dress. "Don't say that. Not even in jest."

He turned his head halfway so it was silhouetted by the moon, his features austere and suddenly cruel. "I assure you it's no jest."

Gabrielle sat up, alarmed. "What do you mean?"

He said nothing, methodically donning one piece of clothing after the other. The quiet clung to the willows, distancing her from him as effectively as a wall of glass.

"Answer me!"

Slowly, he came to her and gently ran the back of his finger along her cheek. "I can't tell you."

"Can't—or won't?"

"As you wish."

It took tremendous effort to swallow the hurt that was threatening to choke her. "But you *are* coming back—"

He froze, his hand dropping abruptly from her face.

"Rodrigo?" she said, trying to squelch the panic.

He didn't respond.

She raised herself to her feet. "Then take me with you. Now. We can leave tonight—"

"Ah, Gabé. You don't understand. You just don't fit in with my plans."

She was truly shocked. "How can I *not*? We have the same dreams!"

He turned from her. "You're mistaken. Our dreams aren't the same at all."

"But Rodrigo, how—"

"Please, don't ask me any more. Don't make me hurt you more than I have to."

A chill of foreboding settled in her heart. "My God, Rodrigo! What are you going to do?"

He gave her a look she hadn't seen for years—the cold, empty glare of the boy he'd been. "I'm finally going to get my revenge."

# One

*The pirate kicked in* the door and stalked across the lady's cabin. He surveyed the scene of huddled, frightened women, and jerking his head to the ladies-in-waiting, barked out his command. "Out!"

Casting helpless looks at their mistress, the servants scrambled out the door, leaving her alone with the infamous brigand—Rodrigo Soro, the scourge of the Indian Ocean.

With arrogant grace, he stepped to where she lay trembling on her bunk, crammed against the wall in a futile attempt to back away. Leaning, he jerked her to him and overpowered her with a kiss.

She shoved him away, her anger making her strong. But it didn't faze him. He pulled her back and with a savage yank, ripped her dress, exposing a bare shoulder. A gasp of voices was heard all around.

"You'll have to kill me," she cried, her breast heaving with her breath. "I shall never submit to your mad desires!"

With a confident smile, he sneered, "You used to feel differently about me."

"That was before you became a vile rogue."

"You liked me being a vile rogue when we were children," he reminded her.

"But that was just pretend. That was before you began destroying my country's ships for your own foul greed."

"And what has your country done for me," he cried in outrage, "but hang my father and steal my name? I care nothing for England, *carícia*. I care only for you."

As he approached once again, she turned away. "You had your chance, Rodrigo. You loved me, then left me to pursue your evil designs. Fiend from hell! I shall never believe another word you say. I shall never trust you again."

The pirate stepped away from her and struck a melodramatic pose as the lights around him dimmed. With a heavy sigh, he raised his voice with his hand on his heart. "My name is feared all across the Indian Ocean, from the Horn of Africa to the Celebes Sea. I've looted ships and collected bounty worth a king's ransom. But without the woman I love, I'm only half a man!"

From the distance, a voice cried out, "Ahoy, Captain. English frigates on the horizon."

The pirate looked back toward the spot where he'd left his lady love in the dark. "I never wanted a woman the way I've wanted you. I'm a fool to leave. Yet leave I must, if only for a time. But mark me well, my only love. This is not finished between us!"

The curtain fell. There was a moment of silence. Then, a thunder of applause. The lights went up, the lady stood, and walked offstage. The pirate moved to follow, but the applause swelled to a deafening pitch. To acknowledge it, the curtain rose again. Frozen in transit, the pirate stepped to center stage to take a deep bow. As the audience stomped their feet, the brigand swept the plumed hat from his head, put a hand to the golden hair, and tugged. Off came a wig, displaying a netting of bound hair underneath. The net was tossed aside and a tumble of rich chocolate curls dropped about the shoulders of the pirate. And in his place stood Gabrielle Ashton-Cross, the toast of the London stage.

Slowly, she extended a trim leg clad in thigh-high boots and bowed with a masculine flourish so her nose nearly touched the ground. It was a maneuver that never failed to elicit an astonished gasp—so piratical and sensational was it coming from one who was so obviously a woman, yet who, for a few hours in the dark, had fooled them all.

Gabrielle stood with the footlights as a barrier, taking her bows, feeling little relation to the hordes she'd conquered so completely with her performance. They were but a means to an end. She smiled perfunctorily and looked toward the wings, where she would have a brief respite before the final act.

There, she caught sight of her younger brother, Cullen, who wore a look on his face she'd never seen before.

He was a boyishly handsome young man of twenty, five years her junior, with sandy hair and sad blue eyes. The bastard children of the duke of Westbury and his mistress, they'd clung together since early childhood, when their mother had died and they'd been foisted on the duke.

It wasn't unusual for Cullen to be there, watching and hanging around backstage. Some weeks he came every night, he was so lost without her. As she rose and smiled at him, he waved his hand, prompting her off-stage. This was so unusual, it pricked her curiosity.

With a final bow, Gabrielle left the stage to a chorus of disappointed groans, and went to see what the excitement was about. Nodding distractedly at the congratulations of her fellow actors, she brushed through them like an arrow toward her goal.

"I must speak with you at once," her brother told her above the din.

Before he could say more, the stage manager, Humphrey Hollingstead, stormed through the assemblage.

One glance told Gabrielle he was fuming again. "Miss Ashton-Cross, you've altered your lines once again."

"Why, yes, Mr. Hollingstead. I believe I have."

He clutched his thickly curling hair and made dramatic gestures as if ripping it out by the roots. "You're driving me to distraction! Always tampering with the lines. I never know what you're going to say. Every night it's a new play."

"It felt right to do so," she explained with a dismissive shrug. "I did, after all, write the play. Isn't that so, Cullen?"

At her intimation that she might involve her brother in this quarrel, Cullen paled.

"If you don't desist," Hollingstead warned, "I shall take action and discharge you."

Cullen opened his mouth to speak. Knowing her brother's propensity for capitulation, Gabrielle stepped in front of him. "You need me, Mr. Hollingstead. It's the air of scandal I lend to this production that keeps the audience coming."

"I'm warning you, Miss Ashton-Cross. I want the lines performed as written in the final act. *As written*, Miss Ashton-Cross. That's an order."

"An *order?*" She cast a sly glance at Cullen, who diverted his embarrassed gaze. She didn't take well to orders, and they all knew it. Hollingstead certainly did. He'd commanded Gabrielle into his bed and she'd refused.

Already, admirers were swarming backstage, elbowing Hollingstead aside. They were mostly male, some with gardenias in hand, all with the eager looks of suitors hopeful of a kind word. Their ranks contained all manner of artists, dandies, and swells from London's fastest crowd. Baron Swalberg and his expatriate circle, including his lecherous hunchback cousin just over from Germany. The earl of Lygate and his whoremongering hangers-on. The novelist Bulwer-Lytton, with his subtly groping hands. And a host of other upper-class rakes whose licentious impulses seemed to have been liberated by the air of reform sweeping England. All of them endlessly drawn to the shocking sensuality of the play—and to her.

When they spotted Gabrielle, they rushed forth in a mass, nearly crushing her with their exuberance.

"We can't talk here," she called to Cullen. He began to coax a path through the swarm, and she followed in his wake.

"I told you she wouldn't stop," one poet said to another. "She never does."

"Maybe they're right," surmised the other. "Maybe she *isn't* interested in men."

"I hear she really knew the rogue when he lived in England. *That's* why she plays him so convincingly."

He turned and stared at the vision coming toward them.

"*I hear*—" He put his mouth to the other's ear and whispered waspishly.

"No! It can't be true!"

Ignoring the gossip, brother and sister made their way through the crush and noise to her dressing room, where already the tables were piled high with gardenias. The *Spectator* had reported once that the actress was known to be fond of them, so ever since, she'd been deluged by the flowers to the point that she could no longer bear their heavy scent. "Why the urgency?" she asked, moving to gather the blossoms and take them outside.

"Father's sent for you."

She took a moment to absorb the words, then turned as if in a trance, dropping the forgotten flowers to the table.

"Sent for me?"

"His note said you were to report to him at once. He's waiting for you at Westbury House."

She looked up and met his gaze and saw that he, too, realized the significance. Never once, in all the years since she'd left his country estate in the middle of the night, had Douglas Cross sent for her.

As Cullen left, Gabrielle turned to the mirror and began to cream her face. She caught her hand trembling, and chided herself for a fool. If the duke had sent for her, it could only mean one thing: She'd won some kind of victory. All at once, a great excitement bubbled inside her. What else could it mean?

She could hear her brother outside diplomatically explaining to her admirers that she'd been called away and her understudy would take her place. In a rush, she left her dressing room, still wearing her pirate costume with the shockingly tight men's pants, red shirt, yellow sash about her waist, and peacock jacket that was folded back on the right side to display her sword.

She was a beautiful woman by anyone's standards, with strong features that, with greasepaint and the austerity of pulled-back hair, could pass for a man's. Her voice was deep, as resonant as that of many men, which aided the illusion. But with her paint removed and her rich brown curls framing her face, it was difficult to see how she accomplished the feat. Her eyes were that of a woman, the distinctive cobalt blue of her French grandmother, smoldering with suppressed passions so they gave the impression she'd just stepped out of bed; but wary and defensive as if daring any man to challenge the barriers she'd erected around her heart. She wasn't aware that they served as an invitation to men, but the fact was widely remarked on in the backrooms of London.

A murmur of disappointment erupted from the crowd. "*Must* you leave?" wailed one of the poets who'd been afforded backstage privileges. "I've waited four dreadful months to see you!"

They thought her brilliant, gifted, a creature of magic. It reminded her now of how unacceptable she was to her father and his world of perfect British order and respectability.

Once again, she felt an uncharacteristic flutter of nervousness coil inside her like a snake. In her father's house, she was nothing. What would she find when she arrived?

Cullen accompanied her to the stage-door alley where he had a hansom cab waiting. Gabrielle paused for a moment before entering the coach, looking her brother in the eyes. Silently, with a small touch to his hand, she assured him that all would be well.

The cab lurched off into the enclosing fog. Gabrielle sat back and took a shaky breath, her mind vaulting forward. *Could* this be the moment she'd been waiting for? Was it possible that all the work, the determination, the suffering, had come to fruition at last?

She gripped her hands together in her lap, trying to still their excited tremors, thinking back to a time when she was seven years old. She and two-year-old Cullen had just come to their father's country house, soon after their mother's tragic death. The duke took them in, but under constant pressure from Hastings, his spiteful legitimate son and heir, Douglas Cross denied his parentage, finally even bowing to Hastings's insistence that the waifs be made to earn their keep. Gabrielle became a servant of the house, and when he was old enough, Cullen was turned out to work in the stables.

For years, Gabrielle secretly cried herself to sleep every night. Cullen was too young to remember, but she missed her mother, missed the feel of someone tucking her in late at night, of holding her close—even if more and more the breath of the one who kissed her reeked of gin. She couldn't understand what her mother had done, or why she'd been taken away.

But as she grew up in the duke's household, she began to piece together her mother's story and to feel her rage. The tropical island home that was stolen from her,

Beau Vallon, became the cornerstone of Gabrielle's dreams.

When she was seventeen, after being deserted by her only love, and enduring the worst night of her life, she roused Cullen from bed just after dawn, and together they fled Westbury Grange forever. With no place to go, Gabrielle stopped an elderly woman in Hyde Park, asking her for any work she might have. The woman turned out to be the incomparable Sarah Siddons, the greatest actress of her time. An old woman, Mrs. Siddons had long since retired from the stage, but something of the courageous determination of the beautiful young girl captured her heart.

She took them in, utilizing Gabrielle's striking appearance as a background player in several of her friends' productions. Gradually, she recognized in her young ward the flicker of an authentic talent, but also saw in her an impulsiveness and lack of discipline that needed to be conquered. Handled properly, Mrs. Siddons advised, a career on the stage might be the gateway to the attainment of anything she might want in life. So the great actress tutored Gabrielle in the rudiments of drama, which came easily, and discipline, which didn't. She then sent her to the provinces, where Gabrielle clawed her way through a barrage of insignificant roles, temporarily suppressing all other desires to learn her craft painstakingly.

It wasn't an auspicious time to be in the theater. The country had been in the throes of financial crisis for years, and audiences were dropping away at an alarming rate. Plum women's roles were dominated by stars, so Mrs. Siddons—deciding to utilize Gabrielle's unfemininely deep voice as a strength rather than a weakness—suggested she disguise herself as a man. Gabrielle did so in a number of forgettable roles in the course of a year, perfecting her impression until she played Iago to rave notices. Soon theatergoers were trekking up to Stratford to see her performance. Before long, *Othello* was brought to the Haymarket, where it was an even greater success.

She was growing weary of acting when at last she saw her opportunity.

The falling fortunes of her father's British East India Company were fueling the empire's economic woes. And in the far-off Indian Ocean, its problems were being exacerbated by the now notorious Rodrigo Soro, who was terrorizing British shipping with a boldness and swagger that had been unknown since the golden age of piracy a hundred years ago. In a thunderbolt of inspiration, Gabrielle realized she could use her intimate knowledge of the scoundrel to create a play that would both humiliate her father and sweep London off its feet.

The story of Rodrigo seemed made for the stage. He was the son of a pirate who challenged England's hegemony over the waters around the Seychelle Islands. When the pirate was captured and hanged, the duke brought the lad to England, took him in. Determined to civilize the young savage, the duke anglicized his name to Roderick Smythe, saw to his education, sending him eventually to Haileybury, the training school of the East India Company. Rodrigo had been an apt and willing student, bearing the prejudice that his fellow schoolmates—and Hastings in particular—heaped on him with a calmness and seeming unconcern that had fooled everyone, including Douglas. Then, on his initial Company voyage to the East Indies, Rodrigo betrayed them all by putting a sword to the captain's throat and boldly taking charge of the ship. Not only did Rodrigo become a pirate, he became the most effective pirate those waters had ever known, largely because of the education he'd received at the hands of the Company. He was known as Simba—the Lion—no doubt because of his unusual golden Portuguese beauty and striking lion's eyes, and not even the best efforts of the Royal Navy could bring him to heel.

Gabrielle knew this story better than anyone, knew

intuitively how to play the character. She made her name with *The Lion's Revenge,* but her real motivation for writing the play, of course, was to force her father's hand. To create a scandal and to embarrass him personally to the point that he could no longer ignore her. To force him to give her what she demanded, even if it was just to silence her.

Now her father had so uncharacteristically called for her in the middle of a performance. Surely that meant her scheme had succeeded at last!

# $T$wo

$Westbury\ House$ was a four-story building in Grosvenor Square adorned with majestic statues of medieval warriors. The fog, which filtered and drifted eerily in the moonlight, caressed the granite figures like stealthy cloaks, lending them a pervading impression of menace. It was an imposing structure meant to intimidate, to announce to the world that a preeminent man dwelled within.

Shivering in the spring night air, Gabrielle stood before the house she'd passed so many times, but had never entered. On the steps, several men were just leaving, the kind of important men of government she'd often seen from the edges of the duke's world. She recognized the powerful Judge Martin Matson, unmistakable because of his uncanny resemblance to a wharf rat. As they passed her, she overheard their angry mutterings and the words "slavery" and "Buxton." When they'd gone, she knocked on the door.

She was greeted with strained civility by the majordomo and ushered inside. All about her were the gloom and ancient armor of a fortress. Swords, lances, and shields lined the cold stone walls, creating an atmosphere of harsh masculine dominance.

"His Grace and His Lordship are expecting you," the majordomo announced, his hushed voice vaulting off the silence of the walls.

"His Lordship? Is Hastings here?"

"The marquis of Breckenridge is in attendance," the servant corrected.

It wasn't happy news. She despised Hastings, and had ever since they'd first seen each other, when her mother was on trial for her life. After Gabrielle and Cullen moved to Westbury Grange, thirteen-year-old Hastings—who never for one moment gave credence to her claim of being his sister—set out to make their lives miserable with a vindictiveness and calculated cruelty that had taught her a harsh lesson about human nature and made her grow up fast. And every time she thought she'd witnessed the limits of his amazing capacity for deception, he surprised her with some daring new innovation.

The marquis had been in the Indian Ocean for the past eight years, the last two of them as governor of Seychelles. A month ago, he'd returned to England on leave. Gabrielle had made it a point not to see him. Even when he'd come to the theater and demanded an audience, she'd had him turned away. It had afforded her great satisfaction to be able to deny *him* for a change.

She followed the butler through the massive tomb of a house and up three flights of stairs. At her father's bedroom, the servant bowed deferentially, opened the gargantuan portal with a white-gloved hand, and waved her soundlessly inside.

"If Your Grace needs me, I shall be at hand," he pronounced stiffly.

Douglas Cross, twelfth duke of Westbury, fifth marquis of Breckenridge, earl of Blandfordshire and surrounding lands, lay propped in his four-poster with a mountain of crisp pillows at his back. Even in bed, he displayed an impressive demeanor. His hair was white now, but with a striking silver tint that made him look all the more distinguished. He was so patrician in appearance that no one could ever mistake him for other than what he was, an influential member of the peerage and a director of the powerful British East India Company.

Hastings Cross sat in a chair by his side, upright as always, under a large framed map of the Seychelle Islands. Dark-haired, he had a sharp nose that lent him the countenance of a bird of prey, and dark, darting eyes that showed his cruelty. His hands were curled round the arms of his chair like the talons of a hawk.

The sight of him under this map emphasized the outrage of his appointment as governor and reminded her of this family's obsession with these islands. Douglas first went there as a much younger man when the islands were still a colony of France, falling in love with their incomparable beauty and serenity, convinced it was the earth's one true paradise. While there he met the young and lovely Caprice Ashton, daughter of one of the archipelago's original French families. Her parents had died within a year of each other, leaving her a struggling cotton plantation, Beau Vallon.

When she met Douglas Cross, he seemed like a godsend. The wealthy duke was smitten with her at once. He was married, but he convinced her it was a marriage of convenience. That he couldn't bear the sight of his wife. That she was frigid and only graced his bed in an attempt to bear a son and heir. That she'd tried unsuccessfully for years, and when at last she'd succeeded in becoming pregnant, she'd abandoned the duke for his country estate and put herself in bed for the nine months it took her to bear Hastings. After which, she'd kept to her bed, a virtual invalid, complaining about her husband's lack of feeling.

The story touched Caprice, made her sorry for the lonely duke. She became his lover, but when he asked her to return to England with him, she refused. The idea of leaving the place where she'd been so happy, so wild and free, bathing in the year-round sun, was abhorrent to her. All his pleadings fell on deaf ears. So one day, Douglas simply bought up the mortgage on Beau Vallon and made a bargain. If Caprice followed him to England and remained for two years as his mistress, he would give her the deed free and clear.

She made the journey, hating every minute of being away from her paradise. The two years stretched to three and then four, and still Douglas—who seemed to be obsessed with her even more with each passing year—found some excuse not to give her back the property.

Gradually, she realized he never intended to give it back to her—that it was his hold over her, the thing that kept her in bondage to him. It would have done her no good to have left him for another man. No matter how wealthy the pursuer, Douglas wouldn't have sold the property at any cost. Even though she was only seven when her mother died, Gabrielle never forgot the anguish in her mother's voice as she told the tale. "I should never have left Mahé," she told her daughter before bursting into tears. "I began to die the moment I left Beau Vallon." They were her last words.

When first Gabrielle and later Cullen was born, the duke became more determined than ever to keep his beautiful French mistress under his thumb. Their relationship deteriorated under the strain. Crazed with jealousy and the growing suspicion that she was sharing her bed with other Englishmen, Douglas flatly denied his paternity when she tried to sue for his Seychelles property in their name. Sensing that her situation was hopeless, Caprice took to discouragement and drink.

She fought with Douglas to no avail until, in utter frustration, she bolstered her courage with a healthy dousing of gin, talked her way into Westbury House, and confronted Douglas with a pistol, demanding that he hand over the deed. They struggled and the gun went off just as the duke's wife—Hastings's mother—walked in the room to see what the fuss was about. The stray bullet hit the duchess in the chest, and she died almost at once.

During the publicity and trial that followed, it was never once mentioned that the murderess, Caprice Ashton, had been the mistress of the distinguished duke of Westbury. Rather, it was maintained that she was a crazy French woman he didn't know. She was hanged publicly at Newgate Prison because of his silence.

But it was Hastings who turned Gabrielle's life into a living hell. He came to the foundlings' home where she was staying temporarily and, pretending to befriend her, took her by the hand through the streets of London and forced her to witness her mother's execution. As the life was choked from her mother at the hangman's noose, Hastings leaned over and whispered, "That's what we do to bad girls in England. We hang them." When she'd looked up, terrified, into his black eyes, he'd added, "Don't make me angry, or we might do the same to you."

He held it over her head for years. At every infraction of her father's rules, she'd been terrified that he'd have her hanged as he had her mother. To this day, she had nightmares of being hanged while Hastings watched, laughing, from the safety of his table at the Magpie and Pint. It was the only thing she'd ever been afraid of in her life.

Hastings looked up to find her still in costume. "Good lord, you look foolish," he rebuked her.

She remained still before him, chin raised at a fighting angle.

"Did you summon me here to criticize?" she asked in her best haughty tone—one she'd learned from him at an early age.

"You would do well not to bait us, young lady, after all you've put us through," admonished the duke.

She met her father's gaze and felt the same sadness she always did when in his presence. Sometimes she thought she could feel some of the love he'd felt for Caprice. Though he'd never voiced such emotions, she sensed that he, too, suffered because of her death. There was a time when she'd thought he might feel something for Caprice's foundered children. Until Hastings had poisoned his mind against them. Until he'd seen to it they didn't have a chance.

"My name, *Your Grace*, is Gabrielle. You might try using it once in a while." She called him "Your Grace" in the way he demanded, but always with a tinge of sarcasm in her tone.

"Your name," he countered, "is not Cross, although you insist on using it to shame a noble family."

"If my name *isn't* Cross, it's only because you deny me the use of it. By now, everyone in London knows I'm your daughter. What good does it do you to deny it?"

"Everyone knows because of your blatant flaunting of it. Not only do you use the name without my leave, you disgrace it by teaming it with that of your mother's and using it to publicize that outrage you call a play!"

"You didn't seem to mind *what* my mother's name was when you took her to your bed without benefit of matrimony."

"I shan't allow you to speak so to me!" he raged.

"Contrary to your opinion, *Your Grace*, you hold no sway over what I say or do. You think to deny me my name and birthright, yet retain the privilege to criticize my every move. What a hypocrite you are!"

"You call me *hypocrite* because I deplore the outrages you perpetuate? Because you defile yourself by executing this perversion on the stage? Because you choose to *glorify* that ungrateful pup?"

"I never set out to glorify Rodrigo. Only to humiliate you."

"You're a heartless girl."

"I wonder where I got it?"

Suddenly, Hastings laughed. "Ah, Gabby. I'd imagined in my absence that you'd changed. Perhaps become the soft woman your appearance seems to promise. Before you open your lovely mouth and show your fangs."

How she hated him! She turned toward the door, ready to leave. "I can't abide this. I'd thought you summoned me here to say you've decided to give me what I want. If you've called me here to demoralize me—"

"The trouble is, Gabby dear, we can't quite get it straight what you *do* want. You're a complicated woman. And you seem to want so very much."

She turned on Hastings, her eyes flashing. "You know very well what I want. The same thing I've wanted since the day I was thrust into that sorry excuse of a prison you call a home. I want my freedom from this society that rejects me, not because of who I am, but because of the mishap of my birth. You wouldn't understand that. You take for granted your place in this world. You don't know what it's like to feel an outsider in your own country, your own home. To feel shame because you happened to be born on the wrong side of the sheets."

"You're right," Hastings drawled, studying his nails. "I wouldn't."

"I want to leave England and take Cullen with me. I want my independence from the two of you. And I want what's rightfully mine—Beau Vallon. The land you, Your Grace, stole from my mother and held over her head. The land you gave to this precious son of yours on his twenty-first birthday, though it wasn't yours to give. The same land he's been holding to keep me chained to him, just as you did to my mother. You owe me that, for all you've put me through. I shall settle for nothing less."

Hastings turned to Douglas. "You see, Father, she wants us to favor her, yet she retains the right to spew forth her venom at every turn. A little gratitude might be in order, Gabby. Say what you will, you still seek to embarrass us above all else."

"Once Cullen and I leave, I shall have no further

need of embarrassing you. In fact, we shall both be happy to relinquish the Cross name. Frankly, we're ashamed to be one of you."

"*You're* ashamed. The Delilah of the London stage and her spineless pup of a brother. I should think you *would* be ashamed, at that."

"Hastings, you're pathetic. Governor of the Seychelles, what a sorry jest. You're still the same cruel little bully who's jealous because we all have a bond with paradise and you don't. So you want to own it."

"That's enough," Douglas countered. "I've brought you here to say you've won."

She stilled, suddenly alert. "Won?"

"You may have what you desire. Hastings has generously agreed to hand over his possession of the plantation on Mahé. You're welcome to it."

She eyed him suspiciously. "In exchange for what?"

"In exchange for your leaving the country forthwith. I'm fed up with this nonsense. You're to relinquish use of the Cross name. And you're to give up your career. No more acting. No more perpetuating this farce you call a play. You're to deny permission for it to be performed ever again. Those are my terms. Take them or leave them. I shall have your answer now."

"I'll take them," she said. Finally, after all these years of struggle, she'd been afforded what she really wanted. Finally, she could make her mother's dream come true. Caprice would not have died in vain.

"I want the deed signed over to me by a solicitor of my choice," she insisted. "Not that I don't trust you," she added, looking sarcastically at Hastings. He gave her a grin like a falcon who'd just devoured its prey.

"It will be done," the duke agreed. "You're to leave in a fortnight. Hastings will precede you on an earlier ship, and arrange for your arrival. Use the time to get your affairs in order and bring a halt to that atrocity of a play."

On her way out, she paused with her back to the

room. It was silent as a vault. She could feel their eyes on her, waiting to see what she might do. She turned and looked her father in his watery eyes. "It's a pity about us," she said softly. "We might have found a way to bridge the gap between us, if not for Hastings."

Then, she turned and looked at her loathed half brother. She'd hoped to see some defeat on his face. But if he'd lost anything in this meeting, there was no hint of it in the calculating gleam of his predator eyes.

# Three

Dockland was a nasty neighborhood, but Gabrielle walked through it unafraid, with the reckless freedom of someone so accustomed to her environment that she no longer sees the dangers. She'd always loved the area along the river where, as a child, she and her mother liked to come and watch the great East Indiamen set out for the Indian Ocean. In those days, the East India Company—known to its vast family of employees as John Company—was king of the seas. The most prestigious and powerful company of merchants the world had ever known, it worked around the clock to keep up with the imports of spices, cottons, saltpeter, porcelain, and tea. Now, the Company was in serious decline. There was even talk of retiring the grand old ships in favor of steamers that would reach India in half the time—another sign of a rapidly changing world. In an effort to hang on to her memories of her mother, Gabrielle still chose to live close to the docks Caprice had so loved.

Tonight, in the predawn fog, the East India Dock was quiet as a tomb, its cracked stone walkways empty of all but the night watchmen who walked their beat.

She crossed the Isle of Dogs, where many of the

newer docks resided, with the smell of the winding Thames in her nostrils. Here, other sounds and smells mingled to create an aura of cosmopolitan chaos and decay. On the way she passed by Chinatown, where the aroma of pork and ginger reminded her she'd forgotten her post-performance meal. She wandered through communities of Irish and Indian lascars, playing native music for hearty dancers long into the night. She saw several families of Africans who'd been slaves and had been freed by the antislavery society. England had been riding a wave of reform in the last few years since the death of George IV. This very month, after a near revolution in the rural north, a sweeping reform bill had finally passed the House of Lords, enfranchising large portions of the middle and working classes and threatening to change the whole makeup of Parliament.

Tonight, though, she gave no thought to politics, for her mind was focused on the news she had to tell her brother. How happy she'd be to get him away from London and all its perils for a boy like Cullen. She adored him, but knew better than anyone that he was helpless and weak. It was the curse of the Ashton men. Her uncle and grandfather had been this way, taken care of by their women. She could still hear her mother's voice ringing in her ears. *You must always protect Cullen, Gabrielle. He's weak. He has the Ashton blood. A man's fate is written in stone, and none more so than the Ashton men.*

Through the fog, she spotted the lantern swinging before the Duelist Public House. It wasn't difficult to guess that she'd find Cullen there—a crush on the tavern keeper's daughter, Hallie, sent him worshiping at her altar whenever he was out of Gabrielle's sight. It had been an old dueling tavern in the days when midshipmen from Haileybury used to battle each other for honor, and the favors of young maidens. For some time now, it had been more of a museum, with crossed swords lining the walls alongside portraits of some of the more illustrious patrons of days gone by. Long abandoned by the Company's officers and gentlemen, it was now mostly frequented by dockers, coopers, stevedores, and other working men responsible for the loading and unloading of the tall ships. It had fallen into disrepair, and was now a spot where the sideslip son of a duke could moon after his lady love with some measure of anonymity.

As she was drawing close, Gabrielle heard a commotion inside—raised voices and the scraping of tables along old wooden floors. Curious, she pushed the door open and was assaulted by a wave of smoke and the odor of beer, tobacco, and male sweat. She heard angry voices before she could see what was happening.

"Hold him, lads," cried a coarse East End voice. "We'll tar and feather the bugger before this night's through."

As her vision cleared, Gabrielle spotted a group of men holding another pinned to a long table. She recognized them at once as the Rotherhithe crowd—two brothers and their three smarmy friends who regularly popped across the river to make trouble. They were a cruel, burly lot, accustomed to long hours spent unloading cargo and swabbing decks. As they twisted the arm of their victim until he screamed, their faces were contorted with barbarous sneers. At just that moment, their victim turned his head and Gabrielle was not surprised to see that the agonized face belonged to Cullen. Every time she looked away, he was in trouble of some kind or another.

He spied her at the same instant and croaked out a plea. "The cat, Gabby. They were torturing Hallie's cat."

One of the bullies raised a frizzled orange cat high above his head. "This the cat you mean, little man? Yer so sweet on the creature, how'd you like him for supper? He's a fetching little bugger at that. Be more fetching still with his hair in flames."

Swinging the cat toward the roaring blaze, the bully cackled his glee as one of his mates yanked Cullen's arm back again and made him cry out in pain.

Gabrielle stepped toward the thug holding the spitting animal, reached over, and took the cat in one quick swipe, surprising the tough so he didn't have time to react. The cat screeched, obviously hurt.

"What the hell, lads?" said the bully with a philosophical shrug. "We'll torture this little nancy boy instead."

As he moved toward Cullen, the others jerked him up. One grabbed his hair and yanked his head back while another punched him in the gut.

Setting the cat gently aside, Gabrielle moved toward them. "How many times have I told you," she addressed her brother. "If you're going to get on in the world, you have to learn to deal with ruffians like these."

The door opened again and a man came in, bowed over a bucket of molten tar. "Here's the tar, lads. Let's have done with it."

The bucket was brought closer, the biting stench of tar overwhelming the place. Gabrielle, feeling the first flash of anger at his torturers and not at her brother, drew her sword.

"What do you think of that, lads?" laughed their leader. "The wench thinks she's goin' to come to the rescue. Where'd you come from, deary?" he added, observing her clothing. "A costume swah-*ray*?"

His mates laughed, the distinctive chortle of men with havoc on their minds. Gabrielle made a few quick lunges to move them aside, and put the blade to the newcomer's throat just as he was scooping out some of the burned tar. He was Willy Wilkins, the cruelest of the bunch.

"I'm afraid I'll have to ask you to desist," she told him regretfully.

Willy looked startled by her words. For a moment he

stood fixed, tar oozing from the stick onto the rotting floor.

Then one of his mates cried, "Heads up, Wilks!" and, pulling a sword from its rusted hooks on the wall, he hurled it over the heads of those gathered so it caught the feeble light. A flash of steel and the dockman's brawny paw dropped the club, and reached up to grasp the hilt of the sword above his head.

"Sorry, girlie," he said with a grin. "Looks like we're going to have our way with your milksop of a kinsman, after all."

"It shall be my pleasure to disappoint you."

Gabrielle assumed the guard position, her body angled sideways, her heels at right angles, her right arm in the line of attack.

"What the bleedin' hell is this?" her opponent sneered. "Is this how a woman wields a weapon?"

She wasn't surprised by his skepticism. She'd assumed the Italian fencing stance, less familiar in England than the French. While standing sideways to her opponent reduced her target area, it also called for greater agility and flexibility. But let him think what he would. She merely saluted him with a smile.

Willy made the first thrust. She parried it lightly, toying with his steel to get the measure of his mettle. As she retreated, he laughed. "Take a gander at yer old mate, lads. Crossing swords with a chit."

As the last word escaped his lips, Gabrielle took an expeditious lunge and cast the sword from his hand. Open-mouthed, he watched the blade fly through the air and land, sliding, at the booted feet of one of his comrades. She wasted no time. As the men gaped at her, disbelieving, she wheeled, slashed at those holding Cullen pinned to the table, and smiled smugly as they scattered. Cullen sped to the corner to comfort the buxom Hallie, who was sniffling over her injured cat.

The lad at whose feet the sword had landed picked it

up and swaggered forth. "Make a fool of my mate, will ye?" he leered as his drooping blond mustache danced.

Gabrielle moved with agile feet, her sword waggling before her, watching his every move. She could hear the redhead crying in the corner, hear Cullen's efforts to soothe her. The tavern keeper bellowed his disapproval, but made no attempt to join in. She tuned it all out as she'd been taught, concentrating on the quick, slashing circles of the lad's blade.

"You'll be sorry you made a fool of my brother," she warned in her distinctive, smoky voice.

"I know her," one man cried. "She's the tart what plays the pirate onstage."

"Then I'll have no trouble making short work of her, will I?"

She never took her eyes off her opponent. When he thrust, she angled back, awaiting her opening. He jabbed harder and she parried, her left hand in the air to balance the weight of her sword. He turned to his friends with a grin and a shrug, saying, "This is too easy, lads," when all at once she lunged and snipped off a bit of mustache with her blade. His hand flew to his cheek and came away with a splash of blood. Angry now, he charged and retaliated, his sword crashing into hers, determined to undermine her with his might. But she pranced before him, hair flying, parrying and counterparrying as he swung with ever-increasing fervor. In spite of the vehemence of his attack, he never once touched her. She was too quick, too dexterous. Too delighted by the prospect of making him pay for his abuse.

She'd studied with Signor Siffredi, the same Italian fencing master who, years before, had inadvertently readied Rodrigo Soro for a life of mayhem on the seas. Gabrielle had done so in the beginning as a way of meeting the physical demands of her role. But she'd found to her amazement that she loved the noble sport, even had a gift for it. Master Siffredi saw in her a quality he called *Intrépido*—a rare form of courage found in only the masters of the foil.

Gabrielle disarmed her opponent, then turned toward his waiting companions, taking on two of the brutes. Unhampered by cumbersome skirts, she leaped onto a table and used her boot to kick one of the brothers against the abandoned bucket. It tipped over, spilling tar in its wake, and from that point on, she used her expertise to back her competitors into the sticky mess. There, they became enraged by their ensnarement in the resin and lost their advantage. Her years of training served her well. While the dockmen were panting, she hadn't even broken a sweat.

"I've some news," she called out to Cullen, laughing as one of their opponents tripped and fell over the other, face-forward in the tar. She sliced upward, nicked the back of her adversary's hand, and announced, "They've acquiesced, Cullen. Beau Vallon is ours at last."

"Ours? What do you mean, ours?"

"They've given it over, free and clear."

He stood with the cat in his arms, looking decidedly puzzled. "Are you quite certain?"

"Of course. The arrangements are all made."

"But Gabby, why would they do such a thing? After all these years?"

"What does it matter? The important thing is we've won. Beau Vallon is finally ours."

For several moments she couldn't talk. One of the combatants backed her against the bar. With her hands behind her, she heaved herself up so she landed with her boots on the counter. Then she put her foot in the boy's face and kicked him out of range.

"It's not really like them, is it?" Cullen called after a bit.

"I shamed them into it. Cullen, do be happy. It's our dream come true. Finally we can retaliate for all they did to Mother. Her life will have meant something, through us."

"Surely they want something in return?"

"For me to disappear and stop embarrassing the family name, which I shall happily do. And my agreement not to allow any further performances of *The Lion's Revenge*. My days of playing pirate, it seems, are behind me. And so is our life in England."

"But Gabby . . . do you really think I should go, too?" He turned and looked longingly at Hallie. "Perhaps I could—"

"*Of course* you're coming with me! Do you think I can leave you to this? I'm taking you where you'll be safe. Home, Cullen! Home to Beau Vallon."

She glanced at her brother in time to see one of the blond giants sneaking up on him from behind.

"Watch your back," she warned.

He wheeled and was nearly overpowered. Suddenly, they were surrounded by a host of champions who'd earlier been content to observe the fun. They advanced with swords, clubs, and fists, intent on avenging their chums. Gabrielle grabbed Cullen and thrust him behind her, fighting against the odds, tiring now as wave after wave of burly dock workers surged toward them. The mood had changed from one of a disbelieving lark to one of vengeance.

"But Gabby," Cullen persisted, hardly noticing their predicament in his distress. "There are pirates there! Rodrigo's hiding out somewhere near the Seychelles, isn't he?"

Seeing that their only hope was to run, Gabrielle shoved Cullen toward the door.

"Rodrigo be damned!"

# Four

*Cullen weaved his way across* the bustling quarterdeck on shaky legs. "Well!" Gabrielle greeted him. "It's the first time you haven't looked green since we left England."

He did, however, look emaciated, as if he'd been through some excruciating convalescence. She could see his ribs beneath the finely tailored shirt. His sandy hair seemed dull and flat. His gentle blue eyes had the vaguely blearly look of a drunkard on a lengthy binge.

In contrast, Gabrielle was a fetching sight in fashionable cobalt satin, the color of her eyes. Her hair was streaked slightly golden by the sun, so it resembled a delectable concoction of chocolate and butterscotch melted and swirled together by the heat.

The sea voyage had been difficult at best. It was a momentous pilgrimage from their berth at Gravesend, twenty miles down the Thames from London, to their eventual destination: by way of Madeira, then across the vast Atlantic toward Brazil, veering southeast to round the Cape of Good Hope, then to Madagascar and on across the Indian Ocean to Mahé, the main island in the Seychelles archipelago. A twelve-thousand-mile journey on a twelve-hundred-ton East Indiaman with an incongruous collection of passengers who would continue on their way to India—soldiers commissioned to the Company army, fortune-seeking rapscallions, fugitives from justice—their only company for five seemingly endless months.

From all outside appearances, the *Drake* was exquisite, majestically adorned in floral gold leaf, its rounded oak hull and oriel windows protruding from the stern and quarter galleries, lending it a capricious splendor. But for the most part, accommodations were closed and stuffy. Gabrielle and Cullen, because they'd wined and dined the captain royally before departing, and through their obvious connections, shared the roundhouse, the more spacious and airy quarters at the far stern of the ship. Through the use of movable partitions, it had been divided into two cabins and stocked with sumptuous furnishings from home. The other passengers had small domiciles without windows in the bowels of the ship, where light and air were but distant memories and the stench of the ship was smothering.

It had been a rough crossing with the worst of it just behind them. Around the Cape of Good Hope, storms buffeted them so violently, they feared the ship would turn turtle. During this time, few passengers showed up in the cuddy for meals, and those who did often followed them by rushing to the rail. Cullen suffered the worst. He couldn't keep anything down and spent most of his voyage languishing in his cabin as Gabrielle recited snippets of Shakespeare to raise his spirits.

But all that changed once they sailed into the Indian Ocean. It was hot as a fired pistol, but the sweet breezes off the African coast scented the air. The warmth of the sun felt healing. The sea was calm, soft and rhythmic, almost lyrical as the ship padded through the brine.

Gabrielle had never felt such incredible warmth in all her life. While others complained of the heat, she gloried in it. "I feel I've never been warm before," she said, tipping her face to the sun.

"It's the first time I've felt good in months," Cullen agreed.

This region was so different from anything that Gabrielle, landlocked in England, could ever imagine. So lush, so inexplicably foreign, so improvidently romantic. The heat, the very air they breathed, was fraught with sultriness and sensuality. In these alien waters, she felt alive for the first time, like a blossom kept too long in the shade, and suddenly bathed in sunshine.

The destination of this voyage—the Seychelles—was one of the world's true storybook visions of paradise. In the exact middle of the Indian Ocean, a thousand miles from both India and Africa, they were a remote cluster of granite islands—in fact, nature's only granitic island chain—with their own special world of flora and fauna. So far off the beaten track, they were uninhabited until a hundred years ago. The pirates came first, then the French took possession in the 1760s, naming them after Louis XV's chancellor, Viscount Jean Moreau de Séchelles. The British took control at the end of the Napoleonic Wars. Over all the Europeans who came there, the islands seemed to cast a magical spell.

Looking outward, Gabrielle could see remnants of the gale they'd left behind. Storm clouds drifted on the far horizon, the only trace of gray in a world otherwise resplendent with rainbow hues. The water beyond the stormy stratosphere was in turn scarlet, orange, violet, turquoise, and the most unusual and striking shade of green. Captain Watkins called it quintillion green. He said it was unique to this part of the world, and would become richer the closer they came to the Seychelles. She felt in that moment that she'd never seen color before, never been free from the skulking, ever-threatening haze of English grey.

"I miss Hallie," Cullen sighed, for perhaps the hundredth time since leaving England. "I wonder if she thinks of me, as I do her."

"I wager she'll be fine without you. She has other—

admirers. Were I you, I'd concentrate on the future, and not the wishful past."

"Except that when I think of the future, I begin to fret about pirates."

Captain Watkins walked by in his blue jacket and impossibly hot black cloak and, overhearing, paused to scoff. "Mark my words, lad, there'll be no pirates on this trip."

Cullen said, "We're told Rodrigo Soro haunts these waters. Is there no possibility of an attack?"

"None whatsoever. The Royal Navy chased the fiend out of these waters months ago. Primarily, I might add, because of the notoriety of your play. You'll forgive my mentioning it, but it proved such an embarrassment that the Admiralty could no longer ignore the situation. Regardless, they've chased him into the Amirantes. He knows better than to come anywhere near the Company sea lanes. There's a fleet of royal frigates waiting for him if he does. No man, pirate or not, would be fool enough to brave such jeopardy."

"Why, then, did we take on a battalion of soldiers at Madagascar?"

"Company policy. We carry a great deal of gold aboard. Soro did us one service and taught us to take precautions. As you can see, we're prepared for any contingency."

It was true. The deck was so full of the soldiers they'd taken on at Madagascar that it was difficult to navigate it without running into them. Their red wool coats looked smothering in the heat, their brass buttons shining as befitted representatives of the Crown. They hadn't been on board an hour yet, and already they were busy checking ammunition, oiling cannons, and preparing to protect the cargo from a threat they knew wouldn't come.

"Merely precautionary, I assure you," the captain added as he walked away. "Relax and enjoy the rest of the trip. It will be smooth sailing into Seychelles."

Turning to watch the soldiers, Gabrielle felt reassured. The leader was a tall Scotsman, Lieutenant Wallace. Red-haired and freckled, with an open, friendly face, he'd impressed the sailors of the *Drake* with his good humor, enthusiasm, and the dash with which he carried out his orders. He seemed an exceedingly accomplished man who, if he had any doubts about his or his men's ability to repel unexpected pirates, wasn't showing it. Within minutes of boarding, he'd made himself indispensable, and also found time to flirt outrageously with Gabrielle. The only woman on a ship full of men, she'd become accustomed to such ogling. But as the crew grew sicker with fever and malnutrition on the way across the seas, they'd ceased to do anything but gaze longingly at her from afar. In contrast, Lieutenant Wallace seemed healthy and virile, toughened by the same punishing climate that was wilting the English sailors. He gave the aura of a man who could take care of Rodrigo with his bare hands. Captain Watkins was right. The Portuguese would be a fool to defy such a barricade. And Rodrigo was no fool.

"Just think," Cullen was saying. "All those years ago, when you used to play pirate with Rodrigo, did you ever dream he'd actually grow up to become one? I suppose we should have expected it. Everyone else did. After all, his people have been pirates for generations. Did you know he comes from the first Portuguese settlers? They've been fighting everybody: the Arabs, the French, the British. Can you imagine—generations of the same family battling for all they desire?"

She shuddered a little as a ghost of a memory drifted through her mind. The masculine smell of Rodrigo's sun-browned flesh. The taste of him on her tongue. "Can I imagine? I've had to fight for everything I want, as well."

"Do you think he'd remember us?"

She felt the old anger returning, so she clamped her teeth shut and said nothing. She'd never confided in

Cullen about how her childhood friendship had turned into a brief adult intimacy.

"I was so young when I used to toddle along behind the two of you," he continued in a musing tone. "Yet I remember him vividly, wearing an eye patch and brandishing his wooden sword. I thought he was some sort of god in those days. Who would have thought he'd turn out to be a true villain?"

"Yes, a true villain," she repeated. *More of a villain than you know.*

"I do believe I'd be afraid of him."

"You have nothing to fear from Rodrigo," she said confidently. "But should we see him again, hold on to me for dear life."

He gave her a quizzical look. "For my protection or yours?"

"For Rodrigo's. If you don't hold me back, I shall kill him with my bare hands."

The edge in her voice prompted him to change the subject. "I think I shall take your advice and concentrate on the future. Tell me about what our new life is going to be like." Even though she'd told him a million times before, he'd never paid much attention. He'd never thought this would actually come about.

At once, Gabrielle brightened. "We're going to start over in our true home. We're going to have the life we were supposed to have. We're going to be free."

"I wonder. Dr. Johnson wrote, 'He that cannot live as he desires at home, listens to the tale of fortunate islands, and happy regions, where every man may have land of his own, and eat the product of his labor without a superior.'"

"These aren't pipe dreams," she snapped. "I wish you could have heard Mother talk about Beau Vallon. She said it overlooked the most beautiful beach in the world. So beautiful we can't even imagine it. They have white sand, Cullen, like we've never seen in England. Like silk to the touch. She said she used to sit in the sand for hours, just rubbing it in her hands, it was so smooth. And birds like you've seen nowhere else in the world. I used to dream about it at night, just to keep from going insane. Seychelles. Remember we couldn't pronounce *say-shells?* We always called it *sea shells.*" She put her arm about him and smiled lovingly. "You'll be well in the sun. You won't be ill so much, as you were in the ruddy English climate. And you'll be safe. I'll see to that. There'll be no pirates beating down *our* door."

At that moment, Lieutenant Wallace was passing by and overheard the comment. "Since you're so interested in pirates," he said, "maybe you'd care to help me with a special task."

He moved to the flagpole and leisurely began to lower the flag. Gabrielle and Cullen seemed the only two who noticed, as the others were intent on their duties. Puzzled, Cullen left his sister and went to investigate.

"Hold this, would you?" the lieutenant said, handing him the Union Jack. Then he reached into his bulging breast pocket and withdrew a thick triangle of material, obviously another flag.

Just then the captain observed what was going on and called out, "You there! Mr. Wallace! What do you think you're about?"

The soldiers from Madagascar drifted from their duties and began to gather round. Heedless of the commotion, the lieutenant indifferently shook out the rectangle of cloth and fastened it to the rope.

"Good God," Cullen breathed.

For the banner the Scotsman was raising was a gold embroidered lion on a rectangle of black silk. *Rodrigo's pirate flag.*

# Five

The Madagascar soldiers drew pistols, shoving the stunned crewmen aside. The first mate lurched toward Wallace, attempting to wrench the halyard from his hands. Unperturbed, the Scotsman calmly drew his pistol and shot the mate squarely in the face. It exploded beneath the roar of the gun, and as the smoke cleared, he fell face-forward, his blood spilling across the deck.

Securing the flag, Wallace drew his sword and turned to a group of sailors rushing to overpower him. Dazed by the horror of the mate's death, Gabrielle snatched Cullen's hand and backed him away from the fighting. Single shots were fired from pistols, but as reloading was impossible in the crush, they were quickly discarded in favor of sabers.

It was clear by now that Rodrigo had substituted his own men for the soldiers at Madagascar. His pirates fought brutally, unmindful of the gentlemanly conduct of war. Gabrielle watched them slash mercilessly at the surprised crewmen as, in the distance, a frigate bore down on the scene.

Suddenly, the sultry air was split by the bellow of a cannon, halting the action. The combatants turned to look as with one blast, the main mast was severed with surgical precision. Amidst the splintering of wood, it toppled to the deck, pinning to the ground several crew members who'd stood rooted, staring as if they couldn't believe what they'd just seen. As if time, in that moment, stood still. Captain Watkins peered out to sea, a look of grudging admiration flicking across his face for the man who could engineer a shot of such astonishing accuracy.

The frigate continued coursing their way, her sails swooping toward them like a hawk on the wind. At the side of the bow were painted in artistically scripted lettering the words *El Paraiso*. "The Paradise."

The ship was a beauty, heavily embellished in gold, the figurehead a strikingly painted lion gracing the bow, its mane blowing back off its face in the wind. But it was the man who stood above who commanded attention, a godlike conqueror with his foot on the rail, his elbow leaning on his bent knee as he watched the massacre with cool concentration.

"*Rodrigo!*" Gabrielle cried, and ran to the rail. Her breath trapped in her lungs, she gripped the brass with white knuckles as his ship advanced on them like a battering ram.

Nothing on earth could have prepared her for seeing him again. He'd been beautiful always, but he was older now, and the maturity of hard-won experience suited him. Any softness, any vulnerability she'd mistakenly attributed to him was but a memory. He was harder now, more virile, his body toughened by the rigors of the ocean, his face hard and sculpted like a crag at sea. His hair was short as she remembered, caressing his forehead in the breeze, but it was enriched by the elements so it gleamed like a doubloon in the glinting sun. Unblinking, his eyes reminded her as always of a jungle cat stalking its prey. He was dressed in severe sparsity, in tight buff pants that hugged muscular swordsman's thighs and a billowing white shirt rolled up at the sleeves. Around his trim waist was a brown leather belt the span of an opened hand, and about his strong wrists were matching leather cuffs that called attention to the power of his forearms, lightly tinged with golden hair. Everything about him was harsh, unrelenting, from the bronzed leather of his skin to the way his hand, dangling over his knee, was clenched in a fist. Even from this distance, he radiated a potent masculinity, seemed to dominate the expanse of sun and sea and air.

Gabrielle stood transfixed, staring at him with wide, burning eyes. She'd never even imagined—never guessed, in spite of the stories she'd heard—the magnificence of his sovereignty, the dynamic, irresistible force he presented. Barreling down on them as he was, he seemed omnipotent, incapable of defeat. A man whose very presence could force a strong contender to surrender without a fight. A man who inspired awe and commanded respect by the presence of indomitable will.

A man, she understood in that moment, whose stage was the bow of a ship, and whose audiences were the victims his theatrics overmatched.

Suddenly she felt Cullen's grip on her arm, heard his scream in her ears. Like a sleepwalker, she became aware that the pirate ship was coming at them at an alarming speed. That if they didn't move fast, the bow would split them in two.

She dove with Cullen as the conquering ship crashed broadside, plowing through the hull of the *Drake* and hurtling them to the other side of the deck.

Shoving aside the disheveled curtain of her hair, Gabrielle looked up and saw a terrifying sight. Pirates swarmed over the rail like locusts, descending on the ill-prepared crew in a punishing force. The freebooters were composed of a mixture of races, many of them Africans. She'd been amused when she'd first heard Rodrigo called Simba, but she could see at once that, like any good showman, he'd put the pseudonym to use. His men wore tight pants the color of a lion's skin, some topping them with brown cotton shirts, others bare to the waist, their muscular torsos shimmering in the sun. The combination of black skin and animal breeches afforded them a ferocious air. With swords, pistols, knives, and fists, some subdued the crew as others poured below to the holds and began to drag up trunks of treasure.

Passengers, forgetful of their assigned battle stations, ran blindly now, but were grabbed and stripped of their valuables before being knocked to the deck. The air was thick with the smoke from gunshots and cannon fire, acrid with the smell of fear. Trying to rise, Gabrielle slipped in something slick and realized, to her horror, that it was blood.

Captain Watkins broke free from the fighting and stumbled to her, helping her to her feet. "Get below," he gasped. "If they see you—"

One pirate, passing by with a trunk full of gold, gave him a caustic bow. "Appreciate the booty, Cap'n."

Enraged, the captain lunged, grabbed him about the throat, and rashly tried to snap his neck. Using the cumbersome trunk for leverage, the pirate shoved the Englishman back, and let the spoils crash to the ground. Then he drew his sword, and in a single motion, cut off half the captain's ear. It gushed blood and he cupped his hands to it, screaming a curse.

The outlaw grinned at his victim and told him bluntly, "If you wasn't the captain, deary, you'd be dead."

Without thinking, Gabrielle stepped forth to upbraid the ruffian. "You bloodthirsty cur," she accused, before the suffering captain could warn her off. She saw his look of alarm too late, but it wouldn't have altered her defiance. She was so appalled by what was occurring, by how horrifyingly different it all was from anything she'd imagined or written in her play, that the spurting of vengeful words brought some relief.

But it didn't last. The brigand turned on her with interest in his eyes. If he hadn't noticed her before, he did now, as a hard gleam brightened his glare. He gave a slow grin and stepped toward her.

"My compatriots," he called to no one in particular. "We've been misinformed. The treasure's over here."

Captain Watkins assumed a protective stance in front of her, only to be tossed aside like a sack of meal and held back by a burly black man with a gold ring through his nose. The smoke had shielded her until now, but with the bandit's announcement, the marauders contemptuously left the ailing crew and began to flow in her direction. In a matter of moments, she and Cullen were surrounded by a dozen or more frightful creatures, each of whom looked as if he could eat a real lion for a midnight snack.

The men circled them with measuring, hard-bitten eyes, rubbing bristled jaws or bulging forearms as they chuckled to themselves. It began as an individual snicker, but like a battle cry was taken up by another and yet another until, like the mounting rhythm of native drums, she could feel the lusty guffaws beneath her skin.

"I need a sword," she hissed to Cullen. But his shock rendered him incapable of action. His gaunt face was completely drained of blood, his blue eyes glazed and stricken with panic.

She backed away, but they followed, teeth showing now; some yellow above hairy beards, some severely white inside thick black lips. More gunfire was heard and she jerked, her nerves taut, truly alarmed now as she recalled the cavalier way Wallace had shot the mate in the face, the casual indifference of the pirate lopping off the captain's ear.

Captain Watkins was heaping abuse on their captors, but Gabrielle couldn't understand the words. There was a stark ringing in her head that warned of incomparable danger. She had to get her hands on a sword. As a woman, she couldn't overpower them on her own. But with a blade in her hand, she could even the odds.

A swift inspection of the deck revealed a sword lying beside a slain sailor. It was wet with his blood, but she couldn't afford to be choosy—not with Cullen freezing under fire, and nothing to aid her but her courage and skill. She made a lunge for it—actually had it within her grasp—when the grinning pirate thrust out his boot and tripped her. She went sprawling to the deck and he kicked the sword aside.

In a panic, she scrambled to her feet and ran. She heard their laughter behind her, could sense their rising lust. Her flight was now but a game to them, adding spice to the chase. One of them grabbed and flung her so she stumbled back against the giant wheel of the helm. Then they descended upon her, their patience with games at an end, pinning her flailing arms back against the wheel so she couldn't resist. Their hands were on her then, lifting her skirts, securing frantically kicking legs. She screamed like an animal, thrashing wildly, determined to break free. But it was to no avail.

Weakened to the point of pain, she felt herself sinking into darkness, so at first it didn't register. Then she felt the imperceptible shift. The mates slavering madness turned to alert respect.

They moved from her like a parting sea as a figure stepped through the smoke. Gabrielle's heart stopped. Standing before her, with a fierce scowl on his face, was the one man who could tame these brutes—the pirate lord Rodrigo.

"*Ella â minga,*" he snarled. *She's mine.*

# Six

*In one swift motion*, he picked her up and threw her over his shoulder. Roaring orders to his men in Portuguese, he strode with her across the deck, then took a length of dangling rope in his hands and swung across to his own ship, which was now drifting back from the collision.

She caught a glimpse of ocean far below as they soared through the air. In that moment, she remembered everything she'd forced herself to forget. The feel of him, corded like steel, the hands strong and masterful, gripping her with the determined possession of a corsair claiming his plunder. She felt weak with relief when his boots touched the deck.

He swept her below in long strides. A door was opened, then closed. Placing her on her feet, he left her briefly to lock the door. She felt dizzy for a moment, having been righted so abruptly. As her head cleared, she glimpsed his cabin, stacked high with books, rich with ancient Portuguese furnishings, the far wall lined with a valuable collection of vintage knives and swords. They gleamed with gold and jewels, as in days of old. She wondered briefly if they'd belonged to his pirate ancestors. But she was immediately distracted by the sight below. For the cabin was dominated by a wide wooden bunk with brilliant scarlet sheets. She stared at it, at the flagrantly sexual invitation the rumpled silk offered from across the room.

Rodrigo was on her in an instant, seizing her in stalwart arms, crushing her to him with an impact so demanding, it knocked the breath from her lungs. In the same motion, he lowered his head and claimed her mouth with his.

She'd forgotten the seductive power of his kisses. So passionate, so devastating, so compelling. As if he could spend a lifetime exploring the luscious sectors of her mouth. As if he meant to plow down her uncertainty with the compulsive invasion of his tongue.

Lifting her in mighty arms, he carried her across the room, depositing her in the jumble of scarlet silk. She couldn't think. She'd spent the years since his desertion suppressing any thought of their time together, discounting in her anger and sense of betrayal any memory of her attraction to him. Now she felt the old longing surge to the surface, exhilarating and frightening her at the same time.

He lowered himself on top of her, his body hard and unrelenting. Grasping both sides of her head, he plundered her mouth once again, holding her immobile as her heart hammered against his chest. She could feel his erection, straining against her like a barbarian fighting to be free. What sweet temptation he was. And how desperately she wanted him!

She moaned and clasped his head to her, all her stunted passions reignited. It was so good, so unbelievably delicious. Her body felt alive beneath his expert mouth, sizzling like the equatorial sun.

"I've waited years for this moment," he said, never taking his mouth from hers. His voice was more heavily accented than she remembered, as if being away from England allowed his true nature to reassert itself. "Years of thinking about you, dreaming about you, worshiping your memory. Years of torture, needing you in my arms, and knowing you bedded no other man."

He couldn't possibly have said anything that caused her more pain, that picked worse at the scab of her one secret wound. She wrenched her mouth from his. "How do you know I've been with no other man?"

"My spies watched your every move."

She gasped, truly startled by this confession. She tried to remember if she'd ever felt herself followed, and couldn't recall.

He raised his head and met her awestruck gaze. "Did you imagine I would leave you so readily? That I would not keep track of what was mine?"

*Ella â minga,* he'd told his men. *She's mine.*

He was so confident, so secure in his own autonomy. Yet there were some things even his carefully placed spies couldn't know. Things that had long ago closed the door on any future with Rodrigo—even if he hadn't thrown his life away to become the bloodiest pirate of the seven seas.

She thought of that night, eight long years ago, when they'd said their farewells. She'd seen the proof back then of his dark passions, of the menacing sensuality of the inner self he'd hidden from an unsuspecting world. Of the cold, ruthless way he could pursue his goals. Hadn't she learned that night to pursue her own aims just as coldly, just as ruthlessly? But she'd never seen this anger, this impression of raw, unrestricted violence that sparked the air between them. It scared her suddenly, as she realized for the first time where she was —alone in a locked room with the one man who was truly dangerous to her designs. With her skirts up about her hips. With him pressing his all-too-persuasive body into the softly yielding flesh of her own. With an erection fueled by years of frustrated desires.

As if reading her thoughts, he softened his tone. Still holding her head in his massive hands, he said, "But that's over. We're together now. I've come here to rescue you."

She put her hands to his shoulders and pushed him away. "Just what is it you're rescuing me *from?*"

"From the clutches of England, of course."

She couldn't believe what she was hearing. "I rescued *myself* from England, thank you very much! Did you imagine I'd wait all this time, like some damsel in distress, for you to fashion a miracle and rescue me? When I had no indication that you ever thought about me at all?"

His hand stilled in the act of reaching for her breast. "I thought about you always. I never stopped longing for you."

"You never sent me word. Was I supposed to read your mind? Wait for a man who walked out of my life without so much as a backward glance? Without regrets of any kind?"

"You're wrong, Gabé. I regretted very much having to leave you behind."

"You *regretted?* You knew what you were going to do and you didn't tell me. You could have made any number of choices. You could have taken me with you. If you'd told me what you were doing and asked me to wait, even . . . but you'd have had to *trust* me, wouldn't you? I might have told my father—whom I despised—what you were up to. I can't believe the arrogance of you thinking you could waltz back into my life and dictate my future after all you did to me."

His hand made the arrested journey and slid over her breast. "Is a future with me so formidable a prospect?" he asked in a husky tone.

She shoved him away and fought to sit up. "Future? What kind of life would I have with you? A pirate's wench? Hunted by the law? Hung by the neck till I'm dead? You don't seem to understand, Rodrigo. You stand in the way of all I hold dear. You once told me I didn't fit into your plans. Well, now you don't fit into mine."

"You have no feelings for me at all, I suppose?" he said in the tone of a man who was beginning to feel rejected.

She lifted her head defiantly and said, "None!"

His eyes narrowed and a hard, calculating gleam replaced his vulnerable gaze. "You wanted me once."

"*But I thought you were someone else!* You played your part so well, I believed it. I thought we'd be married and you'd bring me out here, and together we'd revive Beau Vallon."

"Beau Vallon is an empty dream, Gabé. It always was."

"It's not an empty dream to me. And it's what I've always wanted from you. What feelings I had for you died the minute you deserted me. I've achieved everything I always wanted, with no help from you or any other man. I'm not the innocent girl you left behind, looking to you to remedy the injustice of my life. I'm a grown woman who knows what she wants and knows how to get it. I just don't need you anymore. I don't even need what you once provided. It was fun pretending with you, I won't deny it. But you were an escape from a life I found intolerable. I have the life I want now. And you just stand in the way."

"So you choose Beau Vallon." He got up and began to pace the cabin. "You don't know what you're choosing."

"That's none of your concern."

"If you didn't care about me, why write a play about me, and act out the part yourself? Why show me to the world as the image of your secret longings?"

She had an eerie sense that she was once again an actress in her own play. Except that she'd changed roles, and *he* was the one in control. "What I *longed for*," she said heatedly, "was for my father to give me what he'd stolen from my mother. *I used you*, Rodrigo. I knew if I could push the duke far enough, he'd give in to my demands. What better way to do so than to portray the pirate who was humiliating him in a play so sensual, it was calculated to shock the whole of England? I assure you, it was not intended as invitation for you to finish where you left off. If you misunderstood, I'm truly sorry. But you can hardly blame me for not divining your intentions."

"*Sorry?*" He took her wrists and wrenched her up from the bed so she came crashing against his chest. The blow was like colliding with a brick wall. "A curse on your apologies. I *know* you. I know the passions of your soul. It matters not what you say. You're mine now. This time I surrender you to no man. I made a mistake with you once before. But that," he added bitterly, "is a blunder I won't make again."

*You're mine now.* Staking his claim. Taking possession of her like a bauble he fancied. As if she had no feelings. Permitting her no say at all.

"I shan't let you do this," she vowed. "Your men already tried to take me against my will. Do you think I'd fight them off, just to let another pirate succeed where they failed?"

He was insulted, as she'd intended. She could see it in the tightening of his jaw, in the ferocious flare of his lion's eyes. She pulled away, but he followed, pushing her back to his bunk as he stepped toward her with stormy eyes. As she moved across the expanse of red silk, she came up sharply against the wall—the one with the collection of weapons within handy reach.

He caught the flash of the blade as she retrieved it from the wall. Incensed, he grabbed her arm and yanked her to her feet. But he didn't know what an expert swordswoman she'd become. Determined to fight him, she swung the sword around and put the cutting edge to his throat.

# Seven

He stood perfectly still, but his eyes were hurt, disbelieving. "You'd kill me?"

"To keep you from ravishing me, I'd be willing to hurt you so badly, you'd wish I *had* killed you."

He moved to step forward, but in one swift motion, she shifted the blade to his groin, freezing him in his tracks.

He didn't blink. "I don't have to ravish you," he said in a tight, controlled voice. "I could make you want me so badly, you'd beg me to take you."

Ignoring the erratic flutter inside, she tightened her grip on the sword. "I want you outside."

Still oblivious to the blade at his crotch, he gave her a long, considering look. "I warn you, I won't let you go. When I sail for D'Arros, you come with me."

"Move!" she commanded.

She quickly transferred the sword to his throat and forced him outside and up the stairs. When they were abovedecks, some of his men stopped short.

"*Capitão. . . ?*" one said, uncertain.

Gabrielle didn't even pause. The fighting had ceased, and the two ships were now tied together. In the aftermath of the battle, the dead had been laid out in rows on the deck. Groups of wounded men moaned pitifully. The smell of gunpowder blistered the air.

Using the blade as incentive, she urged her captive to the boarding plank. As she forced him across to the plundered vessel, Rodrigo's men stared in disbelief.

Finally, she stopped. Rodrigo stood, head held regally high in spite of his handicap, his hands clenched in tight fists at his sides. She could see the anger seething beneath his facade of studied calm.

"*Capitão*," cried one of his men, "how can this be?"

Clearly, they'd never seen their captain in such a disadvantaged position. Rodrigo's eyes stared straight ahead, his humiliation mingling with his wrath. She admired his cool. His leonine grace. It couldn't be easy, being made helpless before his men by application of his own sword.

When she'd last seen Cullen, he'd been huddled on the deck, trembling. Now he stood in a group of other prisoners bound to one another in a circle around the mizzenmast. "Gabby . . ." he said, staring aghast at his sister.

She ignored him, concentrating all her energies on keeping the sword lodged against Rodrigo's throat.

"I want your promise that you'll let me go," she told him so all could hear.

He said nothing.

She applied pressure to the sword.

"Say it," she ordered. The action drew a drop of blood.

"I promise," he ground out.

"Say it so your men will understand."

By now, all his men had gathered round. Rodrigo gave an impatient jerk of his head. As he did, the saber cut him. Blood trickled down the strong column of his neck onto his white shirt.

"I promise to let you go."

"Me, the captain, and crew of our ship."

"You, the captain, and crew," he agreed woodenly.

She impelled the sword just the slightest bit. "On your family's honor, Rodrigo."

He met her eyes. The look in his almost blasted her back against the rail. "My—family's—honor," he said, in the way of a man tested to his limits.

"Very well," she conceded. "I shall trust you to keep that oath."

Rodrigo reached up with a fist and contemptuously removed the sword from his throat. It cut his palm, but he didn't seem to notice. Gabrielle backed up instinctively, expecting him to retaliate once he was out of danger. Instead, he merely wrenched the weapon from her, turned, and walked away.

His men looked after him with wary eyes, as if they couldn't decide how to handle this unexpected turn of events.

Lieutenant Wallace called after him. "You mean, man, that we've come all this way to get her, and you're going to let her go?"

The pirate captain paused for a moment, gazing out at the sea as he considered his options. Then his eyes flicked back to Gabrielle and she felt stripped raw by the force of his gaze.

"Take the brother," he ordered.

It was a moment before his words settled in her mind. Not until three pirates began to untie Cullen did she realize she hadn't imagined this awful and unexpected turn of events. Determined not to let her guard down, she said in a contemptuous tone, "Don't be a fool, Rodrigo. What would you do with Cullen, when it's me you really want?"

He didn't answer. One of the pirates wrestled Cullen's arms behind him. She heard his groan, followed by a desperate plea. "Gabby!"

"He's been ill," she tried again, turning back to Rodrigo. "He doesn't travel well. Remember what you used to say? That he slowed you down, tagging along behind? He hasn't changed, Rodrigo."

Even as she spoke, the pirates forced Cullen across the deck and lifted him onto the rail. With him struggling every step of the way, they grappled him across the boards to their own ship.

"Gabby, do something!"

She was truly scared now. Rushing after Rodrigo, she took his arm in her hand and spun him around. "You made me a promise, remember?"

He merely arched a brow. "I promised to free you, your captain, and the crew. There was no mention made of your brother."

This wasn't a joke. It wasn't a bluff. He meant to kidnap her poor brother. She couldn't allow it. It was monstrous of him even to think of using Cullen like this.

Swallowing her pride, she said as calmly as she could, "Very well. Take me instead."

A faint smile grazed his sensuous mouth. "Too late, Gabé. I've already given the command."

"Then rescind your command, damn you!"

After a final lingering look, he walked away. She followed and grabbed him again, speaking in low, earnest tones. "He's little more than a child, Rodrigo. He can't get along without me."

"He's what? Twenty years old? I think it's time he learned. I was thirteen when your countrymen hanged my father and stole me from my homeland. Did anyone consider that I was but a child?"

"It's not the same. You were never like Cullen. He's —you know what he's like. He doesn't have your strength."

"If you mean he still hides behind his sister's all-too-convenient skirts, I consider it my duty to snatch the boy. Your father decided it was in my interest for him to make a new man of me. I now return the favor. You were always too protective of Cullen and his damned

Ashton blood. It kept him weak. Six months at sea and we'll make of him the man you couldn't."

He took the rope in his golden hand and as before, swung the distance to his own ship. As he did, Wallace came up behind Gabrielle and held her arms tight, making it impossible for her to follow. She fought him like a wildcat, desperation making her strong. But he held her easily. "Now, lass," he cooed softly, as if this were of no import at all. "Don't get yerself in a snit."

Ignoring him, she called after her old lover, this time with more of a pleading tone than she'd have liked. "Rodrigo, you can't do this. You of all people know what Cullen means to me. He's more than a brother, he's like my son. I swore when my mother died to die protecting him if I must. You can't take him from me."

From his own deck, he turned and gave her a cold look. "It's done," he said simply.

She fought Wallace again, crying out in frustration as his beefy arms tightened on her and she couldn't get free. "This won't make me love you again. I shall hate you till my dying day." When he ignored her, she threw back her head and called out to him in a voice she used to reach the last row of the theater. "If you do this, Rodrigo, I swear I'll make you pay. I shall have my revenge if it's the last thing I do. Do you hear me? Hastings will come after you with all his might. I never thought I'd say this, but for once, I shall be on his side. We'll destroy you for this!"

He stopped and looked back at her for a moment. Even from where she stood, she could see the hatred in his eyes, the sense of betrayal that she should use his lifelong enemy against him. She thought he'd speak to her, perhaps capitulate, so intense were the emotions that flicked across his face. Instead, he shifted his glance to Wallace. In a toneless voice he ordered, "Fire the ship."

# Eight

Standing at the rail of the ship with the other passengers, Gabrielle looked out on the island of Mahé—the largest of the Seychelle archipelago.

It was an odd and fascinating sight. Mountains of black granite and lush green vegetation in the middle of nowhere, jutting out from the ocean suddenly after passing nothing but flat coral reefs. She'd been told by the captain that these islands were submerged mountains, and that's exactly what they looked like—the tops of mountains rising out of the tide.

Those mountains were misty now, covered with varying shades of grey clouds that drifted along the tops of the hills dreamily—not angry, but as if stroking them with loving, lingering hands. The black of the granite was stark against the green, protruding from the vegetation as if asserting its supremacy over the landscape. The trees bowed reverentially in the sultry breeze, like subjects paying homage to majesty.

It was raining when they arrived. Not the chill rain of England, but a heavy, warm rain that nonetheless cooled Gabrielle's fevered skin. The heat was surprising and oppressive, the air thick and humid, but strangely soft and caressing at the same time. Long before they'd come into the rain, her clothes were clinging damply to her skin and her brow was dotted with perspiration. She was so uncomfortable, she longed to rip off her borrowed clothes and hurl herself into the sea.

The harbor was small, protected as the island curved around it on either side, and astonishingly uninhabited, with only a few ships and smaller vessels riding the waves. A far cry from the bustle of Thames harbors back in London. Beyond, she could see the meagerest glimpses of a town. Here and there a red-roofed French colonial house dotted the hills. In the distance, glimpses of plantations were shrouded in clouds. She thought of how many times she'd imagined this awesome moment, and how now it had been ruined. Maybe when she saw Beau Vallon . . . She wondered where it was, and if she could see it from here.

Onshore was a tiny dock skirting the beach of white sand. She could see a cortege of Europeans awaiting them, huddled together beneath black umbrellas as if at a funeral. As they drew closer, she recognized Hastings standing alone.

The passengers were loaded into smaller boats and rowed in to shore. By the time Gabrielle arrived, Hastings was already hearing the story of what had happened from one of the members of the battered crew. How the passengers and crew were forced into longboats, to be set adrift without provisions. How Captain Watkins, still suffering from the loss of his ear, had decried such treatment even as the Scotsman, Wallace, had reminded him another ship would be along in a matter of days. How the sails of the proud East Indiaman were set to flame, and the victims watched from a distance as it burned and sank before their eyes.

As she heard his words, it brought back memories she'd rather forget. Only Gabrielle seemed to care that her brother had been snatched from their midst. The others, suffering from lack of supplies, kept their distance, silently blaming her for their troubles. It was

Gabrielle the pirate wanted. If she'd gone with him, they'd have been spared the loss of a valuable ship and all the possessions the passengers had in the world. She'd brought this on their heads. Seeking a scapegoat, they shunned her, glaring their accusations with self-righteous eyes.

Only the thought of going after Cullen kept her sane. Her urgency gave her the courage she needed. She had to get her brother back, away from Rodrigo's savage clutches.

She could see Hastings's anger before she could hear his words. He was dressed stiffly in black broadcloth as if he were still in England. As he grew angrier, he let his umbrella slide down his back, as if it were too much to fume and hold it steady at the same time. His black hair grew slick with rain, but he didn't seem to notice. As she approached him, she could hear his voice raised in indignation.

"Took the *brother*? This is unconscionable!" In a temper, Hastings flung his umbrella to the dock. An assistant scrambled forth to retrieve it. "That damned Portuguese," he added. "He jumped the gun."

Suddenly she understood. A moment ago, she'd been bent on burying old rivalries to seek a union of peaceful cooperation. Now, boiling with anger, she charged at him, grabbed his arm, and wheeled him around. "You used me! You brought me here to use me as bait, didn't you? Thinking I'd lead you to Rodrigo so you could destroy him."

He looked down his nose at her, without greeting or welcome, as if continuing an argument that had raged for days. "And what did you expect? That I brought you out here out of the goodness of my heart?"

"You sniveling bastard! It's your fault Cullen's in the danger he is. You have to get him back, Hastings. Now."

"I don't give a hang about your precious Cullen."

"You don't give a hang about anything."

He stopped short and looked at her closely. "Did you see him? Soro? Face-to-face?"

"I almost killed him."

He began to storm about the dock. She could almost hear the wheels of his brain churning fast. "Did he say anything?"

"What, for instance?" she asked, suspicious.

"Where his hideout was, for instance," he snapped.

His insulting tone was forgotten in the sudden realization that Rodrigo had said something curious. What was it? *When I sail for D'Arros . . .* D'Arros! She'd barely heard it before, hadn't known what he meant. But of course! He'd told her the secret of his hideout. Why? Had he let it slip? He wasn't a man to reveal anything he didn't want disclosed. He'd wanted her to know, then. Why? Certainly not so Hastings could use it against him.

With an actress's calm, she looked him in the eyes and lied. "No. He didn't say a word."

Hastings swore. "I might have known you'd be of no help to me. I'm going to talk to the captain. Maybe he can be of assistance."

"I want to talk to the authorities," Gabrielle insisted. "About getting Cullen back."

Hastings turned and gave her an evil, self-satisfied grin. "But Gabby. Don't you remember? I *am* the authority. You might even say my word is law."

As he continued down the pier, his assistant called after him, "What should I do with her, Governor?"

With a dismissive wave of his hand, Hastings called back, "I don't care what you do with her."

The assistant looked sheepishly at the seething woman standing bareheaded in the rain. "I suppose it's to State House with us. You are the governor's sis—uh, guest, after all."

"Not by choice," she muttered.

"I beg your pardon, mum?"

"Nothing. Mr.—"

"Adamson."

"Mr. Adamson, are you familiar with my plantation, Beau Vallon?"

"Of course, mum. I've accompanied the governor there on occasion."

"Then you know where it is?"

"On the other side of the island, mum. I do."

"I should like to go there at once. Will you take me?"

"Now, mum?"

"Yes, Mr. Adamson."

"Wouldn't you like to refresh yourself first, mum? It's some ways."

"I've come a much longer way to see Beau Vallon."

He ushered her to his carriage and together they drove out of town through the lavish terrain. Along the way, she saw a profusion of plants and trees in shapes she'd never dreamed existed. Huge palms and fronds framing sudden large granite boulders. They passed clear lagoons of light blue dotting the countryside, beautiful French homes as they rose high above the sea. She looked back and saw the town of L'Establishment, still bearing the French name. She smelled French cooking wafting out of French doorways. As they descended the hill on the other side of the island, they left the houses behind, winding their way through luxuriant foliage and huge bougainvillea and hibiscus shrubs splashing rainbows of scarlet, orange, coral, purple, and pink across the lush emerald landscape toward the sea on the other side. It was an astonishingly beautiful drive through the rain, with droplets beating rhythmically on the roof of the carriage. But it was beastly hot on land, so hot she felt she could barely draw a breath.

Adamson tried to make small talk, but he was clearly uncomfortable and she spared him conversation, only occasionally asking a question about the plantation, which he dodged with a diplomat's ease. She was soon to discover why. After an hour or more, the coach drew up to a patch of land high on a hill, sloping down toward the sea. The rain had stoped. The air was fresh afterward, but not cool as in England. In fact, it felt heavy, stifling, as if it could easily rain again.

"I didn't expect it to be raining."

"This is the rainy season. It lasts for about a month. Mahé collects more rain than the other islands because of the mountains. Here you are, mum."

"Beau Vallon?" she whispered.

He nodded but dropped his gaze.

She got out of the carriage and walked about in the rain-drenched grass. It didn't take her long to discover the source of his embarrassment. The land stretching out before her was a tumble of overgrown weeds with grasses as high as her waist. The fields of cotton were long gone, reclaimed by a nature that was wild and free. Caprice had spoken often of the unusual fertility of this land. You could almost toss a handful of seeds to the ground, she'd said, and watch the sprouts grow. Apparently, it was true of weeds as well.

Gabrielle made her way cautiously through the bramble toward the main structure. *This was Mother's home,* she thought wondrously. *Where she was born. Where she was happy. Where she tasted her first love.* But as she approached, she found not the home of her mother's romantic memories, but a run-down house, badly damaged by the ravages of nature, neglected for over twenty years. The porch was leaking and the steps sagged. It was difficult to determine what color the paint had been. It looked grey now, and most of it was peeled off in streaks.

"Where are the gardenias?" Adamson stared at her as if he didn't know what she was talking about. "The *bois citron?* My mother said they were everywhere."

"Oh. There haven't been any here for years. They grow on some of the other islands, I think."

She looked out over the horizon, hearing her mother's words in her ears. *We had a hammock stretched between two palms, with gardenias all around. I used to lie about in it for hours, smelling the perfume of the flowers, reading Molière, and dreaming my dreams.* What would she think of her dreams now, if she could see this ruin? Gabrielle looked in vain, trying to find something that lived up to the magic her mother had woven in stories that had made her daughter dream as well.

The more she looked, the more depressed she became. It was obvious there was a great deal more work needed than she'd ever imagined. And money! Where would she find the money? Not from Hastings. How he must have laughed when he'd signed over the deed.

She had to find something. Just one thing that would make her feel her mother's presence. Trancelike, she climbed down the hill through the thick growth toward the sea. There, she found a beach such as her mother had spoken of. An unbelievable, deserted beach with pure white sand. She bent and touched it. It was too wet to get much of a sense of what it was like. It was sprinkling again, the rain dropping into the accumulated puddles on the beach, making quick circles of ripples to be replaced by others, hardly making a sound. She could see it, but the rain was so gentle, she could barely hear it, except for an occasional splash.

Dropping to her knees, she dug in the sand, trying desperately to find some dry enough that she could feel its true texture. But the sand was moist even deep down. She dug more frantically until at last she began to realize what she was doing. Coming to her senses, she glanced up the hill to see Adamson watching her with a worried frown.

Reluctantly, she got to her feet and slowly climbed the hill. She felt so discouraged, she wanted to cry. But it wasn't in her nature. Action was her forte. She would have to do something about this, and soon.

Halfway up the hill, she stopped, arrested by the sight of activity in the distance. A group of bedraggled Africans were chopping through the thick brush to clear a patch of land. She watched for a moment, then re-joined her companion. "Mr. Adamson, who are those men?"

"Slaves, mum."

She stared at him, horrified. "Slaves?"

"Certainly. All the plantations in this area depend on slave labor. Didn't you know?"

# Nine

*In England, slavery* had been just a word bandied about in newspapers as Parliament struggled with the issue that affected Englishmen only in far-off lands. Gabrielle had never come in contact with it personally before. She'd never really given it much thought. But here, it would soon prove impossible to look the other way.

"Everyone's changing their crop from cotton to copra," she heard Adamson say.

"What's copra?"

"Dried coconut meat. From copra one derives coconut oil, among other products. We shall have to get you slaves to clear the land and plant coconut trees, and other slaves to rebuild the house. When the time comes, more slaves will be needed to get the place livable."

"I'd prefer servants," she interjected.

"No need, mum. Slave labor is cheap and plentiful. And with your connection to the governor, you'll have no problem arranging all the credit you need. I shouldn't worry, mum. You'll have this place fixed up in no time."

"But slaves, Mr. Adamson—"

"Oh, now I understand. Fear not. I too felt a little

squeamish about it all when I first arrived. Flies in the face of our English sensibilities of fair play, I daresay. But I was brought around. Take my word for it. You'll adjust in no time. It really is the only way."

But to own other human beings . . . When she'd become mistress of Beau Vallon, she never once thought that she would have to become a slave owner as well.

Adamson took Gabrielle back to State House, the government mansion on a hill overlooking the small settlement of L'Establishment. In contrast to Beau Vallon's shabby neglect, State House was surrounded by clusters of small frangipani trees with spongy branches and pink and yellow flowers, and brilliant with orange, pink, and purple bougainvillea bushes all around. It was a two-story white building in the French colonial style, quite spacious and luxurious for these parts, where life was, by necessity, more informal than it was in Europe. Inside, what looked like more than sixty Africans were gathered, all wearing the clothes of English servitude, much as she'd been forced to wear at Westbury Grange. Every one was exceptional. Men and women alike had obviously been chosen for their beauty. The men were tall and undeniably well-formed with prominent bone structure and muscular torsos. The women were comely, their clothing designed to show off bodies that were taut and rounded as the majority of English women weren't. She'd never seen such an array of exotically impressive humanity in her life.

She looked at Adamson. "Slaves?" she asked softly.

"Of course, mum."

It was chilling to realize that, while the servants in her father's household had been paid wages for their work, these men and women were bought and paid for.

"I'm sure you'll want to bathe and rest," the assistant suggested. "Ordinarily, we wouldn't be out in the heat of the day."

"Then why was everyone at the harbor?"

"Because the governor requested it."

Something in his tone made her shiver in spite of the heat. As if the people gathered today were Hastings's subjects. "Do they always do the governor's bidding?" she asked, more bitterly than she'd intended.

His eyes flashed to her face, but he only smiled non-committally. He gestured to a tall black man dressed in a snow-white jacket and pristine gloves. "This is Robert. He runs the house. He'll take care of you."

"Follow me, please, *msabu*."

She was led through a house of unquestioned beauty, yet she felt a distinct unease. As she passed by rooms, she caught glimpses of velvet curtains and heavy bro-cade chairs, woolen carpets and brick fireplaces, and paintings done in Flemish oils. The curtains were drawn against the now-glaring sun, so it was cool and dark inside. The slaves, dismissed, moved about their duties on soundless feet.

Then a door was opened at the end of a long hall and she was ushered inside. The room was furnished in deep claret tones, with heavy mahogany furniture and drapes and carpets similar to the rest of the house. It was clear Hastings was a lover—indeed, collector—of beauty. Yet it seemed utterly bizarre. Outside was an-other world, strange and foreign, full of noises, smells, and cultures she'd never known. A realm of sweltering heat. Yet within these walls, King William reigned un-disturbed. If she didn't look out the window, if she couldn't feel the humid warmth, she'd have sworn she was back in London.

"This is Maya," Robert said, interrupting her thoughts. She looked up to see a striking black woman with a wealth of black hair, a perfect aquiline nose, and large ebony eyes, which she lowered when Gabrielle looked her way. Like the others, her body was lush and taut all at once. When she moved, her unbound breasts swayed freely beneath the restraints of her structured blouse. "She's a Somali. She'll be seeing to your needs."

Before leaving, Robert ordered that water be brought for her bath.

Maya struggled with a heavy container of water, pouring it into the tub. Gabrielle went forth and helped her. "You don't have to wait on me, Maya. I'm accustomed to fending for myself."

But Maya turned frightened eyes on her new mistress. "Master is whipping Maya, *msabu*. Maya is for taking care of mistress."

In that moment, the full horror of this homecoming hit her. No wonder Hastings had come to love the Seychelles—he was molding it into a larger version of the world he'd created at Westbury Grange.

She recalled Adamson's words. *All the plantations in this area depend on slave labor. Didn't you know?*

And Rodrigo's face. *Beau Vallon is an empty dream, Gabé. It always was.*

That night, she had a dream. It was so vivid that, even asleep, part of her wondered if it was a vision and not a dream at all. She saw Beau Vallon as it must have been. It was so beautiful that she, the dreamer, felt choked to tears. It was surrounded by water of different hues, sparkling in the sun like a rainbow. Playing in the water were birds of all colors—blue, yellow, red, green, purple —splashing in the water and shaking themselves so that prisms of color imbued the place with an otherworldly magic and charm.

As she walked through the lovely, manicured grounds, she saw her mother, lounging in a hammock in a long white dress, reading Molière aloud. Cullen was sprawled on the grass below her, looking radiant and healthy as he never had in life, playing laughingly with a frisky orange cat. An aura of happiness and peace pervaded the sultry air. She was overwhelmed with an urge to hug them to her, and cry joyfully into their arms.

But all at once, a shadow covered the land. She looked up to see what cloud had cast this gloom when she saw a formidable sight instead. Rodrigo, in all his golden pirate glory, stood above her, legs planted in a stubborn stance, blocking the sun.

Before she could protest, he'd swept her in his arms and carried her away.

Suddenly, she was in Rodrigo's cabin, lying naked in the folds of those scarlet sheets. He was kissing her, devouring her with his mouth, igniting her body with wildly roving hands. His voice at her ear saying softly, *"Beg me."* And this time she did. She begged him to take her, voicing her need to him until at last—*at last!* —he gave her what she wanted. Held her down and vanquished her body with the conquering fury of a storm at sea. She could feel his love, his passion, his need of her that had been denied these many years. And as his body moved over hers with exquisite skill, she was aware of the love that filled her heart. She wanted him so badly, she knew she'd die if she couldn't have him. Calling his name, she gave herself to him completely. As his mouth devoured hers, she heard herself whisper, "Rodrigo, it was always you . . ."

As she did, she was aware of Beau Vallon in the background. One by one, the trappings of the happy scene faded away. As Rodrigo plundered her body and her soul, first her mother, then Cullen, then the dazzling birds disappeared. Then, before her eyes, Beau Vallon withered and turned ugly and overgrown.

But Rodrigo took her head in his hands and turned her gaze to him. "You belong with me," he told her, and looking in his eyes, she knew it was true. Then those hands were on her, parting her thighs and slipping up to play with the reticence of her arousal, until nothing was left but her panting need to have him pumping inside her like a swollen, pulsing heart. He stroked her flesh

and she threw back her head in ecstasy. But at the peak
of their passion, she was jarred by a sound—the echo of
stretching rope. She looked up sharply and saw her
mother hanging above the bed. As she screamed, as she
pushed and clawed at Rodrigo, seeking release, the image above her changed.

She saw that it wasn't her mother hanging there at
all. It was Gabrielle herself.

And Hastings was holding the rope.

# Ten

*During the days*, she was able to forget her dream. Her thoughts were filled with two concerns: rescuing Cullen and reviving Beau Vallon without using slave labor.

Hastings was no help. He came and went mysteriously, staying out until all hours, coming in long after she'd gone to bed. She had no idea where he went or what he did, only that he spent a great deal of time with the Grand Blanc, the descendants of the original French settlers—still a major force in the islands even after the British takeover. Hastings seemed to value their company more than that of his own countrymen. He scarcely spoke to Gabrielle.

When she ventured to the island bank where, as Adamson had told her, credit was freely offered her as the governor's sister, she hesitated at first, thinking Hastings would make trouble for her if he found out. When he did, he merely shrugged. "Dig your own hole, Gabby. Just don't expect me to pay your debts when you find you can't make a living." He had no faith in her mission. Determined to prove him wrong, she spared no expense in hiring servants and took on the work of overseeing the restoration of her mother's plantation to its original tropical splendor.

When she demanded of Hastings what was being done about Cullen, he fixed her with a blank stare and said, "I can't go after him, can I? I don't know where he is."

She didn't dare trust him with her explosive secret—the location of Rodrigo's hideout. She wasn't even certain where D'Arros was. It would require stealth to divine the information she needed without giving Rodrigo away. Any obvious questions would get back to Hastings and likely tip him off.

After a week on the island, she finally found an opportunity.

She was at a reception celebrating the building of an Anglican church and honoring the arrival from India of the new minister, Rev. J. C. Holmes. With much of the island French Catholic, the British were banding together this night to commemorate their new cathedral. As governor, Hastings was required to attend, but he seemed edgy, anxious to be off. He kept pulling out his pocket watch and glancing at it as if it might force the hours to fly by. Clearly, the establishment of a new church was beyond his realm of interest.

But what *was* he doing? she wondered. Why did he keep glancing at his watch as if he had some important appointment to keep? Where did he go every night, to come in close to dawn?

The party was in the lavish estate of Jonathan Lambert, deputy governor of the islands. This, too, seemed suspicious, that Hastings had declined hosting it at State House, leaving him free to sneak away when it suited him.

Gabrielle sauntered through the rooms with their chintz-covered furnishings, amazed as always by the quantity of spirits being consumed. When the guests weren't complaining about the heat, they were drinking to forget it. She'd heard vague rumors of widespread opium use among British officials. She didn't doubt it from the glazed looks of some of them. For years, John

Company had exported opium into China, ignoring the emperor's ban, as a way of supplementing Indian revenues and purchasing the tea that had made them the most formidable traders the world had ever known. It wasn't difficult to imagine that some of it would find its way across the sea from India to Seychelles.

The guests spoke to her politely, showing interest in her acting career. Some had even seen her on the stage in London, years ago. But any questions she asked about her half brother were dodged with a hasty glance at his formidable back.

She began to suspect they were afraid of Hastings.

This was brought home after dinner when she passed by a group of women speaking adamantly in soft tones. She heard little of the conversation, but the word "slavery" caught her attention. It seemed that at every gathering, all they could talk about was the issue of Negro emancipation. She knew a controversial bill was going before Parliament that would ban the ownership of human flesh in British colonies. In England, where slavery had been illegal for decades, the issue was only one of a hundred threatened reforms, and barely made the papers. Here, the subject was an obsession—and London's antislavery leader, Sir Thomas Fowell Buxton, was cursed as the Antichrist. It was all the colonists seemed to have on their minds. But every time she tried to join the conversations, they ceased talking abruptly and gave each other warning looks.

Tonight, she decided she'd had enough.

"I was surprised to find slavery in the Seychelles," she confessed, interrupting them.

The ladies turned to her with arrested looks, like wild animals caught in the beam of the hunter's lantern. To deflect her, one of them said, "We say *Seychelles*, dear, not *the* Seychelles. The way you say England."

"Very well," she conceded, determined not to be thrown off track. "I knew slavery was still legal in the colonies, of course, but my impression was that slave trading by we English had ceased. That the owning of slaves was viewed as an abomination."

Maybelle Lambert, eager to fulfill her duties as hostess, broke the ensuing silence with an explosive expulsion of breath. "Oh, my dear, there have always been slaves here, for as long as anyone can remember. My husband says it would ruin the economy if that fool Buxton ever had his way."

"Why, my dear," added another matron, "your mother's people were some of the largest slaveholders in these parts. Surely you're aware of that?"

Gabrielle ignored the stab. "I was under the impression the trading of slaves has been banned for some time."

"Well," said Maybelle uncomfortably, "officially it is, of course."

"Then how do the plantations keep getting the slaves?"

"Maybelle," someone warned.

Gabrielle could see she was making them uncomfortable. Several of them stole glances at Hastings, causing her to wonder how he was involved. Surely if slaves were coming into the colony, Hastings was allowing it.

"To whom does my brother answer, anyway?"

"Why, the British authorities on Mauritius. It's an island some thousand miles to the south."

"So he was right. He *is* essentially a law unto himself here."

"I don't believe Admiral Fulton would think so. He patrols these waters with a fleet of Royal Navy ships. He comes by every three months or so. He should be here within the month."

"Is he a friend of the governor's?"

"Not particularly, I shouldn't think. They do what business needs doing, but sometimes they seem to be at odds."

So there *was* an authority in the Indian Ocean who wasn't in Hastings's back pocket. This was encouraging news. Perhaps she could persuade him to help her. But a month! Could she afford to wait that long?

Emboldened by this discovery, she pressed a little harder. "There are certainly a great many islands in this part of the ocean, aren't there? I saw dozens on the trip to Mahé."

"Oh, hundreds, my dear," Maybelle jumped in, relieved by the change of subject. "But they're just about all uninhabited. There are some people on Praslin, which, next to Mahé, is the largest. That's pronounced *Prah-lean*, my dear. Aren't the pronunciations beastly, though? Then there's La Digue. And of course, Fregate. That was once the family home of that pirate, Soro. Those are all fairly close by, in the Granitic Islands group."

Recalling Captain Watkins's words, she asked, "Are there some islands called Amirantes?"

"Oh, yes, dear, but they're far to the west—two or three days' sail at least. Highly inaccessible. The coral reefs in that area are treacherous—simply *treacherous*! Sailors are afraid to go there. My husband says they think the pirate Soro hides out somewhere in those dangerous waters."

"What are the names of some of those islands?"

"Why, let's see. There's African Banks, and Rémire, I think, and D'Arros, and yes, my favorite, Sand Cay. They all sound rather romantic, don't they?"

"Yes, indeed," Gabrielle muttered. But she'd stopped paying attention. *D'Arros!* Rodrigo and Cullen were on an island two or three days to the west.

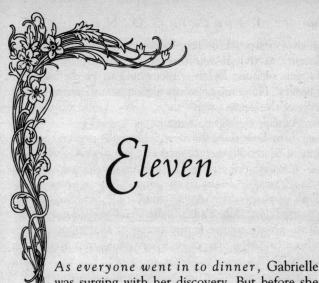

# Eleven

As *everyone went in to dinner*, Gabrielle was surging with her discovery. But before she could think of what—if anything—she might do about it, she saw Hastings look at his watch again and wander out to the porch. Coming up the lawn, she recognized three of the island's more prominent French planters—Delon, Montand, and DeVille. They surrounded Hastings, seeming to argue with him, until he capitulated and allowed them to drag him away. But as he was leaving, she noticed that Hastings cast a sly glance over his shoulder, like an adolescent sneaking away from his parents to go mischief-making.

What was he up to? she wondered again. And decided to follow them and find out.

She was in luck. Wherever the four men were going, they were traveling on foot, speaking softly and chuckling in low tones. Even though it was dark, she had to follow some distance behind so her presence wouldn't be detected. Once or twice she was afraid she'd lost them, but she increased her stride and caught up easily enough.

Less than a mile away, they came to a plantation she'd once passed and inquired about, only to have her queries deflected in the most evasive terms. All she knew was that it was French, owned by the premier French planter, Delon, and seemed to be shrouded in mystery. No one spoke openly of it, and no lady was ever seen to pay a call.

As they walked past the house toward the back, she began to hear the faint sounds of drumming in the distance. She followed them through a grove of coconut trees. Soon a bonfire in the distance lit the way. As she came closer, she witnessed a horrifying sight. A black slave girl was tied spread-eagle to a whipping post, completely naked, her dark skin gleaming like molten chocolate in the glare of the firelight. An African man, naked as well, had her anchored with his hands cupping her buttocks, and was slamming into her mercilessly while she cried out her agony into the night.

Lounging in the surrounding grasses of the steamy night were a group of men she recognized as French planters, smoking opium from long pipes, looking glassy-eyed and dreamy as they watched the proceedings. Slave women were gathered round, their sleek, naked bodies available to the wandering hands of the men. One woman knelt beside one of the planters, parting his tailored trousers and servicing him with her mouth. Distractedly, his hand went to the back of her head, petting her like a kitten.

"What's afoot?" Hastings asked, his gaze settling on the woman being raped before their eyes.

"Oh, she wouldn't cooperate," one of them explained, reaching over to take the smoking pipe. He shrugged philosophically. "What can I say? She's new and inexperienced. But no matter—she'll learn. By the end of the night, we'll all have had her, and she'll be better acquainted with her duties, eh?"

The men laughed as the African man squeezed the bound woman's breasts and increased his thrusts as she cried out in fear and pain.

"God, I love these islands," Hastings sighed, settling himself down on the grass. He leaned back on his elbows as a slave girl ran to retrieve the pipe and brought it to his lips. Letting her hold it for him, he took a puff and reached between her legs, fingering her as he exhaled and watched her eyes. She lowered them, settling back to allow him what liberties he chose.

"If the Buxton bill passes," cautioned Delon, "you won't love them so well. There will be no more debauching for us, *mon ami*."

"It won't pass. I have powerful friends and powerful men under my control who'll make sure it doesn't pass."

"A powerful father, more like."

"Anyway," Hastings pointed out, "they banished trading long ago and that hasn't stopped us, has it?"

"*Oui*, but if they ban the ownership of slaves, what are we going to do? *Hide them?*"

"It's that abominable corsair we must be concerned with at the moment," said Montand. "You remember when he commandeered that shipment of slaves last month and set them all loose? Most of them have joined his ranks, I hear. It's said they plan to attack every slaver who comes this way and free its cargo. Not only is he destroying our business, but all the attention he receives in England aids Buxton and his reformers. One way or another, we must wipe this menace off the face of the earth. And soon."

"Don't you think I know that?" Hastings snapped. "We're doing everything we can. We know he's in the Amirantes, but there are ten islands in the group, all of them surrounded by coral reefs that will rip apart any ship that doesn't know the waters intimately. It's a bloody graveyard of shipwrecks. That's why Soro hides out there. He knows those waters, where no one else does."

"Surely we can find a pilot capable enough to—"

"You might find someone who knows a passage to

one or the other of the islands. But only Soro himself knows them all."

"So, unless we know what island for which we search, and can find someone willing to take us there—"

"It would be suicide," Hastings agreed. "There is one possibility, of course. We're just going to have to attack every island till we have him. Attack till we find and destroy the Portuguese bastard."

"That's not a bad idea."

"I shall need financial backing, naturally."

"But of course."

"We'll do it, then. We shall start next week. We'll gather a fleet, find as many pilots as we can who know pieces of these waters, attack every last bloody island until we find Soro, and kill him and everyone who sails with him. That should take care of the problem."

"What about your half brother?" Delon asked pointedly.

Hastings met his gaze and snapped, "He's not my half brother. And I don't care a fig what happens to him."

"Then we're agreed."

"And while Soro is being blown to bits," Hastings continued, "I shall sail to Zanzibar the first of the month and meet with the sultan."

"Isn't that dangerous at such a time?"

"If I don't go now, I shall be forced to wait another month for the next ship. Believe me, Soro will have his hands too full in the Amirantes to pose any threat to me. Now," Hastings added, rising to his feet, "I should like to forget this beastly business and have a go at this unwilling slave myself. See if she hasn't learned her lesson."

He bent to retrieve a whip, which he curled around his hand. Then he stepped into the eerie glow of the fire, took the black man's shoulder in his hand, and heaved him off the sobbing woman so he went stumbling back. Taking the woman's chin in his fist, he yanked back her head and said in a menacing tone, "Now. Are you ready to be a good slave? Or do you need another lesson?"

As he shed his clothing and some of the others rose to join him, Gabrielle turned and ran. She ran as if she were being chased by demons from hell. She ran as fast and as far as she could, trying to expel the horrid vision from her mind. Her instinct was to fight them, to storm into the clearing and rip the men from the woman and make them pay for their abuse. But reason stayed her hand.

Their words had put Rodrigo in a new light. And she saw her father and Hastings in a different light as well. They were partners in an evil conspiracy, and Rodrigo was trying to stop them.

She ran all the way back to State House. In her bedroom, she paced the floor, panting through burning lungs, asking herself the same question over and over: *What am I to do?*

She knew now, with a woman's instinct, that Rodrigo had told her the whereabouts of his hideout for a reason. He'd wanted her to go to him. He'd taken Cullen knowing she'd eventually decide to do the very thing she knew she must: go after him herself.

If Hastings's fleet got there first, Cullen could be killed in the attack. Still, she wasn't ready to face Rodrigo on his own terms. She needed time to think. But there was no time. Hastings would probably be home soon. She needed an idea. Something daring, something no one would guess. Not Rodrigo. Certainly not Hastings.

Suddenly, she stopped. The perfect scheme seized her in its grip. It was so obvious, why hadn't she thought of it sooner? Impulsively, she sneaked down the hall to Hastings's formal bedroom and threw open his armoire, rummaging through his clothes. Yes, there was just what she needed here—even a man's ceremonial wig. She picked up a shirt, held it to her breasts, and turned to the mirror.

A vision filled her head of a mass of shadowy figures surging to their feet beyond the footlights as she yanked off her wig. She'd fooled them all, she thought, stripping off her feminine clothes. Why couldn't she do so again?

# Twelve

*The gaggle of taverns* in Shantytown was little more than a ragged collection of open huts, fashioned from gayak wood with woven latanier leaves forming roofs in case of rain. There were no walls, no hidden pockets of safety; just enough wooden posts to keep the roof above their heads. Even at night it was warm enough that enclosing partitions were deemed unnecessary.

For Gabrielle, this meant unwanted danger. There were only a handful of taverns, but each was within easy spying distance of the other. Even through the rain, she could look from one into the other and see the collection of French overseers, British seamen, and American whalers sprawled about the rickety tables or huddled over their grog. Already she'd been observed in three of them, asking questions she hoped would lead her to Rodrigo.

It was raining again. She entered the fourth tavern, shaking off the warm water, altering her walk, her stance, the slant of her eye to better fill Hastings's clothes. It was impossibly hot in the suit and cloak, the rain increasing the muggy heat instead of alleviating it. The boots were too big, in spite of the rolled-up stockings she'd used to stuff the toes, and rainwater had seeped in, sloshing maddeningly as she walked. She had to work consciously not to limp or drag them unnaturally. Not for a moment could she forget her role. To be discovered as a woman was dangerous from any standpoint. These men were rough, accustomed to living a thousand miles from the nearest law. What would they do to a woman caught lurking in the dark bower of their midst?

Then there was Hastings. He was clever enough to figure out her intentions. Already, he could have men searching for her. She had to make her escape quickly, if at all. Mahé was an island. The only way to get off it was by ship. She glanced once again at the dhow riding the swells in the harbor and felt a curl of nervous excitement in her belly. Small and flat-bottomed, the vessel was perfect for her plans. Someone had to own it, and she had to find him quickly. It might take time to convince him of her scheme. And time was something she had precious little of to spare.

The men looked the same here as they had in the other establishments: mostly vagrants or men who worked the waterfront. One or two freed slaves sat in the back, away from the whites who disdained them. As she entered, a buxom whore eyed her speculatively, set her tankards down on the nearest table, and sashayed forth.

"I've not seen you here before, *cher*," she greeted in a French accent. Her dishwater hair spilled over her shoulders, her fleshy hips moved toward Gabrielle's. If she didn't stop her, the whore would get too close and uncover secrets that were better left undisclosed.

Thinking fast, Gabrielle took the whore's chin in her fist and with a flick of her wrist, shoved her back like an arrogant rogue. "You move too fast, woman," she said with her best masculine swagger. "I attend to business first. Pleasure comes with the dawn."

The whore licked her lips and ran her eyes along the gentleman's frame. "Then I'll hope for a speedy night."

Inwardly, Gabrielle laughed, feeling warmed by the lack of suspicion in the whore's eyes. So far, her deception had played perfectly. Still, it was dangerous to remain. All the whore had to do was slip up behind her and run her hands along what she assumed was the gentleman's chest, and she'd come in startled contact with Gabrielle's bound breasts. It wasn't a chance she relished taking.

She moved from her, strutting as best she could about the sandy floor strewn with dried palm leaves, making sure her back was never turned to the whore, keeping one eye on her as she surveyed the men.

"Who among you lads owns that dhow out in the harbor?" she asked, as she had in the last three taverns.

The activity went on as before. Some spoke French in quiet tones. Two Americans were flipping coins to see who had first call with the whore. She felt the time ticking away as the rain beat against the leafy roof and spattered in the sand outside. Another false start. She'd have to look elsewhere, yet she was running out of taverns. It was possible the owner was safe in his bed, and she'd never find him.

Then she heard a small voice. "I have that honor."

She looked around but couldn't spot the one who'd spoken. Had she imagined it?

There was a rustle from one of the tables and a man half stood, wavering just a bit. He was a short man with a balding head and a florid face. As she approached, she could smell the fumes of liquor as if he'd blasted them her way.

"That's your dhow?" she asked again, hoping she'd heard wrong. This man, although English, looked neither sturdy nor sober enough to navigate his way so far as the next tavern, much less the impregnable reaches of Rodrigo's hideaway.

"She is."

"And a fine one she is at that," she complimented him, although her knowledge of such things was decidedly limited. All she knew was a smaller boat had a better chance of navigating the dangerous reefs she'd have to sail through in order to find Cullen.

"Thank you, mate. Have a drink fer yer pains."

Gabrielle sat down and accepted the tankard of strong brew the whore slapped before her. She gave the whore a wink and a pat and sent her safely on her way.

"What do you do with such a fine skiff?" she asked the seaman.

"Oh, mostly ferry back and forth amongst the islands." He paused to gulp his drink, spilling suds down his chin. These he wiped away with his shirtsleeve and gave her a grin. "Mostly transporting goods. You ain't drinking."

She took a sip, grasping the tankard by its bowl instead of the handle, the way the other men did.

How best to handle this? she wondered. Appeal to his masculine pride.

"Well, as I said, it's a fine-enough-looking boat, but I don't reckon she'd hold up on longer voyages."

The skipper raised himself up in a show of outraged dignity. "I'll have you know, laddy, I've been to the outer islands and back with this beauty with nary a scratch on her."

"Ah. Then you must be a navigator of exceptional skill."

He shrugged. "Jonah Fitch does all right, that he does." He peered at her then, as if suddenly realizing the man before him was asking a goodly number of questions. "Say, now. Don't know as we've seen the likes of you in these parts before," he said, leaning closer so his breath singed the inner flesh of her nostrils.

"I came in on that ship that was attacked by that pirate."

"Oh. Bad business, that."

"Indeed. I've a mind for some solitude after such an ordeal."

"There's solitude aplenty in these parts," the man agreed.

"I had in mind more solitude than I've found on this island. Some place where a man can nurse his shattered pride."

The blur seemed to recede from the seaman's eyes. "What did you have in mind, laddy?"

This was it. She could succeed or fail all in the next minute. "Ever hear of an island named D'Arros?" she asked carefully.

A Frenchman, overhearing, said, "D'Arros. This place, she is way out in the Amirantes. Dangerous waters, *monsieur*."

"Don't I know that?" Fitch snapped, shoving the Frenchman aside. "Get on with you." When the interloper had left, he turned back to Gabrielle with a noticeably shrewder eye and lowered his voice. "I know where it is, all right. I've been by there, many a year ago. But there's talk now about them Amirantes. Talk that ain't exactly to my liking."

She tensed. "What sort of talk?"

"Some say the pirate Soro haunts those waters."

Either he was onto her scheme, or was dickering for more money. She leaned over in a conspiratorial way, coarsening her accent. "Let's hope not. It'd be just me bloody luck to run into him again, what with this recent encounter. I don't reckon a chap could be that unlucky twice in the same lifetime, do you?"

There was a commotion in the doorway. Gabrielle looked around to see officers dressed in magistrates' uniforms asking questions of the whore as they shook their cloaks free of rain, splashing the patrons, who let out a roar of protest. She recognized them at once. Hastings's men.

They moved through the hut, demanding to know if

a woman had been asking questions about leaving the island, and warning against aiding her cause.

When Gabrielle turned back to Jonah Fitch, he was eyeing her closely. "What would it take for you to skipper me to the Amirantes?"

"It'd take a pretty bit of dosh to make me navigate them reefs. A pretty bit, indeed."

She reached into Hastings's pants pocket and withdrew a silk pouch full of coins she'd pilfered, dropping it to the table. "Is this pretty enough?"

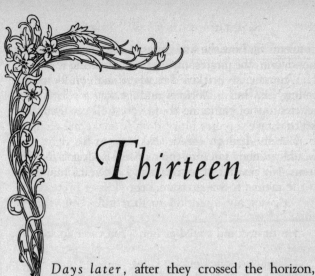

# Thirteen

*Days later,* after they crossed the horizon, suddenly there loomed before them a chilling sight: four armed frigates anchored off the cove, *El Paraiso* foremost among them. Beyond these lay an island heavily fortified with castlelike walls. Unlike Mahé, with its high mountains and huge granite outcroppings, D'Arros was a coral island, relatively flat and covered with varieties of palms. Swarms of large seabirds circled the sky above it.

It was the first sign of life they'd seen since leaving Mahé. Jonah Fitch raised the spyglass. "Pirates!" he croaked. "Hang on, matey. We're putting our tails betwixt our legs and running like dogs."

"Not so fast." Something in Gabrielle's voice stopped him. She was still disguised as a man, but her appearance had altered. By now, she'd refashioned Hastings's clothes so they more closely resembled the ragtag attire of a man of the sea. She'd slid her sword into the sash at her waist, which she'd made from a torn bit of Hastings's silk cloak.

It had been tricky, fooling the skipper with her identity for so long. She'd had to claim a gentlemanly modesty when attending to her own needs. But her greatest concern was how she was going to convince him to turn her over to the pirates, once he saw what she was about. Her conscience pricked her when she considered not telling him her intentions until it was too late. If he reacted out of panic, he could very well get them both killed.

But she had no choice. No man in his right mind would willingly sail into the midst of Rodrigo's fortifications. No amount of money could convince him.

"No time to waste, mate," the skipper protested.

"It's not my intention to turn tail. This is why I came."

He turned and stared at her. "You came looking for Soro?"

"I came to join him."

"*Join* them?" He looked out at the ominous ships riding the tide. "Well, too late to turn back now." With efficient motions, he raised a flag of truce.

When he was finished, Gabrielle gave his back a manly slap. "That's the spirit. Now let me do the talking. If we don't convince them we mean what we say, there could be consequences."

"To say the least."

While waiting for the signal, Gabrielle adjusted her appearance as she'd planned. To disguise her distinctive cobalt eyes, she wore a patch over one and squinted the other. If she was worried about what the skipper would say, she needn't have bothered. He eyed the black silk patch she'd also made from Hastings's cloak and said, "Have you got one for me?"

"Sorry."

"I could pretend to have a wooden leg."

"I wouldn't," she advised, adjusting the patch to fit more comfortably. "If they find you out, they'll likely kill us both. Not anxious, are you?"

"Anxious?" He put on a good show of bravado. "Mate, I've faced King Neptune himself in some of these storms. Once you've braved the sea, men don't seem so fearsome." Yet he gave her a keen look that betrayed his true feelings. "What about you?"

"A touch of stage fright, that's all. It will pass."

"Odd choice of wording, that. Stage fright."

She reminded herself to watch what she said in the future. If this uneducated skipper who hadn't seen a theater for twenty years had caught her slip of the tongue, Rodrigo was sure to as well.

Once the white flag was spotted, they were waved in toward the main ship, guns leveled at them from all around the deck. Gabrielle's heart pounded as they drew close, looking up at the vessel of terror that loomed before her, wondering if Rodrigo was striding the deck.

"Permission to come aboard, sir," called the skipper, a formality that would never have occurred to Gabrielle.

The red hair and bearded face of the Scotsman, Wallace, came into view.

"To what purpose, man?" he asked. "Don't you know these waters are treacherous? Cutthroats lurk in these parts, so we hear."

The pirates laughed.

"We hear you're recruiting men for a big battle," Gabrielle called in her most masculine voice. "We've hopes of joining your particular band of cutthroats."

A disbelieving snicker circled the deck. "And why is that?" Wallace called down.

Without hesitation, she called back, "Because we've as little pity for the masters of slaves as you."

The laughter stopped. Suddenly the sea and everything around them resonated a silence she could hear in her soul. Wallace left his post at the rail, spoke to someone in low tones, then returned.

"Permission granted. The captain's onshore. I'll row you there meself. But I'd watch me step, lads. We tolerate no tricks on D'Arros."

Wallace settled himself into their skiff, which bobbed about in the surf beneath his weight. As the man who'd joined him rowed them in, Wallace disarmed the newcomers, tucking Gabrielle's sword under his arm. They said nothing rowing in. Gabrielle kept her face turned toward shore, lest the Scotsman should recognize her beneath the disguise.

When they came at last to the reef that surrounded the island, a group of barefooted sailors met them and guided them over the treacherous coral. It was a fearsome struggle, as the churning tide fought to free the boat from the sailors' grip. The skiff beached at last on a white sandy surface and the guests were helped ashore. As she descended, Gabrielle couldn't help noticing the thick calluses on the feet of the men who'd helped them, as if years of traversing the coral had toughened them.

Even from the water, Gabrielle had noted the trappings of a community. The far beach was littered with a profusion of huts made from tree trunks and palm fronds. The island was flat with a natural habor, but more barren than those she'd passed to get here.

There was some activity here and there, but most of the inhabitants of the island were gathered up the beach. Wallace led them through the thick sand with sure, steady strides. There, a collection of a hundred or more men, mostly freed slaves, huddled in a mass—some looking determined, some casting glances about the pirates as if unsure. Fires roared from an assortment of tin barrels, while a number of the pirates held into the blaze long metal spikes, as thin as needles, about eight inches in length. Beside them, on tables fashioned from native trees, was a collection of large wooden bowls.

"Wait here, out of the way," Wallace told them. "You're just in time to witness the taking of the oath. If you can stomach *this*, lads, we might well address your suit."

Gabrielle didn't like the sound of it. A feeling of trepidation permeated the novices. From some she sensed outright fear. What was going on? She glanced about the beach and spotted Cullen, watching from the sidelines. She barely recognized him. He looked different from the man Rodrigo had stolen from their ship. Where once he'd been ill and pale, he now radiated a robust well-being. His sandy hair, without its taming pomade, was long and wild, but it shone with health, glinting with streaks the color of pale wheat. His skin, once so pallid, now glowed red from the sun.

"I'll be back," she told Jonah, then hastened to her brother's side before her companion could stop her.

"Cullen," she whispered. When he gave her a startled glance, she put her finger to her lips to signal silence.

"Gabby!" He hushed his voice immediately, looking around him. "How'd you get here?"

"With great difficulty. And now we're getting out." She caught the flash of fear in his eyes.

"Rodrigo will never let us off this island, Gabby."

"Why do you think I came in disguise?"

Abruptly, the air changed. An electricity flicked through the assembly like a bolt of lightning. The men straightened. The crowd cleared. And there stood Rodrigo, wearing the fierce scowl of the pirate king.

He strode about the beach, inspecting the men who congregated before him, some of them shaking visibly as he caught their eye. They'd obviously heard ferocious tales about the pirate, and at this moment of truth, didn't know what to expect.

When his back was turned, Gabrielle crept as unobtrusively as possible back to Jonah's side.

"You've briefed the new men?" Rodrigo asked without preamble, looking at no one in particular.

"Aye, Captain," someone answered. "They know what to expect."

Rodrigo paced before them with the grace of a lion, his hands behind his back, his boots striking the dry sand like cracks of a whip. He looked fearsome and proud. She suddenly wondered what she was doing matching wits with him. But just the thought of his power here, in his own domain, beyond the reaches of the law, made her all the more determined to succeed in her quest: to get her brother safely out of here.

He addressed the men. "Once you sign the articles of faith, you will be officially inducted into the service of *El Paraiso*. We fight for a noble cause, and we use whatever methods that cause requires. No man is welcome who does not hold these principles dear. I am master here, make no mistake. But you are not slaves. You answer to me of your own free will. For this reason, we ask of you this test of faith. If any of you are squeamish, if you don't love the cause we serve, we invite you to leave. My men will escort you to safe waters once you've given your oath not to reveal the whereabouts of this outpost. But be forewarned, my hale and hearty men. We brook no deceit. If you break your oath, we will know it. And on my honor"—he paused to look each individual dramatically in the face—"we—*will*—hunt—you—down."

A man behind her gulped.

"However," Rodrigo continued, "if you decide to join us, the wearing of our mark is the commitment we make to each other and our cause. None of us does this lightly. The British authorities know I will never force any man to wear this mark. Therefore, they will automatically hang anyone who bears it. So be forewarned. Once you've worn the bird of freedom, there is no turning back."

With a gesture of his hand, Rodrigo motioned to one of the African members of his crew, who stepped forward and repeated what he'd said in a language Gabrielle couldn't place. Some African dialect, she supposed, although she thought she caught a few words of Portuguese thrown in.

When his interpreter was finished, Rodrigo added, "Now, who among you wishes to part company with my men?"

He paused, waiting, but there wasn't a sound.

"Very well. We begin."

A table was quickly brought up at the side of the secluded beach. Behind that was placed a chair, and on the table a heavy leather-bound book.

Rodrigo sat in the chair, opened the book, then dipped a quill in the inkwell his men had provided. "Once you've braved the brand, come to me and sign your name among those of our men."

Braved the brand? Gabrielle watched in mounting horror as the long iron needles were removed from the fire and dipped into the wooden bowls. All around them, the recruits began to remove their shirts.

"If you want to join us, get in line," Wallace told her as she stared aghast. Numbly, she stepped into the closest line of men. Staring at the naked, masculine back gleaming with sweat before her, she fingered the buttons of her shirt and wondered how in God's name she could get out of this one.

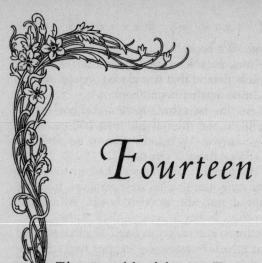

# Fourteen

*The test of faith began.* Ten men at a time were brought to the tables, where they were folded over and given a thick length of rope to place between their teeth. Then, with swift efficiency, the needles were dipped in dark ink and inserted again and again into the underlayer of the men's flesh. The mark was etched on their right shoulder blade with the same swift, efficient pinpricks. Gabrielle heard the grunts of the men and saw the sweat streaming down their faces before the tattoo was finished and a special ointment smeared on top. When the first of the men stood, wavering shakily, she could see the raw outline of a bird in flight.

"What's the mark?" someone asked in a weak voice.

"A frigate bird," said Jonah Fitch.

Gabrielle cast him a questioning glance.

"Frigate birds are the pirates of the air," her companion whispered. "They wait for some other bird to catch a fish, then attack that bird and take the food. A pirate bird, you see? Soro's family used to own the island named for the birds, once upon a time. Afore it was took from them."

She could see some twisted sense in it, but she had

more pressing matters on her mind. Somehow or other, she had to think of a distraction before her own shirt was ripped to her waist, and her identity revealed.

Scores of men were tattooed, then made their way to Rodrigo, where they signed the book and shook his offered hand. She noted that he said a personal word to each, but too softly for the rest of them to hear.

Just then, in the instant before the needle scarred him, one of the few white men jerked away with a cry of fear. He spit the rope from his mouth and turned on Rodrigo with pleading eyes.

"On my honor, sir, I want to be one of your men. I'm a fugitive from the penal colony in New South Wales— and an Englishman who abhors seeing my countrymen pander in slaves. But I have me doubts that I can do it."

"Can't you?" Rodrigo asked. He stood, then put his hands to his shirt and ripped the buttons from it in a single wrench, yanking it in the same fluid motion to his waist. "I did." Turning, he displayed a sun-browned back broad and taut with muscles. And just at the right shoulder blade was the unmistakable brand of a pirate bird in flight. Twice as big, it was beautiful, etched into his skin like a lovingly fashioned work of art.

Gabrielle had to admire the theatrics of his display. No one could see the scene without being moved by the sheer visual splendor of it—of a leader so willing to assume the same risks he demanded of his followers.

At the sight of it, the reluctant recruit hung his head. "You've shamed me," he said. "If you'll still have a sorry cur like me, I'll be more than proud to wear your mark forever."

As Rodrigo watched with suspicious eyes, the man fixed the rope firmly in his teeth, then refused to bend over, taking the piercing of his flesh as he stood. He nearly turned blue from holding his breath so fiercely, but when the deed was done, Rodrigo surprised them all by laughing aloud. Tugging the ruined shirt from his breeches, he tossed it aside, rounded the table, and crossed the beach to hold out his hand.

"What's your name?" he asked.

"Higgins, sir." But he didn't take Rodrigo's hand.

"You're a good man, Higgins."

"I was nearly a coward, sir."

"Coward?" Rodrigo asked as if he couldn't believe what he was hearing. "Tell me if you would, good Higgins, what glory there is in being born fearless? I assure you, there isn't a fearless man among my crew. We've been slaves, every one of us, in one manner or other. The very definition of a slave is one who, through no action of his own, is forced to live in fear. Sooner or later, every man among us comes face to face with his own terror. It's the *conquering* of that terror that makes us brave, and strong. It's through the banding together of our collective horror that we can fight that which we fear most—the injustice that brought us here in the first place."

So seductive were his words that when he stopped speaking, Gabrielle had to remind herself to breathe. She, too, had suffered injustice in her life. A form of slavery forced on her by Hastings's jealous paranoia. It would be so easy to become lost in Rodrigo's words of hope and retribution. She gritted her teeth, forcing herself to be strong. To reject the emotions his words threatened to unleash.

With a straightening of his stance, Higgins took Rodrigo's hand and shook it heartily with both his own. "I thank you, sir, indeed I do. And I pledge to our cause my fealty, for what it's worth."

Rodrigo put his hand in a comforting gesture to the back of the man's neck. "Go sign the articles, Higgins, then go rest." Then, turning to scan the rest of the crowd, his gaze fell on Cullen. "And you, boy? Would you care to wear our mark, and swear loyalty to me as your captain? Or do you prefer to stay my prisoner?"

For an instant, Cullen's eyes flicked to Gabrielle,

where she stood in line debating her dilemma. She caught the fear in his eyes, the hesitation. Once again, he was looking to her to protect him. And for a moment, even though she'd have to stop it, she wished he'd have the courage to do it. Reject his Ashton legacy, walk to the front of the line, bare his back, and for once in his life, startle her with some resource of gumption.

But it was not to be. Cullen dropped his gaze and said timidly, "Thank you, sir. Perhaps another time."

Rodrigo looked at the boy thoughtfully, then, with a slight nod, moved off without another word.

At that moment, the man before Gabrielle stepped forth to offer his back. She knew it was now or never. Raising her voice, she turned and addressed Rodrigo directly.

"I, too, question whether I care to be obligated to you, sir—a man who is clearly my inferior with the blade."

There were gasps all around. She felt at once that she was in the theater, and the climactic scene was at hand. All around her, she heard murmurs. "Dangerous words," said one. "He's never been bested with a sword," cried another in outrage. And still another suggested, "Hang the scoundrel."

Rodrigo just stopped in his tracks, his back still to the scoundrel in question. Slowly, he turned, and she saw the sensual mouth turn up ever so slightly in an engaging grin. "Bold words, indeed, lad. But I assure you, if you can best me with your sword, I'll wear *your* mark and call you Captain."

"Retrieve my sword and we shall see who deserves the title. *And* the respect."

Wallace made a move to apologize but Rodrigo raised a restraining hand. He rounded her slowly, looking her over with great care. She quailed inside but vowed she could do this.

"You look pretty frail, *menino.*"

"I'm not a boy."

This seemed to amuse him. He crossed his arms over his bare chest and put a thumb to his chin, considering her. "You speak Portuguese, too. A man of many talents, it would seem, eh, Mr. Wallace?"

"A man of many boasts," scoffed Wallace, enjoying himself now as much as Rodrigo. "Have you no' heard of the captain's prowess with a sword?"

"The question is, has he heard of mine?"

Rodrigo grinned. "The gentleman's sword, then, Quartermaster. And my own."

As the swords were brought, Rodrigo readied himself for combat. Sitting in the chair, he extended his boot and one of the Africans ran to kneel before him, pulling it off. The other boot was removed and he stood before her in his bare feet, with no clothing to encumber him now save a skintight pair of breeches.

Gabrielle tried not to think how Hastings's stuffed boots might hamper her, and she dared not remove them and reveal the feminine curves of her feet. But she dismissed it as unimportant. She knew something Rodrigo didn't. Both had studied fencing with the same master. She knew everything the maestro had taught him. She could anticipate his every move. As he took his sword and faced her, she gave him a cocky grin.

It never once occurred to her that she might lose such a battle—not just of skill, but of wills.

# Fifteen

*They faced each other* and Gabrielle saw the flicker of surprise when she matched his Italian stance. "Very nice," he murmured as he gave her leeway to make the first thrust.

As they danced about the sand, she tried not to look at him, but to keep her focus on his steel. It was difficult at best. He'd never looked so like a lion before, his pale breeches clinging to his muscular frame, his skin a golden brown and streaming with sweat, his hair falling in wayward waves over his eyes. His body exuded a raw, fierce domination held in check—like a lion lazily swishing his tail before suddenly pouncing on his prey. She raised her gaze to his chest. That was hardly better. She recalled too well the feel of it, hard and tempered, remembered how easily his nipples hardened beneath her tongue. She watched the muscles in his arm coil and expand as he wielded the heavy sword with an ease that bespoke his expertise.

She had to concentrate. She must think of her mission. She must think of Cullen. She must cling to her fury at Rodrigo for taking her brother and forcing her into this position. What she mustn't think was how beautiful he looked with his golden hair shimmering in the sun. With his feline's eyes flicking contemptuously over her frame. With his grin showing impossibly white teeth in a bronzed and handsome face.

She lunged, launching the attack, but he danced away so quickly, she barely saw him move. His bare feet made him nimble, glancing off the hot sand of the beach as if propelled by a vault. As she chased him about, he moved like a phantom, like mist beneath her blade, there one moment, dissolved into thin air the next. But she knew the moves. So she began to anticipate what he might do, then test him to see if she was right. Invariably, she was. If she lunged just so, he moved to the right to prance easily out of reach of her blade. She let him get away with it several more times, varying her attacks so he wouldn't guess her aim. So far he hadn't touched her with his steel.

Then, suddenly, as he veered right, she pivoted and slashed her blade up the front of his leg. It cut through the skintight breeches in a long slice, drawing blood, exposing the gash on his sleek, hairy thigh.

Now he knew she meant business. Glancing at his wound the way he might express annoyance at a buzzing fly, he asked in a deceptively gracious tone, "Why didn't you tell me you wanted to play rough?" Then he whirled and engaged her for the first time. As his saber clashed against hers, the force of it reverberated through her arm, numbing it to the point that she nearly dropped her sword. She could scarcely believe the force of the blow. No competitor she'd ever fought, no matter how strong, had ever matched the might of Rodrigo's attack.

He swung at her again and again. She feinted and parried, but soon enough, she was completely overwhelmed. The wound to his leg didn't faze him. He pounced on her with the grace, stealth, and power of the king of beasts stalking its prey. She'd seen such brutal yet lissome swordplay only once before: when she'd watched her half brother, Hastings, fencing with his coach. Yet, she felt instinctively that Rodrigo was using only a fraction of his potential. That while she was losing ground fast, he was merely warming up.

On the defensive, she backed away from him until she came flush against the table. She put her hand to the wood and hoisted herself up so she stood on the edge above him. But her boots made it awkward. As he feinted, she nearly fell backward.

He caught her just in time. His hand on her arm sent shock waves of a different sort rushing through her. As if he'd swallowed lightning and was transferring it to her. With a single pull, he righted her and sent her sprawling to the shore. The boots tripped her so she slid along the sand. It was so hot, it blistered her hands. Looking up, she saw him coming toward her with resolute intent. But her eyes settled, unwillingly, on the gaping breeches of his thigh. She noticed the crisp golden hairs matted with blood. The bronze of his thigh that matched his naked chest. How close she'd come to severing him for life.

"Need some help, *menino?*" he taunted with a trenchant grin.

She was panting, nearly exhausted from her efforts. Her arm ached beneath the increasing weight of her weapon. But her pride mounted her to her feet. She charged him with a growl, but he easily sidestepped, sending her hurtling back to the table.

It occurred to her then that if she could anticipate his every move, he could do the same with her. He proved it by feinting and, avoiding her blade with a quick riposte, slashing up to knock the hat from her head. She watched it fall backward and drift like a feather toward the surf as she wondered if she'd felt her wig slip, or if it had just been her imagination.

"You must be heated in such finery," he commented. In spite of her alterations, he'd noted the quality of Hastings's clothes. Did nothing escape his attention?

She was about to find out.

"But this is hardly fair," he said smoothly. "I fight

bare-chested, and you're confined by clothes. If you follow my example, it might give you the advantage you need."

Too quickly for her to anticipate, he ripped her shirt with the point of his blade so it gaped open, revealing the length of cloth that bound her breasts flat underneath.

Suddenly she understood that he'd known all along. But when had he guessed?

Effectively put on the defensive, she fought with all her strength and skill to keep his blade from her chest. But he fooled her again with a quick movement and the blade cut upward to sever the cloth in two. It was an amazing maneuver, for though it stripped the cloth from her, it left her flesh unmarred.

As he contemptuously flicked the cloth away, she felt her breasts sway freely.

"You devil!" she breathed and he laughed his glee. Angrily, she lunged at him, but the boots tripped her instead. Seizing his opportunity, he flicked his sword-tip at the side of her head and the eye patch went the way of the cloth. His blade missed her eye by a hair's width.

While she was recovering, he made a quick circle with his blade and, with a mighty swoop, sent her sword flying to the other side of the beach.

Incensed, she reached up and yanked off the wig. Her hair fell to her shoulders and she stood before him like a wild thing, her hair a shambles, her breasts heaving with her breath.

He laughed and, tossing his sword aside, swooped down on her, parting her ruined shirt with large hands and running them up her ribcage to cup her breasts firmly.

"Ah, Gabé, I knew if I took your brother, you'd come to me. But I never expected such a marvelous charade."

He lifted her easily, guided her breast to the level of his mouth, then clamped his lips on her with a moist, hard suction that jarred her with its suddenness, even as it curled her toes within her ridiculously overstuffed boots. She heard a passionate moan and realized with a shock that it was coming from her own throat.

But she wouldn't give in. He'd abandoned her once before. He was a man *without* a heart, a man who gave himself only to a cause. But she had a cause of her own. And she had no intention of letting him distract her from that goal.

Grasping his shoulders, she heaved herself away. She stood before him, her body damp and steaming, her breath coming in erratic gasps, staring him down as she shoved her tousled hair back over her shoulders.

"Very well. If it's your desire to expose me to your men, allow me to assist you, by all means. I'll merely rip the shirt off my back, as you did yours."

She moved her hands to do so and he was on her in a flash, grasping the sides of her open shirt and wrenching them closed so roughly, one of the side seams split. She stared defiantly into his face, hers gleaming her triumph.

"Shall I fetch the needles?" he countered. "I'd relish seeing my mark on your flesh."

"I'd rather die!" She tried to jerk away but couldn't. "I came to get the brother you stole from me."

She reached up to slap him, but he jerked her to him so forcefully, she couldn't get her hand past his arms. She heard her shirt rip again, but she was beyond caring.

"I went to a great deal of trouble to get you here. On my order Jonah Fitch braved exposure in Mahé and waited for you to come to him. So if you think I'm going to let you collect your brother and sail away, you're sadly mistaken."

"And if *you* think I'm going to kneel before you and call you master, you're out of your bloody mind!"

He stared into her eyes. She locked her gaze with his, refusing to look away, watching as any tenderness or mercy left their depths to be replaced by a cold and cruel desire.

"Quartermaster," he said quietly, without looking away.

She felt Wallace's presence beside them. "Sir?"

"This woman is henceforth my captive. Rummage through the booty and find her a dress to wear. See that she puts it on if you have to strip her and place her in it yourself. Then—"

His eyes searched hers and caught the rebellious raise of her chin.

"Then, Captain?"

"Then secure her in my cabin."

There was a momentary pause. "*Secure* her, sir?"

Rodrigo's hands dropped from her shirt as if he could no longer bear the touch of her skin. "Lock her in my cabin. If she tries to escape, tie her." His eyes flicked back to hers, full of the quiet confidence of a man who knows his orders will be obeyed. "I'd like to see you escape me this time," he added, before she was dragged away.

# Sixteen

For hours, Gabrielle fought back the panic that threatened to make her scream. Wallace had done his dirty work well. He'd dressed her in the only frock he'd been able to find, a rich gown of ivory satin embossed with lace. Without a corset, the gown was too small, cutting into her waist and crushing her breasts so they throbbed from the constant pressure. When she'd tried to gouge his eyes, the quartermaster had tied her hands behind her back. In the process, her breasts were thrust forward, pushing the deeply cut bodice farther down the generous globes of flesh.

But that wasn't the worst. She could suffer the indignity of being dressed for a pirate's pleasure, as if going to a ball—or like an unwilling bride. She didn't even mind so much that her tangled hair was falling in her face, and without her hands, she couldn't effectively fling it back. She could survive the cramped muscles from staying hours in one place. What she *did* mind—what terrified her and kept a scream lurking at the back of her throat—was the heavy iron chain around her neck.

Rodrigo had made it clear he would brook no chance of escape. In order to accomplish this, Wallace had forced her to kneel by the stove in his master's cabin. After fastening her wrists behind her back, he'd wrapped a thick metal chain about her neck, securing it to the black stove behind her. She had just enough of a tether that she could lower her head, giving her aching shoulders a rest. But it was impossible for her to stand, or to alter her position in any way.

Since the age of seven, when Hastings had forced her to watch her mother's execution, she couldn't abide having anything about her neck. Even a soft silk scarf caused her to feel she was choking. Being chained by the throat brought back that dreaded nightmare—the one of watching her mother hang and slowly realizing it wasn't her mother at all they were hanging, but herself. It had left her with a premonition that she, like her mother, would die of hanging.

It was one of the many reasons the life of a pirate filled her with such horror. If she gave in to temptation and accepted Rodrigo in her bed, she knew she could never let him go. By joining forces with him, she'd effectively be placing her own neck in the noose.

She was so close to tears, they burned in her throat. As the hours passed and the room grew dim, then darkened to a deep pitch, she struggled with the blackest visions of her tormented soul—all that she forgot during the day but relived at night in visions of atrocities that left her drenched and trembling in her bed. In daylight, she was a fearless woman, but in the dark, she became a child again—the child who'd shaken in her bed night after night, longing for a comforting touch, only to be awakened by Hastings whispering in her ear. "They hang bad girls like you."

She couldn't stand it. She couldn't stay for one more moment with this wretched chain around her neck, seeing her mother's face as her once-beautiful eyes bulged in death. Hearing Hastings's voice at her ear, sinister and pleased. If she had to brave this one minute more, she felt she'd go insane.

Her only distraction was focusing on her hatred of Rodrigo—hatred fueled by the humiliation of her unexpected and effortless defeat in the duel. If she concentrated on Rodrigo, the anger made her strong.

Concentrating on Rodrigo wasn't hard. She could even *smell* him in the room. He'd always had a distinctive aroma, partly man and partly the sea. But there was something else. She recalled it sharply now, as if the years had disappeared, and she was kneeling before him, a girl of seventeen, on their island of love. She'd reached for him, caressing him with her hands, bringing him to her mouth. To worship his beauty with a kiss. To breathe deeply of his scent. Ever after, she'd associated that scent with forbidden sensual desire.

The worst of it was that, as she grew more weary by the hour and her mind began to slip, another vision flashed of Rodrigo entering the cabin, yanking the chain back, and entering her as she was, bound to his stove on her knees. As shocking an image as it was, she couldn't get it out of her mind. Her breasts, spilling over the binding boundaries of her dress, ached to be crushed and molded by his pirate's hands; the nipples, hard and tight, longed to swell beneath his tongue.

Just then she heard the bolt slide back. She swallowed, realizing how dry her throat was, how parched and swollen her tongue. Nervously, she licked her lips but couldn't wet them. Her heart raced in her breast and she cursed it, bade it to be calm.

He entered then, with a candle in his hand. She couldn't see him at first. All she could see was that single blinding light. Accustomed as her eyes were to the darkness, the flare of light obscured his features. The door closed behind him, but he didn't move. He just stood there looking at her as if time stood still. With a valiant effort, she raised herself higher on her aching knees and tossed her head to try to pitch her hair back. But it was useless. It was too heavy and it fell like rib-

bons over her face, forcing her to look in his direction
through a gauzy veil.

Eventually her eyes adjusted and the beacon took its
true perspective, becoming just the meager flickering of
a candle's flame. He walked forward soundlessly and his
face came into focus. The wide forehead. The high
cheeks. The Roman nose. Those full, sensual lips. The
golden hair that gleamed and beckoned her fingers like a
trunkload of Spanish coins.

He set the candle aside without taking his gaze from
her face. In his other hand he held a heavy golden goblet, mellowed with the age of a hundred years, and brilliant with rubies. They winked in the light and
reminded her once again of rumpled scarlet sheets. He
held it negligently, dangling from his palm, the stem
between the third and fourth fingers of his hand.

She looked away because the sight of that hand,
cupping his goblet as he earlier had her breast, seemed
too intimate a sight for her present shattered state. Lowering her lashes, she rested her gaze on the gash she'd
inflicted on his thigh. It had been cleaned of blood so
only the flesh wound remained. But she could see the
flexing of muscles beneath the overlay of golden hair.
Her eyes followed the inevitable line to the juncture of
his thighs and saw him harden perceptibly beneath her
gaze. A shiver of excitement rushed through her. Her
lips parted in an effort to draw air.

"What have you been thinking about?" he asked in a
hushed voice.

She looked up and, with difficulty, met his gaze
through her hair. "Of how dearly I'd like to kill you."

It was then that he noticed the chain. With a sudden forceful lunge, he wrenched it from the stove. Un-
wrapping it from her throat, he let it clatter to the floor
as he pulled her to him in a fierce embrace and put his
lips to the soft, bruised flesh of her neck.

"I didn't know," he murmured into her flesh.

She stiffened in his arms. "If you think that's going to make up for what you've done to me—"

He let her go so suddenly that she lost her balance. With her hands still tied behind her, she couldn't reach out and right herself, so she fell in a crumpled heap at his feet.

Squatting on bent knees, his elbows resting on them for balance, he brought his face close to hers. With his free hand, he gently brushed the hair back off her face.

His soft touch startled her. It made her weak, opened her to him in a way demands never would. It frightened her, so she jerked her head from his grasp and willed him to wither before her gaze. But he merely traced the line of her bare shoulder. Then he slipped his finger beneath the straining material that bound her breasts, and coaxed it down, exposing her completely to his gaze. With her breasts bared before him, she felt the veneer of civilization fall away with her frock. She felt him stroke the softness of her flesh. Not hesitantly. Not asking her permission. Just grazing her with the back of his finger as if asserting his right to do so. She felt more helpless, more enslaved by the involuntary exposure of her breasts than she did by the tethers at her wrists.

She tried again to swallow and couldn't. She was struggling for a self-possession she couldn't grasp. Struggling against his siege. The vibrations he emitted through the touch of his hand, the whispered power of his words, were so provocative, they threatened to sweep her away. She felt flooded with flame, mowed down by images and sensations so intense they left her trembling and breathless in their wake. Never had she come across a force so trenchant, so utterly seductive. It was like reliving the temptation of her dream all over again. The dream where she gave herself to him completely and begged for more.

His eyes lifted from her breasts and bore into hers, the eyes of a wild beast.

"Come," he coaxed. "Quench your thirst."

He put the goblet to her lips. She could smell the wine, heavy and rich. But she knew he didn't mean the thirst of the afternoon. She knew he wanted her to slake her desires in the temptation of his touch. He dangled the bait before her like a devil inducing her soul. It would be so easy to drink her fill. But at the last moment, she turned her face away.

She felt his rage before he moved. Then, suddenly, with the spring of a lion, he was on his feet. His fist tangled in her hair. He jerked back her head, put the goblet to her lips, and poured. She had to open her mouth or it would flood her face. The fear of choking won. She parted her lips and swallowed convulsively as he forced it down her throat.

When she'd drunk the contents, he withdrew the cup. But he stood over her still, keeping her face turned to him by yanking back her hair. Her lips were pursed. She didn't say a word, just stared mutinously into his eyes. Slowly, his hand still in her hair, he lowered himself to her level once again. With his face inches from hers, she spat the wine she'd saved in her mouth into his face. It spread and dripped from him like blood.

Red as rubies. Scarlet as those accursed sheets.

So calmly it frightened her, he wiped the elixir from his face. "You spilled some," he told her. With his finger, he scooped the drop of wine from her chin. Then he put it to her mouth and made her suck it off.

"I know what you want," she said in a voice vibrating with passion. "But I won't do it. You'll have to kill me first."

"You used to feel differently about me," he said lightly.

"That was before—"

She stopped, realizing suddenly that they were in the midst of a bizarre reenactment of her play.

"Before I what, *carícia*? Became a vile rogue? As I recall, you liked me being a vile rogue when we were children."

Obviously, he'd read the play more than once, and was now taunting her with her own words.

"You're not playing your part, *carícia*. I believe your line is: 'You left me to pursue your evil designs.'"

"Fiend from hell!" she cried, falling into his trap. "I shall never believe another word you say. I shall never trust you again."

He stood then and, looking melodramatically into her eyes, put his hand on his heart and said: "'My name is feared all across the Indian Ocean, from the Horn of Africa to the Celebes Sea. I've looted ships and collected bounty worth a king's ransom. But without the woman I love, I'm only half a man!'"

She sat back on her heels and glared. "How dare you mock me?"

"Ah," he said in his natural voice, with the ghost of a smile flickering at his lips. "You do not see the absurdity of it all? You curse me now, but I have fond memories of you as a wild little girl with flying hair and a taunting laugh, boasting that she could best me at swordplay as she ran across the English hills with her skirts about her knees."

He helped her to her feet, then untied her hands. Gently, he rubbed her wrist where the rope had chafed. Realizing that he was trying to disarm her, that she was yielding to that part of herself that loved him still, she pulled her hand from his and settled the bodice back over her exposed breasts. Then she spoke seriously, if without the anger that had earlier colored her words.

"Rodrigo, you want to decide for me what my future should be. Just as my father and Hastings did. But I refuse to be told what to do, what to think, what to want. Beau Vallon has been my dream for most of my life. If I let you take that dream away, I've done the same thing my mother did. For whatever reasons."

He thought a moment, taking a turn about the cabin. "Some things are more important," he said at last.

"It's my home, Rodrigo."

"Seychelles is my home, too. But the problem, Gabé, is that in order for you to build *your* home here, you must destroy mine."

"I don't understand."

"Then I shall make sure you do." He was quiet for many moments, as if musing to himself. "You will go on a journey with me tomorrow."

"Rodrigo, you have no time to waste on journeys. I heard Hastings say he and the Grand Blanc have gathered a fleet to come after you, island by island, until they've blown you apart."

Unperturbed, he said, "That would be extremely foolish of them. Not knowing these reefs, they wouldn't have a chance in the Amirantes. And I daresay they know it."

His lips curled slightly, and she sensed the challenge in his next words. "No, the trouble lies not with Hastings but with what I am going to do with you."

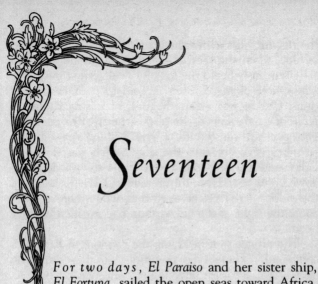

# Seventeen

For two days, El Paraiso and her sister ship, El Fortuna, sailed the open seas toward Africa, flying over the waves like phantoms fueled for speed.

Gabrielle was dressed like Rodrigo's sailors in lion breeches and a soft cotton shirt covering her bound breasts. Rodrigo had found her some boots that were closer to her size than Hastings's had been. She was free to move about unhampered, but she felt weighed down by concerns.

No one answered her questions about why they were at sea. She was told only that they were intercepting an Arab vessel sailing out of Mozambique. One of the infamous sultan of Zanzibar's personal fleet. But she'd overheard Wallace expressing his worry about the impulsiveness of this journey to Rodrigo. "We've precious little preparation, man. We know not how many men are onboard. 'Tisn't like you to be so rash, when so much is at stake."

Gabrielle's one happiness came from seeing Cullen so enthusiastic about life at sea. The Indian Ocean might make a man of him yet.

On the morning of the third day, she'd retreated to

the rigging, high above the quarterdeck, in a vast world of blue, when she spotted the ship on the horizon and simultaneously heard the lookout's call. All at once, the atmosphere changed. Men jumped to their battle stations. Cullen was given the task of raising Rodrigo's pirate flag. His fingers fumbled as he tried to fasten it, but once he'd hoisted it, he gave Rodrigo a proud grin.

They gave chase to the ship, which was slow and bulky, and it wasn't long before El Paraiso was looming down on its bow. From this distance, Gabrielle could see the sailors' dark faces beneath their white robes, see the panic the sight of the golden lion had instilled in their hearts.

The pirates were readying the cannons at Rodrigo's command. "There'll be no firing into the ship," he called. "I don't want anyone hurt who needn't be." As he spoke, he moved toward a cannon that had been wheeled to its place on deck. Motioning to Cullen, Rodrigo began to explain what he intended. "What we want is to knock off the main mast and immobilize the ship. I'm going to show you how it's done, but you can't learn just by watching. You must go by instinct as well. This is my favorite cannon," he explained, running his hand along it as if caressing a lover's thigh. "She never fails me. You want to be sure to put in just the right amount of powder. Manuel will work with you on that." The Spaniard grinned as he rammed in the powder. Picking up the cannon ball, Rodrigo hefted it in his hand. "The ball must be perfectly round. I have these honed for hours." The ball was inserted into the cannon's body. Then Rodrigo lowered his head level with the weapon and aimed it carefully, speaking as he did so. "You must always accommodate for the curvature of the earth. Never fire a straight shot. With practice, you develop an eye for judging."

Finally the wick was lit. Gabrielle's heart raced as she realized Rodrigo was actually going to fire on the sultan's ship. The weapon exploded, lurching back, and in instants, the main mast of the enemy ship was severed with the same surgical precision that Rodrigo had used on the East Indiaman. With a mighty creak and groan, the mast toppled to the deck.

A cheer arose from the pirates as they swarmed to the rails. Before they could board the conquered ship, Rodrigo called them to a halt. "Let's allow the lady the honor of boarding first."

They turned to look at Gabrielle. Most of them had witnessed her duel with their captain. Some remembered the way she'd forced him on deck of the *Drake* at the point of her sword. As she gazed at them in shock over Rodrigo's words, she saw the respect reflected in their grins of consent.

Rodrigo had picked up a hat and was holding it out to her with an inviting hand. In a daze, she felt herself climb down the rigging, walk toward him, take the hat, and tuck her hair up under it as she placed it on her head. Nervousness slithered through her stomach like a snake. What was this game Rodrigo dared her to play?

She felt Cullen come up behind her, his excitement receded, his face white. "Gabby, you could be killed!" he breathed, frightened now that the ramifications had struck home.

"Oh, that's right," drawled Rodrigo. "I'd forgotten you're but a *stage* pirate. You have trouble with reality." Taunting her with a sword, his grin widening, he added, "Didn't you put your sword between your teeth in the play? I hear it brought the audience to their feet. Damn fool thing, for a *real* swashbuckler. You could get your head cut off if you should slam against the ship."

He was goading her—to what end she didn't know. But she wasn't about to let him reduce her to a sniveling heap in front of his men. Ignoring Cullen's whispered warnings, she stared Rodrigo in the eyes and said, "Head cut off, be damned. I'll show you how a pirate boards a captured ship."

Rebelliously, she put the sword between her teeth,

grasped the rope he held out to her, and with her best theatrical flourish, swung across the ocean to knock over three Arabs and land on her feet on the opposite deck. From the decks of *El Paraiso*, she heard a rousing masculine cheer.

But there wasn't time to feel her oats. Assuming she was a man, the Arabs charged with drawn swords. They carried scimitars, curved and deadly-looking as they glinted in the sun. Gabrielle drew the sword from her aching teeth and engaged in a fierce battle that called for every bit of her concentration.

There appeared to be no more than ten sailors on board. Puzzled that the pirates should send only one man, they held back for a time, allowing her to duel with one at a time. Soon she was besting them easily, so they came at her in pairs. She was in her element, slashing at one while she danced out of the way of the other's swinging blade.

She knocked the sword from the hand of a sailor and, gleaming in triumph, turned to face four men surrounding her on all sides. Her swordplay, she'd soon found, was superior to theirs, even if her strength was not. She could handle two of them easily, but it was impossible to defend her back at the same time. As she paused, taking a precious second to ponder the difficulty, she felt a swish of wind beside her and heard the heavy thump of boots. Glancing aside, she saw Rodrigo, sword drawn, looking like the pirate he was, kicking one of the Arabs at her back and engaging the other with his sword.

With the two fighting side by side, it wasn't long before the Arabs were subdued. As the pirates swarmed on deck, Gabrielle fought to breathe. She was pouring sweat and the air was burning like fire in her lungs. Rodrigo put his arm about her shoulders and guided her. "Come, Gabé. Let me show you something."

On frightfully shaky legs, she went with him past the stairwell to the middle of the quarterdeck. As the pirates

from his ship went about the task of binding the conquered vessel's crew, Rodrigo reached down to a latch
on the floor of the deck. Grasping it, he pulled up a
hatch. A portion of the deck rose with his arm.

As it did, a ghastly smell hit her like a wave, almost
knocking her down. She hesitated, thoroughly confused.
But he took her arm in a firm grip and pulled her down
the steps behind him. On the way, he retrieved a lantern and paused to light it. It sputtered and fizzed before
settling into a gently swaying flame.

As they descended into the darkness, Gabrielle began to see a sight of such horror, she knew she'd never
forget it. There, in the cramped hold of the ship, were
hundreds of Africans chained to the floor. Men, women,
even children, all hid their eyes from the glare of the
light, as if they hadn't seen any for the two weeks they'd
been on board. As they walked through the bodies,
Gabrielle's flesh began to crawl. The captives were grue-
some, some with open, running sores that hadn't been
tended. They were surrounded by their own filth. Some
had vomited blood and lay in the remains. Some, she
could see when Rodrigo nudged them, had died during
the voyage and been left where they lay. Those who
were alive were so emaciated, their bones showed
through their skins.

They began to cry out to them, a ghostly wail that
made her want to cover her ears and run. She felt herself inside some Hieronymus Bosch vision of hell. She
could feel their suffering, their agony, the desperation of
their fear. The hand at her mouth was shaking so that
she couldn't control it.

She became aware that tears were streaming down
her cheeks. Soon, she realized Rodrigo was looking at
her and she raised tear-streaked eyes to his face.

"Look at it, Gabé," he told her. "*This* is your Beau
Vallon."

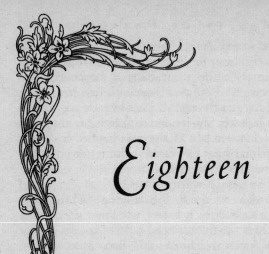

# Eighteen

*For hours, Gabrielle* forestalled her grief by throwing herself into the process of helping the rescued slaves. Carefully, she helped unchain their limbs, weeping inwardly at the crusted blood that caked their ankles and wrists. Again and again she made the trip up those rickety steps, supporting the weight of a woman or carrying a child in her arms that was so light, it felt more like a sparrow than a human being. In the process, she stopped seeing them as one mass of brutalized humanity, and began to feel for them as individuals, each with wounds and needs that she felt insufficient to meet.

Once the Africans were transferred to the sister ship, the slaver scuttled, and its crew put adrift in a longboat, Gabrielle helped tend to the human cargo. She put salve on raw burns and open wounds. Rodrigo, of course, had known their mission all along, had brought her specifically to see this abomination, so he'd come well-prepared with medicines and bandages and barrels of fresh water to cleanse their injuries. After hours of this, Gabrielle felt numb and drained, as if she couldn't feel anything if she tried.

She was so exhausted by the time she returned to *El*

*Paraíso* that she was fairly catatonic. All she could do was watch helplessly as *El Fortuna* sailed back toward Africa, taking the frightened captives home. She was vaguely aware of Rodrigo's hands on her shoulders, urging her to rest. She heard his words as he ordered Wallace to take her to his cabin so she could. She had a sensation of movement as she was guided down the gangway. But nothing registered. Nothing but the horror her mind fought to reject.

When the door to the cabin closed softly behind her, she stared about her as if she'd never seen the room before. Rodrigo had relinquished his cabin to her for the duration of their journey, so she'd slept in his bed, tangled in the scarlet sheets that had taunted her so from the day she'd first seen them. Now, she stared at the bunk without recognition. It was all she could do to make herself walk toward it. To reach for it with a quivering hand. To crumple like a severed leaf to the floor before the bed. To lay her forehead on the sheets and close her weary eyes.

When Rodrigo entered minutes later to check on her, she was sobbing with all the passion she'd never allowed herself in all her years of anger and frustration as the bastard daughter of a duke. Her shoulders shook with her pain. Her throat burned. Her breast heaved with the intensity of her despair. She cried for those she'd vainly tried to help. She cried for all the years she'd wasted, hoped, and dreamed. She cried, she had to admit, for herself.

She heard his voice above her. "*Carícia.*" Just a quiet breath of a whisper. But in that word was all the pain he'd borne through the years. All the loneliness. All the frustrated desires he'd sacrificed for the good of the many.

"How could you do this to me?" she cried.

She stared up at him accusingly, to find him gazing down at her with the most compassionate look in his eyes that she'd ever seen. "I remember well the first time

I saw such a sight. I know all that you feel, for I've felt it all myself."

"Have you?" She didn't realize she was angry, but suddenly she was consumed with it, so angry it drowned out the confusion and disillusionment for one blissful moment. "You tricked me. You did this purposely."

"I wanted you to understand."

"And what have you left for me, Rodrigo? You knew if you showed that to me, I could never go back to my former life. I can't go home and see slaves everywhere around me without thinking of what I've seen this day. You knew that when you brought me here. But what do I do now? I'm caught between two worlds. I can't go back and I can't go forward. A part of me knows I had to see this. I couldn't go on as I was. But there's another part of me, Rodrigo. A part that hates you for showing this to me." She felt the sobs shake her once again. "Beau Vallon was all I had. It's all I've ever had. And now you've killed it."

"I told you before. Beau Vallon was always an empty dream. Your desires are illusions. They're built on evil."

"But it was *my* dream! Where do I go now? What do I do?"

He was quiet for a moment. When he spoke, it was in a soft, compassionate tone. "What did you want before you wanted Beau Vallon?"

"Nothing. I never wanted anything else."

"I don't believe that."

In despair, she suddenly cried, "I want to stop having to fight so hard for what I want. All my life, I've had to fight for what others take for granted. A roof over my head. A good-night kiss. A home. I've fought so *hard*, Rodrigo! So many years, so many struggles. Without help from anyone. I've had to fight for my very name— for the right to *use* my own name." She looked up suddenly and realized, from the blue blaze of his eyes, that she could be talking about him. "And it's come to noth-

ing. I want to stop fighting. I want what's mine by right.
I want—" She tried to put it in words, but couldn't.

"Some things are worth fighting for."

"I no longer care about the fighting. I want peace."

"In short, you want paradise. But paradise isn't a
place, Gabé. Paradise is living by your convictions.
Knowing in your heart that you're doing the right
thing."

"Yes, that's it," she said, quieting. She pushed herself
up stiffly and sat perched on the edge of the bunk. "I
want peace in my own heart. But if Beau Vallon won't
give it to me . . . what will? Don't you see? I had
something to believe in. And you took that away from
me."

"Perhaps what I did was bring you back to the place
you were meant to be."

She stared at him uncomprehendingly.

"As a child, you always championed the underdog.
It's why you took the responsibility of looking after Cul-
len on your shoulders as if you were looking after the
Holy Grail. I always admired that quality in you."

"It's not a quality I'm known for."

"Perhaps not now. I imagine it's been lost in ambi-
tion, in your need to fight for everything you wanted, as
you've said. But as a child, it was your most dominant
trait."

She tried to recall. It had been so long since she'd
thought of anything but getting what she wanted.

"Do you recall when I first came to Westbury
Grange? Thirteen years old, my father murdered before
my eyes, snatched from the only home I'd ever known.
Angry with the world. You befriended me when no one
else would. I was spit on at school. Called names that
would make you blush even now. They called me
Roderick, and every time they did I felt they'd stolen
some small part of my soul. You understood that about
me, because you'd felt it yourself. You called me Rodrigo
and gave me the pride I needed to keep going. You,

Gabé, saw my soul for what it was. You befriended a suffering boy with an open and loving heart. I don't know that you ever realized what that meant to me. How I loved you for it, even as a child."

Their eyes met and she felt for a moment the empathy of their youth.

"I saw in you then a compassion that Hastings's evil has tried to kill. But somewhere, Gabé, somewhere deep inside, that compassion lives. Such compassion as can't help but weep on seeing what you saw today. In any case, now you see what I'm fighting for."

Mention of Hastings made her draw away. She stood, needing to put distance between them. "Hastings is trading in slaves, isn't he? And you're fighting him."

"Yes, but not Hastings alone. My people have been fighting such invaders since we first came here. It's a family mission, if you will. You remember I told you the Soros were the first to settle these islands? They were Portuguese explorers who fell in love with them on Vasco da Gama's second voyage in the sixteenth century and stayed. They lived in peace, growing or making what they needed to survive."

"It sounds like heaven," she said wistfully, thinking that was what she'd hoped to find when she'd come.

"It was, of course. But when the French came, they brought their avarice and their slaves. My great-grandfather saw how they were destroying his home and turned pirate to try to turn them away. It was fruitless, of course. Yet we never ceased in our battle. There has passed through the Soro family a sacred trust, to do what we must by any means at our command, until slavery is abolished in this land. I'm the fourth generation that has turned pirate toward this aim."

"So when they hanged your father—"

She felt him tense. "They hanged him because he believed in the rights of man. I watched him die and knew in my heart that it was my turn to take up the gauntlet. It burned in me, this knowledge that I was now the successor to a valorous cause. I grew up that day, ready to fight the English that had taken over where the French left off. I would have slaughtered them all, given half a chance."

"But instead—"

"Instead, they took me to England. As cold and bleak a land as the hand of God ever created. Douglas took me in, and set out to fashion the perfect English gentleman and Company man."

"I never understood why he did so."

"The same reason he kept your mother, perhaps. Because I represented paradise to him. He never could abide the thought of losing the paradise he'd glimpsed here as a young man. You know, I've always felt a certain odd sympathy for Douglas."

"Odd, indeed."

"I sometimes think if he could ever escape the clutches of his pernicious son, he might be capable of a truly honorable act."

"I suppose you also feel sorry for Hastings," she said with more bitterness than she'd intended.

"A little, perhaps."

"Then you're a more magnanimous person than I am."

He was quiet a moment. "I used to suspect he was half in love with you and didn't know it."

Everything inside her stilled. Turning from him, she held her breath.

"It would help explain why he's never accepted you as his sister."

Seeing that it made her uncomfortable, he returned to the subject at hand. "Now you know why I had to leave you and come back here. And now I tell you that I've always loved you. Never, for one day since I left, did I stop thinking of you, longing for you. I saw your face in every sunset. I heard your voice in the wind. But I had to put my own needs second."

"And mine," she murmured. "I gave you the secrets

of my soul, yet you didn't trust me enough to tell me the most important thing in your life." He stood and reached for her, but she brushed him off. "You don't know what it did to me when you left. You have no idea of the consequences I had to pay because *you* wouldn't trust me!"

The silence reverberated through the cabin. She couldn't look at him. If she did, she feared she'd say more than she wanted to reveal.

"Perhaps that's true," he said at last, his voice a coaxing hush. "But that's all past. What's real is you and I here now, and this malignancy that's spoiling our paradise. You and I have fought Hastings before. Will you help me now to do what I must?"

She sat down and struggled to organize her jumbled thoughts. "What is it you hope to accomplish?"

"I want to stop Hastings."

"And how will you do that?"

"Ideally, I'll capture him, take him before Admiral Fulton, and make him confess."

"But of course he'd never let you take him alive."

"That's probably true."

She suddenly saw Hastings's evil face in the cold white light of a Bedfordshire dawn. And she saw the faces of those African families in the hold of that slaver. She remembered then a bonfire where a slave was tethered, awaiting her master's pleasure. And Hastings's voice, talking about his plans, sailing for Zanzibar the first of the month. That was just a few days away.

She faced Rodrigo and said softly, "Maybe there *is* something I can do to help."

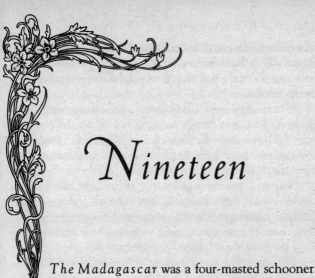

# Nineteen

*The Madagascar* was a four-masted schooner that made a regular run between Diégo-Suarez, Mahé, and Zanzibar. It was French-owned, and held a complement of twenty sailors, plus room for another twenty passengers—surprisingly luxurious for this part of the world. Disguised as a French couple, Rodrigo and Gabrielle boarded it in Mahé. They'd made a midnight landing on the far side of the island, where they were met by two of Rodrigo's spies, given a change of clothing, and booked passage under the name D'Allard.

Wallace had not wanted her to come along, but Gabrielle had pointed out that a French couple would be the least likely candidate for such a clandestine operation. Cloaked in layers of petticoats and a veiled bonnet, Gabrielle felt stiff and uncomfortable, suffocating in satin after her days dressed in the easy freedom of the sailors' clothes.

She was rightly nervous about being spotted. It turned out that all of the passengers were buzzing over the fact that a mysterious and important passenger was aboard, complete with a small detachment of guards to protect him. He was ensconced in the captain's cabin, where two heavily armed guards were posted at all times. With Rodrigo's usual supporting players aboard, they ran a deadly risk that they might be recognized and overpowered.

When they were under way, as Rodrigo waited on deck, he surprised her by sending her down the passageway to have a look. Reluctantly, Gabrielle sauntered toward the guards in her best dramatic shimmy, and gave them her most brilliant smile. In French, her tone lowered so whoever was on the other side of the door couldn't hear her, she said, "I'm told we have a distinguished passenger aboard. My, but he must be important, having you strong men to guard him *personally*."

The guards exchanged self-conscious looks.

"When will I get a look at this man of mystery?"

"Our charge has no intention of leaving the cabin for the duration of the journey, *mademoiselle*."

"But never? Surely he must need sustenance, as we all do. He *is* human, is he not?"

They chuckled a little at the comment. "There are rumors to that effect, *mademoiselle*. However,"—the guard leaned forward and lowered his voice conspiratorially—"we sometimes have our doubts, those of us who work for him."

In a stern tone meant to make up for his partner's informality, the other guard said, "The gentleman will be taking all meals in his cabin. We have orders that he is not to be disturbed."

"Even," added his partner, "by such a charming *mademoiselle* as yourself."

"He's never to leave," she murmured, as if regretful. "The poor man. How awful for him. But that, one supposes, is the price of power, is it not, *messieurs?*"

With a smile full of seductive promise, she left, giving them a view of her best sashay from behind. She looked perfectly calm, but her body trembled and her heart pounded, thinking of Hastings being on the other side of that door.

Up on deck, out of hearing range, she told Rodrigo what she'd found out. "He's being extremely cautious," he noted.

"He's always been cautious—in his own diabolical way."

"Maybe a little too cautious for someone who thinks his forces are pounding me to death in the Amirantes."

"He's never been one to leave anything to chance. So what do we do now?"

"If he comes out and spots us, we'll have to move. If the guards are correct and he doesn't come out, we'll wait till midnight, then we'll take over and take the ship due south. *El Paraiso* will be waiting just off Ile aux Vaches."

They'd been under way for the last couple of hours, and no one seemed to suspect them. Buoyed by the prospect of accomplishing their mission, she barely noticed Rodrigo's growing concern as they stood at the rail and he stared off wistfully into the distance.

Soon, they passed an unusually beautiful island, lush with palms and serene beaches, with mountains at either end. Like most of the granitic islands, it resembled a fried egg; the greenery inside forming the yolk, the surrounding white sandy beaches spreading out from the center. They'd sailed on the afternoon tide, and now the sunset cast the island into emerald relief, glistening in a burnished orange glow. It was six o'clock, and the sun was setting like clockwork, as it did every day. Just as the sunrise always came twelve hours later, no matter the season.

"What is it?" she asked.

It was a moment before he spoke, so lost was he in his thoughts. Finally, he answered, "Praslin. The second-largest of the granitic islands. There are plantations on either end. But in the interior of the island, buried deep in a primordial jungle, is a haven like nothing you've ever seen. You recall me telling you of *meú avô*— my grandfather, Reis?"

"Of course. The one who raised you because your father couldn't stay at home with you."

"Yes. After my mother died, he was my closest friend. He used to bring me to this place. It's the most mystical place I know. The French call it the Vallée de Mai. But *meú avô* said it's the Garden of Eden. Plants have survived there that exist nowhere else on earth—including the *coco de mer*."

"What's that?"

"It's the forbidden fruit the Bible speaks of. Sometime I'll show it to you. When you see it, you'll know why."

His talk of mystical places endeared him to her. She, too, felt the energy of the place, as if she could feel all the emotions that had passed within the confines of an enclosed area. What would it be like, she wondered, in a jungle believed to be the Garden of Eden?

"*Meú avô* always said if I was in trouble to go there. It's a difficult journey, straight through the jungle to the center. That, and the superstition about its origins, keeps people away. He always said I'd be safe there."

He turned his head and their eyes met. She had the feeling he'd told her this as more than conversation. His face once again took on a troubled shade, and he stared out to sea.

Later, when she was slipping into her men's clothes, her heart was pounding with excitement. With her hair tucked up under a hat, she met Rodrigo on deck, careful to keep her footfalls quiet. Above them, in a sky of liquid ink, sparkled millions of stars that were rarely, if ever, visible from the northern climbs of England.

"On second thought," he reconsidered, "why don't you stay in the cabin?"

"Fifty of your best pirates couldn't keep me in that cabin, Rodrigo."

"Then keep your eye on me and do as I say. Should anything go amiss, I don't want you hurt."

"You don't have to worry about me," she assured him. But she was touched that he did.

Rodrigo strolled over to where the captain stood beside the boatswain, who was steering the ship. When the captain greeted him, he nodded his head once in salutation. Then he drew his sword so swiftly that Gabrielle barely saw him move. Just as quickly, Rodrigo had the blade of the sword to the captain's neck.

As quietly as she could, Gabrielle moved behind the sailor, who stood at the wheel. At the same moment that he noticed his captain's distress, he felt the point of her blade in his back and froze with his hand still on the wheel.

Gabrielle could hear Rodrigo's voice but not his words as he spoke quietly to the captain. The night was sultry. She felt damp beneath her men's clothes. But her hand was steady as it held the sword. She had no doubt that she could do what must be done.

The captain tipped his head back and opened his mouth to speak, only to gasp as Rodrigo tightened the connection of blade to throat. She heard his soft warning before allowing the captain room to speak. "Boatswain," the captain said in a strained voice. "Change our course for Ile aux Vaches. At once."

It was less than an hour later when they caught the first flickers of the lanterns signaling El Paraiso's location. As they drew up to the ship, the pirates silently boarded the passenger vessel and took over for them, filing out to muffle any crew members and passengers that might seek to make trouble. As one, Rodrigo and Gabrielle ran down the gangway toward their ultimate goal. At the door of the captain's cabin, Rodrigo said to the guards, "Your ship has been commandeered by the forces of Rodrigo Soro, gentlemen. It is my intention to open the door you guard so jealously. Were I you, I should be sensible and relinquish my post while I might still be allowed to leave unharmed."

Sensible or not, the guards had no intention of

abandoning their post. Gabrielle and Rodrigo were forced into swordplay. But soon, other pirates joined them and the guards were quickly subdued. Panting, Gabrielle turned to the locked door with a skipping heart.

As the guards refused to divulge the source of the key, Rodrigo was forced to break the door down. He did so at last after several tries, severing the wood from its hinges. Gabrielle followed him inside, anticipating the sight of Hastings trembling in a corner.

It took a moment for the truth to settle in. There was no Hastings. There was nothing at all save an empty room.

# Twenty

After an exhaustive search of the *Madagascar* turned up no sign of Hastings, the passenger ship was permitted on her way. *El Paraiso* then rendezvoused with Rodrigo's other two ships, and Rodrigo ordered the flotilla to flee southeast, away from the Amirantes and away from Seychelles. He seemed troubled, pacing like a caged lion, barking orders sharply, as if the greatest urgency were spurring him on.

When they were well underway, and Rodrigo was free to leave the deck, she followed him to his cabin. He answered her knock distractedly. When she entered, he was bent over, poring over charts that he'd spread out on his table as if searching for some hidden clue.

"What are you doing?" she asked.

He brushed aside the charts and began to pace once again. "You *distinctly* heard him say he'd be on the schooner for Zanzibar?"

"Yes. Distinctly."

"Then what happened?"

"I suppose he changed his mind. Maybe he went with the fleet to the Amirantes."

He considered this, and nodded. After a moment, he finally looked at her. What he saw was a pair of stricken cobalt eyes, staring at him without the slightest reserve or hesitation. It was the face of a woman in love.

"Gabé . . ."

"I just realized something."

"What's that, *carícia?*"

"That every moment with you is precious. I can't control what happens in the future. I can't even guess what's in store for us. I only know that all I have with you is right here, right now. And I want you to know, I lied to you before."

"When?" She had his full attention now.

"When you asked me if I ever wanted anything but Beau Vallon. I did want something else. But I thought I couldn't have it. That night you left me . . . it changed my life forever. It changed *me*. I didn't think it was possible to want it ever again. I didn't think I dared allow myself. But I do. I can't help it, Rodrigo. I want it now more than I've ever wanted anything else."

He took the steps that closed the distance between them. "And what is that, *carícia?*"

His breath was hot on her cheek. She could see his eyelashes, long and golden, fringing eyes that were suddenly smoldering with desire and a certain victorious glint. He knew damned well what she wanted.

She couldn't bring herself to say it. Not the whole truth. To say *I love you* seemed tantamount to flinging her fate in the faces of the gods. Asking for retribution too soon . . . too soon . . . If this was all she could have, she would find a way to cherish it now. For once in her tired life, she would let the future take care of itself.

She swallowed and, actress that she was, changed her breathy voice to a teasing tone. "I want to make love with you on those wretched scarlet sheets."

His eyes flicked to his bunk in surprise. It was the last thing he'd expected her to say, she could see it in the raise of his eyebrow as he settled his gaze once again on her face. "Are you saying you love me for my sheets?"

"Who said I loved you?"

He put his hands on either side of her head to hold her in place and lowered his mouth to hers. "Ah. It's just a tumble in my sheets you desire?"

"In your oh-so-enticing *scarlet* sheets. It isn't decent to have such sheets."

His lips still a fraction away from hers, he murmured, "It wasn't decency that prompted the choice."

Her breath mingled sweetly with his as she asked, "What, then?"

"The thought of what you'd look like, spread across the folds. I always thought you fetching in red."

"No English gentleman would be caught dead with such scandalous sheets."

"You don't need to flatter me." He rubbed his thumbs along the hollows of her cheeks. "I shall make love to you all night if you like. For eternity, if you will. You may have all the scarlet sheets your heart desires."

"Eternity is too much to ask. Kiss me, Rodrigo. Kiss me and let us make the most of the moment."

He kissed her neck instead, sending shivers to her toes. "In all the time I've known you, I've never once heard you talk about the moment. It was always the future that was on your mind."

She looked up at him, allowing all the love she couldn't express to shine like a beacon in her eyes. "All I want right now is you. And the moment is all we have. Hurry, Rodrigo. Before the moment passes. I'm yours for the taking. Take me like the pirate you are."

Her velvet voice inflamed him. He pulled her to him so hard that her breath left her in a puff. She'd egged him on, but suddenly she felt dominated by him, by the sheer power he exuded as he commanded her body to respond to his. His lips were hard against hers, forceful and demanding, asserting his right to kiss her with all the authority at his command. Her body ignited like a blaze as he pressed into her, shoving her back against the table so she could feel his rampant maleness pressing into her thigh. It felt so right, so welcome and familiar, as though she'd felt this exhilaration a million times since he'd left her—the exhilaration she knew only he could provide.

"Rodrigo," she panted, "I've missed you so. I didn't even know how I'd missed you until this moment."

As she'd been talking, he'd been kissing her neck and kneading the soft flesh of her bottom in his hand. There was nothing hesitant about him. He devoured her with a raw, animal passion that was as elemental as the scorching equatorial wind. Her body was alive and throbbing beneath his hand, crying out for him as the roar of her desire sounded in her ears.

Suddenly he picked her up and swung her in his arms. Gasping with passion, she felt joyful, loving, free. Completely open to his roving mouth.

In true piratical fashion, he laid her back into the folds of the scarlet sheets, assaulting her with his lips, moving down her sailor shirt to press them once again against the barrier of soft cotton. Impatient with it suddenly, he began to open her bodice, tearing the buttons in his haste to taste her on his tongue, only to come across the cloth that bound her breasts flat. He gave a potent Portuguese curse.

But as he opened his eyes, his gaze softened on her face, on the look of open invitation ablaze in her eyes. As suddenly gentle as he had been commandeering, he took her dark hair in his fingers and brushed it out against the red of the sheets, like a fan. "I never looked at this bed that I didn't imagine you in it. I never went to bed at night that I didn't long to hold you in my arms. Are you real? Or am I dreaming once again? I imagined you here so many times. If I touch you, will you disappear?"

She reached into her shirt and tugged at the knot of the cloth. Pulling it out in a long strip, she tossed it to the floor. Her breasts tumbled before him, beckoning his hands. "Touch me and find out."

But he paused, looking down at her with the leisurely perusal of a man with endless time on his hands. "Tell me," he coaxed. "Is it just my sheets you desire?"

"Yes."

A knowing look flicked across his face as the corner of his mouth curled in a wry smile. He moved back and she sensed that he felt he'd begged enough, that he was enjoying her throwing herself at him when she'd resisted with such alacrity in the past. Two could play that game, she decided, enjoying herself as much as he. They'd always played together. It came as naturally as breathing the same air. As he sat over her, looking down with amusement fluttering in his eyes, she ran her hands along the silk sheets at either side of her head, stretching her body up toward him, her breasts displayed before him like a benefaction, summoning him to feast on her at will. When he just smiled, content to watch her, she tossed her diversion to the winds and flung herself at him with such intensity that she surprised even herself. With her arms round his neck, she pulled him back to her, demanding the carnal heat that had left her so bereft when he'd taken it away. Now it was her lips that devoured his, tasting greedily as she rubbed herself against the telltale bulge in his pants.

"Tell me," he urged softly. "For once, sweet Gabé, I long to hear you voice the truth."

His lips were so close, but when she moved to kiss them, he gripped her tighter, causing her to cry out in pain. The laughter was gone, the wry amusement of a man toying with the one he loved. His intensity gripped her as fiercely as his hands on her arms. He shook her, so her hair flew about them, enfolding them both. "Tell me, Gabé," he insisted. "Tell me you love me. *Tell me!*"

All she wanted was to kiss him again, to run her hands through his sun-kissed hair, to feel his roughened mouth, hard and insistent, on her quivering, exposed flesh. "Make me," she challenged.

She never found out what he might do. As his face changed, as she noted his resolution to rise to her provocation, the roar of a cannon blast split the silent night. They froze as one in each other's arms. Then, as swiftly as he'd gathered her into his arms, he was racing across the cabin to peer out of the porthole. With a curse, he grabbed his sword and, calling back for her to stay put, hastened out the door.

Shaken, hearing the repeating round of cannon fire blasting outside, Gabrielle ran to the porthole to see what Rodrigo had spied. There, in the starlight, was an ominous sight. They were surrounded by a fleet of ships.

Ignoring his orders, she grabbed her sword and dashed upstairs to find pandemonium above. Rodrigo was calling out orders as his men scampered across the deck to obey. Gabrielle joined him, distracting him with a hand at his arm. "Hastings?" she asked.

"Who else?"

"Then it was a trap. This whole charade—him not being on that ship—"

"A plot to get us out here, where he could ambush us."

He called out another series of orders, readying the cannons for fire. "But how?" Gabrielle insisted.

"He let you follow him, knew you overheard him. He was counting on you telling me."

"But—"

For a brief instant, he gazed into her eyes, his look piercing in the light of the stars and the distant flare of the fleet's torches. "We underestimated him, Gabé."

As he rushed away across the deck, calling for her to get below, she paused to take her first close look. They were surrounded on all sides by the vigilante fleet, which had bottled up the other two pirate ships as well. As she watched, their cannons spit fire, exploding into the night. The ship took a direct hit, then another, then another. Soon they were being rocked by the blasts. Belatedly, she began to think of Cullen. She finally found him manning a cannon. But as she started toward him, she saw the rail where he was take a direct hit. A portion of the ship was blown completely away. Screaming for her brother, she felt the crash of another explosion, felt the deck shatter beneath her, a motion of falling, an enveloping wet warmth that welcomed her in its depths. Then there was nothing but darkness.

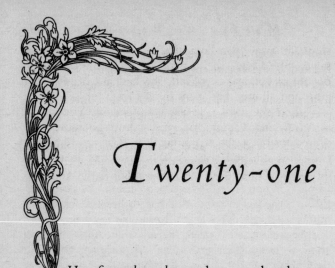

# Twenty-one

*Her first thought* was how wondrously warm the water was. It opened to her, embracing her in summery arms that rocked and soothed. She must have drifted in and out of consciousness. She found herself hanging on to a large piece of what felt like wood—flotsam from the ship, no doubt. In her hand she clasped something cold as if her life depended on her holding on. She wasn't certain what it was. Her mind, clouded by shock and the explosion, couldn't seem to function. She felt confused, disjointed.

For a time, all the world seemed still. Then, as her shock receded, she became aware of pained cries all around her. The explosions continued, splitting the night with blasts of fire and fury. Eventually, the blasting stopped. She heard men's voices from above. Enemy voices that would happily hang her for her part in this night's work. *Don't make a sound*, she willed herself again and again. *Be dead.*

She began to drift in the water, away from the disaster. It didn't occur to her to look for Rodrigo or Cullen. She'd never find them in the dark. Besides, her mind was so weary that she was having trouble thinking at all. When she glanced up and saw the lamps of the invading ships far away, she knew the tide was taking her to safety. She'd have to trust the sea. Hoisting herself up on top of her makeshift raft, she laid her head in her arms and allowed her spent mind to rest.

When she awoke, it was getting light. She wasn't sure how much time had passed, but she must have drifted for hours, on the strength of some current. Her body was stiff and sore. As she raised her head with difficulty, she saw that she still clenched her sword in her fist. When she pried it open, needles of pain shot through the numb hand. She had to flex the fingers for minutes before she could get the circulation going again.

Eventually, she roused herself sufficiently to look about at her surroundings. She was surprised to see in the dawn mist that she was in the middle of a pocket of three islands. It took her a while to get her bearings. But when she did, she recognized Praslin, the largest of the group. She suddenly remembered Rodrigo's words. *The Garden of Eden. It's the most mystical place I know. Meú avô always said if I was in trouble to go there.*

If Rodrigo was alive, he'd be there, waiting for her.

Restored by this hope, she began to paddle for land. Close in, she rode the surf, scraping herself up on the thick coral reef as she was buffeted to shore. Only when she tried to stand did she realize that she'd badly injured her leg, no doubt in the explosion that had blown apart the ship.

On inspection, she found that her leg was uncut but frightfully bruised. She could find no evidence of broken bones. Little more than a severe sprain, she guessed. With some time off her feet, she should be fine. But there was no time, and no luxury to mend. She had to reach the valley Rodrigo had spoken of.

After dragging herself along the beach toward a cluster of trees, she scouted a likely-looking limb and set about fashioning a staff. When that was finished, she was dripping with sweat. She still wasn't accustomed to the punishing heat. It was imperative that she keep her fluids replenished. Spying some coconuts lying about, she cracked several open with her sword and drank the milk. Further fortifying herself with the meat of the nut, she resolutely set out for the interior of the island, praying for the strength to find her way.

She didn't know what to look for. She had no descriptions, no landmarks to guide her way. All she knew was that she must head directly for the middle of the island, and that she had a sense she'd recognize the valley when she saw it.

So she set out on her solitary journey, determined to be strong, resolving to be brave. She wouldn't allow herself to think. If she did, she'd think of Cullen, who, no doubt, had died because of her, and of Rodrigo, who had likely been blown to bits. So she turned off her mind, thinking only of her need to reach the valley.

It was a horrifying journey. Alone, barely able to move her leg, not certain of her direction once she'd left the sight of shore behind, she battled exhaustion, and the impulse to give up. On the second day, she began to penetrate the interior. The terrain was rocky, and the growth so thick it was utterly devoid of trails. It was dark in the jungle, so she could barely see the filtered rays of the sun high above. She stumbled continually. She was scraped by sharp branches and her bare feet were raw and bruised from stepping on the protruding rocks she was too tired to avoid.

It was also so hot and humid, she could barely breathe. She sweated without end. The ripped shirt she'd tucked into her breeches was perpetually soaked, chafing her fevered skin. Dizziness overwhelmed her and she had to stop at intervals to lean against a tree while her senses settled once again.

Finally, she was so exhausted, she thought she couldn't go on. But some instinct told her she was close. Bleary with fatigue, she kept herself moving. At last, with darkness falling fast, she heard the rustle of a stream. Nearly delirious by now, she threw herself down and drank greedily from its depths. Her thirst slaked, she rolled over and discovered she was in a wide valley that seemed to have been landscaped with strange primeval plants, including a huge variety of palms she'd never seen before. She gazed up at their heights and noticed that some held fruit that looked shockingly like a large male erection. At their bases, lay a collection of fallen coconuts that were perfect replicas of the female vulva. *The* coco de mer. *The forbidden fruit. When you see it, you'll know why.*

She was in the Vallée de Mai. The Garden of Eden.

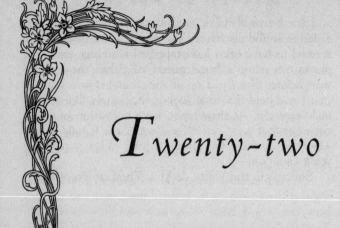

# Twenty-two

*The next morning*, as she awoke, she was aware of feeling purged. As if all the poisons had been discharged from her body. As if she'd been enlivened with a slowly building sense of renewed strength. She heard birds singing sweetly in the trees. A trickle of water teased her ears. The natural bed of leaves beneath her felt soft and soothing. She stretched, feeling alive and refreshed. And opened her eyes to a wondrous sight.

What in the dusk had seemed merely beautiful now looked like an artist's vision of heaven. Giant palms with lushly green leaves as tall as a man draped over her. The sun filtered through like rays of light through stained-glass windows. It was the most magnificent display she'd ever seen. She felt herself in a cathedral fashioned by God's own hand.

Everywhere she looked, she was surrounded by trees and fronds and prickly stalks the likes of which she'd never imagined. Pushing herself up on one elbow, using a hand to shift her tangled hair from her face, she saw that she lay by a streambed that traversed the valley. Huge granite rocks lined a path, creating a waterfall of the stream as it danced and slid along the slopes.

She heard a scuffle and turned, expecting to see Rodrigo smiling down at her in welcome. Instead, she spied a green gecko a foot long scrambling for cover beneath a plant whose leaves looked like fingers of a prickly hand.

Her impulse was to search the valley for Rodrigo, but she knew she must attend to her own needs first. She was battered and sore. She needed nourishment and rest. She needed to care for the leg that was swollen and throbbing with every touch.

Limping weakly, she set out to gather tropical fruits and lay them aside as a cache of food. She had no idea how long she'd have to be here, fending for herself. Then she used her sword to build a small shelter, a crude structure fashioned from thin tree-trunks draped with the gigantic palm leaves. She washed her clothes, scrubbing them against the smooth surface of rocks. As they dried slowly in the muggy atmosphere, she bathed in the warm stream, absorbing the healing essence of the garden around her.

Her surroundings were so exotic, a magical valley of great proportions with cascading waterfalls, treetop aeries, and shaded pathways guarded by massive granite boulders. The paths meandered up and down steep hills, and the azure sky seemed alive with birds. Some flew in pairs, some alone. Some were white, some black, some showed flashes of brilliant orange or red. They dipped and swayed, circling the island again and again as if the most joyous thing they could think of was to fly through the air. She remembered how her mother loved the unique birds of Seychelles. And she recalled her dream, where the multicolored island birds had represented paradise and Rodrigo and his dark passions had threatened it.

She wondered now who that woman was, the one who'd rejected the man destiny had given her like a gift. She'd give anything to turn a corner and find him standing there, whole and compelling in his golden beauty, his arms outstretched to welcome her home.

But although she spent the next few days searching the area for him, she never found a trace.

On the fourth day, a storm swooped down on the island.

Perched on a huge boulder just at the entrance of the valley, she heard the rumble of thunder in the distance, smelled the tang of rain in the thick, sodden air. The wind gusted, and the strange palms looked menacing as they bent and swayed in the gale.

Panicked at the thought of being alone in the onrushing storm, she lowered herself to the ground, intent on reaching her shelter quickly. As she made her way along the path of dead brush and leaves, darkness suddenly descended like a theater curtain. She realized with horror that she could no longer make out even the haziest forms. The storm was upon her now, as if the sky had opened and let drop a flood. Rain beat against the canopy of the towering palms, drenching her in a relentless shower.

She was terrified. She heard the noises of creatures scattering in her path, but she couldn't see them. In her bare feet, leaning heavily on her staff, she blindly raced ahead. But her camp wasn't where she'd thought it was. She'd lost her bearings.

She was stumbling now, tripping at every step. As a flash of lightning split the night, she jumped and lost her staff. Her frantic fumblings couldn't locate it, so she was forced to go on without it. Many times she fell and scraped her arms against the jagged edge of rocks or the prickly skewers of the ghostly palms. She'd been so brave for so long, keeping her apprehension at bay. But the storm had rooted up all the worst of her fears. This paradise that had offered her safety had suddenly become an arena of unimaginable horror.

And just as she reached her moment of total despair, she heard a human voice calling through the squall. It was thickly accented, and full of the same alarm she felt coursing through her veins.

The voice seemed demonic, a cruel joke, part and parcel of the aberrant ether of the night. She rushed from it—and collided hard with something coming her way. She was startled by the contact, by the abrupt halt of her flight against a barricade as strong and unyielding as any prehistoric tree. By the unexpected warmth of bare flesh as her hands reached out to right herself and came in contact with human form.

"*Carícia*, thank God."

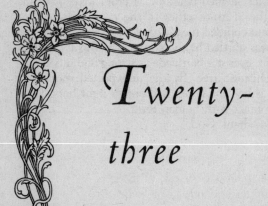

# Twenty-three

*In one glorious moment*, she felt his lips on hers. She was drowning in his kiss in the pouring rain. Then he heaved her up into his arms, his mouth devouring hers as he swept her away.

"Rodrigo . . . Rodrigo . . . Rodrigo. . . ." she called above the wind.

"I thought you were dead, Gabé. I thought you were dead!"

He was sobbing with relief. She could taste the salt of his tears.

Whatever questions she might have asked went unspoken in the heat of his touch. Those questions could wait for a more dispassionate time. The turbulence of the storm, his finding her in such an untamed state, had fueled his desperation for her as surely as her awareness of it fueled her own. It suddenly seemed like the most natural thing in the world that he should show up from out of nowhere in the midst of a violent storm to swing her into his arms.

Slowly, as if in a trance, she slid from his arms to stand before him. In the flash of the lightning, she saw his gaze fixed on her breasts beneath the plastered shirt. They felt on fire, as if he'd set them to flame. He didn't touch her, yet in her mind, she could feel his mouth clamp on her nipple. She could hear her moans low in her throat.

"I love you," she breathed into his ear. She couldn't bring herself to stop saying it. "I love you. *I love you!*"

"As I've always loved you."

She could feel him against her, hard as any granite boulder, his body steaming with hot rain and untempered desire. She pushed away so she could see his face in the spasmodic streaks of light.

"I need you so, Rodrigo."

Somewhere above, thunder crashed and a streak of lightning split the blackness of the sky. In the flash, she looked up and caught a glimpse of a long, thick fruit that jutted above her like a man's erection ready for the plunge. The *coco de mer*.

By now the wind was lashing strands of drenched hair like whips across her face. She felt his hands reach for it, clench the tendrils in tight fists, felt him tug her to him by her hair. Felt the warm, heart-stopping contact as he slammed her up against his chest. In an instant his mouth was on hers, claiming her as his own.

His mouth moved to her breast, sucking through the damp cotton, moving with persuasive skill. He raised his head. Her breast felt cold without the succor of his warm mouth, but his hand quickly took its place. It yanked down the shirt so she felt herself exposed to the storm.

She wanted this above all things. His presence had unleashed such a volcanic yearning that she knew she must have him or die.

The shelter was forgotten. Gone was any thought of refuge. Security, protection, these were words from another realm that seemed so much less real than what was transpiring in this mystical, storm-thrashed world.

She slipped the soaked clothing down her body so it fell at her feet. As she stepped out of it, it seemed to symbolize the baring of her naked soul for his pleasure.

Gently, he took her hands in both of his and came close so his mouth was at her ear. "Legend says on stormy nights, the male *coco de mer* uproots himself from the earth and goes to the female to mate. No human has ever seen such an occurrence. Were we to witness it, we'd be struck dead, so we would tell no tales."

She glanced up at the giant tree above, believing in the magic, thinking she almost saw its fruit move and shift and become a man. Lightning cracked against the sky, sounding like the wrenching of ancient roots from the hard earth at their feet.

It reminded her of when they were children, his telling her fanciful tales. Then, like the man of action he was, he picked her up, swung her around, and laid her down on a soft, grassy bed, making her forget the child he'd been in the man he now was.

His mouth was on her, at the mound of her breast, the curve of her belly, the fragile, pulsing tissue of her inner thigh. He licked and nibbled and nipped with a constantly moving mouth, the mouth of a virtuoso, the mouth of a man who loves the taste of a woman and can never get enough. He moved over her, not in a sensual, slow-moving trail, but in a swift fashion that carried with it the tantalizing element of surprise. In the dark, she couldn't see. He played on her defenselessness, enhancing her awareness of his mouth by kissing her first on her shoulder, then on the balls of her feet, raising a leg to lick the back of a shapely buttock, then nipping at her nipple with the grinding friction of gently gnawing teeth. She never knew where his mouth would surface next. The not knowing made her hot, made her forget everything else in the delicious anticipation of his next move. Just as his mouth settled on a breast, his fingers played with the damp evidence of her hunger, causing her to cry aloud, then moved too quickly to trail a fevered path along her calf to circle the cap of her knee. By now, her body was on fire, wanting his touch so much, she grew impatient to have him sheath himself in her.

She reached for his breeches, caressing the manifest bulge. "Don't tease me, Rodrigo. Come inside."

Her hands ripped at the fastenings. He brushed them aside and she heard the wet material slide down his hardened skin. Then she gasped as he lay atop her, his body warm and hard, and utterly masculine, the body of a man who knows his own desires. She felt his erection against the opening of her thighs. He angled himself so he was rubbing against her, back and forth, slowly, slowly, until she opened her mouth wide and panted, "I want you so."

She arched her hips to increase the lovely friction of him rubbing against her, his erection now slickly moist from the juices of her lust. He grabbed her hair in a fist that was neither caring nor compassionate. Like a caveman claiming his woman in the wild. It thrilled her.

Then he took himself in hand and for some time, he teased her, parting her wet curls, sliding back and forth, then circling her cleft, goading her to a state of turmoil that intensified her passion and caused her to thrash her head from side to side. She lunged up, trying desperately to coax him inside, but he put a halting hand to her collarbone and pushed her back to taunt her some more. Her senses began to slip. Everything inside her melted away—her exhaustion, her terror, even her relief at finding him alive. She forgot everything but the need to open herself to him, to be *taken* by him. To be elated beyond reason by the unbelievably exhilarating torment of his touch.

Just as she felt her climax building—when she no longer cared what he did or how—he entered her with a savage thrust. He pierced her like a man who could no longer wait to seize the woman he loved. He plunged into her like a hurricane at sea, lifting her hips and thrusting with the same mad grace with which he wielded his sword. Unconquerable. Impossible to guess where he might strike next. As he drove into her, his hands wandered to her breasts, her throat, to thrust his fingers in her mouth. They were everywhere and nowhere, urging her body to new heights of desire, inciting her hunger and quenching it all at the same time.

She was panting and gasping so loudly, she couldn't believe it was her. She'd never made such noises, such untamed noises, like an animal of the wilderness. She bit down on his fingers and tried to quiet herself, but he sank into her like an arrow hitting its mark and she threw back her head and cried out loud.

"Go ahead and scream," his voice said at her ear, hot and hushed like a fever. "There's no one to hear you. Civilization is miles away. There are no rules of decorum. It's just you and me, *carícia*, and the heavens and the sea. Surrounded by a jungle few men have ever seen. Wild things, all. Tonight, you control your own destiny. Tell me what you desire."

He nipped her ear, sending a spiraling heat pulsing through her senses. His words had taken hold of her. She felt like a savage creature, stripped of its human bonds.

She'd waited so long for him. She'd wanted him like she'd wanted nothing and no one. She'd fought him, denied him, but always she'd known it would come to this. To her panting helplessly in his manly arms. To her begging him to give her what she'd denied she'd wanted for so long. The inevitability of it was dazzling. It stole her breath in great gulping sobs.

"What is it you desire?" he coaxed.

"Harder," she gasped. "*Harder*. HARDER!"

Her words enflamed him. He hauled her up and obliged her, sending her soaring until her head dropped back, her mouth gaped open, and she screamed her fulfillment to the stormy skies.

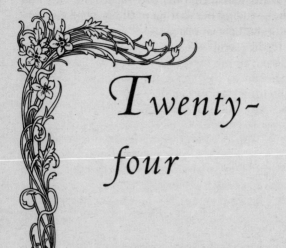

# Twenty-four

*Gabrielle awakened* with her head between Rodrigo's legs, her cheek resting on his inner thigh. It was sticky, the dark gold hair slicked down by the issue of their night of passion. A torrid night of unimaginable bliss. Her blurred gaze followed the sleek line of his swordsman's legs to the apex of his thighs, where he lay flaccid but still huge—a symbol, a manifestation of manhood, of power, of . . . liberation. They'd slept under the stars like children of God, with no clothes to cover their nakedness or impede their roving hands. When he'd reached for her repeatedly in the night, his rough palm was greeted by warm and willing flesh: the soft glove of a breast, the curve of a tender thigh. This morning, here in the Garden of Eden, in her lover's embrace, smeared with the proof of their passions, she felt truly reborn.

Overcome with gratitude, she lowered her head and, with an eager tongue, took a long, lingering lick up his thigh.

He stirred and came awake. Feeling him move, she grinned at him, took him in her hand, and kissed him reverently as she felt him spring to life beneath her lips.

"I still can't believe you're here," she murmured with a sigh. "It's like a miracle. I'm so grateful, I never want to let you out of my sight again."

"You're not as distraught this morning, I see," he observed with an amused smile.

"I feel stronger. It's as if you passed some of your strength—your energy—to me."

"I have. The Shona of Africa believe that when a man climaxes, he transfers his energy to the object of his desire. And I've got eight years of energy built up. No wonder you have such a glow about you."

"I don't flatter myself that you waited eight years for me."

"Mentally, I did."

She laughed at his sheepish expression. "Well, *physically* you've improved. Not that you needed improvement." He looked embarrassed. "How *did* you get to be such a . . . *formidable* lover?"

He just shrugged, as if he'd prefer to drop the conversation.

"Come on, Rodrigo." She gave him a nudge with her elbow. "Tell me."

"I had . . . a teacher."

"A woman?"

"Yes."

"Was it Shayla?"

He was truly flabbergasted. "How do you know about Shayla?"

"Oh, that's easy. When we were children, whenever a damsel was to be rescued, you always named her Shayla."

"Did I really? Well, Shayla was a Shona woman from deep in Africa. She was eighteen and I was twelve."

"Twelve! And she taught you lovemaking?"

"It was a tradition in my family. My father and

grandfather had both been taught the love secrets of the Shona at the advent of manhood. You see, Gabé, the Shona are the descendants of a lost civilization that once existed in central Africa—Zimbabwe. I've seen the ruins of their great cities. They had an advanced culture, more advanced, I think, than anything that has ever existed in Europe. Their men and women were equals— true partners. They understood how the willing exchange of power in a relationship could create an authentic balance, and a level of trust that is unheard of in your European love affairs. They made lovemaking into an art form, the secrets of which have been carried down through the centuries by their Shona descendants. Though that knowledge seems to be slowly dying out."

After a pause she asked, in a vulnerable tone, "Did you love her?"

"I adored her. As a pupil loves his teacher."

"Shayla is a beautiful name."

"I always thought so."

"And just what *were* these secrets she taught you?"

"Well . . . it's hard to explain in words."

"Try."

"They involve restraint, submission, and the playing of roles to break down inhibitions. As an actress, you should like that."

"Restraints . . . really?"

"Among other things. And, of course, there was my graduation exercise—the greatest of the lost love secrets of Zimbabwe. That's something I can never speak of aloud." He turned and looked at her with a glint of mischief. "Only perhaps show you someday."

She felt the heat of his implication curl down her spine. "When?"

But he didn't answer. He just gave her a kiss that was more enticing than any answer he might give.

"What happened to her? Your Shayla?"

She felt him stiffen. "The slavers got her. She was a goddess, and they tried to make her into a slave. But she died before they could put her on the block at Zanzibar. She was too free a spirit ever to adjust to *that* life. She just stopped living."

A sudden sadness permeated the air. Neither of them spoke for several moments, until Rodrigo said, "Does it surprise you to learn I had such a secret in my past?"

"A little."

"I'll wager you have secrets of your own."

Drawing up, she said, "Would you like me to tell them to you?"

He studied her a moment, then said, "Only when you feel ready."

She didn't respond. In the silence, they felt the magical mood of their lovemaking slip away and the cold, hard reality of their situation set in.

She asked, "Did you lose many men in the battle?"

"A great many, I'm afraid. Most of them. I tried to find survivors, but all I saw was the sea littered with corpses. I can only hope there were survivors and that, like you, they escaped to safety."

"Everything was so confusing . . . it was too dark . . . I don't suppose you saw . . . Cullen?"

He was quiet for a moment, as if measuring what he should say. "I saw him take a direct hit. I never found his body. I fear, Gabé, that we must count him among the dead."

"I swore to protect him, and in the end I failed him." The guilt curled around her heart like a fist.

"You can't protect people, Gabé," he said gently, putting a comforting arm about her. "Often, when you try, you hold them back from their own growth."

"There was no growth. He was an Ashton, and the fate of the Ashton men is written in stone. Doomed to a life of helplessness . . ." She couldn't afford to go on thinking about Cullen. If she did, she'd go insane.

A skink the size of a large cigar crawled over her foot and she jerked her leg, causing her to wince in pain.

"What's that?" he asked. She realized he was looking at her badly bruised leg. It was yellowing now, but it still looked frightful, with most of the thigh discolored and swollen.

"I hurt it in the explosion. I had a staff somewhere, but I lost it in the storm."

"And you walked all this way, on such an injury?" She saw the pride in his eyes. "You're as brave, *carícia*, as any of my finest men."

She felt warmed by the praise.

"I can make a salve for your wound from takamaka bark. I'll venture out and find some."

"I'll go with you. I just need a staff."

He rose and, gloriously naked, used his knife to cut a limb and shave it for use as a staff. It was so quickly done that she couldn't help but recall the way she'd struggled with the same process.

They walked slowly through the valley as Rodrigo looked about as if he'd just come home. At one point, he took her hand, gesturing with a sweeping motion of his arm. "Look around you, Gabé. This is the heart of paradise. There are no predators here. Nothing is poisonous, not a plant, not a spider, not a snake. See those birds?"

She looked up through the foliage and saw once again a cloudless blue sky animated by the joyous flight of the birds.

"What are they doing?" she asked.

"Displaying themselves."

It seemed a charming phrase. As if they knew their beauty and were offering it to the world.

"Come," he said, leading her along the path. They came at last to a hollowed-out root in a tree. "A ferry tern," he said, pointing. There, a lovely white bird sat close to her chick. When they approached, the mother bird looked up with the softest, most trusting black eyes Gabrielle had ever seen. No fear. No alarm. No instinct to protect her young. Just a look of such sublime welcome that Gabrielle felt moved to tears.

She bent so she was within inches of the bird's sweet face. "I've never seen a bird who wouldn't fly away at this close range. Or at least become upset and want to keep you from her young."

"They don't know danger here," Rodrigo explained. "They don't even build nests. They just lay their eggs on the branch of a tree and fly away. It never occurs to them that anyone will harm them, because no one ever has."

She looked up at him with a new understanding in her eyes. "That's why you love it so."

"It's why my family has loved it for hundreds of years. It's why we've fought to protect it from the greed of evil men who want to spoil it."

"Men like Hastings." Once again, she felt the fist of guilt squeeze her heart. "I can't believe I allowed him to trick me as he did."

"I wouldn't be too hard on myself about that. Hastings is very clever—he certainly fooled me."

"Why do you think he's so evil?" she asked.

"Who knows how the twig was bent?"

"He's always been that way. There's something missing in him. He has no feelings for other human beings. He has only contempt for our father. His mother was just a smothering burden. And I know he was relieved at her death. And yet he's so relentless in his pursuits. What drives him? What does he want?"

"Sometimes I look back on that mean little boy and think of how he was excluded from the bond of Seychelles. You, me, Cullen, Douglas, and Caprice: We all had these roots in paradise. Hastings had heard all the stories of its splendor from his father. How jealous he must have been. It's only natural that he'd grow up to be obsessed with Seychelles and want to possess them. He just wants what everyone wants: paradise."

"Is that what this fight of yours is all about?"

"Of course, Gabé. Everybody wants paradise. What makes our situation so unique is that the paradise that all the characters in this little drama want is so tangible. We can feel it, touch it, smell it. It's real. It's all around us."

She'd never thought about it in this light, but it was true. Douglas, Caprice, Rodrigo, Hastings, even Cullen, and of course, herself; they all wanted paradise. *This* paradise. "So you and Hastings are locked in a struggle to see who will be master of paradise?"

"You could say that."

"So you will have to kill him."

"Probably."

"And then what? Won't there be other contenders? A whole society of plantation owners? An entire economy based on slavery? And like Hastings, won't this endless succession of enemies all have the power of England behind them?"

He said nothing. There was nothing he *could* say.

In that moment, Gabrielle understood for the first time just how hopeless Rodrigo's stand really was. She suddenly realized that he was locked in a battle that, in the scheme of history, he couldn't possibly win.

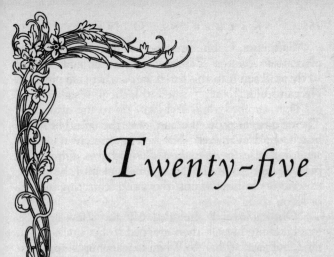

# Twenty-five

"*Is it safe?*" Gabrielle asked.

Over the last few days, as they'd taken the time they needed to recover their strength, she'd been overcome by a sense that they must never leave the sanctuary of this valley. Toward this end, she'd hidden from Rodrigo the fact that her leg had all but healed, still using the staff to walk. She no longer needed it, thanks to the salve he'd made, but she knew if Rodrigo discovered how much better she was feeling, he'd insist they leave. To face certain defeat. Ever since her realization of his hopeless struggle, she was loath to hurry him into a situation that was sure to end in his destruction. So while she mended, she'd engineered her efforts toward distracting him enough—making him happy enough—that he'd want to stay.

For a couple of days, her plan succeeded. Rodrigo had wanted her for years, and the thought of having her for the taking in this paradise of his heart seemed to him, at times, too good to be true. He could spend hours making love to her as if there were no tomorrow, and no pressing business at hand. But he'd begun to grow restless and long for a change of scene. So she was indulging his yearnings by following him through the jungle to a distant beach.

"Safe enough," he answered. "There are only two plantations on the island, one at either end. It isn't likely we'll run into anyone. If we do, there are plenty of places to hide."

They climbed a hill and came down the other side. There, glistening in the sun, was the most beautiful beach she'd ever seen. Not a long stretch of endless sand, but a series of small, secluded coves dotted with palms. Huge granite boulders jutted out into the ocean, the waves crashing against them and scattering in a sea of foam.

"Oh, it's lovely!" she cried. She ran a few steps before catching herself, then dropped to her knees in the sand, burying her hands. When he came up behind, she smiled up at him. "It's just the sort of sand my mother used to tell me about. Feel it, Rodrigo! It feels like silk."

"Let's find some shade," he suggested. "I don't want you staying in the sun too long."

It was easy to underestimate the severity of the equatorial sun. Already, her skin had turned a rich golden color. There was no way of avoiding it. But she'd learned that even an hour of unprotected exposure could lead to a painful burn.

They found a spot where two silver-trunked takamaka trees leaned horizontally toward each other, their leaves creating a protective patch of shade. Dropping to the sand, Gabrielle hugged her knees, looking around her with appreciative eyes. The beach, closer to the water, was strewn with long strands of green kelp and smooth white coral. Across the sea, she spotted islands all around, the hills shaded in light and dark greens, with rocky areas that looked almost pink in the afternoon light.

The sea was clear and clean. With the tide in, the shallow water covered slabs of granite interspersed with sand, so that part of the water looked so green it was almost black, while a portion was so clear she could see the tan of the beach underneath, and patches showed in various shades of aquamarine. In the distance it was all swirled together so that it looked striped—or like a thin layer of aqua covering buried islands. To the left of their cove stood round rocks shaped like mounds of wet clay the artist had squeezed with a fist, letting the clay ooze through his fingers, then leaving it to dry.

Beyond the coral reef, breakers rolled in, creating a rim of white. As Rodrigo settled down beside her, all was quiet except for the far-off roar of the waves and the gentle singing of the water lapping up on the beach. Occasionally, the warm wind blew and the water surged forth to embrace the sand, like a lover that had been too long away.

Gabrielle instantly fell into the mood of this peaceful setting. She wasn't a woman who welcomed inactivity. Her mind was too turbulent and full of roiling thoughts, her body accustomed to movement and the pursuit of goals. Yet she looked about her with the new appreciation of one who'd recently faced death, and felt the serenity of her surroundings seep into her soul. Even the palm trees angled toward the sea, almost lying on their sides, looking as if they could drift down and take a nap.

She looked at Rodrigo, lying back on one elbow, surveying the sea with an expert's eyes. When they glanced at each other, they merely smiled. There was no need for words. They could read their thoughts in each other's eyes. In the days they'd spent together, they'd rediscovered the effortless affinity they'd shared as children. They found no need for endless chatter. Being silent together, simply holding hands, was as companionable as their most riotous nights of love.

She turned onto her stomach and put her cheek to the sand. It was unbelievably tranquil. She felt no need to move, or even think. The earth sang a lullaby to her, soothing her cares, assuring her of the rightness and order of things. It was like being at the very end of the world. Stretching her arms wide, she felt she was embracing all of creation. As if she were truly one with it and all its rhythms. None of the old worries mattered. She couldn't even recall the things she'd considered important in her other life. *This* was what life was—to lie with her ear pressed to the sand and listen to the hymn of the sea as it resonated to chords in her own soul.

"I can't believe this," she said dreamily after an hour or more had passed in which she'd done nothing more than run her foot back and forth along the unbelievably sensuous sand. "Normally, I'm anxious to leave after staying in one spot for too long. I become bored with sitting. But I could stay here forever, under this odd tree that's so obligingly sheltering us from the sun. It seems I've been here always, at peace, knowing I belong."

She rolled over on her back and looked up to see him smiling down at her. "You do belong here," he told her.

"I never felt that I belonged anywhere before. Even when I came here, I didn't seem to fit. Nothing my mother told me seemed to be true. I thought her stories were just the fanciful memories of a young girl denied. But I do feel I belong here . . . with you. Without people and their restrictions, I feel light of heart—free to be who I am. Shall I tell you a secret?"

His eyes lit with amusement. "Please do."

"Sometimes I think I don't really like people. I could stay here always, and see no one but you, and be completely happy for the rest of my life." She paused as a feeling of melancholy marred her good humor. "Why can't it always be like this, Rodrigo?"

He reached over and ran the back of his finger along her shoulder. "It can," he promised.

With his thumb, he slipped the torn shirt off her shoulder and leaned to plant a kiss on her heated flesh. She grinned, a feeling of happiness bubbling inside. "Feeling like playing, are we?"

"You're not dressed for play."

"I'll take mine off if you will," she teased in the tone of a taunting child.

They laughed as they stripped off their meager clothing and tossed it aside. But Gabrielle's laughter snared in her throat as she caught sight of the magnificence of his body. Her gaze rested on the coiled biceps and lean forearms, the strength of which was accentuated by the thick leather cuffs he wore at his wrists. It gave him the look of a fierce warrior even when he smiled. As if his every thought, his every waking desire, was how to conquer her trembling body with the creative mastery of his will.

Her eyes traveled the length of him, down the stalwart chest, lightly tufted with hair of gold, to the taut, flat belly, to the potent proof of his desire as it throbbed and pulsed. A pagan god in all his glory, struck from molten gold, empowered by the sun. "You're so beautiful!" she exclaimed. "No man has the right to be so beautifully formed."

She sat up and began to scoop sand into a mound.

"What are you doing?" he asked.

"Paying tribute to you."

He watched her with a curious frown as her hands moved in the sand, patting, shaping, using her fingers to carve in details. Occasionally, she glanced at him for inspiration, then went back to her task. As it developed, she leaned over it, shrugging him away when he bent to see. "Wait till it's finished. An artist must be free to create unimpeded. You wouldn't crash my rehearsal, would you, before I learned my lines?"

Finally, she gave a triumphant sigh. "There!" she announced, glancing at him with twinkling cobalt eyes. "It's perfect!"

He looked to see that she'd made a duplicate of his erection out of sand. Like his, it was veined and hard, full of life and character. The head was clearly defined, even down to the indentation at the tip. It could have passed for the real thing.

She ran her hand over it. It was tightly packed and seemed vital and active beneath her touch. "This sand is so soft, I swear this is real."

"Which do you prefer," he asked in a voice as heated as the sun, "the flesh or the sand?"

"Oh, let me see . . ." She pretended to consider as she continued to stroke her fingers over her handiwork. Leaning, she kissed the projection of hard-packed sand.

"So you like the sand, do you?"

"Well, now that you mention it, this is the most incredible sand I've ever felt. I can't seem to stop touching it. It's so . . . sumptuous."

"It's granitic sand. That's why it's so soft."

"I don't care why. I just love the feel of it."

"Then, by all means, don't let me deprive you."

He pushed her down on her back in the sand. When she laughed and said, "What are you doing?" he held her pinned down. Her struggles forced him to hold her tighter. Soon, she was breathing heavily in the heat, his locking her beneath him stirring her blood, the quivering pulse inside her quickening with every lurching beat of her accelerated heart.

He took a palmful of the silken sand and let it sift through sun-browned fingers onto her pale skin. He trailed it along one breast, then the other, until each nipple was rimmed in a circle of white sand. He sprinkled it between her legs, the light touch of the silt tantalizing in its gentle padding against the sensitivity of her most vulnerable core. Then he took his hand and rubbed the luxurious grains into her skin. Her cleft grew wet. Her abdomen coiled like a fist. Her nipples hardened as a suffocating sound escaped lips that parted beneath the systematic storming of her senses. He scooped up another fistful and palmed it over her breast. This he kneaded into her like dough, the friction of the gentle grains delectably sensual, shooting through her with mind-numbing pleasure, awakening a coarse and lurid ache in her loins.

"How does it feel?" he asked.

She was so insensible, she didn't want to move. But glancing at him through eyes that were drunk with passion, she couldn't resist the urge to touch. As with a priceless vase in a museum, she felt the impulse to run her fingers along the contours of such heart-wrenching beauty. Her mouth watered as she saw his erection magnify before her eyes. Just for a touch . . . just for one delicious taste . . .

"See for yourself."

She shifted, took a handful of the velvety ground granite, and rubbed it against his erection. She felt him swell even more beneath her fist. When he was covered with it, she laughed and pointed to her facsimile. "You see? I told you it was perfect. I'd be hard-pressed to tell one from the other."

"I guarantee you'll know the difference."

With tenacious hands, he compelled her back against the ground.

An erotic longing gutted her like a spear. She felt hot, feverish as she hadn't in the throes of her illness, fueled by his lust that curled her toes on a sibilant sigh, and made her feel like the most desirable woman on earth beneath his practiced hands. Her body readied itself with blissful expectation.

With sure hands, he spread her arms wide, like a cross, then parted her legs. As she watched, he took both hands, filled them with sand, and dribbled it over her body. More sand followed, and more, leisurely, as if he had all the time in the world, until the sand began to accumulate in heavy mounds. As he dug deeper, the sand was cooler, moist, like dough. With as much concentration as she'd called on earlier to make her idol in the sand, he buried her body from her ankles to her chin. All of her body, that is, except her feet, her hips, her breasts, and her hands. Then he stepped back to observe his handicraft.

She couldn't move. She was completely immobilized

by the heavy, damp sand, as effectively bound before him as if he'd tied her spread-eagle with ropes. Then he got up and wandered off toward the sea.

"You're not going to leave me here like this!" she cried.

He said nothing, leaving her to wonder why he'd left her more tender, vulnerable places open to the torrid air. She saw him bend and pick up a long length of sea kelp, then move to the water to retrieve another, this one wet. On his way back, he stopped to scoop up the frond of a palm that had fallen in the sand.

"Have you ever wondered what kelp would feel like against your skin?" he asked.

"Never."

"For instance, what would this dry kelp feel like on the bottoms of your feet?" As he spoke, he put action to his words. The kelp was dry and crackly, and it tickled her toes. She squirmed and laughed, but it was impossible to move away. "Or what if it were wet?" He trailed the wet kelp along her exposed breasts. It was slick and slimy, but slipped along her nipples, highly charged. She could feel herself go wetter still.

He played with her for a torturous length of time, trailing the insidious wet kelp along her face and throat, sliding it up between her thighs like a greedy snake, igniting in her loins a shrieking surge of unadulterated lust. Each place he touched vibrated to the tease, the light torment of a touch without touch. He lingered on her cheek but slid all too soon away from her clit. She tried and tried to angle herself so he'd touch the places she wanted him to touch most, but nothing would persuade him. Even as she began to beg him in a voice made breathy by the undulating friction. "Where?" he'd ask, with a smile. "Here?" Then he'd touch her briefly— oh, too briefly!—and slither away.

He used the tools of nature as toys to amuse himself and drive her insane. The palm frond was stiff. Rubbed against the underside of her foot, it tickled her so badly, she had tears streaming down her face. Stroked against her nipple, it made her long for the crushing weight of his palm. It was excruciating, wanting more of him as he plagued her with the all-too-brief promise of audacious pleasures to come.

The sun had shifted, so it was angled over her. It was hot and stimulating against her exposed skin. She began to perspire beneath the cool, damp sand. The heat, the seductive sand, the open sky of azure blue, the birds displaying themselves overhead, just as he'd displayed her to his eyes, all simmered together to stir in her a passion as hot-blooded and reckless as the roaring sea. When he moved so his erection brushed her bound hand, she grabbed on to it and pumped it with relish, straining to bring it to her mouth. The feel of flesh was exquisite after the torture of makeshift toys.

"What do you want now?" he asked. "Sand or flesh?"

"Oh, flesh, *by all means*." She could no longer stand being denied. If he denied her now, she'd perish in the hellfire of her own clawing need.

"Where do you want it?"

"In my mouth."

He obliged her by straddling her face and bringing himself to her. She stuck out her tongue and just barely touched him before he moved back. Heavy-lidded with passion, she let out an agonized cry. She wanted so much to surround him with her mouth. The need was as elemental as the scorched and steaming air she heaved into raw lungs. Her blistering ardor enveloped her like flames, incinerating everything as it coalesced in the scalding compulsion of her desire. She could taste him already. Yet every time she reached for him, he jerked away.

Her lazy mood, her lingering, drifting sensibilities, were shot, a mere remembrance from an afternoon long past. She was as hot as she could remember being, both from the penetration of the sun's parching rays, and from the boiling of her blood as he drove her to distrac-

tion with a game of give-and-take. Her disposition was
titillated now to mindless, famished need. As his hand
found her hot, pouty folds, she whimpered and sought to
arch against it, only to find herself restrained. Her im-
prisonment of sand electrified her longing for him. He
rubbed the rigid length of himself along her face, teasing
her cheeks, then moving lower to the voluptuous invitation of her breasts. With one hand, he held them together as he shamelessly thrust himself between; with
the other, he stroked her with light and sensitive fingers
that contrasted with his rugged thrusts, jettisoned any
pretense of pride, and made her cry out for more. As he
propelled himself between the lush globes, the head of
his erection barely touched her mouth to be quickly
yanked away. The torture was so sweet, she felt on the
brink of some shattering revelation. He thrust harder
now, penetrating and withdrawing, the propulsion
bringing him flush against her lips. As he did, she
opened her mouth and reached for him with her outstretched tongue, striving with a manic need to taste the
essence of his aggressive passion. But she could never
quite reach him as he moved like quicksilver. And when
he withdrew his hard-muscled body completely, her
head fell back with a disappointed wail.

She wasn't disappointed for long. He put his mouth
to hers and, after kissing her with searing ardor, said,
"You drive me wild." Then, as if he couldn't wait any
more than she, he moved between her extended thighs
and slid the hard, corded length of his arousal into her,
plundering her warmth, penetrating her, invading her,
white-hot as a branding iron singeing her flesh. Plung-
ing deeper, he buried himself in her just as he'd buried
her helpless limbs in the sand. That sand, coating his
erection, created an unexpectedly blissful friction as he
pumped like a madman with ferocious, unmanageable
strength. He fell over her and pressed his hands into her
upturned palms, reiterating his domination, making it
impossible even to curl her fingers around his palms as

the pleasure shot through her in wave after wave of inexpressible, rapturous joy. She shivered in the heat, arched as best she could beneath a searing shot of yearning that rattled her sagacity and shattered her soul.

When they'd spent themselves, he lay atop her, his body heavy as an anvil, breathing like a furnace pumping at high speed. "*Deus,* what you do to me," he gasped, as if he couldn't draw air into his lungs. He lifted his golden head and peered down at her with heartfelt eyes. "I've never loved another woman in my life," he told her. "I've never wanted a woman the way I want you. My dreams are destroyed, yet I'm happy here with you. I, too, feel as though I could live forever with you by my side, with no·other companions."

"Just the two of us," she murmured, smiling lovingly into his eyes. "With no distractions. No rules. No one to tell us what we must or must not do."

"You can't know what it was like, all those years without you. I thought I was lonely as a child. But I never knew loneliness until I tasted of your love, then had to leave you behind. I never guessed that you'd insinuated yourself into my heart the way you did. But night after night, as the sun set on my beloved islands, I looked into its golden glow and saw only your face."

"Was my face covered with sand?" she teased. "I'm so full of sand, it's in my teeth."

He answered her smile. "I can do something about that." And he brushed away her cell of sand, but bit by bit, slowly, with courtly fingers, so by the time she was freed, she was stimulated anew.

He read the craving in her eyes and smiled. "Let's go wash off," he suggested, then bounded up and headed for the sea. He was already crossing the coral reef and wading into the deeper waters beyond by the time she reached the edge of the water. He began to swim, cutting through the brilliant green of the water with robust, effortless strokes.

But she was too lazy to swim. The sun, combining

with her climax, was making her sleepy, in spite of the discomfort of the sand on her sweat-drenched skin. She looked around and eyed the granite rocks with the waves crashing over the top. The surface of them dipped naturally in the form of a body. Perfect, she thought, and scrambled up to the top, gauging her progress between waves.

Then she settled herself in the curved indentation, lying on her back with her face to the sun. Closing her eyes, she waited for the next swell of surf. When it came, it crashed over her, drenching her with a spray of the warmest water possible from the sea. It lapped and pooled about her, washing away the sand, as she stretched in dreamy luxury on the surface of the smooth-washed rock.

She could easily have fallen asleep, with the water wooing her every now and then. But Rodrigo's cry startled her awake. She rolled onto her side and saw the fin of a gigantic shark cutting the water toward him. It rose from the depths and she realized it was immense—perhaps as much as forty feet in length.

"Gabé, look!" he called.

With her heart in her throat, she watched Rodrigo swim toward the beast, grab hold of its protruding fin, and ride it some distance until it started heading out to sea. Then he let go, laughed mightily, and swam back toward her.

"Do you realize what that was?" he said excitedly. "A whale shark—the largest fish in the ocean. They're very rare. You could spend your lifetime out here and never see one. Some people consider them bad luck."

"You scared me to death!"

"They're perfectly harmless. Come swim with me. It will strengthen your leg."

"Won't the shark come back?"

"If it does, we'll both take a ride."

But she could see he was teasing. The whale shark was by now far out to sea.

She left the boulder and crossed the barrier of the reef with care, holding her arms out at her sides to keep her balance. The coral was sharp and cutting on her tender feet. The water was so clear, she had no trouble seeing the millions of shells and bits of oddly shaped coral covering the reef. She bent to scoop up a handful and came out of the water with some of the most beautiful shells she'd ever seen. Every one was exquisite and delicately formed. Some were white, some brown, some a deep cobalt blue, the color of her eyes. The coral in turn was white and smooth, or bright red and jagged. She held a small shell to her ear and heard the roar of the ocean from within.

Rodrigo swam to meet her when she reached the sand beyond the reef. There, the water deepened sharply and it was possible to swim. The breakers carried her up and back with a lulling rhythm. She looked up at the sky and drifted on the swells. But she couldn't stop stealing glances at Rodrigo. Wet and gleaming golden in the sun, he was an enticing package of hard-coiled muscle and masculine grace. Feeling playful, she swam to him and put her arms about his neck, wrapped her legs around his waist.

"I've got you now," she teased. "You can't get away from me this time."

Then she slid down the length of him, and as her face came in contact with the water, she added, "I've been wanting to do this all afternoon."

She dove beneath the surface. Holding on to his waist, she floated toward his erection, which was swaying with the rhythm of the water. She was buoyant in the water, coming close then drifting away. Finally, she succeeded in getting her mouth around him and a wave came crashing in and toppled him from beneath her. When she came up sputtering and laughing, he was lying on his back, exposed to the sun.

She tried again. Each time she thought she'd succeeded, the tide would foil her, carrying him away.

Soon, they were hysterical with laughter, Gabrielle determined to achieve her goal, Rodrigo happy to let her try.

"What does a woman have to do to get her mouth around you?" she grinned.

Finally she gave up. She wrapped her legs around him again and held his shoulders to keep from floating away. "You'll just have to put it somewhere else," she vowed. And moved her hand beneath the water to guide him in.

Suddenly, she felt his change of mood. His shoulders stiffened, and his hand grabbed her wrist and pushed her away. Glancing up at him, her laughter frozen on her face, she saw that his alarmed eyes were fixed on a point in the distance. She turned to look. Her gaze began at the base of the hill and traveled upward, scanning the horizon. She, too, stilled inside as she spotted the intruders high on the hill.

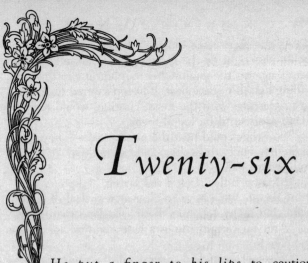

# Twenty-six

*He put a finger to his lips* to caution silence, and stared hard at the two men who stood at the top of the hill, looking out over the horizon beneath hands that shaded their eyes. From his stern glare, it seemed Rodrigo recognized them.

The men started their gradual descent down the hill toward the beach. As the interlopers turned to feel their way down a particularly steep granite slide, Rodrigo took her hand and pulled her along behind him. The coral cut her feet as they ran through the water. She had to bite her lip to keep from crying out. In a quick dash, Rodrigo scooped up their clothes, then raced with her for a nearby granite boulder.

From there, they could track the progress of the two men. They came relentlessly, pausing now and again to survey their surroundings as one pointed and the other listened with apt attention. Gabrielle now recognized one of them as Delon, the man to whose plantation she'd followed Hastings the night she'd left Mahé. Seeing him brought the memories back as freshly as if they'd just occurred. It brought with it a renewed hatred for her half brother, and a wave of grief for Cullen. All the things she'd managed so successfully to suppress.

As the men came closer, it became apparent they would pass right by the hiding place. Gabrielle pressed herself against the granite, her toes burning in the sand, willing herself to disappear. If Delon spotted them, he'd go to Hastings with the news. Hastings would tear the island apart until he found them.

Soon they could hear the men's voices. They spoke in French, but both Rodrigo and Gabrielle spoke French and understood.

"It's a bit hilly," Delon was saying. "I'd prefer something flatter. We'll have to clear a great deal of land to plant that many coconuts. Better flat land than hilly."

"Are you certain this is a wise venture?" asked his companion.

"We feel confident copra will become the new money crop. Wait and see, my friend. Soon there will be copra plantations on all these islands. We'll simply be the first."

"But where will we get the money—not to mention the slaves—for such a venture? If I understand your plans, this will be one of the biggest plantations these islands have ever seen."

"Don't worry about that, my friend. The governor has guaranteed it. There will be no end to the money or the slaves."

"Speaking of Cross, where is he? I haven't seen him for weeks."

"He's taken over the old Soro place on Fregate."

"Fregate? Why there? It's so inaccessible."

"He likes that about it. Besides, how could he resist occupying the throne of his old enemy?"

Delon's companion laughed at the image, but soon again frowned at the terrain they were surveying.

"Perhaps farther along, we'll find land more hospitable. I must be honest and say I don't take a liking to these hills."

They moved along. Gabrielle slumped in relief, sitting with her back against the boulder, staring out at the

sea. She didn't have to look at him to feel Rodrigo's
tension. Where he'd been relaxed and indolent earlier,
he was now as taut as a rope stretched to its breaking
point.

She didn't want to speak. But someone had to say
what they both knew was on his mind.

"Please tell me you're not going to Fregate."

He was silent.

"I don't want to leave our valley," she said.

"We can't stay there forever."

"Why not? What else is there out there for us? Cullen is dead. You've taken away Beau Vallon. And you
admit that you're fighting a hopeless cause! I've been
happy here for the first time in my life. *The first time
. . . happy!* I never even knew what the word meant!"

When he spoke, his voice was gentle, but resolved.
"Gabé, we can't just crawl into a hole and hide while
evil takes over the world."

She saw it was useless to argue. "Very well. But don't
underestimate him again. He's sure to have guards everywhere."

"True. But his defenses will be down. He thinks me
dead. Besides, I know every inch of that island. Don't
forget. It's my home."

The way he said the word *home* made her heart con-
strict in pain. She looked at him then and saw the anger
in his eyes.

"I have to know what he's doing there," he said.
"You can stay here."

Sensing his determination, she stood and began to
pull on her clothes. "No. If you go, I go with you."

# Twenty-seven

They landed their makeshift raft at a beach Rodrigo identified as Anse Parc. Even from the water, Gabrielle could see the old pirate walls, now badly deteriorated from the elements.

On the day-long voyage to Fregate, Gabrielle had experienced an acute anxiety. A sense of impending doom that overcame her the moment they left their magical valley. But she brightened somewhat as she felt Rodrigo's excitement—his sheer joy at the sight of this island.

"My great-grandfather built those walls," he said.

It took some doing to float in over the coral reef. The tide was choppy, making it perilous. Gabrielle clung to the rope that held the sail he'd fashioned from dried palms.

"You can see why he chose the island," Rodrigo called to her. "It's the most isolated of the granite islands. Also virtually impregnable. There's no way to get on the island during the southwesterly monsoons because of the tides. He could hide out here and no one could follow. But at times like these, during the northeasterly monsoons, the island is open to assault from this direction. That's why he built the walls. To keep those brave enough to navigate the reefs out of his fortress. They're still fortified with old cannons. There, see?"

Taking her hand, he helped her from the raft.

"Where did you live?"

"The house is on the other side of that peninsula." He pointed to a hill above the beach.

They climbed the hill. By now, Gabrielle was acclimated to the heat. She made the trudge without much more than a heaving breath. At the top, she gasped. There before her on one side was a valley spreading out from the hill, covered with giant trees—bwa-d-fer and gayak mostly—mixed with palms and wild native grasses. The palms rustled in the sultry breeze, glistening in the sun. On the other side, they looked down at the beach from which they'd just come, an idyllic white-sand cove surrounded by distended rocks and the old pirate walls.

"I've never seen anything more lovely," she told him sincerely.

He nodded, looking out over the unusual, startling green of the ocean with serene eyes. "I used to love this spot as a boy. I would sit here and look out at the sea, and relive my grandfather's stories of the family adventures."

"That would be your grandfather Dario?"

"No, Dario was my great-grandfather, the first pirate Soro. He was a real pirate. Ruthless as sin. Stole everything he ever had. My great-grandmother included."

"Stole her?"

"Kidnapped, more precisely. She was Danish. Golden-haired, like me. He saw her one day in Capetown, took a shine to her, waited for dark, then threw her over his shoulder and sailed off with her."

"And she stayed?"

He smiled. "Turned out she was a bit of an outlaw herself. She liked being the kidnapped wife of the most notorious pirate in this part of the world."

Gabrielle laughed. "I think I'd have liked your great-grandmother."

"I think I would, too."

"And your grandfather, the second pirate Soro?"

"*Meú avô*—raised me after my mother died when I was a baby. He was long retired by then, of course. Reis had also been a pirate, but he was more of an idealist than his blood-and-thunder father, Dario. By the time Reis grew to adulthood, the French—your mother's people—were drifting in. With their cotton plantations and slaves. Reis hated them. And always seemed more interested in destroying their slave ships than in amassing booty. They attacked this island a half-dozen times over the years, but never could roust him from it. God, I loved that old man!"

"And your father? The third pirate Soro?"

"Silvera Soro. Yes, he was a pirate, too—of sorts. He inherited a lot of Reis's idealism and love for these islands. Even more than his father, he felt they had to be protected from the outsiders who would spoil them. By his time, the British were taking over the islands. He attacked slavers and occasionally British shipping and John Company outposts. But his operations were mainly out of the Amirantes—D'Arros, in fact. I rarely saw him. The British watched this island carefully. After *meú avô* died, he'd come back to see me at least once or twice a year. They finally caught him on one of those visits, in fact, and hanged him without a trial."

She looked at him and felt a swelling of love in her heart. For the first time, she felt she understood him. That she'd glimpsed who he was and what he loved. She could feel it reverberating through her own soul. She went into his arms and held him close, realizing that, come what may, they'd made the right decision in re-

turning to his home. Perhaps it would strengthen him
for the fight to come—strength he would need.

His arms tightened about her and he held her for a
long time, saying nothing.

"Be still," he whispered momentarily. Expecting
danger, she stiffened in his arms. "Stay quiet and look
behind you."

She did. Instead of the threat she'd been expecting,
there was a small bird resembling a pigeon but with the
tiniest wings she'd ever seen.

"It's a white-throated rail. The last flightless bird in
the Indian Ocean. Kin to the dodo. You've heard of
them, haven't you? My grandfather remembered seeing
dodoes on Mauritius in his youth. Now, of course,
they're extinct. Killed off by cats and dogs because they
couldn't fly. You're looking at the last of these kinds of
birds left in the world. Only a handful remain in a few
havens on the islands."

The sight of the bird gave her a renewed surge of
anxiety. The truth was, she felt her lover every bit as
endangered as this bird. Once again, she wanted to rush
back to *their* safe haven in the Vallée de Mai.

"Come," he said, moving away but holding out his
hand. "I'll show you my home."

They walked for quite some time, down the meadow
and up another hill, through dense foliage and partially
cleared fields. Rodrigo explained that much of the old
brush had been burned off to plant the coconuts, bread-
fruits, takamakas, casuarinas, and banyans that were all
around them. As they neared the house, they passed
through fields of sugarcane, vanilla, tobacco, sweet pota-
toes, maize, coffee, cinnamon, papaya, bananas, and
vegetables, all gleaming in tropical splendor.

"There are your gardenias," he said.

She looked to where he was pointing. A luxuriant
bush some thirteen feet high was ablaze with small
white flowers with purple spots. "The *bois citron?*" she
asked in a breathy voice. When he nodded, she walked

to the massive shrub in a trance. These flowers had
come to symbolize her longing for this Seychelle paradise. The blossoms were small and delicately feminine,
with a sweet, lemony scent. Lovely and fragile, much
like her mother, who'd loved them so.

She had tears in her eyes as she buried her nose in
them, drinking in their scent. She hadn't found them as
she'd expected at Beau Vallon. Instead she'd found them
here—at Rodrigo's stolen home.

"We must go," he reminded her gently.

Reluctantly, she followed him. But not before she'd
picked a tiny blossom to smell along the way.

They had to be careful. Occasionally they heard a
sound and were forced to hide in the nearby brush. By
the time they drew up on another hill, it was growing
late. Soon the sun would slip down over the horizon,
leaving behind a brief orange glow. But it was still hot.
Gabrielle was damp and her tongue felt swollen from
thirst.

"There," he said simply, pointing down the hill.

She followed his gaze to a lovely but simple two-
story wooden plantation house. It had an open, covered
porch curling around the perimeter so the inhabitants
could sit out in the shade at any time of day. From
where they stood, they were afforded a side view, so she
could see the huge banyan tree out front, with its aerial
roots forming an archway that led to the front door. It
seemed a gracious, comfortable home overlooking the
most beautiful ocean in the world, just strolling distance
from the most extraordinary palm-lined beach.

But the sight was marred by the appearance of a
number of half-clothed African slaves. One was a
woman whose child—a young boy of no more than four
—clung to her legs, his cries piercing the aura of serenity and calm. A white foreman strode forth to see what
was happening, striking out with his riding crop as one
of the male slaves stepped forth to offer assistance. The
whip lashed the would-be samaritan's face, and he fell

back, groaning in pain. As the child increased his screams, the foreman made a gesture of contempt and arrogantly strutted up the stairs and inside Rodrigo's house.

When Gabrielle glanced at Rodrigo, he was livid, clenching his fists in balls of rage.

He swore viciously in his own tongue, turning away from the sight. "*Bastardia!* They kidnapped me from my homeland. Forced on me their language, their customs, their narrow sense of justice. Stole my name, my home. The God-given right to freedom. They enslaved me as surely as—" He turned tortured eyes on her, reminding her of a wounded beast who, in his pain, readies for attack. "You wish to know what it is to be in chains? *This.* Being forced to watch as they destroy your hopes and dreams and the very soul of your land—and being powerless to stop them."

Her heart ached to see his pain, that pain that he'd revealed to no one during his long confinement in England—not even her. Reaching out, she put a gentle hand on his arm, felt it bunch and tighten beneath her touch. "Then we're both in chains." He looked at her, accusingly suspicious of her words. "For I'm bound by my love for you."

It was a moment before the words penetrated the furies of his mind. When they did, he dropped rigid shoulders and pulled her into his arms. "I want my home, Gabé," he groaned into her hair. "More than anything, I want to walk through that front door with you at my side."

She moved back and sought his eyes. "As what?" she breathed, afraid for him to voice the words.

"*Cómo mi espôsa,*" he said. "As my wife."

A thrill rushed through her. *Wife.* It had always seemed a detestable word. As if the person saying it really meant *appendage.* Suddenly, it seemed the most beautiful word in the English language.

She looked down on the lovely house that had once

been his home. Tried to imagine strolling through the majestic roots of the banyan tree, looking up in awe as she passed beneath. Tried to envision herself mistress of such a home. Saw him come up the walk, full of salt and sand. Saw her throw herself into his arms and kiss him in joyous welcome. Saw golden-haired children gathering cheerfully at their feet.

Children who didn't have to worry about their pirate father being hanged.

"How do you say 'home' in Portuguese?"

His mouth formed the words. "Like Spanish. *Casa.*"

She tried it tentatively. *"Meú casa."*

Briefly, he smiled. But it was a sad smile, and his mournful lion's eyes drifted once again back to the sight below. *"Sem lar,"* he said softly, more to himself than her.

"What does that mean?"

"Homeless."

An abrupt ache in her heart burst her happy picture of home. "Rodrigo, let's go back. Let's go back to our valley, before it's too late."

Before he could answer, there was a noise behind them. They whirled to the sight of four men leveling pointed guns.

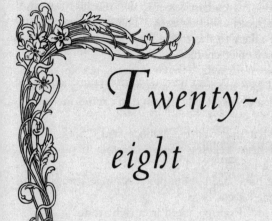

# Twenty-eight

*There was a joyous cry* and the men lowered their weapons and stepped forward. Gabrielle stared dumbly, trying to adjust as her heart slowed and she realized the intruders were members of Rodrigo's old crew. There was Higgins, the fugitive from New South Wales so reluctant to be tattooed, and her old friend Jonah Fitch among them.

Then there was a rustle in the bushes and a tall man with wild red hair and a thick beard stepped out. It was like looking at a ghost as she recognized Wallace, who she thought had been blown to death in the explosion.

"We're the sole survivors of the attack," Wallace explained. "We knew if you made it out alive, you'd come here eventually." He turned to Gabrielle and added, "Glad to see you made it too, lass."

Jonah Fitch stepped forward with a grin. "I second that, ma'am."

"And Cullen?" she asked hopefully.

They shook their heads. "I'm sorry, ma'am," said Jonah in a sorrowful tone. "We looked and looked, and never found him."

To cover his embarrassment, she reached out and pressed his hand affectionately. "Thank you for that. I see you've taken to the pirate life," she said lightly regarding his former charade.

His grin returned. "I have, indeed, ma'am. And I must say, I like you more as a woman." His eyes flicked to Rodrigo and he added, "If you don't mind me saying so, sir."

Somewhat impatiently, Wallace said, "Suffice it to say, we've been keeping an eye on your house. Cross moved in a month ago. I don't mind telling you, Rodrigo, there have been some pretty strange things transpiring since he got here."

"Such as?" Rodrigo asked in a tight tone.

"There's slaves coming and going in ungodly numbers. And them Frenchmen come and stay a day or two, then leave and others replace them."

Rodrigo turned back to the house he'd grown up in. "For once, I'm grateful to be the last of my line," he said bitterly. "I'd hate for the other Soros to see what's transpiring in their own home."

As they watched, Hastings came out of the house to see what the commotion was about. The boy was still screaming, turning his face upward as tears streamed down it, while his mother tried desperately to hush him. Even from where she stood, Gabrielle could see the woman's fear. She would be beaten if her son didn't stop crying, and the look on her face said she knew it.

They were too far away to hear anything but the boy's shrieks. But the stubborn set of Hastings's shoulders spoke volumes. Gesturing toward the boy, he watched as his foreman wrestled the child forcibly from his mother's arms. As the boy screamed louder still, the foreman tossed him to another slave, who carried him off. His cries drifted away, and soon all was silent. So silent, there was a ghostly still of terror in the air.

Slowly, Hastings walked around the African woman whose son had just been wrenched from her. He looked her up and down in a leisurely fashion, as he might a horse he was thinking of buying. He fingered her hair, making the woman start. He came before her and pried open her mouth so he could see her teeth. Then he stroked her face tenderly in a gesture that froze Gabrielle's blood. He said something and jerked his head toward a room upstairs. Cringing, the slave looked up at the window he'd indicated and shook her head, as if pleading not to be taken. Hastings didn't even bother to punish her. He just nodded to his foreman, who grabbed the woman and hauled her through the banyan tree and up the porch stairs.

Wallace had moved to his captain's side so he could speak softly in his ear. "The oddest thing, *Capitão*. He takes these women and rogers them. Sometimes two or three a day. One of the boys sneaked up and peeked in the window to make sure. Makes them do all manner of unspeakable things. Things I wouldn't mention in front of a lady. We hear them screaming sometimes."

By now Rodrigo was seething, pacing like a caged lion, his fists clenched in rage at his sides. "They defile my house in this manner, doing their dirty work in my mother's bedroom." He was so incensed, he began to rant in Portuguese.

"Well, it's breaking our hearts, *Capitão*, I can tell you that. The things we've seen . . ."

"We'll wait until dark," Rodrigo interrupted crisply, very much the pirate captain now, very much in command. "Then we'll go in. The two of us, Wallace."

"Where to, *Capitão*?"

"To cut the heart out of a vulture."

"I'm going too," Gabrielle said to him.

He gave her the dismissive glance of a leader with

more pressing things on his mind. "Not this time," he said.

Her chin firmly set, she asserted, "I can't just crawl into a hole and hide while evil takes over the world."

Stiffly, he said, "Very well."

# Twenty-nine

*Gabrielle followed* as Rodrigo and Wallace noiselessly climbed the rail of the porch and swung themselves up onto the sloping roof that led to the bedroom windows upstairs. She had little trouble pulling herself onto the roof. Her years of fencing had made her agile, and her legs strong.

It was a hot night, as usual, and the windows were open. Earlier they'd heard grunts and screams coming from the room. Now all was quiet except for the gentle rhythm of a man's snores.

Moving stealthily to the window, they peered inside. It was a spacious, airy room with high ceilings, cool and inviting. A large four-poster bed with Hastings sleeping in it dominated one wall, conspicuous for its absence of mosquito netting. Above it was a collection of ancient swords much as Rodrigo had displayed on his ship.

The furnishings were fashioned from light bamboo. A small gecko slept undisturbed on the wall above Hastings's head. In the corner was a lovely tropic bird in a golden cage, its long white tail sticking out of the bars.

But her impressions were fleeting as Hastings began to stir. Rodrigo, on his way to rouse him, stopped suddenly and stared at something at his feet. Following his gaze, Gabrielle gasped softly. The slave woman was lying on the floor, tied by a rope to the bed. She was awake, but she didn't lift her head from the floor. She merely lay as she was, staring up at the intruders with eyes that were wide with terror.

Rodrigo leaped to the wall where the swords were kept with the unseeing instinct of one who knows their positions well. His hand came to rest on a gold-encrusted saber. Seizing it from the wall, he slashed the ropes from the frightened girl with a heave that sent Hastings bolting upright in his bed. Ignoring him, Rodrigo took the girl's arm gently and lifted her to her feet.

"Go to your son," he told her. When she didn't seem to understand, he repeated the command in Swahili. She stared at him to make sure she understood.

Wallace, on his way to the bed where Hastings was demanding to know what was going on, paused and gave the girl a meaningful glare. "*Mkombozi*," he said, jerking his head toward Rodrigo in introduction. It was what the freed slaves called him, Swahili for "the Liberator."

"*Mkombozi!*" The woman's mouth formed the word as if it were a prayer. Then she quickly ran from the room.

Even as she did, Wallace's fist was grabbing hold of Hastings's nightshirt. Rodrigo joined him and together they hauled their prey from his bed onto the floor with a heavy crash, where he lay sputtering indignantly, sprawled with his nightshirt up about his legs. With one quick motion, Rodrigo's knees straddled him, one pinning each of his shoulders to the floor as he held the blade of the sword to his throat.

Wallace was hovering over them, his hands flexing convulsively. "Let me kill him, *Capitão*. Let me do it slowly, with great pain. 'Tis only rightful justice for all the men he slaughtered."

"No," said Rodrigo, in a feral voice Gabrielle barely recognized as his. "He must be killed, but we'll have no fun with it. And I must do it myself."

Gabrielle felt a wave of satisfaction sweep over her. She realized she felt no remorse for what was about to happen—just a sense of justice being dispensed. But as Rodrigo put the sword to his throat, Hastings cried, "Wait, Roderick!" It was the squeal of a man who knew he was about to die. *"Rodrigo,"* he corrected belatedly, through clenched teeth.

"Think fast, old friend," Rodrigo taunted. "Your time is running out."

Wallace took Gabrielle by the arm and began to pull her away. She fought him off.

"I have something to trade for my life," Hastings rasped.

Gabrielle stopped cold. She was suddenly terrified of what might leap from his infinite resources of treachery.

Rodrigo gave a caustic chuckle. "What could you possibly have that would be of more interest to me than your life?"

"If you deem it worthy, make me a promise you'll spare me."

"Why should I promise you anything? Now that I know you have something to offer, why shouldn't I just torture it out of you?"

"Because I'm strong. You know that. It would take you days to break me. I may even last a week. By then, it may just be too late for the information to be of any use to you."

Rodrigo glanced at the others, then back to Hastings. "All right, then, if I deem it worthy, you have my word."

Hastings said one word so it rang out in the room. "Cullen!"

At the name, Gabrielle came back to life. When

Wallace reached for her again, she shoved him back and stepped to Rodrigo's side.

"What about Cullen?" she demanded.

Hastings's eyes darted to her and she saw his surprise to see her—surprise which, with effort, turned into a characteristic smirk, even with a blade to his throat. "So you've joined your dear lover at last, Gabby."

She kicked his shoulder, causing the sword to slip and cut him, dripping blood to the floor. "Hastings, you serpent, tell me what you know about Cullen, or so help me I'll give Rodrigo leave to slit your sorry throat."

With an evil glint, he spoke the words slowly and deliberately, enjoying every one. "Cullen's alive. I gave him to the sultan of Zanzibar."

Cullen was alive!

In a fury, Rodrigo grabbed Hastings's hair in his fist, drew back his head, and made ready to slice his throat. Wallace stayed his arm. "Wait. What if he's telling the truth?"

"I know he's telling the truth," Rodrigo ground out tonelessly. "Giving the boy to the sultan of Zanzibar is exactly what he'd do."

"Then the information *was* worthy," Wallace pointed out.

"Yes. But I think we should kill him anyway."

"But *Capitão*, your word!"

The shock in his quartermaster's voice penetrated the hunger for revenge. Not moving his eyes from Hastings, Rodrigo said, as if it pained him, "Very well. I suppose this will have to wait for another time."

Gabrielle watched the scene, but none of it registered in her mind. The only thing she could think of was that Cullen was alive.

*Cullen was alive!*

# Thirty

*The supply schooner* was anchored off the island, about five hundred meters out to sea. From the brush that lined the clean white beach, Rodrigo, Gabrielle, Wallace, and the others lay in wait, watching the small dhow ride the waves, attempting to circumvent the coral reef. The tide was unpredictably choppy today. Three times they'd tried to land, and three times had been forced to choose another spot. The day before they hadn't been able to land at all, but had returned unsuccessful to the schooner to await the morning tide. If they weren't able to land this time, they'd give up and go around to the other side of the island, hoping for better luck. It was just the sort of inaccessibility for which Dario Soro had chosen the island a hundred years ago.

Finally, the dhow caught a wave and sailed onto the reef. Its crew jumped out, stepping lively on the biting coral, and grabbed the small boat, guiding it to shore. Once anchored on the beach, they began to unload their supplies, eager to be off while there was still a friendly tide.

Soundlessly, as prearranged, Rodrigo and his men stalked the beach and sneaked up from behind. Jumping the crewmen, they took vines they'd gathered earlier and swiftly secured their hands and feet. Then Rodrigo waved Gabrielle from the brush and helped her into the dhow as the others guided it back into the sea.

"Should we leave them in the sun?" Wallace asked, looking back at the struggling crewmen lying like frying bacon on the sand. They'd burn beyond repair in a matter of hours.

"Their compatriots will join them shortly," Rodrigo assured him. "They'll set them free."

As a supply ship that ferried from one island to the other, the schooner was unarmed. Rodrigo's men found little resistance as they scaled the sides and overpowered the crew. There was a brief skirmish when the crewmen realized what had happened, but the intruders had both surprise and expertise as allies. Within minutes, they tossed the crew overboard to swim for shore.

"Won't this ship be missed?" Higgins asked as Rodrigo gave orders to man the sails.

"There won't be a ship out here for weeks," Jonah Fitch answered for him. "This is the end of the line for this schooner. No one will miss her for a month. By then we'll be in Zanzibar."

"And we'll have Cullen back," Gabrielle said.

Placing his hands on the helm, Rodrigo muttered, "God willing."

She didn't like the way he said that. He was worried. What did he know that he wasn't sharing? "Rodrigo—"

She was interrupted by one of his men, an African who pointed to the sea, gesturing emphatically to make a point. Gabrielle thought she recognized a word of Portuguese now and then, but it didn't sound like any Portuguese she'd ever heard. The only word she remembered hearing before was *mkombozi*. The same word Wallace had used to the slave in Hastings's bedroom.

She went to Wallace, who was listening closely with

a frown puckering his red face. "What language is that?" she asked.

"Swahili."

"I thought I recognized some Portuguese."

"Swahili is a mixture of Arabic, Portuguese, and some African tribal languages," he explained. "A kind of trader's tongue." But he said it distractedly as he glanced out at the sea in the direction in which the man was pointing.

She moved to Rodrigo's side. "What was he saying?"

"He says this is not a good time to embark on such a journey. This is cyclone season off the coast of Africa. The winds make it treacherous to sail there this time of year."

Jonah Fitch came rushing across the deck. "There's no cows."

"Cows?" Gabrielle asked, confused.

"Sea cows, ma'am. They're normally all over the rocks in this part of Seychelles. Seafarers in these waters consider the dugongs good luck. Their absence is a bad omen, ma'am. Maybe we should wait, sir."

"We can't wait!" Gabrielle cried. "Who knows how they're treating him? You, yourself, have said the sultan is a monster."

"The sultan," spat Wallace, "is a monster of . . . inconceivable proportions."

She felt dangerously close to hysteria. Seeing this, Rodrigo took her hands in his and made her face him, willing her through his determined presence to focus on what he said.

"I know you want to rescue him, and I want to help you. But we can't do anything foolish. Zanzibar is a fortress. The sultan is protected by his own personal army of guards and a fleet that's only gone for a few days out of the month to patrol his holdings on the African coast. When the fleet's gone, the palace guard is diluted to watch over the docks. That would be our only chance. If the fleet's in, there's nothing we can do but wait for it to leave. We'll need some luck."

Her eyes were blind with tears. "He needs us, Rodrigo. We've got to get him out of there. I can't make the same mistake again. I can't lose him one more time. Don't you understand? No matter what it takes, we *must* get him out."

# Thirty-one

Zanzibar. As a child, the very name had conjured for Gabrielle images of romance and exotic adventure. Every English youngster had heard tales of the mysterious island off the coast of eastern Africa, where the mighty Arab sultan reigned supreme. She'd often formed the word on her tongue, savoring the magical texture of it. Zanzibar.

But when she arrived there, it was for her not a vision of extravagant fancy. The sultan was no longer the stuff of legends, but a chimera of unimaginable proportions, who clutched the tender soul of her baby brother in his cruel fist. A fiend whose obsessions were so unspeakable that no amount of pleading would loose the stories from Rodrigo's tongue.

Dressed as Arabs in flowing white robes, and headdresses that covered their hair, Rodrigo and Gabrielle traversed the main district of narrow alleyways and rough stone squares where Arabs and Indians loudly peddled their wares. All around them the sweet smell of cloves drifted in on the hot breezes. The sultan was planting cloves over most of the island and exporting them to a spice-hungry world. It was proving to be a surprisingly lucrative venture, giving him a great deal of credibility in the European money markets. He'd reaped almost as many profits from his first shipments of cloves as he'd made in the same period trading slaves.

The heat was oppressive. Even Rodrigo's clothing clung to his skin. Dust and squalor were everywhere, kicked up by sandals, circling in the breeze. The smells of exotic spices singed the air. They passed warrens of buildings with tall, heavy, intricately carved doors. Some of the most beautiful doors in the world, lavishly fashioned from Burmese or Indian teak or jackfruit wood with fish, lions, peacocks, flowers, spices, and fruits. Some had heavy metal spikes jutting out like the gangplank of a keep. Each door was symbolic of the householder's interests. Rectangular doors were Arabic; those with round or gothic arches signified Indian possession. No two were alike.

The slave market chilled Gabrielle. An open square facing the beckoning blue of the ocean, it contained a long stone slab for the exhibition of slaves, and a number of crude granite posts fastened with rings where the human merchandise could be chained. A small crowd was gathered as they passed—little more than a handful of people. Gabrielle didn't know if it was a slow day, or if they'd arrived so late in the proceedings that most of the customers had already gone home. A single slave was being auctioned, an African woman of indeterminate age, with eyes sunken in her face. The auctioneer yanked the robe from her to reveal her body to the gaping assemblage. Her breasts were huge and hung heavily, swaying as the auctioneer took her shoulders from behind and shook her to better display his goods. Her hips were full and ripe. He pointed, obviously expounding on what everyone could see—this was a woman with limitless sexual potential. The bidding started—in Arabic, Gabrielle thought, although she couldn't be sure—and soon the woman was bundled up in her robes again while her new owner paid the coin.

He then put a chain about her neck and hauled her away.

They spent the afternoon watching the sultan's palace. All around it were guards armed with wicked scimitars at the sashes of their robes. The men were huge and threatening, obviously chosen for their ability to infuse fear in the hearts of the sultan's subjects. There was no end to them. Each story of the building was safeguarded. Every door was barred by at least two burly men. No one entered or exited the building without first being questioned by the sentries. Gabrielle couldn't understand what they said, but their voices alone were enough to impose the fear of Allah in a less-hearty soul.

"There's a fair-skinned boy being kept in the sultan's chambers," Rodrigo said. "That must be Cullen. And of course, that would be on the top floor, where it's hardest to penetrate."

"What's your plan?" she whispered as they watched one man being thrust up against the wall and searched, then hauled off by a bulwark of a sentinel.

Rodrigo gripped her arm and pulled her away from the scene. She resisted, dragging her heels in the dust.

"I have no plan," he ground out between his teeth. "We can't get in."

"What do you mean, can't get in?"

"You can see for yourself. His fleet is in. His personal guard is very much in presence here. We didn't get the lucky break I wanted."

"Then we'll wait till the fleet leaves."

"I'm afraid not. As soon as the warning comes from Hastings, it won't leave. It will never leave again while we're still alive."

Her heart sunk. But something caught her attention. A couple of decrepit old men in rags were pleading with the guards. In their hands they held out crude wooden bowls. With a cursory nod, the doors were opened and they were ushered inside.

"Those men got in," she pointed out.

"They're beggars. It's against the sultan's religion to turn away the poor. He houses them for the night and gives them food. But they're kept in the basement, away from the rest of the house. There's no way we could get by the guards once we were in."

He began to walk through the narrow, crowded streets.

"Then what are we going to do?" she asked.

Turning, he motioned her to silence. "Don't let them hear your voice," he growled. "Do you have any concept of what they'd do to you if they knew who you were? A beautiful white woman? They'd get a fortune for you on the block."

She lowered her voice. "Very well, I'll be quiet. But what are we going to do?"

"Nothing. We need time."

He began to walk off again.

"Time?" She rushed behind him, struggling to keep up with his hectic pace. "Time for what?"

"To gather men. And ships. We need to build a navy to destroy the fleet, attack the palace, and get Cullen out."

"That will take too long. He could be dead in the time it would take us to—"

"To do anything else would be suicide."

They argued all afternoon. All through the time they were seeking shelter at an inn. All through their meal of spiced meat and turmeric rice. Gabrielle simply refused to accept any postponing of her brother's rescue. But nothing she said would persuade Rodrigo to act.

Frustrated and angry, she took the bottle of wine he'd provided, sloshed it into her goblet, and drank it down. With the cup half empty, she was struck by an idea. She removed the goblet, wiped the wine from her lips, and set it down.

"Let's not argue any more," she said. "Here." She filled his glass and passed it to him. "Let's forget it for tonight. There's nothing we can do now. Maybe you won't be so stubborn in the morning."

When he glared at her, she smiled as if she'd been teasing him. He softened a little and drank the wine.

"It's not that I don't want to get him out," he explained, more reasonably. "It's just that we must do so with caution."

"With caution," she repeated. *When her brother's life was at stake? Over her dead body!*

She mustn't capitulate too easily, or he'd suspect her motives. To throw him off guard she said, "Perhaps you're right, after all. I'm not making any *promises*, mind, but I shall consider the possibility. I was in a play once. *A Lady's Lesson.* Dreadful rubbish, before I was being considered for decent parts. The heroine defied her husband and caused a great deal of trouble for herself. You may well guess that a *man* wrote the play. At the end she offered a rather pithy apology for her stupidity in disobeying him. All about having learned her lesson—hence the title of the play. Rather a lot of rot, really, but if it will make you feel better, I'll offer up a private performance."

By the time she'd stopped speaking, he was smiling. She poured him another glass of wine. He came to take her in his arms. She put a hand to his chest to halt him.

"Drink your wine," she said. Then she took a sip from her goblet, put her lips to his, and passed the wine into his mouth.

Later that night, when Rodrigo was sleeping off the three bottles of wine she'd managed to get into him, she rose from their bed and silently took her Arab robes outside. Moving out of hearing distance, she held the garment to the light of the moon in calculation, then carefully ripped the robe in several places. She had to make certain none of her womanly curves would show, while at the same time making a convincing show of wear. As Arab women were allowed no freedom of movement, she could only succeed by convincing them she was a man.

With that accomplished, she tossed the fabric to the ground and stomped on it, grinding it into the dust. She retrieved it, shook out the excess, then looked it over with a critical eye. Retrieving one of the torn strips, she bound her breasts flat against her and slipped the robe over her petticoat. She tied her hair back in a makeshift turban, placed the headdress on her head, and wrapped the remaining cloth around her hands to hide their delicate lines. Then she took a small club and hid it in the waistband of her tight petticoat, under the flowing robes.

Without a backward glance, she stole through the bright moonlight, creeping down narrow alleys, trying to recall the way. Twice she took a wrong turn and felt hopelessly lost before she found a familiar landmark. Eventually, she came to the sea. She stood for a moment, looking out over the deserted slave market, feeling a chill that had nothing to do with the cooling breezes off the water. Palm trees rustled in the wind. Her robes brushed softly against her legs. The silence hung like fog over the night.

She took a moment to collect her nerve. For an instant, she feared she couldn't go through with it. It was too daring. Suicide, Rodrigo had called it—he who was the most daring of men. But he'd also said she possessed the courage of champions. She couldn't stand around while her brother was imprisoned by a monster. The urgency to free him ate at her soul.

*I'm just playing a part*, she told herself. *I'm standing in the wings, awaiting my cue. It's always the same. Stage fright so bad, I feel I can't go on. And then, as if by magic, I hear my cue, and see my key light, and suddenly I become the character, and I know I can do no wrong. I'm a beggar asking humbly for alms. Deaf and mute, so they won't hear me speak. They can't turn me away. I know I'll get inside. What I do after that is up to me. . . .*

She bent over and ran her bandaged hands in the dust. This she coated on her face. A fountain provided sprinkles of water to turn the dust to mud. The better to disguise her features. She wedged dirt under her fingernails with shaking hands. *I'm a beggar*, she repeated. *They can't turn me away*.

With a drumming heart, she walked toward the sultan's barricade and extended open palms to the guards.

# Thirty-two

*Gabrielle was in a dungeonlike basement* with several dozen beggars. The odor was stupefying—a mixture of unwashed bodies, illness, and decay. One old man, unused to eating, had vomited on the floor after devouring his rice. The guards had merely tossed him some hay and ordered him to camouflage the mess.

If the sultan welcomed the poor, he didn't treat them with any semblance of hospitality. They slept now on the cold floor, huddled in their rags against the chill of the stone dungeon. No attempt was made to clean them up or make them comfortable. The barest requirements were met, that the sultan might salve his conscience and placate his God.

By now it was two or three in the morning. The guards—two massive Arabs with the faces of devils—had fallen asleep over some Oriental board game, snoring contentedly in their chairs. Still, their scimitars gleamed at her from their belts, sinister reminders of the tenuousness of her position.

She removed the sandals Rodrigo had procured and stole across the room on bare feet. Club in hand, she crept up on the guard with his back to her and hit him hard on the head. He lurched, snorted fitfully, then slumped onto the table with a heavy thud.

The noise awoke the other sentinel. As he jerked awake, Gabrielle hid the club in one hand behind her back. He rose to his feet, towering above her, and spoke in angry words, pointing to the floor, where she'd apparently been ordered to sleep. In the midst of a sentence, though, his eyes drifted to his partner, who was silently sprawled across the table. His gaze lifted to her face in sharp suspicion.

Gabrielle didn't stop to think. With the instincts of an actress in the midst of a role, she worked extemporaneously with the tools she had. Her free hand opened the robe and let it fall to the ground, displaying the tight petticoat clinging to her womanly form underneath. One tug sent the binding around her breasts flying, allowing the pale globes to fall free.

She could see his lust at once. He seemed mesmerized by the gentle swaying of her breasts in their boundary of white lace. A thick tongue darted out in an attempt to moisten wind-blistered lips. When his gaze rose to her face, she gave him an enticing smile.

He was on her instantly, grabbing her to him and burying his mouth in her neck. He held her so tightly, it was difficult to maneuver. He seemed as massive as Gulliver as she struggled to circle his barrel of a chest with her arms. They barely spanned the breadth of him. She had to angle her elbow to bring the club in line. Even then, she knew she wasn't strong enough. From this position, she couldn't knock a fly from his head.

But she had to try. He was mauling her now, his sense overcome by the bulge of an erection beneath his robes, which he continually thrust into her hips. Instinct emphasized her danger. If driven too far, she could never stop him. He'd rape her here on the cold stone floor, then turn her over to the sultan. She had to make her move while he was still stunned by his good fortune —before his lust made him too strong.

Gritting her teeth, she willed all her concentration into her arm and flung it back to smash the club against his head. It hurt enough that he shoved her from him in surprise. She didn't pause. Taking the stick in both hands, she swung with all her might, cracking his temple. He reeled back. She followed and whacked him again, the sound of it sickening in the silent gloom. This time, he swayed and fell to the floor.

With great dispatch, she struggled to wrest the clothes from him, then slipped into his robes herself. They were far too large, so she had to improvise, tucking yards of material up into the sash at her waist, rolling up the sleeves. She fastened the headdress tightly about her head. The disguise would fool no one for long. She wasn't a small woman, but she was no match for the stature of the sentries. As she'd done when playing Rodrigo, she'd have to assume an attitude that would compensate for and distract from her size.

She took the key from the guard and turned it in the lock. The door creaked open. To her relief, no one stood watch outside. Fingering the scimitar at her sash, she crept along the passageway until she came across a flight of stone stairs.

Halfway up, she heard the flap of sandals. She raised her head and there before her was another imposing guard tromping down the stairs. He said something as they passed, which Gabrielle couldn't understand. She swept past him on bare feet. But two steps above him, she sensed the change. He stopped and was glaring at her by the time she turned around. An image of Cullen's peril flashed through her mind. Just as swiftly, she drew her sword and thrust it into the guard's gut. Surprised, he clutched the bloody mess and stumbled backward down the stairs to land in a blacked-out heap below. He wasn't dead—she could detect his rasping breath—but neither was he capable of calling out for help.

With distaste, she wiped the bloody blade on her black robes. As skilled as she was with a weapon, she'd never found it necessary to draw blood. To feel the ghastly slice of flesh beneath her blade. She had to fight the nausea with an iron will. Time was essential.

The building was quiet this time of night. She searched the long, wide hallways without knowing what it was she sought. Rodrigo had said the sultan would likely have her brother with him. She must find his rooms. Then she'd decide how to get inside.

On the third floor, she stopped as she was about to round the corner. A door had just opened. From it came a group of guards similarly attired in black. Speaking among themselves, they headed up the hall toward the grand marble staircase, which they mounted with grins of anticipation.

Cautiously, she followed the men up the staircase, waiting for them to round the corner before ascending to the top. There, she peered around the wall and saw, at the end of an extensive corridor, a pair of majestically carved white doors the size of a normal-sized wall. Before them, two guards stood erect, their arms crossed about their chests, scimitars within handy reach.

She could see at once that this was the sultan's inner chamber. She understood, too, what Rodrigo had meant. There was no way to pass those guards. Their orders were likely to keep out all threats on fear of their lives. Even if she spoke the language, no amount of rhetoric would convince them to let her pass.

As she watched, the sentries opened one of the colossal doors and the new guards went inside.

She waited for what seemed an eternity, wondering how to get past the guards. They stood rigidly erect, never moving, never speaking. She supposed she could just present herself, but if she spoke to them—

The slap of sandals sounded again on the tiles. Looking around the corner, she saw another small group of guards heading down the hall and recognized her chance. It was risky. So easy to be caught. But if she didn't grab the opportunity, who knew when another would come along?

She waited in a crouched position until they'd just passed her, then sprang forward and joined them at the back. It was quickly accomplished. She marched with them up the long hall to the gargantuan doors. There, she stopped short with the other guards, keeping her telltale blue eyes lowered to the floor.

Finally she felt a flutter of movement. She forced herself not to flinch, not to imagine them seizing her arms and hauling her up before the sultan's wrath.

Then the door opened wide. It didn't creak—it wouldn't dare—but she saw the opening on the floor where once the white door had been. As the guards began to move, she swallowed her nervousness and took a cautious step inside.

# Thirty-three

A *wide hallway continued on*, stretching toward closed doors at the back. At her side was a huge anteroom that seemed to lead to the sultan's quarters, elaborately furnished with silk tapestries and ornaments of brass and gold. She could see before her an intricately latticed screen with an ornate passageway leading to the main hall. As the guards continued on their way down the long hallway, she fell back behind the screen and waited as their sandals echoed out of sight.

Gabrielle slunk closer, pressing herself against the far end of the screen where she hoped she wouldn't be spotted. From there, she could see the anteroom. It was large and cool with bright silk pillows scattered about the gleaming tile floor. A Moorish window was open to the breeze. Beyond it she could see the glimmer of the moon on the sea.

The room seemed to be empty. It was so quiet, she could hear herself breathe. Then, just as she was wondering where to find Cullen, she heard a movement. Her eyes searched the hall and found a figure at last, looking small and inconspicuous as he lay on his side among a pile of pillows. He was robed in splendid silk, embroidered with gold threads. He seemed to be painting. It was the clink of his brush against a glass bowl that alerted her to his presence.

Her heart jolting with joy, she cautioned herself to look carefully for guards. He must be closely watched. How else to explain the open window, and his indolent lack of notice?

But as prudently as she searched, she could find no one else in the room. Puzzled, she stepped around the screen and said, "Cullen?"

He looked up in surprise. Then, happiness splashed across his face, as if he'd taken his paints and spattered color all over his skin. "Gabby! Oh, I'm so glad to see you! You have to help me. You must get me out of here."

She was so stunned, she could hardly move. It was a surprise to find him in such luxurious surroundings, seemingly pampered, and even more surprising that no one appeared to be guarding him. Casting a look about the room from this more advantageous vantage point, she could see there was, indeed, no one guarding her brother. "Quick, Cullen, we're both climbing out that window and—"

"Gabby, take care!"

She'd started toward him. But in midflight, she was caught from behind and lifted from the floor. A thick arm held her in place as she struggled to break free. She was hauled around to face two guards beside the one who held her pinned against his chest, her legs flailing maniacally above the ground.

As she struggled, she slipped, and his hamlike arm came in contact with her breasts. He froze, said something to his compatriots, and set her on her feet. As he held her fast, the others ripped the guard's robe from her shoulders and gaped at her.

She heard Cullen's whimper somewhere behind. "Gabby . . ."

"Go to the bazaar. Find Rodrigo," she snapped. "Now!"

The guards peered closely when they heard her speak. They began to whisper heatedly among themselves, casting glances back over their shoulders at the sultan's quarters beyond. One guard pinned her arms behind her as his fellow sentinels chattered and snickered softly as they pressed her swaying breasts with rough hands. As she struggled, they began to torment her, raising her robes to see her legs, and the soft, downy hair between her thighs. They ran dark hands along her golden skin, murmuring indecipherable words of appreciation.

"Gabby—"

She craned her neck and saw a guard taunting Cullen with the point of his scimitar.

It was more agony than she could bear. Not just their ravishing, but the anguish of having come so close to succeeding, only to be yanked away. The frustration, the bitterness of it choked her like acid in her throat. If only she could get loose. If only she'd moved one minute sooner. If only . . .

She was lost in this fight. She wasn't strong enough. All she could do was fight with aching limbs, and live with the knowledge that this had all been in vain.

Just then another guard entered and, catching sight of them, barked out an order. They dropped her to her feet instantly as the man—obviously in charge—rounded her with narrowed, assessing eyes. He scratched his chin as he took in her disheveled state, reached over, and slipped the headdress from her head. Her hair fell to her shoulders as his eyes watched in appreciation. Then he spoke in a low tone. Reluctantly, the others nodded their understanding.

With a jerk of his head, the guard holding her thrust her out into the hall and closed the giant doors behind. To her surprise, he began to drag her down the long hallway. He wasn't taking her to the sultan, then. But where?

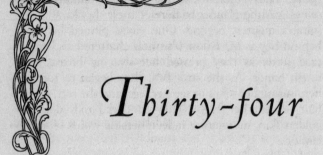

# Thirty-four

*She was dragged* through long corridors and down numerous flights of stairs. Eventually, she lost track of which direction they were heading. She only knew they were in a different part of the building from where the beggars were kept. The guards stopped at last before a heavy iron door with a massive lock. They spoke in low tones, and the attending guard retrieved a set of chains. With her still struggling, they manacled her neck, wrists, and feet, and shoved her through the door to fall to her knees on the stone floor. Then the door clanged shut.

Looking up, she saw that she was in a room filled with Africans of all descriptions—men, women, children of all ages. Most appeared healthy, some were even enormously attractive. All were manacled just as she was. Some of the men's wrists or ankles chafed against their chains, and were caked with dried blood. Instantly, it brought back images of the slaves *El Paraiso* had rescued from the slaver. Slaves that were to be sold by the sultan of Zanzibar.

She tried to talk to them, to ask what was going on, but no one spoke English or French. They simply stared at her. If anything, she thought she detected pity in their eyes. What was happening? She sensed these were slaves of the household, but she couldn't understand why she'd been brought here.

Unless . . .

Once again, Rodrigo's words came back to her. *They'd get a fortune for you on the block.* A vision of the slave market assaulted her mind. But no . . . it couldn't be true. . . .

The chain at her neck was oppressive, bringing back the old horrors. She scooted back against a cold wall, trying not to shake, but trembling helplessly nonetheless. She felt a mad impulse to try to disengage the shackle from her neck—to bloody her hands in the effort—anything to get free. But she knew the futility of such a foolish action. Instead, she struggled to swallow her panic. Not knowing her fate made it all the more frightening. What were they going to do to her?

Shivering—from cold or fear, she didn't know—she clutched the fetter at her throat, gripping so tightly her hands went numb. And all the while her mind cried out, What am I going to do? *What am I going to do?*

The sad realization was, there was nothing to be done.

Somewhere in the night, one of the African women noted her terror and took pity on her, sliding on the floor to her side and taking the trembling woman in her arms. It touched Gabrielle deeply. When she looked up, the African flinched away, as if expecting to be chastised for daring to touch a white woman. But Gabrielle gave her a tentatively grateful smile, and the African took her into her arms again and rocked her to sleep, humming soothingly all the while.

Gabrielle awoke feeling deadened from her fitful doze. The guard who'd just kicked her awake passed her a crude bowl of some foul-smelling meal. Revolted, she put it aside. She wasn't even remotely hungry.

After the bowls had been collected, an Arab woman entered the dungeon. She was dressed in pale blue silk with a long veil covering the lower half of her face. Of middle age, she carried the signs of a once-great beauty. Her large, dark eyes were rimmed in kohl, giving them a mysterious depth. She drifted in on a cloud of perfume that made Gabrielle's surroundings seem all the more surreal. She was followed by a trio of guards who carried with them buckets of steaming water, sponges, towels, and a silver tray gleaming with an impressive assortment of oils and perfumes, all in colorful and exotically shaped bottles. While one guard held her still, Gabrielle was stripped completely. The woman then set about the elaborate and drawn-out task of cleaning her while the guard bent her this way and that to better accommodate the sponge. No one gave a thought to the fact that a roomful of people watched from beneath lowered lashes —people that included men and children. Or that the guard took discreet liberties as he bent her to the woman's will, brushing a breast or grazing an inner thigh. She was treated without any of the dignity she'd come to expect as a human being. She was treated in the same brusque but careful fashion a breeder would use when bathing a prize dog—or a slave-monger a slave.

She was forced to suffer the insult of having her most intimate places scrubbed until her skin glowed. Then a portable table was brought in and piled with pillows before being draped with silk. Gabrielle was made to lie on the table while the woman lingeringly massaged oil into every inch of her skin. She must have worked on her for an hour while the Africans pretended not to watch or averted their eyes in embarrassment.

Finally she was doused in perfume and her hair was brushed dry. It was allowed to fall free in rich chocolate waves. Then a dress of rare indigo silk was brought in and draped over her pampered body before a long matching veil was fastened to cover the lower half of her face. Without having uttered a word, the woman departed with the guards, leaving Gabrielle swathed in the luxury of silk and rare perfumes, with manacles at her neck, ankles, and wrists.

No one said a word. No one looked her way. She felt ridiculously foolish, mortified beyond words. But a more menacing thought dominated her mind.

Why was she alone, of all the people in this room, being given this special care? No one else was so much as bathed, much less coiffed and perfumed. What was she being prepared for?

Perhaps she was being taken to the sultan after all. In spite of the ominous implications, her heart skipped a beat. If she was taken to him, would she see Cullen again?

They came for her some indeterminable time later. First, all the Africans were herded together with a long length of chain connecting the leg irons one to another. Then a couple of guards seized her, one on either side, and fastened a set of chains to her neck brace. These they each held as they guided her along through the fortress behind the row of Africans, like a dog on two leashes, divided by two masters. She didn't know why she was accompanying the Africans or why she was being guided along separately. It took all her courage to steel herself for a fate she couldn't guess.

They were led through a maze of corridors, then suddenly came upon the front hall. With a start, Gabrielle realized they were being led outside. The bright African sun pierced her eyes so she had to lower her head. Instantly, the guard cuffed her chin so her head was held high. Then they hauled her down the steps and out into the street.

A crowd was gathered, she realized, as they let out a cheer. In fact, as she was shoved ahead, she detected a path of bodies lining the way. The mob moved with them, staring, calling out things she didn't understand. Looking up, she saw they were staring at her. As if she were the starring attraction in some circus.

She was pushed along through the crowds in the

debilitating Zanzibar heat. She began to perspire so the silk of her sheath clung to her skin, outlining her curves. The veil was sucked into her mouth as she attempted to breathe the thick air, so her lips were visible through the gauzy silk. The sandals at her feet skipped over the stones as she was pushed this way and that.

She was paraded through the streets like a horse for sale. Then suddenly the crowd seemed to part and she saw before her the terrifying possibility she'd been forcing from her mind on this long trek—the notorious slave market of the sultan of Zanzibar. She knew, of course, what her future was now. Someone would buy her, and once she was in his clutches, he'd be free to use her at his will. Arab law treated women as chattel without rights. But slaves weren't even considered. Her new master could kill her if she displeased him, and the law would pat him on the back and tell him he'd taken the proper course.

She looked ahead at the slave block and saw the sight she must make. A diaphanous silk gown clinging to her body. Her golden skin and sensual cobalt eyes. Blue eyes, the prize of the East. Defiant eyes that challenged every man there to tame her to his will. In a matter of moments, she'd be thrust up those stone steps and put on display for all comers to bid.

# Thirty-five

Gabrielle was forced to watch, held in place by her guards, as one after the other the Africans were put on the block and sold. She observed with mounting horror as each was stripped and perused by prospective buyers, poked and prodded like an animal. They were made to open their mouths so their teeth could be inspected. Women's breasts were tested, their legs parted so new owners could feel inside.

Gabrielle felt incensed that anyone could treat fellow human beings with such persecution and contempt.

She held her head high even as she suffered for the others. Her gaze scanned the jeering mob and she felt her heart sink at the impossibility of her situation. There were hundreds of robed men in headdresses that hid most of their faces. Even if Rodrigo had guessed by now what had happened, even if he was here in the crowd, there was no way he could rescue her in front of all these people. It would be folly to try.

Time dragged on. The Africans were sold one after the other, carted off in chains by their new owners. Some carried whips and cracked them against flesh to make their new property dance to their will. It sickened

Gabrielle, but she made herself look. *This is what Rodrigo's fighting,* she thought. This inhuman display. From her ordeal was born an empathy she would never otherwise have felt. She was one of them now, a piece of flesh to be bartered to the highest bidder. She'd felt their pain, their terror, and made it her own. Now she understood.

Still, the time passed. The sun was fierce above in a cloudless sky of blue. As blue as Gabrielle's eyes. People stared at those eyes as they would covet a priceless jewel, so she lowered them and tried not to think. But she could see from beneath her lashes that there were few Africans left in the line to be sold. Obviously, they were saving her.

One, then another, then another was forced up on the block. That left only one remaining, a black youth of fifteen or so. She couldn't understand the bidding, but she could comprehend the meaning. The boy's muscles were fussed over. Obviously he was being sold to work in the fields. Her heart went out to him. So young, with so little life ahead. She thought of her years of servitude in her father's home. It had been awful, but she'd always had the knowledge that she could leave. What must it be like to know you have no say in your own destiny for the remainder of your life?

She reminded herself she was about to find out.

The youth was led away and the guards tightened their hold on her chains. She was escorted through the crowd to the podium. At the foot of the stairs she stopped, her heart freezing like the blood in her veins. She couldn't make herself take another step.

The move was made for her. She was shoved toward the steps so that she stumbled up them, suddenly aware of all eyes on her, hardly believing what was happening. The auctioneer stepped forward and began to point as he spoke, highlighting her finer qualities, no doubt. She was turned so they could see her back. A hand ran itself over her backside and patted her like a filly. In another moment, she would be bought and paid for like all the rest.

Someone in the crowd called a command, accompanied by a rousing cheer. As if in a nightmare, Gabrielle felt herself being stripped of her silk sheath in this most public of places. The silk slipped from her with a swish and she felt the hot air on her skin, the sun beating down on her tender breasts. She heard men, women, even children giggling as she was revealed to them. She began to struggle, becoming panicked, and they laughed again. Children jeered at her. Men licked dry lips and began to call out bids.

She'd never felt more exposed in her life. Her face flushed as men came closer to inspect her. They touched her and she flinched away. Angered, the guards jerked her back on her chain. Her display of spirits only caused the men to pursue her more. The auctioneer said something and the others laughed and nodded their heads. As if he'd said, "She'd be fun to tame," and they'd all agreed.

With mounting hysteria, she scanned the crowd, wondering who among them would own her, body and soul.

A frenzy of bidding mounted around her. She could tell by the gleam in the auctioneer's eyes that she was fetching a handsome price. For perhaps a quarter hour, there was a constant calling of bids as the auctioneer looked her over with a satisfied gaze. Then, as the price escalated, most of the men dropped out, groaning their disappointment, but taking the opportunity to ogle her just the same.

The bidding eventually narrowed down to two men —an Arab in white robes and an Indian with a pristine turban on his head. They juggled back and forth for a few minutes, but as the price increased, they took several moments to consider their next bids. There was a long pause after the Arab replied, then a gasp of astonishment as the Indian offered another sum. It seemed that time stood still. The mob held its collective breath as it waited to hear how the Arab would reply.

Silence hung over the square where once bedlam had reigned. Not even a stir of breeze broke the deadly quiet. Gabrielle's nerves throbbed and screamed.

With infinite deliberation, the Arab walked forward and mounted the stairs to the block, his long white robes trailing in the dust. She could see little of his face, except for a strong brown jaw and finely shaped lips. His robes hid his body, so it was difficult to tell his physique, but he stood erect, with the bearing of one who's accustomed to getting his way. In his strong hand he held a walking stick, elaborately carved from a stalk of ebony. He walked with straight, sure strides, leading her to believe the stick was purely for decorative purposes.

With a graceful arrogance, he stepped before her. He didn't so much as look her in the face. Instead, his eyes fell to her exposed breasts. With his walking stick he prodded them, testing their firmness, letting them bounce a little on his stick. Her humiliation caused her to back away. But with a jerk of his head, the Arab let it be known he would brook no such rebellion. She was brought back in place.

Then, abruptly, he nodded to the auctioneer. Without turning, he held out his hand to the man below him and accepted a heavy white bag of gold. This he tossed to the auctioneer without even looking to see if he'd caught it.

Something in the gesture reminded her of other times. Of a pirate lord strutting across the deck, roaring orders he knew would be obeyed. Not even bothering to check that they were. Her heart leaped at the thought of it. Rodrigo! Of course! He'd disguised himself as an Arab and bought her so he could take her safely away.

But after the first flush of relief came a wash of anger. How dare he put her through this! Toying with her in front of all these people. The thought of it made her seethe. She thought of all the things she'd rail at him when she got him alone.

Then, for the first time, he lifted his eyes to Gabrielle's face. Black eyes, not gold. Arab eyes, as cold and impersonal as death. Eyes she'd never seen in her life. The cool brittleness of his expression changed to one of challenge. He seemed to promise her with his look that he'd break her if it was the last thing he did.

She was so devastated, her knees almost buckled beneath her.

He descended the stairs and his man scampered up to take his place. Taking her chains from the guards, he tugged to get her moving. She realized in that moment, with a heavy sinking of her heart, that she'd actually been bought. She belonged to the cruel Arab who'd silently vowed to break her spirit. There was nothing she could do.

She was led away from the market toward the sea. There, a large ship of Arab design waited in the harbor. It took her a while to realize she was being transported directly to the ship. When she did, she went wild. She knew if they succeeded in placing her on that ship, she was done for. No one on earth could stampede that vessel and carry her off alive. And if it sailed, her hope sailed with her. Rodrigo couldn't possibly pursue them. Thanks to Hastings, he didn't have the men or the ships.

She struggled hysterically, breaking free and running a few steps before she was grabbed again. Voices were shouting now, but they sounded distant in her ears. She was so terrified, she couldn't tell if the screams she heard were her own or someone else's. She only knew it was better to die trying to escape than ever to set foot on that ship. Her agitation mounted as she realized there would be no escape.

A small sedan chair was brought with long handles carried by slaves. She was forced, struggling all the way, inside. Then the door was slammed shut and the conveyance began to move. But just as the one door closed, the opposite door opened. Insensible by now, she caught a glimpse of golden hair and lion's eyes. Then a huge bag was dropped over her body. She was enclosed by darkness and hauled in a heap over his shoulder. She heard the door close behind, then she was carried away, bumping against his back the whole way.

She waited with held breath for the sounds of alarm. None was forthcoming. No shouts. No rushing feet. Just the normal hubbub of a market at the close of a sale.

She felt herself lifted onto something and detected the shape of a saddle beneath her. She felt him mount, then the horse lurched away, galloping over the stones and through the alleyways at breakneck speed. The pommel of the saddle dug into her ribs, bruising them. Crushed as she was into the rough canvas bag, she bounced painfully against the horse's side. It was unbearably hot and stuffy in the parcel, breathing her own breath. *But she was safe!* She was no longer the property of a stranger bent on her mortification. She could breathe a sigh of relief.

Finally, after what seemed like hours of bouncing along, the horse was drawn to a halt. She was lowered and she felt a tugging of the ropes. Then a ray of light penetrated the darkness of the fabric. She was helped to her feet and she caught a good glimpse of Rodrigo's cherished face. Shackled as she was in chains, she nonetheless threw herself into his arms.

"Oh, Rodrigo, it was so awful! They *sold* me, as if I were a possession, and not a person with a soul. Can you ever forgive me for not understanding?"

He hugged her to him, trying to hush her as a hand soothed the back of her neck. "I'm only glad you're safe. And back where you belong."

She pushed herself away and looked into his eyes. His beloved cat's eyes that beheld her now with love and relief and some of the fear he must have felt in getting them both out alive.

"You risked everything for me," she told him. "And now I'm ready to risk all for you. I don't know what the future will bring. And I don't care. All I know is that from now on, Rodrigo, I want to do everything I can to help your cause."

# Thirty-six

*It was dusk.* They were camped at a tree-enclosed spring somewhere in the interior of East Africa. The soft air of the African highlands was cool and filled with lovely scents. Higgins and two of the recently freed slaves were building a huge bonfire out of slender trees knocked down by a herd of elephants that had wandered by. Small groups of Kikuyu warriors, all of them recently freed from slavery, squatted nearby and were chanting a song in celebration.

They'd fled Zanzibar three weeks ago. Since then, they'd been slowly making their way into the uncharted interior of the continent. Rodrigo knew the area well. He'd been brought here as a boy by his grandfather, who, in his younger days, had used the vast plains as a hideout when he could no longer reach his home. As the African continent was the one place Europeans hadn't explored, and were afraid to enter, it had served the same purpose for Rodrigo over the years. He knew the landscape, had made the acquaintance of the various tribes. Now he was using this knowledge to gather men in any way he could to launch an effective attack on Zanzibar.

Rodrigo picked up a branch and went to join Gabrielle, who sat on a large log facing the fire. During these weeks on *safari*—the Swahili word for "journey"—they'd worked with a fierce determination. The first order of business was to finish what they'd started: rescue Cullen from the palace. Then they'd band together to stop Hastings and his cohorts once and for all.

"When will we have enough men?" she asked him as he sat by her side.

"I'm not certain. Our task is difficult at best."

She tried again to swallow her impatience. He was being cautious, as always, and her impulsive nature chafed against the restraints.

"But enough of this for one day. Let's go for a walk, Gabé. Before it gets dark."

Having difficulty letting it go, she reluctantly nodded and stood. He took her hand and guided her down a narrow gully, through a grove of spreading acacia trees. Their welcoming branches were silhouetted against the deepening lavender of the sky. Stars were beginning to dot the heavens, stars that would, in the inky blackness of the African night, seem so large and bright, they would appear to spring from some long-forgotten childhood dream. The sounds of insects and birds that only came out in darkness began to mingle with the Kikuyu's distant songs, blending together into the one primal rhythm of Africa. There was magic in the air. Slowly, she felt herself succumbing to it.

"I really love it here," he said, his voice sounding hushed in the still twilight. "In a way, it's the opposite of Seychelles. There, it's humid and the air is heavy. Here, it's cooler and dry. And the air is soft. Do you feel it?"

"I've never felt such soft air in my life."

"In Seychelles," he continued, "nothing can hurt you. There are no natural threats. There, nature is luxurious. Here, there's danger behind every rock. Nature is harsh, even in its beauty. But I love it all the same."

She smiled as her concerns for Cullen were distracted by the tenderness of his tone. "I admit its savage charms are hard to resist."

He moved closer and took her in his arms. Suddenly, they heard a scraping sound close by, and a faint, guttural grumble. His arms tightened about her. "Be still, Gabé."

"What—"

"Lions."

She jerked in his arms. "Where?"

"Under that tree," he said, gesturing. She could make out the vague outline of two beasts lying on the ground and facing each other. "They're mating."

"Oh, my God, Rodrigo, if they see us—"

She moved to run, but he grabbed her instantly, pulling her to him so her back was pressed against him. Instinctively, his hand crept to her mouth to silence any outcry.

"They're not interested in us. Only each other. Look. The female is showing the male she's ready. In the mating season, they'll join together every fifteen minutes for weeks."

As they watched, their eyes now adjusted to the darkness, the male calmly came around and mounted his mate. She stretched herself up to accommodate him. The male grabbed her neck with his teeth, pumped savagely, and let loose with a mighty roar. It only took moments, but it was ferocious and primal. Then the pair stretched and walked off into the night, leaving their audience behind.

Gabrielle was breathing hard against his palm. She'd forgotten she still stood with him pressed against her, his hand at her mouth. She'd forgotten everything in this awe-inspiring display. It reminded her of the days of their intense lovemaking in the Vallée de Mai.

"It's quite a process. The male masters her completely, but only when she lets him know she's ready."

In the ensuing hush, her voice was but a tentative sigh. "Rodrigo . . ."

"Hmmm?"

"I've been thinking about Shayla."

She saw him smile. As if he'd known she'd get around to this, sooner or later.

"What have you been thinking?"

"I want you to show me some of what Shayla taught you."

He laughed. "That requires a particular frame of mind."

He was tweaking her curiosity. "What sort of frame of mind?"

"When I was with Shayla, I was myself, naturally, but I was also . . . playing a role."

"I'm an actress. I excel at playing roles."

"What I mean is, I left my own will at her door and did everything she asked. If I couldn't willingly accede to her will, I didn't learn. Nor did I experience the full measure of arousal that was possible. It required turning off the mind and moving to a higher level of feeling. Of existing for the moment, with no expectations, and no limits of the mind. I existed only for her pleasure, and in doing so, attained a level of satisfaction and fulfillment that was beyond imagining."

"I want to know that pleasure. Show me."

He paused for a moment. "Now?"

She moved so that her body slithered up the length of his. "Yes. Right now." She'd wanted him so badly, had ached for him so in her denial of his caress, that she felt she could abide it no longer.

He hesitated, considering.

"I mean it," she coaxed. "I want to know. Not your graduation exercise, of course."

He laughed as if to say he wouldn't anyway.

"But something. I want to put myself in your place. I want to know what it was like for you."

He shifted so he could look into her eyes. His face,

or what she could see of it in the light of the savanna moon, was serious, more thoughtful than was his custom.

"I warn you. You'll have to turn yourself over to me completely. Submit to my desires. You must trust me in all I say and do. Do you understand? Because I'll only do this with your total and willing consent."

A thrill shot through her. "I understand."

Her heart was beating wildly now, like a bird about to fly the coop. She felt as if she'd had no life before this day. That she'd been born when she'd opened her eyes in this African wonderland. Yet, how could his promise of sexual domination feel so liberating? Why, she asked herself—endeavoring to be rational in the face of his rough, masculine presence—was it so absolutely appealing to think, not just of giving herself to him, but of being *taken* by him? Why was his threat of sexual power such an aphrodisiac? And why did the prospect of it make her feel more of a complete woman than she ever had before?

He took her face in his hands and looked at her for a long time. "You're sure?"

She nodded. "I couldn't have done it before. Not when I felt we were divided. But now, I want to give myself to you completely, unreservedly. Give you something I'd never give any other man. Only—"

"What, Gabé?"

"What if it goes too far? What if I become frightened and want you to stop? How will you know when I really mean it? And how do I know you will?"

"Ah. You want to know how far you can trust me. If you like, we'll use a safe word."

"A safe word? What's that?"

"Shayla always had a safe word in case things went too far. A word you wouldn't normally use. When you say it, I know you need to stop. Saying it assures you that you're safe."

"Oh, I rather like that."

"Then what's it to be?"

"*Simba*," she said at once. "I won't use it except in extreme need."

Still, an idea was forming in her mind. He was right. In spite of everything, she *did* still need to know how far she could trust him. This suddenly seemed the perfect way to find out.

He led her back to their small hut, the chief's hut in a place of honor away from the main village, surrounded by trees thick with growing vines. Here, he knew no one would disturb him. The night birds, frogs, and insects sang their native songs. He seemed to belong here, a king among beasts. As the drums beat a primal rhythm, he turned and faced her. Her heart jumped into her throat.

Slowly, gently, he extended his hands so his fingers were locked with her own. Like the most tender lover, he turned her hands up and kissed each palm. Then, slowly, but with a bold resolve, he forced her arms behind her back and brought his mouth to hers.

His kiss alone would have buckled her knees—as fierce and passionate a kiss as she'd ever received. But with her wrists held fast behind her back, it was absolutely transfixing. She swayed into him, opened her mouth and moaned aloud.

He let go of her hands then and put his to her shoulders. Taking his mouth from hers so she cried her denial, he put his mouth to her ear, and whispered, "Get on your knees."

She hesitated. It was what she'd sworn never to do. But with a persistent pressure, he pushed her down so her mouth grazed the coils of his chest, his flat, narrow waist, and, as her knees touched the ground, the bulge in his torn breeches. His hands left her and came into her range of vision, moving swiftly to open his pants and bring his erection out into the steamy, moon-washed night. She'd never seen anything more beautiful. In the celestial light, his erection looked exalted—

huge and bestial, ribbed and corded, full of a life and character all its own, as if carved from marble by an artisan's hands. She reached for it, dying to touch it, remembering the outer softness pulsing against the rigid inner steel. But as her hand approached, he pushed it away.

She couldn't believe the erotic effect of this simple act of denial. After his relentless pursuit of her, over twelve thousand miles of land and sea, to be denied, at this moment, what she desired most, made her sticky between her thighs in a way no power on earth ever had.

She licked her lips, staring at him with hungry eyes, already wanting him in her mouth. "I want to touch you," she insisted. "I want to taste you." He took himself in hand and rubbed the head along her mouth. When she parted her lips to take him inside, he moved away, grazing her cheek, not letting her taste him even when she moved her head and tried again.

"You want to suck it?" he asked.

"More than anything."

He considered her a moment as he grazed her cheek with the soft head. Then his voice, graveled with passion, said, "Put your hands behind your back. Clasp your fingers together. No matter what happens, don't move them. As far as you're concerned, your hands are tied."

She looked up and found his face and saw that he was serious. She knelt as she was, staring up at him in silence. Could she do this? Keep her hands bound behind her as if he'd tied them with rope? She'd promised to do anything he wanted for this one night. Yet she felt she was treading on dangerous ground. To give in to his will so completely . . .

Then she recalled the safe word. *Simba*. It may have meant "lion" in Swahili, but to her it meant safety.

Parting her lips to draw air, she slowly did as he'd requested. Putting her hands behind her, she felt her cold fingers collide. She clasped her fingers loosely together.

"Tighter," he commanded, his voice now that of the pirate lord.

Swallowing, she clasped her fingers tighter together. It was an oddly amorous experience, knowing she had no control, that she was bound to do his bidding without so much as the use of her hands.

But it was difficult to think of her hands when he was holding his masterful erection in her face and taunting her with it. Finally, he guided himself to her mouth and allowed her to draw him in. He was so delicious, she forgot herself and reached for him. Instantly, he grabbed her hair and hauled her head back so he dropped from her mouth. Looking up at him in the darkness now, she couldn't see his face. But she could feel his power. She could feel his fury flowing down his arm into the fingers that yanked her hair.

Alarmed, afraid he'd deny her the astonishing pleasure of having him in her mouth, she crossed her wrists behind her, turned her palms together, and clasped her fingers so tightly, a hurricane wouldn't have shaken them loose.

His hand loosened in her hair and he stroked it back off her face, tenderly now.

He let her taste him again. She began to lose herself in the process. To forget the circumstances. To lose track of her mentally bound hands. To submerge herself in the seductive pleasure of affording him pleasure. Her mouth gripped him like a vise, making up for the fact that she couldn't use her hands. If she was powerless to his will, the least she could do was get him so enflamed, he'd lose control. She knew he was enjoying it. He was so hard, she thought he'd explode. Guttural groans were coming from his throat. He said, "Oh, Christ," and his fist tightened in her hair.

Still, lingering along the fringes of her mind was the awareness of what she was denied. Just knowing she couldn't touch him made her want to all the more. She had to clutch her fingers together so tightly they felt numb, just to keep from reaching for him and pumping until he climaxed.

He must have sensed her designs, for he pulled away and dropped before her on bent legs. His finger scooped up some of the moistness about her lips and he offered it to her, letting her lick it off. Then he leaned over suddenly and kissed her lips, showing her his approval as he clutched her head and pulled her close, drowning her in his kiss.

He traveled the length of her with his lips, enticing lustful sensations in a body already exploding with desire and the heightened stimulation of having her hands willingly bound. He tasted, he teased, nibbling her breasts until her nipples grew pebble-hard, lapping at her navel and her inner thighs. And just when he moved close, when she thought he'd find her steaming treasure and use his tongue to ease her agony of longing, he moved away. His mouth at her thighs drove her wild. Again and again, she felt compelled to free her hands and guide him where she wanted him. But she couldn't release her hands now if she tried. His will was stronger than her own. He kept her captive with his resolve.

"Turn around, *carícia*," he said presently, his command sounding like a sweet caress.

She did so slowly, unbinding her hands to prop them before her. He moved behind her, running a hand along her naked back, negligently reaching under to cup a dangling breast. She heard the swish of his breeches as they dropped to the ground. Then, he was at the opening between her thighs, hard as steel, as much a weapon as any sword. She was so wet that, big as he was, he mounted her without interference. As he moved inside her, his thighs slapping against her buttocks, he reached forth and took a fistful of hair in his hand. This he pulled as he propelled himself into her with reckless force. It was astonishingly carnal, his pulling her hair as he slammed into her from behind. It unleashed in her a surge of lust such as she'd never felt before. She felt like a lioness being willingly mastered by her mate. She knew now she'd never wanted another man. What she'd mistaken as desire paled in the savage onslaught of his invasion. Far from feeling used and abused, she felt frenzied with passion. She forgot herself, her fears, the dark corners of her own mind and found, in the panting woman beneath the pirate, her true and glorious self. She felt the wild woman rise like a phoenix from the ashes of her childhood and make her strong. As she heard him cry out, she knew he was feeling the same.

Her joy was boundless. She'd never been bedded by a man with as much fire and imagination as Rodrigo. He made love with a vigor and aesthetic dedication that spoke as much for his love of her as it did for the vast range of his expertise. His touch was always different. He never ran out of new ways to excite her. Even the smallest caress lit a flame in her. He never asked for any indulgence without bestowing the lion's share on her.

He made love like an African, not a European. When he moved his body, the thrust of his motions came from the hips, centered in his body in a way Europeans' weren't. His African techniques of lovemaking sent her hurtling to the brink of delirium and back. He stayed hard for an hour or more at a time, making love to her with slow, hard thrusts that matched the distant beating of the drums until she felt on the borders of madness. With Rodrigo, making love was like an untamed dance of varied and colorful steps. Just when she thought it was as good as it could get, just when she was certain she could never again be so excited, so fulfilled, so absolutely smitten with the man she loved, he proved her wrong. She'd never been so happy to be proved wrong in her life.

When he yanked some nearby vines from a tree and bound her hands behind her back, she felt a momentary panic. But as he began the delectable process of fulfilling his desires, she became so carried away with the unexpected ecstasy of it that she nearly forgot her designs. She knew, in the reckless reaches of sanity, that she was in control. That her safe word afforded her escape. But the furious torrent of passion washing through her, the familiar heat that sparked her loins and transformed her tranquil breath to an unruly lament, threatened to hold her prisoner more securely than the vines twining her hands. And she realized, in the midst of it, that this was more thrilling than anything that had happened in a life filled with drama and pageantry. That the grandeur of his licentious contrivances was more spectacular than anything she, in her own imagination, could have designed.

She realized in the throes of tumultuous passion that she didn't want him to stop. She knew in that moment that she could spend a lifetime giving herself to him, and never lose her awe at the power of their union.

But he'd brought up the issue of trust. And she had to know.

Greedily, she continued long after she'd intended to call a halt, savoring the surge of sensations that wrung her out and made her doubt her ability to carry through. It was too sublime. How could she deny herself—and him—such exquisite gratification? How could she possibly say the one word that would stall the game?

But she must. She had to know once and for all how much she could trust him.

So she waited until she knew he was in the throes of delirium. Until he was on the verge of melding with the moon and the stars. And then, gasping air into her lungs, for it was difficult to catch her breath, she panted out the word she'd been caressing like a forbidden lover on her tongue.

"*Simba.*"

For a moment, he didn't seem to hear. He was wild with ardor, the sweat dotting his golden form from his strenuous exertions in the balmy night. He grabbed her hair and thrust harder as she felt her climax escalating to a frenetic pitch. It was the hardest thing she'd ever had to do, to raise her head and call out the word that would deny them both the fruits of their passions.

"*Simba*, Rodrigo."

It was a moment before it registered. Then, with an agonized roar, he slowed his pace. "Are you serious?" he asked, incredulous.

She had to be strong. She had to be sure. "Yes. Yes. *Simba*."

He fell over her with a ragged groan. But he withdrew his bold erection from the swollen liquid of her sheath and lay atop her, breathing like a brawler who'd been bested in a fight.

Even as he did, his fingers found the vines that bound her hands and tugged them loose. Her arms came around him with loving gratitude, holding his steaming body tightly in their grasp.

"Are you all right?" he asked.

"Yes," she breathed. "Oh, yes."

"I didn't hurt you?"

"No. Never. It was . . ." She couldn't think of a word to describe the unmitigated thrill of it.

"Then . . ." He was quiet for a moment, as if questioning her motives. Then, all at once, he understood. She feared his anger, but he merely lowered his head and gave her a long, passionate kiss. A kiss that reminded her of her stunted passions. Of how her body, even now, was longing to be joined with his.

"I've changed my mind," she told him, now that she knew he could be trusted to cease. "Make love to me, Rodrigo. Let's do it all again."

But he rolled off her and flattened himself on his back, drawing her gently into his arms. "Not tonight," he said. "I told you I could be trusted, and I'm a man of my word."

He held her tenderly the whole night through, his rampant erection brushing her leg as he stirred restively in sleep. She could think of nothing that night except what she was missing by playing the trickster. She thought how dear he was to give her this assurance. But still, she wished desperately that she'd had the good sense to trust him all along.

So she tossed in his arms long into the night. And cursed herself for being such a fool.

# Thirty-seven

From the cover of the hilltop, they watched the enormous slave caravan trudge its way across the vast African savanna. They'd been struggling to catch up with it for a week, and finally here it was before them.

Their group included an interpreter who spoke several local dialects and some natives who'd volunteered to transport supplies. All carried rifles Rodrigo had liberated from earlier, more modest caravans. They also shouldered the hideous accoutrements of the slave trade. If they happened upon a slaver who was likely to question their designs, the tethers could be fastened about the natives' limbs to convince the intruder they were part of the same brotherhood, and catch him off guard. Twice already the ploy had worked. Two separate traders had wandered into camp to assess the competition. When each had settled in the shade with the proffered drink, Rodrigo's "slaves" had drawn rifles and freed the trader of his ill-favored merchandise without so much as a fuss.

Now they could see their prey winding its way through the grasses below. It was the largest slave caravan any of them had ever seen. A group of Arabs in long robes led the slaves in single file beneath the relentless noonday sun. They were leashed together by the means that had become disgustingly familiar to Gabrielle by now. Two forked limbs of trees were strung together back-to-back so there was a fork the size of a man's neck on either side. These forks were inserted around one male slave in front and one in back, the open ends connected with strips of leather. This was attached to a long rope that was wrapped like a noose around a female slave's throat as she walked behind. Children of all ages traipsed beside their mothers, clinging to their legs. Sometimes there were as many as five or six children grabbing hold and slowing the woman's progress. When that happened, they were lashed—children and all—by whips made of hippo hide: hide that stung on bare skin more than any other whip ever devised by man.

Gabrielle could hear the screams of the children from her perch atop the hill. It was beginning to wear on her nerves, this constant pillaging of human cargo. After each excursion, she had asked Rodrigo, "Now can we go fetch Cullen?" But he was never ready. He didn't have enough men, he argued, even though he'd sent seemingly hundreds back to Mombasa for training under Wallace. Each time, she asked the same question: "When will you have enough?" And each time, she received the same reply: "When I have enough."

The procession was approaching now. Rodrigo gave the order and the natives began to fasten the restraints to their own necks. Then he led the way down the hill. Gabrielle followed behind, dressed in Arab robes to keep her gender hidden.

They stopped before the convoy. Gabrielle took a moment while Rodrigo was conversing with the Arabs to study the faces of the slaves. Their dark eyes looked hollow. She could detect in their dull depths the absence of hope. She felt a mad impulse to go to them, to whisper the secret, to put an end to their suffering. One minute more seemed too long to suffer, after all they'd been through. She caught the eye of one more-daring man who looked up from the ground and smiled. She hoped he might feel some of her sympathy.

But his eyes flicked from her to Rodrigo. She saw them widen, saw the collection of disbelief. Then she heard the name whispered on his lips: *Mkombozi!*

Other slaves looked up and whispered the same. *Mkombozi! Mkombozi!* Gabrielle wanted to rush to them and implore them to be quiet. If they gave it away, it spelled disaster for them. She saw the interpreter put a surreptitious finger to his lips and motion silence behind the Arabs' backs.

The slave who'd first spotted Rodrigo dropped to his knees and held his hands together as in prayer, pleading for help. Soon two more had done the same. Appalled, Gabrielle moved to hide them from view with her robes. But she was a second too late. The lead slaver turned and saw the commotion. Then she heard the name *Mkombozi* on his lips as he turned Rodrigo's way. She could tell from the expression on the Arab's face what he was saying. "*Mkombozi.* I've heard tales of you. I know who and what you are."

It happened so quickly, she thought she'd dreamed it. Suddenly, there were rifles in the hands of Rodrigo's men. Gunshots blasted the stillness of the savanna, and the Arabs fell in a swirl of flowing robes to the ground. Their blood spilled out over the grasslands, and they took their last breath of the soft African air.

Gabrielle was stunned by the swiftness of it, by the sudden savagery. Rodrigo had given them no warning. He'd killed them in cold blood. He had to do it, she realized, but it unsettled her all the same.

All about her, Rodrigo's men were shedding their tethers and freeing the would-be slaves. Rodrigo spoke to them in Swahili, explaining his mission. As he'd done numerous times before, he asked those who would join him to form a separate group. Then he strolled among them, picking out the most able-bodied to join his crew.

Gabrielle sat on the ground as far from the dead bodies as she could, feeling the need to rest her trembling legs. She'd sworn her allegiance to Rodrigo's cause, but she felt repulsed by the brutal ways of Africa. How the landscape could be so beautiful, so welcoming, so caressing; and the reality of its world so harsh. One animal slaughtering another. A plant of magnificent splendor with the poison to kill. Men enslaving men and shooting one another dead.

She looked at Rodrigo. He was just finishing up. It appeared they had an impressive number of volunteers. She rose to her feet to go ask him the same question she had each and every time. Knowing what the answer would be.

"When can we sail?" she asked again. "When will we have enough men?"

Rodrigo looked into her eyes and saw the weariness. He saw, too, the repressed impatience and the assumption that it would find no satisfaction. He glanced at his collection of warriors, then back into his lover's eyes.

"*Now* we have enough," he said.

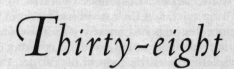

# Thirty-eight

*It was close to dawn*. Rodrigo had sailed his three ships into the Zanzibar harbor under cover of darkness. With nothing but the brilliance of the African stars to light the way, the men had worked silently, readying cannons, guns, and swords for the attack. The atmosphere aboard the ships was charged with electricity. Men paced nervously, checking and rechecking weapons they already knew were in order. Gabrielle could feel the excitement pulsating through her veins. In just a little more time, she'd have Cullen safely back with her. Rodrigo had brought enough men with him to level the city if they had to. In fact, he'd moved beyond the customary objectives of a pirate. The mission bore the trappings of an all-out military attack. There was no doubt in her mind that they'd retrieve her brother this day.

She was dressed like the others, in breeches and a shirt that allowed her freedom of movement. She'd been equipped with boots that fit so she could move with ease.

She'd refused Rodrigo's suggestion to stay on board *El Paraiso Segundo*, his new flagship, taken from an Arab slaver off Lamu and refitted for battle. She wanted to be in the thick of the action. She wanted to see her brother's face when they set him free.

The attack had been skillfully planned. Rodrigo had sent spies in to report on the number of ships in the sultan's fleet, and on the level of activity at the palace. The remarkable news came back that things were relatively quiet, as if their guard had let down in the month since Hastings had arrived with a warning that an assault might be imminent. The governor of Seychelles was still there, the guest of his partner, the sultan.

As the sky gradually lightened, the offensive began. Rodrigo raised his hand, giving the signal, and a barrage of cannon fire split the predawn repose. The smell of gunfire scorched the air. Soon, the smoke became oppressive, making it difficult to see. In a matter of minutes, Rodrigo's cannons had destroyed the two lead ships of the sultan's fleet. They split and sank amidst the protestations of creaking wood, effectively bottling up the other ships in the harbor—just as Rodrigo had planned. Wasting little time, those who'd been assigned to the shore attack leaped into the boats and rowed across the breakwater in soundless unison as the cannons were turned on the sultan's palace. Citizens began to flow out of homes, half-dressed, to see what was afoot. The sultan's guards were on the run, scimitars drawn, fighting Rodrigo's forces as they swarmed onshore.

When Gabrielle reached dry land with Rodrigo, swords were clashing all around. Cannons continued to fire at regular intervals. The enemy was clearly outnumbered and suffering from surprise. Still, they fought valiantly, congregating at the palace door to guard their sultan at all costs. They'd been trained to give their lives for the protection of their leader. Nothing short of annihilation would convince them to open the gates.

"There must be another way in," Rodrigo called to her when he saw that his men were making no headway at the entrance. He motioned for her to follow and they rounded the palace walls. Along the way, they were met by a cortege of late-arriving guards. Rodrigo fell on them at once, battling three at a time with his sword. Gabrielle recognized one defender as a guard who'd grabbed her that night in the palace, effectively halting her rescue attempt and pawing her in the bargain. Incensed, she lunged at him, fighting with all her might and skill until she had him backed up against the wall. There, with a single savage thrust, she ran him through with her sword. The guard looked stunned as she pulled out the bloodied instrument, staggered a few feet, and fell dead at his post.

She stood staring at him for some moments, aware now more than ever of the pervasive smell of gunpowder as she watched his blood seep onto the stones. Her stomach lurched queasily at the sight of her handiwork. But she thought of the look of gleeful lust on her victim's face as he'd pillaged her, and it eased her guilt.

She became aware slowly that Rodrigo was fighting six men at once. He was faltering as they sought to pin him against the wall. Coming to her senses, she nicked his closest attacker with the tip of her sword and, having captured his attention, engaged him in battle herself. She and Rodrigo now fought together side by side, the clash of their steel ringing out like cymbals at the climax of a symphony. As the guards fell around them, Rodrigo grabbed her hand and they ran.

He pulled her to an abrupt halt on the sea side of the palace. There, he stood transfixed, gazing overhead. As she watched him curiously, a look of hatred hardened his eyes. Gabrielle shifted her gaze upward to find a balcony overlooking the sea. Standing behind the stone balustrade were the sultan and her brother, Cullen, looking down on the scene. The sultan was calling orders to his men. Cullen stood numbly beside him. Then, as if from nowhere, Hastings stepped into view. He put a sword to Cullen's throat.

"Ah, Roderick Smythe, my old friend," he called down. "Have you come to pay your respects?"

"I thought it was time we renewed our acquaintance," Rodrigo returned.

"How kind. And I see you've brought company. Welcome, Gabby, to Xanadu. But then, you've been here before, I understand. Had a bit of sport on the block. A close call, what?"

Ignoring his jabs, she put her mind to the quandary of how to get Cullen down safely.

"Come, Gabby," Hastings called. "Cat got your tongue? If so, it's the first time I can recall. We don't, after all, call you *Gabby* for nothing."

Beside her, Rodrigo had moved below the balcony and was removing his boots. "Keep him talking," he whispered so that no one else could hear.

She did as he'd requested. Looking up, she noted in the onrushing dawn the slick dark hair of her half brother, the cruel sneer of his thin, pursed lips. He looked like a hawk contemplating his prey. How she hated him!

"You always were the charmer of the family, Hastings," she called up in her smoky voice. "As I recall, it *required* the edge of a sword to keep people by your side."

As she spoke, Rodrigo moved to the wall below the balcony. The palace was made of rough stone. He tested it with his hands, searching for footholds, then, anchoring the deadly blade of his sword in his teeth, began stealthily to climb. She glanced at him, then quickly back, lest she give away his intentions. Still, her heart slammed in her chest. It was a flagrantly daring thing to do, to climb up and confront them alone. Without knowing how many of the sultan's personal guards were still inside.

"We've come for Cullen," she told Hastings.

"Pity to have made the trip for nothing. I'm afraid, Gabby, that as usual, you're wasting your time."

"Let him go, Hastings. He's your half brother, for God's sake."

"That pup," spat Hastings angrily, "is no brother of mine."

Incensed, she cried, "You're diseased, Hastings. You can't love anyone. You never could."

Almost at once, she knew she'd made a mistake. He was stung by her retort—she could see it in the flash of pain and betrayal that colored his face at the word "diseased," as if she'd broken some unspoken agreement. When he replaced his usual mask, his lip curled in a slow, exacting sneer. As he finally spoke, he enunciated every word in his best stiff-upper-lip manner. "I loved someone once, Gabby. And as I recall, it required the inducement of not a single sword."

Everything stilled. Gabrielle felt numb, as if a glacial wind had frozen her in her tracks. Unbidden, her gaze darted to Rodrigo. He was halfway up the wall, but he'd stopped at Hastings's words and was looking back at her with a hot curiosity burning in his eyes. He saw the blood drain from her face, as if Hastings had just pushed some boundary he'd never broken before. Shamed, Gabrielle lowered her lashes. She suddenly couldn't bear to look her lover in the face.

"Oh, dear," Hastings called down in mock annoyance. "And I'd promised not to tell!"

Enflamed by his effrontery, Gabrielle called back, "Hastings, you fiend. May you rot in hell!"

Rodrigo had started moving again. He was nearly to the precipice of the balcony.

"We *are* going to take Cullen," she added, rallying her strength to give Rodrigo the distraction he needed. "There's nothing you can do to stop us."

"I don't think Cullen is going anywhere," Hastings predicted.

Rodrigo's hand was on the balcony floor. With a mighty yank, he heaved himself up, grabbed hold of the rail, and swung his legs over the side. As he did, all in one motion, he kicked Cullen out of reach of Hastings's sword. It was a flamboyant piece of work that caught Hastings by surprise.

"Oh, good show, Roderick!" he cried when confronted by Rodrigo's blade. "I do so admire your ability to throw people off their guard. Do you know, Gabby, I used to torment this fierce pirate as a boy. Do you remember how I used to do it, Roderick?" Hastings leaned forward and spat in Rodrigo's face.

The sword moved too swiftly for her to see, crashing against the wall just inches from Hastings's head. Rodrigo followed it with a barrage of attacks that would have felled a lesser swordsman. But Hastings was good. He parried Rodrigo's thrusts and, with swift efficiency, put him on the defensive as Cullen crouched in a corner and the sultan ran into his rooms, screaming for his guards.

"Now this is more like it," Hastings called above the clatter of their swords. "To fight like men in battle. This is what you and I were destined for from the moment we met."

They battled fiercely, each bent on the destruction of the other. Hastings had backed Rodrigo against the rail, but he leaped up on the banister and kicked Hastings in the face so he went crashing back into the wall. Rodrigo followed with a brutal assault. Gabrielle watched with her heart in her throat. She knew the measure of Rodrigo's swordplay, for she'd been bested by it herself. But from all that she could see, as ferociously as he fought, as honed was his skill, Hastings was matching him stride for stride.

They fought wordlessly for a time, each concentrating on the battle before him as the cannons continued to fire and men fought below along the shore. Then, as abruptly as it had begun, the cannon fire ceased. A deathly stillness settled over the dawn. For an instant, Rodrigo and Hastings paused, each sparing a glance out to sea. Rodrigo appeared startled, but a look of satisfaction settled on Hastings's features.

"Ah, reinforcements arrive," Hastings gloated.

Gabrielle glanced toward the harbor and saw an alarming sight. A small fleet of Royal Navy ships loomed on the horizon, headed toward the bay. She estimated seven ships before her startled gaze sought Rodrigo's face. It was Admiral Fulton's patrol. Sheer chance that he happened to pull into Zanzibar on this day.

Rodrigo instantly leaped from the balcony. "We have to get to the ships before they box us in," he said to her. Then, looking back up at Cullen, he commanded, "Jump."

Cullen froze.

Her breath coming in gasps, Gabrielle called up to him. "Cullen, jump."

"That's a long jump, Gabby," Hastings laughed. "I'd say there's a guaranteed broken leg in that jump."

"Don't listen to him, Cullen. *Jump.*"

"Jump like I did, boy," Rodrigo ordered. "Now, or we leave without you."

Still, Cullen seemed frozen in place.

Gabrielle glanced back at the harbor. The ships were coming closer. In a matter of minutes it would be too late to get into the longboats and row to their own vessels. "What's the matter with you?" she screamed at her brother. "Just jump!"

"Gabby, I can't," Cullen wailed.

"You can. We'll catch you. We'll break your fall."

When Cullen merely put his hands over his eyes, Hastings gave an evil cackle, glorying in his power to inflict pain. "He never was what the bard called 'made of sterner stuff,' was he?" Cullen turned his back on her.

"You bastard!" she cried.

"No, Gabby, you have that wrong. You and Cullen are the bastards, remember?"

Rodrigo gazed sternly at the approaching ships. "It's now or never, boy."

"Cullen, please. Rodrigo will help you. Just close your eyes and let yourself fall."

His face was awash with tears. "I can't, Gabby. I want to, but I can't move!"

She couldn't believe what was happening. She stood, stunned, staring up at him. Rodrigo grabbed her arm as Hastings threw back his head and laughed. In the distance, she could hear the sound of cannons again as the navy ships fired on their paltry fleet.

"We have to go," Rodrigo told her finally as she dug in her heels.

"I can't leave him."

Hastings crowed, "You heard the boy. That Ashton blood is not to be denied."

"He's not going to do it," Rodrigo said in a severe growl. "And there's no time for me to crawl back up and carry him down."

"No." She looked back at Cullen as Rodrigo dragged her away. She could see the utter helplessness in her brother's eyes. He wasn't coming. "Cullen, please . . . please . . ."

She lost track of what happened after that. Rodrigo towed her away, but she fought him every step, looking pleadingly into Cullen's eyes and screaming his name.

Somehow, they made it to the longboat. Somehow, the men rowed them to the ships. Somehow the sails were unfurled and they sailed away in time. In time to escape the Royal Navy's retribution. In time to see Cullen turn his back and reenter the sultan's chamber because he was too afraid to take the step to freedom.

When they were safely away, Rodrigo came to her and took her in his arms. But she broke from him, from the contact that might have soothed. Grabbing the nearest object at hand, she hurled it across the deck. The unlighted lantern crashed against the deck, scattering glass in all directions. "How could he do it!" she screamed. "How could he stand there and refuse our help? He's a coward. He's always been a coward. He *deserves* to stay!"

Suddenly she realized they were all looking at her. Every man on deck had stopped what he was doing and was staring at her as if she'd gone mad. Her anger and frustration were so intense she didn't care. If a hundred lanterns were lined up side by side, she'd have hurled them all, one by one.

It was a while before Rodrigo tried again. He gave her time to gather her breath. Then he tentatively joined her side. She didn't look at him. Her burning eyes were staring through the dawn, back toward Zanzibar, where this day both brothers had betrayed her in their own way.

For a while all she could do was stare out to sea. She felt the sea breeze, warm and cleansing, on her tear-streaked cheeks before she realized she'd been crying. Finally she glanced at Rodrigo. "It's finished," she said, feeling utterly defeated.

"No, Gabé," he told her evenly. "It's only just begun."

# Thirty-nine

Gabrielle fell into a dark depression. It lasted all through the voyage back across the Indian Ocean. All the time Rodrigo was setting up a new stronghold—fearful that his escape route to the Amirantes was cut off by the vigilante fleet. It all passed in a daze. She was numb, incapable of reacting to anything around her. It was as if the carpet of her life had been pulled out from beneath her, and she had lost the will to pick herself up from the shambles.

They were on Alphonse, an island just below the Amirantes, and a virtual graveyard of shipwrecks that had met their fate on its treacherous coral reefs. Hulks of brigantines still lay abandoned on the sandy beach, looming like ghosts from another era. The island had been nicknamed Dead Man's Reef by wary sailors. As such, it made a perfect hideout. It had been years since anyone had been foolish enough to try to navigate its shoals. Anyone but Rodrigo, who knew the island well.

The first order of business had been the building of thatched huts to house everyone. Long barracklike structures, open on the sides, were erected for the men, who slept in rows in the sand. A more private hut with walls was constructed for Gabrielle to share with Rodrigo. But sensing she needed to be alone, he kept his distance and often worked through the night.

During these weeks, Rodrigo had been vigorously training men for a new goal: an all-out attack on Mahé. He was determined that the only way to end this struggle, to wipe slavery out of his Seychelles once and for all, was a thrust to its depraved heart. To that end, he was building an armada. More ships and more men poured into his personal navy every day. Most of them were either freed slaves or idealists, but a fair number were experienced seamen who had heard of his audacity and just wanted to be part of a good fight. As these men filtered in, they were dispatched to recruit more men and commandeer more ships. Already, there was an imposing fleet of vessels in the natural harbor of Alphonse. It was menacing for Gabrielle to see the long row of masts and rigging bobbing in the tide. It looked like the preparations for the Battle of Trafalgar.

But one day Rodrigo walked away from this enormous undertaking and sought Gabrielle out on the beach. She had taken to spending long hours by herself on the south end of the island, away from all the hectic activity. It gave her some peace of mind just to sit in the sand and watch the giant land tortoises lay their eggs. The gentle leviathans were almost extinct on Mahé but were everywhere on this island, some of them as much as four feet in width. They seemed to have no fear of her. Once in a while, one would turn and spit at her, but it seemed to be more for show than anything else. She kept her gaze fixed on one as Rodrigo approached.

Without speaking, he sat down beside her, using his finger to draw a little frigate bird in the sand.

"I think it's time we had a talk about Cullen."

"Rodrigo, please—"

"It was a big jump. He didn't have it in him."

"You told me once that by overprotecting someone, you cut him off at the roots. Is that what I did with Cullen?"

"Perhaps."

"But he so obviously *needed* protecting. The Ashton men—"

"A pox on the Ashton men. You had expectations and Cullen met them."

"What do you mean?"

"He grew up knowing the Ashton men were weak. No one has to be a slave to his heritage."

She raised a brow. "Really? Look at you."

"There's a big difference. I embrace my role in life willingly."

She thought a moment then said, "So what do I do now? Give up on him?"

"The best thing you can do for him—the only thing —is to let him go. And see what happens."

She saw the inevitability of it all and made her decision. "Then I let him go."

"I'm proud of you."

She didn't respond. He, too, was quiet for some time. When he spoke, his voice was gentle, heavily inflected by his Portuguese accent, the way it was when he cared deeply about what he was saying. "I think you're ready to tell me your secret."

Her throat closed in on her. "My secret?"

"The one you spoke of before. The one Hastings promised not to tell."

She flinched as if he'd hit her.

"He did promise, didn't he?"

She dropped her head to her knees. Rodrigo was trying so hard to be understanding, but there was no way *any* man would understand what she now knew she had to tell him.

He tried again. "Didn't you point out to me how damaging it was of me not to trust you? That night before I sailed from England . . . if I'd trusted you, things would be different. I could have spared us both a great deal of pain."

A single tear trickled down her cheek. Mechanically, she brushed it aside. "I can't tell you."

"Please, Gabé. Don't make the same mistake I made. Trust me enough to know that nothing you tell me will affect my love for you. Nothing can make me leave you again."

"You don't know that. You imagine what you will, but whatever you imagine it's not as bad as what happened. It can't be. No one could imagine—"

When she broke off in a choke, he gave her a moment before asking softly, "Did he rape you?"

She jerked away from him, unable to bear his patient sympathy a moment more. "No," she sobbed. "How much better if he had. At least then . . ."

"At least then . . . ?"

She whirled on him, angry now at being forced into this, the one thing she'd hoped never to tell a soul. This secret, this wretched secret that Hastings—damn him to hell!—had sworn never to reveal.

"All right, you want to hear it? Then hear it in all its ugliness. At least if he'd raped me I might be able to live with it. I could have hated him for his brutality. But as it was . . ."

"How was it?"

She hurled her mind back to that fateful night when, devastated by Rodrigo's cold rejection, a younger Gabrielle ran from the boat up through the sloping fields of apple trees to hide herself in the barn of Westbury Grange. There, throwing herself into a pile of hay, she'd cried her heart out as the horses had whinnied softly in sympathy. She could still smell the tart odor of manure, the sweetness of the hay beneath her wet cheek. She was seventeen and she'd just lost, not for the first time, all she'd loved in life.

"I must have fallen asleep," she told Rodrigo, seeing it all in her mind's eye. "Something woke me. I remember feeling as if I'd been drugged. The pain, after my short sleep, was heavy and oppressive as I recalled our parting. It tore at my heart so I thought I couldn't bear it. Then I heard the soft breathing. Someone was there, with me in the dark. I realized what must have woken me. It must have been the opening and closing of the barn door. It was pitch-black. I couldn't see who it was. But he came to me as if he had cat's eyes, with no hesitation, and took me in his arms as if he had the right. And I remember thinking he smelled of the sea. And—"

She was choking on her tears now as they flowed hotly down her face.

"I thought it was *you*. I thought you couldn't bear the pain of how we'd parted any more than I. That you'd turned about on the road to London and returned to confide your plans in me after all. Then to have one last night of love before you sailed away. One beautiful memory to sustain us both."

For a time, she couldn't talk. The tears scalded her throat so that she was sure she couldn't go on. But he said nothing. She heard nothing but the sea rolling in to shore and an unearthly silence coming from the man she loved.

"I loved him that night with all the passion and heartbreak and love I wanted to give to you. And, feeling renewed, feeling strengthened, feeling that I could, after all, face your departure, I fell asleep in his arms. *In what I thought were your arms!*"

Needing a focus, she turned to watch the giant tortoise who was creeping across the sand with infinitesimal strides. Still, Rodrigo said nothing. She almost wished he would. She wished he'd bellow his outrage. Anything to halt this awful story before it was too late.

But of course it was already too late.

Taking a breath for courage, she went on. What did it matter now? "The next thing I knew, a small shaft of sunlight was awakening me. I remember opening my eyes and looking at it and thinking how beautiful it was. How lovely to wake up in your arms. I'd never done that, and who knew when I would again? I turned toward you with a feeling of bittersweet joy to kiss you awake. And realized with a—" Her voice cracked. The carefully honed voice of the actress, which was trained as an instrument never to fail her. "It was so horrible. How can I tell you? How can you ever conceive the horror of it? Of thinking I'd spent the night making love to you, and finding . . ."

She rubbed her forehead, which was by now pounding like a drum. "I was hysterical. I think I started screaming. He tried to hush me before I woke the whole household. He told me—" She sobbed and hid her face in her hands. "He said he *loved* me. He said, as he always has, that he never accepted Douglas as my father. He kept insisting we weren't related. That he wanted to *marry* me. And all this time, I just kept screaming and screaming. He kept his hand clamped against my mouth the whole time. And soon I began to realize that while I was hearing my screams in my own head, there was nothing coming out. No sound. Just this horrible need to scream out my pain, and not even the ability to do so. He wouldn't even allow me that."

She turned then and looked at him for the first time since she'd started telling the story. "Do you have any idea of the rage I felt? Not just against Hastings. But against you, for what happened to me. For not trusting me with your plans. For not taking me away from that awful place. I swore that day that I'd never rely on anyone else again. I never did. I roused Cullen from bed and took him to London that very day."

There were several moments of silence, in which she struggled to realize what she'd done. That in a burst of agony, she'd relieved herself of this awful burden. To the last person she had ever wanted to know.

"So you see, when you said I hadn't taken any other lovers, you were wrong. I took him *willingly*. That's what makes it all the worse."

Exhausted, she fell onto the sand, feeling drained of

words, of thoughts, of feelings. Drained of everything. It was over now. She'd just thrown away the last thing she loved in all the world.

He was so quiet, after a time she gave up expecting words. He'd digest it and, with the cold, private dignity he'd shown in England, would simply walk away. He'd have a man row her to Mahé. Back to Hastings. To shut out the pain, she focused on the sea, the endless rolling of the waves against the shore, the lap and retreat of the water, the whisper of the breeze. Life goes on, they seemed to promise.

But how? After this, how?

Eventually, she felt him crouch down by her side. "How," he asked in a voice raw with feeling, "could you think it would make any difference at all?"

Her startled gaze found his face. The face of a man who loved her, no matter what. Her heart raced a little, then cautiously slowed.

"You aren't appalled—"

"Appalled! Of course I'm appalled. Appalled that he took advantage of you. Appalled by what I did to you. But Gabé, you did nothing wrong. You turned to another man out of love, thinking he was me. I'm the one to blame."

"But he's not just another man. He's my—"

He put a hand to her mouth to cut her off, just as Hastings had all those years ago. "Maybe. It doesn't matter. You did nothing wrong."

New tears were flowing now, tears of gratitude and relief. "You're not angry? You don't hate me?"

"Hate you?" He gathered her up and pulled her into his warm, strong embrace. His arms seemed to tell her that nothing would ever harm her again. "If anyone is deserving of my hatred, it's Hastings. Not you."

She sobbed into his chest. "Oh, Rodrigo, I was so afraid. I kept asking myself, what would you think of me? I thought I couldn't bear it if you knew."

He pushed her away a little so he could look into her

tearstained face. "Listen to me, *caricia*. Hastings is the bane of our existence. I'm always underestimating him. I've always underestimated his capacity for evil. But no more. Together we shall beat him. You and I. We will triumph over his corruption. This I promise you with my life."

"I don't want revenge, Rodrigo. All I want is you."

They held each other for some time, quietly feeling the peace, the sense of sharing, seep into their shattered souls.

She took his hands in her fingers and kissed them.

"I want to leave all this. I want to go back to the Vallée de Mai. To live like Adam and Eve in the Garden of Eden."

"You know we can't do that now."

"Rodrigo, I'm so afraid that we've lost all we found there. That we can never get it back, unless we return to our magical valley."

He watched her quietly for some time. Then he asked unexpectedly, "Are you hungry?"

She took a moment to adjust. "Hungry? Hardly."

"Thirsty, then. It's sticky hot. Perhaps some cool wine."

"I don't—"

"Come, I want to show you something."

He took her hand and pulled her along, up a path that led to the interior of the island. It was quite a hike. By the time they'd stopped walking, she was so thirsty, his offer of wine was now welcome.

"We're here," he said.

They were standing before a cave. He gestured for her to lead the way. She could see nothing but darkness before her.

"*Where* are we?" she asked uncertainly. "There's nothing here."

"Ah, but you're wrong. This is the gateway back into Eden."

# Forty

"*It doesn't look much like Eden,*" she said as they entered the cave.

"It will," he promised, "before the afternoon is through."

He struck a flint against the rock wall and touched it to a lantern. It hadn't been lit in some time, so it sputtered and protested before spilling a warm, tawny, welcoming light into the cavern. Gabrielle let out an enchanted sigh.

Before her was an intimate grotto filled with aged bottles of wine. There were stacks of bottles, trunks of bottles, bottles piled high on all sides. In the midst of this unexpected wine cellar, beneath a sloping rock ceiling, was a mound of faded pillows, thickly covered in dust.

As she went to one wall to inspect the labels, Rodrigo picked up the pillows, took them outside, and shook them vigorously. When he returned, they were free of dust. The material was frayed with age, but some of its former rich color could be discerned.

Gabrielle was picking up bottle after bottle, holding their labels to the lamp.

"Do you know what you have here?"

"The finest collection of wine in the world, I would imagine."

"These are ancient. Here's a bottle of Madeira from 1703. And brandy from 1692. Rodrigo, what is this place?"

When she glanced at him, he was smiling at her enthusiasm. "*Meú avô* stashed his booty of wines here. He and his pirate *amigos* used to come here and drink their fill, lounging on the pillows you see, trying to top each other with seafaring tales. This collection was once famous all along these waters." He gestured with his arm, encompassing the whole cave. "Behold the buried treasure of *meú avô*."

In her mind's eye, she could see the pirates, scarves about their heads, rings in their ears, dressed in bright silks as they lounged back on the pillows, drinking their booty. "I can see them now. Telling tall tales and debauching women, no doubt."

"No. I'm the first to bring a woman here with the intention of—debauching her."

A thrill shot through her.

"Take your pick," he offered with a gracious gesture of his hand.

It was cool in the cave, so the wines stayed naturally chilled. She took some time rifling through the antique bottles, aware of his eyes on her backside when she bent to look. They seemed to burn through her clothes like a flame. She began to feel wet and steamy between her thighs—as steamy as the sultry tropical afternoon.

She selected a port, and Rodrigo opened the bottle and handed it to her. She glanced about as he chose the 140-year-old Maderia and popped the cork with his teeth.

"Did they bother with goblets, your pirate ancestors?"

He gave her a satirical look. "Do something really

forbidden. Something of which your most proper father would never approve. Drink from the bottle, *carícia*."

She put it gingerly to her lips and tentatively took a sip. When she looked up, he was scowling at her.

"It's not a serpent. It won't bite you."

She felt ridiculously tight inside. "It's always gone against the grain for me to do this," she explained. "Not because of my father. Once he rejected me, I never cared *what* he thought. But I remember my mother, in those last awful days before she shot the duchess. She was drinking a great deal in an attempt to drown her sorrows. She used to come home so befuddled, she swilled her liquor from the bottle without bothering to look for a glass. It's always seemed to me the very definition of unrestraint."

"That's the point," he told her. "Drink." He took the bottle in his own hand and tipped it so she had to drink. "Not like I've put a sword to your throat," he admonished. "*Com alegría. Com entusiasmo.*"

"With joy," she repeated. "With enthusiasm."

"Indeed. That's hundred-year-old port you're drinking. Not to mention, *meú avô* risked his life so you could drink your fill. Drink it as if you *enjoy* it. Savor it, Gabé, as you would savor life."

"How do you say 'savor'?"

"*Sabor.*"

"*Sabor*, then." And she tipped the bottle again and drank this time as if the liquid were ambrosia from the gods. As if she were carrying Rodrigo's very essence over her tongue and down her throat.

She drank down half the bottle in slow, extravagant gulps. When she removed the bottle from her lips, she felt slightly dizzy. She dropped back into the assemblage of pillows and lay sprawled before him, laughing. "It's rather fun at that." Raising the bottle high, she brought it back to her lips with dramatic flair and drank again.

Her giddiness made her sloppy. The wine spilled from her mouth, splashing onto her chin. It caused her to giggle, but before she could raise a hand to wipe it away, he pounced upon her with the reflexes of a lion, falling atop her to lick her chin clean with his tongue. A shudder jolted her to stillness. His lips hovered above hers, so close she could feel them, even though they weren't touching her own.

"I have a feeling that's not the only forbidden thing I shall be doing this day."

His eyes, smiling into hers, looked elusive. "Drink your wine."

"You're not perchance planning to inebriate me and then run off, as I did with you? Leave me here panting for you while you slip back to your duties?"

"Do I appear to you to be a man with plans?"

His body on hers was heavy, warm, absolutely exquisite. She moved beneath him and felt him harden against her belly. "You have a decidedly wicked yet enigmatic look about you. What are you thinking?"

"I'm thinking you've been in a fragile state of late. That I shall ask nothing of you that you're not ready to give."

His elusiveness was more intoxicating than the wine. She felt heady and breathless as his face began to shimmer like a mirage before her own.

"What—for instance—would you not ask of me?"

He considered her. "Were you not ready—for instance—I wouldn't dream of asking you for even so innocent a token as a kiss."

He propelled his bulk over her, pinning her against the pillows. Then his mouth descended on hers in a scalding kiss. When he shifted away, she had to grip his shoulder with her free hand to keep her grip on reality.

"So kind of you not to—overexcite me, in my delicate condition."

He reached for his own bottle and drank a few leisurely sips. When he set it aside, he brought his hand in one fluid motion to ease her skirt up her calf and over her knee. That knee bent of its own accord, like a lioness stretching in preparation to mate. Her heart stopped dead as he slid the soft material in a slow decline down her leg, his thumb playing havoc with her inner thigh.

"Oh, Rodrigo."

Slowly, he grazed his hand back along the path of her bent leg to her ankle. He looked up and met her eager gaze with a smoldering look of his own. Watching her, he took a single finger and drew it up the back of her calf and slowly, delicately, along the back of her thigh. So innocent, so uncalculated, as if he just wanted to feel her with the tip of his finger. Yet she felt as if dynamite had exploded within her, sending doubts and inhibitions flying with the debris of her bruised heart.

"I'd never, for instance, put my lips here, for I know what it might do." As he spoke, he kissed the sensitive inner flesh of her knee, sending chills reverberating through her. "Nor would I trail my tongue along your thigh." He did so, nibbling her inner thigh until she felt helpless to so much as lift her hand. Her head dropped back, her hair falling in a long sheath to the ground of the cave. "And even if I were so bold as to kiss you there, I'd never touch it with my finger, knowing what that might do to *me*." He stroked her thigh, where his lips had been, with the back of his finger. "Knowing how it would make me want to touch you here . . ."—his finger moved higher—"and here . . ."—higher still —"and even here . . ." He reached the nest of wet curls as she opened her legs to him, wide. Gently, he eased the curls away so he could see inside. Then he rounded the triangle of hair with one finger that barely skimmed her. The pressure was so light, she thrust herself against him, wanting more. But he slid away. "I'd never dream of touching you there." Again, he barely grazed her. It was the sweetest torture she'd ever known. She was crying out to be touched, but every time she moved toward his finger, it danced away. "Although I'd want to. *Deus* knows I'd want to. But even seeing how wet you are, I wouldn't dare touch you. Especially not here."

He touched her then, spreading her juices all along her as she cried out. But it was fleeting, so quick that it left her panting for more. She clutched at his hand, desperate to move it back, but he pulled it away.

It was thrilling. The fact that he wouldn't touch her made her want him so badly, she actually ached with need.

"I'd never lick you here," he said. "I'd want to, but I never would." Then he leaned over and licked her with one long slow swipe of his tongue.

Her breath caught in her throat. She was so galvanized by the contact, she felt every part of her throbbing with life. Her fingers itched to touch him. The tips actually felt as if they were flaring and retracting in their need. She'd never wanted anything or anyone more than she wanted him . . . now . . .

She thrust up and met his mouth, silently begging for more.

He leaned over her, his body punishing in its weight. "Will you do anything I ask?"

She felt the hesitation before she could keep it from showing.

"You still don't trust me," he admonished.

"I do. I want to. *Make* me trust you. Show me what you told me you would. Remember? Your graduation exercise? The thing Shayla taught you—the greatest of the love secrets of Zimbabwe . . ."

But he just smiled. "You're not ready."

Defiance flared in her eyes. "Then *get* me ready!"

He glanced at her bottle of wine. Taking it up, he held it to her lips. "Drink this."

She suspected he might want her drunk and more amenable, and she was willing to go along. She drank the wine, finishing it at his prompting. Her head was spinning by the time she was done.

He took the bottle away from her lips and ran his tongue along the opening, licking up the last drops of wine. Then he bent and put his tongue to her, as if comparing the taste of her to the wine. With a groan, he dug his tongue in deep. Then he lifted his head to tease her some more, but, looking at her, was overcome with his own need. Tossing the bottle aside, he grabbed her under her knees, jerked her flat on her back with a sudden savage yank that caused her heart to flare in her breast. Lifting her hips to his mouth, he dove in with his tongue. His head moved like a man starved for too long. The sensations he incited in her mingled with the wine to leave her light-headed and bemused. He reached up and thrust aside her top so his strong hand could squeeze and play with her breast.

She was so hot, she felt on fire. Her breath came rapidly, like blasts of flame. He lowered his weight onto her body again and, replacing his mouth with his hand, put his lips to her ear. "It's not easy to get ready for this," he said in a hushed, intimate voice. "You must lose all your restraints. Show me you have no resistance. Trust me completely. Totally."

She was electrified. She felt in that moment that she'd do anything—anything at all. Anything he wanted, anything he asked. He must have sensed it, for he reached over and took up the bottle again with his other hand. He put it to her mouth and said, "Get this wet."

She allowed him to guide the neck of the bottle into her mouth. As he moved it, she sucked it like an erection. It was oddly erotic. He let her suck it for a while as his tongue began its devastating play. Then he took it away, slid it once into his own mouth, then inserted it into the hot, pulsing core of her body.

She arched up with a moan that came from some primal place in her soul. As he plunged the bottle in and out, he replaced his tongue on her cleft. She could feel the bottle deep inside, moving like a man, but twice as hard. It sent jolts of pleasure and pain shooting through her, made her wild.

He replaced his tongue with his fingers and sat up a bit, watching her. She opened eyes misty from wine and desire and saw that he was watching her face. Embarrassed, she snapped them closed.

"Look at me, *carícia*," he coaxed. "Let me see your beautiful eyes."

She did. At first it was awkward. She couldn't quite meet his eyes. But he increased the thrusts of the bottle, and she forgot everything but the pleasure he was inflicting. She panted loudly, meeting his gaze, seeing the approval and arousal flaring in his animal eyes. "Come for me," he told her.

It was a supreme act of trust. To allow herself to lose control at his hands, not in a darkened room, but in the light of a primitive cave, with him watching her every move. With her eyes open, so she was aware of him watching her. His fingers moved on her, varying their rhythm, and he rammed the bottle into her so she couldn't think. Her mouth fell open and with her eyes locked on his, she relinquished control. She climaxed for him, and it was like nothing she'd ever experienced before. She couldn't stop. In wave after wave of ecstasy, she floated and burned. She was under his control completely. Held in the air by his masterful hand. And she felt that he'd never let her come down.

When at last she did, he gave her no time to rest. He was on her at once, withdrawing the bottle and replacing it with his own swollen erection. He was so much bigger that she gasped aloud, feeling filled and whole, as if the other half of her had just been replaced. As he began to move, she put her hands to the back of his head.

He kissed her passionately as she raked her hands through his hair. As he thrust into her she felt her head begin to swirl. She'd never been so aroused in all her life.

His mouth was at her breast. "I'm going to show you," he said, before his mouth claimed her nipple.

"Yes," she whispered. "Show me what Shayla showed you."

And he did. . . .

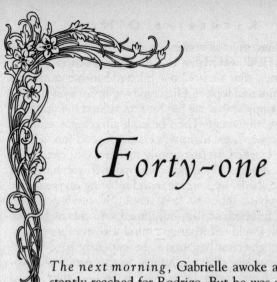

# Forty-one

*The next morning*, Gabrielle awoke and instantly reached for Rodrigo. But he was already gone. Looking out at the sun, she realized it was late. Almost noon. No wonder, she thought, smiling. Their lovemaking had continued for hours and hours. It was dawn before they'd drifted off to sleep.

She dressed, then went out into the blinding sun. Back at the encampment, Rodrigo was training his troops as if he hadn't spent the night giving her unimaginable pleasure. He couldn't have had more than two hours sleep, yet he seemed refreshed. She watched him for a while, watched the way his muscular body moved as he demonstrated with the sword, remembered the way it had moved over her the night before. Her heart wouldn't settle. It fluttered like a trapped butterfly in her breast. Feeling breathless and flushed, she saw some of the men eyeing her with secretive smiles. She must have looked like a woman who'd been thoroughly ravished the night before. She certainly felt like one. With her hair streaming down her back and her breasts still throbbing from the pressure of his hands, from the tickle of his tongue, with her face growing hot every time she thought about it . . . how could they not know?

Rodrigo felt her gaze on him, then paused and turned. He'd never been one to show affection in front of his men. But he held out his hand to her now. She ran to him and took it. She could see in his eyes that he was as happy as she. He put his arm around her and held her close a moment. Then he said, affecting a teasingly British tone, "Last night was cracking good fun, what?"

She laughed, feeling utterly joyous. "Oh, *cracking!*"

The day passed quickly. She spent it watching him from the shade, sipping water and nibbling on breadfruit and jambosa slices to keep cool. By sundown, they weren't finished, so they continued into the night. But Gabrielle could tell Rodrigo's mind was on other things. He kept glancing her way as he patiently tried to explain a concept that was foreign to the Africans' sensibilities. Every time he moved to leave, they asked another question and he was forced to reiterate.

She began to tease him every time he looked her way. To give him a coy smile or an inviting look. To run a hand along her breast ever so subtly, so it caught his eye for a moment before she stopped. She could see that he was becoming more and more distracted. When he looked down at the bulge in his pants and back at her, she threw back her head and laughed, relishing her power to arouse him, to take his mind off his work.

Finally, he broke away and told the men to have their supper. He came to Gabrielle and dropped next to her under a palm tree, lounging on his side with his long legs stretched out before him. Higgins brought them some fish on a leaf and they shared it with their fingers, intimately talking and kissing between bites. As the sky darkened, they could hear African drums in the distance. The new recruits were no doubt entertaining themselves.

"I feel like a fresh-faced lad in the first throes of love," he confessed.

"I don't."

He raised a brow and peered up at her.

"I feel like a woman who's just grown up. Who's just discovered all that love can be."

"Ah. But you've just *begun* to discover it."

He leaned over and kissed her so she fell back into the sand. His body pressed into hers, his lips claiming her own with a wild kiss. Her food forgotten, it slipped from her fingers as she brought her hand up to run it through his hair.

"And to think we owe it all to Hastings," she said, amazed that she felt free enough to speak lightly of something that had haunted her for so long.

He was instantly thoughtful. "I've been thinking about that. You know, Gabé, Hastings never mentioned this before. I know he promised he wouldn't, but it isn't like him to keep such a vow. He never threw it in my face, though he had ample opportunity over the years. Even in Zanzibar, he didn't speak until you so wounded him, he lashed out in pain."

"What are you saying?"

"You said once that he has no feelings for other human beings. And yet, I think he has feelings for you."

"He thinks he does. But what I said was true. Hastings doesn't know what it is to love. He's incapable of love. And I believe that thought is the one thing that scares him. That's why he lashed out at me the way he did."

There was a delicate sound above them, like the soft clearing of a throat. They looked up to find one of the Kikuyu elders standing there in his bright robes, waiting patiently for them to finish. The Kikuyu didn't approve of public displays of affection, and, even though the lovers were well-hidden by the dark, his censure was written on his face.

"Excuse me, *bwana*. These peoples say they are wishing to join your tribe."

Rodrigo frowned, confused. "Which peoples?"

"The Kikuyu. They are wishing to be part of your tribe."

"Tell them they're already part of my tribe." He turned back to Gabrielle.

"Excuse me, *bwana*, but they are seeing for themselves they are not being part of your tribe. They are seeing that some of your men have marks of honor on their backs. Glorious birds whose wings are raising in flight. These Kikuyu are proud, *bwana*. They are wanting such marks for themselves."

"Very well," said Rodrigo. "Another time."

"Excuse me, *bwana*."

With an exasperated sigh, Rodrigo sat up and said, "What is it? Am I to be afforded no peace?"

"These Kikuyu are awaiting your presence for the making of the ceremony."

"What . . . now?"

"They are knowing of such a ceremony, and they are wanting it for themselves. The Kikuyu are not waiting, *bwana*. They are needing your favor now."

Rodrigo sprang to his feet and followed the man up the beach. Gabrielle trailed close behind. Farther along, they began to see the blaze of a terrific bonfire. There, hundreds of men gathered, dancing in the moonlight and the glow of the fire to the beat of the drums. It was a sight of savage beauty, their black, muscular, sweat-gleaming bodies undulating to seductive rhythms.

When they approached, one of the Africans came forth and held out a wooden bowl with a long, protruding needle to Rodrigo.

Wallace came up to him and said, "I've tried to explain that they can't simply demand the ritual, but they won't listen. They refuse to take another step unless they're afforded the same rights as all the rest of us."

"It's a matter of honor," Rodrigo said thoughtfully. "Of respect."

Gabrielle thought back on the day she'd first seen this ritual. It had seemed barbaric to her, a thing of cruelty inflicted on those who didn't know to resist. A way of assuring their death if they were caught. But here, in the glow of the fire, beneath the moon and the African stars, she could see the beauty in it. These men wanted to show they belonged. They wanted the brand of the tribe on their flesh.

Rodrigo glanced at her. "The lady and I have plans for the evening . . ."

"No," she told him firmly. "You must do it. They've worked hard. They deserve this favor."

So Rodrigo turned the tools over to Wallace and sat with her on the beach to watch the proceedings. It transpired much as before, except it now seemed a ceremony of great majesty. The gleam of the beach in the moonlight, the lapping of the waves against the sand, the starlight, the flare of the fire, the mesmerizing beat of the drums.

Then it was over. The tattooed men were dancing. Wallace moved to douse the fire. Rodrigo got up to confer with him. They stood talking, silhouetted by the giant blaze.

Suddenly Gabrielle called out, "Wait!"

She rose. Then, walking forward with slow but steady steps, she lowered the back of her dress, and knelt before Rodrigo with her back to him. He hesitated.

"Are you certain?" he asked.

"I've never been more certain of anything. I know now what it is to be a slave. I, too, want to join your tribe, to offer my devotion, my loyalty, my life. To serve your cause by your side. I, too, want the favor of the brand of honor."

"You know what this means," he warned. "If you're ever captured, you can't pretend to have been kidnapped by me. It's well known I mark no one who isn't willing. This will prove you joined me with an open heart."

"I open my heart to you. Let them see the proof."

Wallace stepped in. "Are you sure, *Capitão*? It's a great deal to expect."

Rodrigo looked down at her in doubt. She said, "I do

this without question, with an open, loving heart. I pledge myself, body and soul."

"You understand what it means?" he repeated.

"It means I trust you completely."

Rodrigo moved around and met her eyes. She looked up at him with all her trust burning in her gaze. "It means there's no turning back," she told him. "I wouldn't if I could. I give myself totally by this, the ultimate symbol of commitment."

He smiled. "Some women would think the ultimate symbol of commitment was a wedding ring."

"I'm not other women."

"No," he agreed. "You're not."

For once, Rodrigo took the instrument in his own hand. As she knelt, waiting quietly, he went to the fire and heated the needle. Her heart beat in rhythm with the drums. He came back and handed her the rope to bite. But she shook her head. "Just let me hold your hand."

Tossing the rope aside, he moved behind her and held his hand out to her. She clutched it tight with both of hers. Then, taking a breath that filled her lungs, she said, "I'm ready," and let it out.

The prick of the needle was more painful than she could ever have anticipated. It continued its assault beneath her skin, again and again, until she thought she could bear it no longer. But he worked quickly, like an artist with a sure hand, and just as she thought the pain was too much, she began to transcend it. She was overcome with a feeling of joy so deep that tears of happiness flowed from her eyes.

She looked up and saw him standing over her in the firelight with eyes as moist as hers. She could see how moved he was by her display of devotion. And it made her love him all the more.

"*Mkombozi*," she said for all to hear.

Then she collapsed to the sand.

She felt a wet cloth at her wound. Then a cooling

salve was applied. It robbed her of a great deal of the sting. But she felt drained all the same. She felt her limp body lifted in Rodrigo's powerful arms. Felt herself being carried from the scene.

In their hut, he placed her gently on their makeshift bed. "I'll get you some grog," he said. "It will help the pain."

But she clasped his hand and wouldn't let him go. "It doesn't hurt. All I want is you."

He looked at her as if he didn't quite understand.

"Make love to me, Rodrigo."

He held himself in check. She could feel the effort he was making to be patient for her sake. She could also see that her act of trust had aroused him greatly. "I don't want to hurt you."

"Only your refusal could hurt me now."

He didn't refuse. More tenderly than she'd ever seen him, he took her in his arms and made love to her with long, slow, hard thrusts. As if each was a measure of his own devotion, to be dragged out and savored. Hushed, intimate. *Wonderful*.

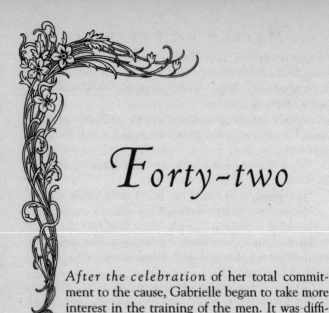

# Forty-two

*After the celebration* of her total commitment to the cause, Gabrielle began to take more interest in the training of the men. It was difficult, because she didn't understand the language.

During the day, Rodrigo usually spoke Swahili—which was the *lingua franca* of the African coast. It was an extraordinarily melodious and joyful-sounding language. But though she derived great pleasure from listening to it, gradually, she began to feel excluded, and, from the worried tones, to sense that some ominous new element had been introduced into the drama.

One afternoon, one of Rodrigo's Seychellois spies returned from Mahé and reported some information that set Wallace arguing in soft but explosive tones with Rodrigo. As she happened by, they switched from English to Swahili. When she asked Rodrigo later what the fuss was about, he sloughed it off as "a difference of policy." He would say no more.

The next day, she went to Wallace as he was sitting in the shade, eating freshly grilled marlin from a large shell. When he saw her, he gestured for her to sit beside him in the sand.

She smiled. "You've been with Rodrigo a long time, haven't you?"

"Long time, lassie. Five years. He took me off a prison ship five days out of Capetown. I was an officer in a Scottish regiment serving at the pleasure of King George. You see, lass, I'd borrowed some funds from the regimental treasury to pay a pressing gambling debt."

"I get the feeling you know him better than anyone."

"Except yourself, maybe."

His words pleased her. "Instinct tells me something's happened. Something I don't know about."

Wallace didn't respond to this. He set his fish aside and rubbed his hands together like a man reluctant to speak. They were dry, and the rustling sound of them scraping together made her cringe. She stared at the shell with the half-eaten fish, looking pearly white against the glimmer of sun-drenched sand.

"I saw you arguing yesterday," she persisted.

"Mayhap you should be asking the captain."

"I'm asking you."

He glanced at her as if wondering whether to tell her the truth. "Well, lass, you're bound to hear it sooner or later. It seems word of our preparations has reached Mauritius. Admiral Fulton is bringing in the entire British fleet from India to protect Seychelles. Twenty fully armed men-of-war."

"Twenty?"

"Aye, lass."

"Then Rodrigo's got to stop. He must give up his plans."

"That's what I've been telling him. But he won't hear of it. He's decided the only way to oust your brother and his dirty compatriots is an all-out war, winner take all. Now or never. No turning back."

A chill swept through Gabrielle. She'd always felt this coming. "But there's no way he can win. He can't take on England herself!"

Wallace shrugged. "He thinks he must. Normally he's a more cautious man, but his mind is set."

"There must be a way to stop this," she said.

"If there is, I don't know what it would be. God knows, I've tried."

"You could refuse to follow him."

"That, lassie, I would never do."

She couldn't let this happen. But what to do? She felt adamantly that he was taking the wrong course. But she knew her lover well. Well enough to realize he wouldn't be swayed by sentiment. What she needed was a concrete strategy that she could lay before him, complete and logical. Something so obvious, he couldn't choose any other path. She thought of all she knew about the situation. Hastings's involvement. Rodrigo's aims. The stories she'd heard of people in England fighting the same issue on a more abstract scale . . . the antislavery society . . . Thomas Fowell Buxton . . . the issue in Parliament over the statute of Negro emancipation.

And suddenly, she had her idea.

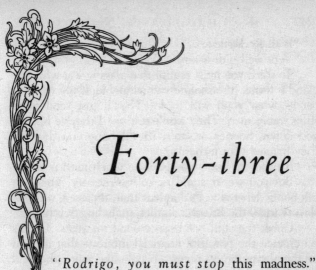

# Forty-three

"*Rodrigo, you must stop* this madness."
She'd taken hold of his arm and pulled him
around to face her as he was in the midst of a
conversation with Higgins and Jonah Fitch. He
turned and glared at her as if he couldn't believe what
she'd just done.

"You can't go on with this. It's suicide."

"You've been talking to Wallace, I presume."

"Something I should have done long before."

"We'll talk about this later."

"No, we need to talk about it now."

"Not in front of the men."

"But I have an idea. Something that will put an end
to this war and give you everything you want without
losing the life of a single one of your men."

"I'd hear 'er out, Captain," said Jonah Fitch. "Her
ideas are outlandish, I'll grant you that, but they usually
get the job done."

"Well, if *you* say so, Mr. Fitch, then naturally," Rodrigo said in a faintly sarcastic tone.

They left the others and walked toward their
thatched hut on the beach. "This must be quite an
idea."

"It is, Rodrigo."

"Very well. I'm listening."

"To start, you must realize that waging war with England is futile. It's absolutely unwinnable. If you win this battle, what good will it do? They'll just send more ships, more men. They won't rest until they've hunted you down. Sooner or later, they'll hang you the way they hanged your father."

"It's nice to know you have so much faith in me."

"But you see, it could be so unnecessary. There's a bill being debated in Parliament that, if passed, will ban slavery in all the British colonies, including Seychelles."

"Gabé, that bill has been around for years. There's no chance the powerful financial interests that depend on the plantation economy—people like your father and his friends in Parliament—are going to let that statute ever become law."

"Rodrigo, in the last two years, an avalanche of reforms has swept over England. That bill is coming to a vote in the next session. It's all anyone in Mahé is talking about."

He mulled over her words. He held the thought a moment, then rejected it. "It'll never pass. The fight is here, not there."

"You may tell yourself what you will. I'm telling you this battle must be fought in London. If you want to win, sail with me for England. Do what you can to influence Parliament. There's a man there, a Mr. Buxton, a powerful man who's spent his life fighting for the abolishment of slavery. We can go to him and tell him all we know. We can tell him about Hastings and Douglas and their friends in Parliament. Tell them about the underground slave trade. How British officials and officers of the East India Company are involved. Don't you see? The scandal alone will ensure that we're heard. This will be a tremendous boon to the antislavery forces. They've been waiting for just such evidence to tip their hand. We'll help them get this law passed. But it has to be done now, Rodrigo. If they deny the bill, it will be years, perhaps decades, before they consider it again."

"As if they'd listen to a pirate over a duke."

"If you don't see the logic of this idea, then all those years you spent studying England's legal system were in vain. You learned to think like us. Use it against them. Use your intellect instead of your sword. Douglas is always complaining how you took the education he financed and turned it against him. For the love of God, for those you seek to protect, do so on a higher order. Beat them at their own game."

He just shook his head. "You're dreaming. Were I to show up in England, they'd hang me on sight."

"No. I just told you, there are people in Parliament who need you. They'll protect you. You have to trust them." She paused a moment and added more quietly, "You have to trust *me*."

He met her gaze and saw the challenge in her eyes. "It's not a matter of trusting you. It's a matter of doing what's right."

"It's a matter of doing the intelligent thing. The thing that will work. And I'm telling you, Rodrigo, if you wage war you haven't a chance. You might as well slit your own throat. But if you go to England, you can win."

"My battle is here, Gabé," he said firmly.

She thought for a moment, wondering if she should voice her thoughts. "If you refuse this sensible course of action, then maybe I should go to Hastings and attempt to talk some sense into *him*. He can't really want this war. And you yourself said he must . . . care for me. Perhaps I can persuade him—"

He turned on her in anger. "If you think I'd let you go to him, you're mad. He's not someone you can deal with on those kinds of terms. No matter what his feelings are, underneath it all he's evil. I've always underestimated him in the past. Don't make the opposite mistake. Don't overestimate him."

Angrily, she retorted, "Then at the very *least*, let's go to Admiral Fulton and present our case. I've heard he's a fair man."

"Gabé, sometimes you're so naive."

"You stubborn, short-sighted—" She checked herself from going further.

He was still for a moment. Then he said, "I'm sorry. But what you're suggesting is a pipe dream. Strategy is not what you're good at. You must leave this to me."

"I see." She stood up and started to pace, sweeping her arm angrily as she spoke. "I'm supposed to trust you so completely that I allow you to mark my flesh to prove my devotion. But when I ask you to trust me—"

"It's not the same thing!" he roared.

She felt as if she were seeing him with newly awakened eyes. "You don't trust me. You've *never* trusted me. You want me to trust you with everything, but the first time I ask for your trust in return, you refuse. I'm *right* about this, damn you! I grew up listening to Company officers discussing politics as I served their meals. I know how they think, and how they work. And I know that the way to win this war is to go to England and change this law. Whatever we have to do to get there, however dangerous it might be along the way."

"It's rash and impulsive, just like you."

"It's a way to *win*—if that's what you really want to do. But maybe that's not what you want. Maybe you're just in this for the glory. Maybe what you really want is to be killed in battle, so people will write folk tales about the great *Mkombozi* who *died* fighting for his cause!"

"I won't be spoken to in this manner," he raged.

"Then you won't be spoken to at all. You've betrayed me, Rodrigo. You ask of me what you're not willing to give. If I could, I'd scratch the brand from my back and throw it in your sorry face!"

Later that night, she crept to Jonah Fitch's bed and shook him awake, hushing his protests.

"I have a mission for you," she whispered. "We're going on a journey."

"Will you be going as a man or woman, ma'am?"

"You're taking me to Mahé. And I'll be going as myself."

# Forty-four

Gabrielle stood with Jonah Fitch behind the frangipani trees of State House, awash in their perfume, watching the shadows flit by the lighted windows of the residence. It was night, and a party was in full swing. The music drifted out on the hot breeze from an open veranda. They could hear the chatter and laughter of the guests.

One of those guests was Admiral Terence S. Fulton, the earl of Coventry. He'd sailed into Mahé a week ago with the seven Royal Navy men-of-war he'd taken to Zanzibar, which now lay anchored in Mahé's harbor. More ships were due to arrive from India any day.

Gabrielle spared a final moment before walking boldly inside.

"I can't say I'm comfortable with the prospect of ye walkin' into the viper's pit," her faithful companion grumbled in low tones.

"I'm banking that the circumstances will serve to defang the viper. Admiral Fulton is my security. He's not affiliated with Hastings in any way. He's known to deplore slavery of any sort. He can have no wish for a war of this size. If I can get to him, tell him what Hastings has been doing, convince him of Rodrigo's honor, then I'm sure he'll become our savior."

"That might take a powerful performance, ma'am."

She straightened her shoulders. "That's what I do best, Mr. Fitch."

"Indeed you do, ma'am," he agreed.

"Now listen up. If something happens, if Hastings somehow prevents me from getting to the admiral, I'm counting on you to go to him, tell him I'm here, and that Hastings has me prisoner."

"That I will, ma'am. You can count on me."

The door was opened by Robert, the tall, white-gloved African who saw to the running of the house. He bowed to her, then, when he recognized her, appeared startled. He cast a quick glance back over his shoulder, as if warning her away. She sensed his sympathy. Word traveled fast on these islands. It was said the Africans always knew things without being told.

As if reading her thoughts, the butler asked softly, *"Mkombozi?"*

"He's safe. But he won't be for long. Not if I can't speak to Admiral Fulton."

"Take care, *Umbu*. The governor is here."

"What was that you called me. *Umbu?*"

"It means 'sister,' *Umbu*."

She was so touched, she reached for his hand and gave it a squeeze. But he drew away at once, casting another worried glance over his shoulder.

"What's your name?" she asked.

"I'm called Robert."

"No, I mean what's your real name?"

He squirmed uncomfortably. It was forbidden in Hastings's house for a slave to speak his or her real name. "Kaninu, *Umbu*," he whispered.

"Kaninu, is my room still in readiness?"

"It is, *Umbu*. Your belongings have been left as they were when you departed."

"Can you sneak me up there without anyone knowing?"

"I believe so, *Umbu*."

"Then do so. I have to face the admiral tonight, and I want to be dressed for the part. I return to this house not as a beggar, but as the daughter of a duke."

Quickly he led her to her room and had a tub of hot water delivered. She soaked in the tub, washing the salt and sand from her skin and hair. As her hair dried, she perused her closet and chose her outfit with care. The frocks looked like the wardrobe of another woman—so stiff, so formal, so uncomfortably binding. The clothes women wore when they were slaves to fashion, and other peoples' ideals.

Her former maid, Maya, was sent to her to help her dress. Maya chatted away as she fitted her with layer after layer of confining material. A corset. A chemise. Yards of petticoats. Then embroidered silver satin with a full skirt and train that weighed twenty pounds. By the time Gabrielle was dressed, she felt trussed up like a Christmas goose, stuffing and all.

But Maya's words distracted her from her discomfort. She told of how all the slaves knew of *Mkombozi*'s efforts on their behalf. How they knew the white rebel girl had run away to fight by his side. She knew Gabrielle had been to Africa. She knew everything, it seemed. She even fingered the mark of the frigate bird in flight on the back of Gabrielle's right shoulder. She didn't say anything, but Gabrielle understood she knew the significance of that as well.

"All will aid *Mkombozi*," she told her.

As she was finally ready, her hair piled atop her head in sensual curls, the jewels gleaming at her throat and wrists, Kaninu reentered the room. Excitedly he said, "Now is your chance, *Umbu*. The governor is in his den. The admiral is in the drawing room. If you go to him quickly . . ."

But as she looked at herself in the mirror one last time, she was overcome with a sudden strange pity for her half brother. She thought of Rodrigo's words: *He must love you very much indeed.* Could there be something in his seemingly worthless soul worth salvaging? Didn't he deserve one last chance to evade the noose that was at the end of her plan? In spite of Rodrigo's warning, she felt she must try to reach the one last vestige of goodness that he might have left. She knew if anyone could reach it, she was the one.

"Kaninu, go to the governor and tell him I want to see him."

"But *Umbu!*"

"Go now."

She entered the den only moments after Kaninu announced her presence. Hastings stood there with two of his henchmen. He looked severe in black evening clothes, his black hair slicked back, his tailoring as impeccable as if he'd just returned from Bond Street back home. Only the jittery fluttering of his eyes hinted at his sinister character. There was a bit of the actor in him as well. He could convince anyone he was the perfect English gentleman, biding his time in the tropics while waiting to take his rightful place as the duke of Westbury.

His eyes flicked over her, taking in her appearance. "I must say, dear Gabby, you seem to have an infinite capacity to surprise me. Has our old friend Roderick sent you packing?"

"I shan't keep you long, Hastings. I'll make my business brief."

"We have business?"

"I've come with dove in hand."

"It's an improvement, I must say, on wielding a saber beneath my nose. But tell me, what prompts this sudden charitable gesture?"

"Because underneath all this, we're family. I thought perhaps we could make a peace."

"You know perfectly well I don't accept you as family. God only knows how many men your mother took to her bed."

With great effort, she suppressed her wrath, assuming

a calm and rational tone. "I've been doing a great deal of thinking since we last met. I've realized that I've been wrong about many things in my life. I was wrong about Rodrigo. I was wrong about Beau Vallon. And I was probably wrong to raise poor, dear Cullen the way I did . . ."

"Is there a point to this maudlin story?"

"So, I thought there might be some off chance that I was wrong about you as well. That you might have a streak of decency in you somewhere."

Hastings perched his hip on the windowsill and crossed an ankle over the other knee. "What *are* you saying, Gabby? Haven't you learned yet to come to the point?"

"The point is, I've come here to offer you a way out of a desperate situation."

Hastings looked at his henchmen and chuckled. "Do I look like I'm in a desperate situation, gentlemen?"

"You will be when I get to Admiral Fulton and tell him what I know about you," Gabrielle stated.

Hastings grew quiet a moment, then said to his henchmen, "Step outside for a moment. Stay by the door. I shall call you if I need you." When they'd closed the door, he turned back to her and said, in a serious tone, "What is your offer?"

"Stop all your slaving activities. Give a pardon to Rodrigo. Give him back his home on Fregate."

"And what do I get in return for all this charity?"

"The knowledge that you've prevented a war. And our vow of silence regarding your nefarious activities."

He considered her for some time. There was a different look on his face than she'd ever seen before. A softer, more open expression. "You've touched me tonight, Gabby. I'm taken off guard."

Hope leaped in her heart. "Oh, Hastings, if only you'd listen to reason about this. If only for once in your life you could make a grand, magnanimous gesture."

He seemed to be struggling with his decision. She moved closer, took his hand in hers.

"And what if I were to say to you, my dear Gabby, that I would do all this, but I ask one thing in return? Do you love him enough to make the ultimate sacrifice?"

She snatched her hand away. "Don't be disgusting."

"What if that's the only way you could save his life? By giving yourself to me?"

"And if I said yes, what would you do?"

"We'll never know until you give me your answer. I may take you up on it and let your lover go. And then again . . ."

When he didn't finish, she prompted irritably, "Then again—?"

"Then again, I may just pity you for your vanity and laugh in your face."

"You despicable cad! I was right about you all along. You *are* diseased."

His face darkened. "That's enough!"

"Oh, far from it! You're a monster. You never cared about anyone."

"I cared about *you*," he shrieked. "I came to you and gave you my love and you spat in my face!"

She'd never seen him lose his composure so completely. It took her a moment to formulate her next words. "Well, dear brother, now's your chance to prove it. If you really love me, Hastings, if you care for me as deeply as you've professed over the years, do as I ask. Not for your own personal gain. Not because it will benefit you in any way. But because you love me. And because, underneath it all, you really do have a human heart."

She could see the emotions battling across his face. Slowly, he went to the door and opened it, gesturing his henchmen in. He looked back at her thoughtfully, regarding her with watery eyes, as if moved by her words.

Then, smiling suddenly, showing pointed teeth, he turned to his men. "Lock the bitch up."

His henchmen moved on her as Hastings walked away. She began to struggle, her surprise aiding them in securing her. She called to Hastings, but he kept walking.

At the door Hastings paused and added, "And lock up that scum we found lurking outside. That Jonah Fitch."

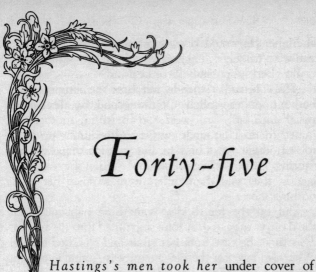

# Forty-five

Hastings's men took her under cover of darkness up the hill from State House to Grand Trianon, an old French plantation house overlooking L'Establishment—and the home of one of Hastings's French benefactors.

She was placed in a top corner bedroom with the door locked behind her and a guard posted outside, to spend a sleepless night trying to formulate a plan.

The next morning, she was up before dawn. Clouds had gathered on the mountaintops and it began to rain. Undaunted, the contingent of guards stationed out front kept their vigil, obviously taking no chances on her escaping. She could hear the sounds of the household downstairs—maids cleaning, voices calling to one another as if they didn't have a prisoner cloistered above.

She settled in to wait. Hastings would have to make the first move, and like any good actress, she'd take her cue from him. She spent her time asking the same questions over again. Why was he keeping her locked away on this hill? To keep her from Admiral Fulton, no doubt. But why such a collection of guards? Even if there was anyone to report to Rodrigo, it would take three days for word to reach him, and for him to arrive at Mahé. He would know Hastings was setting a trap, and wasn't likely to obligingly walk into it. What, then, could Hastings possibly have in mind?

She courted patience by watching the activity of the harbor from her window. On the second day, three more naval ships sailed into port. On the third, another two joined them. That made twelve frigates lining up to go roust Rodrigo out of his den. But still, Hastings kept her waiting. He didn't even send word. When she asked the guards, they said their orders were to keep her here, nothing more.

But on the fourth day, something happened that she'd never expected. A lone ship sailed into the harbor. This time she rose from her chair and clutched the sill of her window. For the new vessel was Arabic in design, sleek and beautifully arrayed. On its bow were painted the words *El Paraiso Segundo*. Rodrigo's ship.

But what was it doing sailing boldly into Mahé harbor in defiance of twelve naval frigates?

The sight of the ship stunned her. She'd never expected rescue, yet it appeared Rodrigo was taking action after all. Perhaps it was a ruse. To throw them off guard while he slipped in and carted her off. It was clever, she'd grant him that. Hastings would rush to the harbor, thinking he had his old enemy at last, and meanwhile Rodrigo would be snatching Gabrielle behind the governor's back.

As she watched, the pirate ship fired a single volley. Then, after a moment, a white flag was raised. A flag of surrender.

There was a flurry of activity in the harbor. An English longboat sailed out toward the pirate ship. Meanwhile, she could see carriages leaving State House for the harbor. A skiff rowed from *El Paraiso* to the British longboat. They stayed together for a while, then the longboat returned to the harbor.

After some time, a carriage pulled into the driveway. There was a knock on the door and some voices below.

Then she heard boots on the stairway. They came down the hall toward her door. *Rodrigo!*

The lock was sprung and she rushed to the door. But on the threshold, she stopped. For it wasn't Rodrigo who stood in the hall. It was the contingent of Hastings's guards.

"What's amiss?" she asked, alarmed.

"We've orders to take you to the harbor," one of them explained.

"The harbor? Why?"

"We don't know, miss. The governor sent word, that's all we know."

Hastings. Why would Hastings order her to the harbor? And where in bloody hell was Rodrigo?

They took her down the stairs and ushered her into the carriage. The ride through the lush greenery was lost on her as she tried to figure out what was going on.

When they arrived at the harbor she saw at once what had happened. Admiral Fulton stood on the dock conferring with some of his officers. And beside him was the man they called the Liberator in irons.

"Rodrigo!" she gasped.

His head came up at the sound of her voice. But they weren't the eyes of a captive she beheld. They were the eyes of a lion, fully in charge, knowing what he was doing every step of the way.

Suddenly she understood. He'd raised the white flag himself. He'd given himself up!

His steady gaze seemed to assure her that all would be well. But there was something more. A look that told her all she needed to know. That his giving himself up was an incredible act of trust. Of saying he'd trust that she was right. He'd risk his life and all he'd worked for as an act of faith. To show her he believed in her, as he'd asked her to believe in him.

She was so moved, she took a step toward him, but Hastings blocked her way. When she glanced at her half brother, she could see by his face that he was furious. It made no sense to her. He should be pleased. Wasn't this what he wanted—to see Rodrigo in chains?

"What's happening?" she asked.

"Your lover has just given himself over to the admiral," Hastings ground out between clenched teeth. "He's made a bargain for himself. He's turned himself in to be tried in England for piracy."

"And the admiral agreed?"

"Yes, damn it."

"And me?"

"He told the admiral you were my *guest*. After all the pains I went through to keep your presence here unknown."

"So we're both to be tried in England?"

He turned vengeful eyes on her. "Don't think I don't know what he's up to. He thinks to use the trial as a sounding board to influence Parliament in the passing of the Emancipation Bill. But it won't do him any good."

She looked past him at Rodrigo, standing tall and proud, looking straight into her eyes with a calm and confidence that made her heart skip a beat. It was what she'd wanted—for him to go through legal channels to avoid a war. She understood his reasoning, and how clever was his plan. Admiral Fulton would be fair. He'd see Rodrigo was granted as fair a trial as was possible for a pirate of his stature. The publicity of his capture would ensure that the antislavery factions heard his case. She prayed it would go this way. If not, she would bear the responsibility for what happened.

As if reading her mind, Hastings added, "What you'll get for your pains is a fast trial and a hangman's noose—both of you. I'll see to that. You see, sister dear, I've convinced the admiral to allow *me* the honor of escorting you back to England."

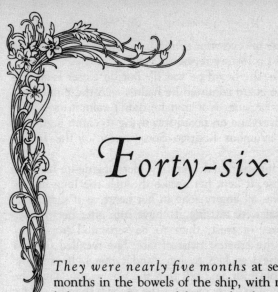

# Forty-six

They were nearly five months at sea. Five months in the bowels of the ship, with no daylight, no air. Separated from each other with no life but the life of their own thoughts. With no visitors allowed, except the guards, who brought them food twice a day and were warned to keep their distance.

For Gabrielle, it was, in the beginning, the worst kind of torture. Not that they mistreated her. She was given the best food the ship could offer. Fresh fruits and vegetables were provided in the earlier months as they provisioned along the coast of Africa. She wasn't manacled—she was allowed to move about her cabin at will. As time passed, the guards even chatted with her a bit, telling her what the weather was like, describing the blue of the sky.

But she had no idea where Rodrigo was, or if he was all right. When she questioned the guards they were vague. She received sketchy rumors but had no way of ascertaining if they were true. She did learn he wasn't afforded the same mobility as she. They'd chained him like a wild dog. A guard was posted near him at all times. The story of how he'd seized his first ship was foremost in everyone's mind. They were taking no chances on history repeating itself.

Once, she heard he was ill. But on closer examination, the guard admitted he hadn't seen the pirate, and couldn't be sure. Not that he didn't want to see him, mind. Everyone on board was dying to catch a glimpse of the infamous Rodrigo Soro, terror of the Indian Ocean.

She missed him desperately. Her longing for him was so intense, it kept her awake through the long nights. There was an empty ache in her heart, as if something elemental were missing. To have him offer her this supreme act of trust, then to be separated from him, seemed the cruelest twist of fate. She recalled the last words she'd spoken to him, and cringed. If only she could hold him, and tell him she was wrong. That she knew he didn't care more for the acclaim than he did for peoples' lives. How could she have said such a dreadful thing?

But sometimes, in the dead of the lonely night, she felt his forgiveness. Sometimes, if she imagined hard enough, she felt that he came to her. That he was there with his arms tightly about her, holding her close to his chest. She could feel his love and comfort embrace and warm her, and make her whole. Finally, feeling his presence strongly, she would fall asleep in his arms.

Still, it was agony, living in the cell of her own active mind. There was no way to find out where he was. A guard was posted outside her room during the day and much of the night. He was free to come and go as he pleased, opening the door to check on her periodically at any hour. If she dropped something, the key would turn in the lock and the door would swing open. The lack of privacy was horrifying at first. She felt like a laboratory specimen, being kept for observation. She wondered at the sense of it. Surely they didn't think she could break down the door and escape? It was a month or more before she discovered the reason.

Late one night, when the guard was no doubt asleep outside her door, she was awakened by some sound. Confused, she lifted her head from the pillow and listened. She'd just decided she was dreaming when it came again. A soft tapping from the side wall.

At first she thought it must be rats. She clutched the covers to her and nearly called for the guard. But then it came again, in the same rhythm as before. This wasn't accidental. Someone was rapping purposely on her wall.

Throwing back her covers, she padded across the wooden floor in her bare feet. The sound came again, low on the wall, as if from someone in the next cabin. She crouched on the floor and it came once more. Softly, almost imperceptibly, in the exact cadence as before. Reminding her of an African drum.

Then she knew why she was so closely watched. Rodrigo was being held in the next cabin. Chained to the floor, no doubt, without any thought to his comfort. Her heart broke for him. To think of him so close, just on the other side of the wall . . .

The tapping came again and she put her hand to the bulkhead, as if she could feel his fingers against the wood.

"Rodrigo!" she called softly. The tapping stopped. She called again, *"Rodrigo!"*

Suddenly the key turned in the lock. She wheeled around as a shaft of light pierced her eyes and the guard stood like a demon in the threshold of her door.

"What goes on here?" he demanded.

She wasn't an actress for nothing. Instantly, she clutched her nightgown to her and began to pant in heaving breaths, willing herself into a hysterical state.

"I heard thunder!" she cried.

He cocked his head. "I didn't hear it. No, there's no storm expected. Not tonight."

"But I heard it, I tell you! I can't abide thunder. Ever since I was a little girl and my father beat me during a thunderstorm. I shake in my bed every time there's a storm."

He came into the room. "You must have dreamed it," he said, soothing now. "There's no thunder tonight."

She backed away from him and banged against the wall, in case he'd heard the tapping. He'd assume she'd done the same thing earlier. With tears streaking her cheeks, she kicked her legs at him, then clutched herself into a trembling ball.

"There, there, Miss Ashton. You're imagining things. It's the being without daylight for so long, I'll warrant. Maybe I can get permission for you to go topside now and again. Would you like that?"

Like a child, she looked up at him and nodded.

"Good. Then let's get you back to bed, now, and be done with childish imaginings."

As he settled her into the covers, she knew she'd made an ally.

But the minute he was gone, she leaped out of bed, dried her eyes, and ran back to her place on the floor. Very softly, she tapped out the rhythm she'd heard. But all was quiet on the other end. Rodrigo must have heard the commotion and decided to spare her any more danger.

She put her hand to the spot where his must earlier have been, and rested her cheek against the wall, willing him to feel the comfort, the love she was sending his way.

There was no more tapping for a fortnight. When it came again, she refrained from calling out to him, realizing she'd be overheard. Instead, she repeated the rhythm and waited for his reply. When it came, she sank back against the wall in relief. He was all right. He was communicating with her. She could actually feel him on the other side of the wall.

It was agony not to be able to call out to him. Knowing he was so close, yet so far out of reach. She began to live for those taps, when she knew he was thinking of her, wanting her to feel his love. She didn't dare instigate the transmission. She had no idea when he was guarded. If her knocking was overheard, he'd likely be severely punished and moved so he couldn't call on her again.

Halfway through the voyage, she was awakened one night by a different sound. Instead of tapping, this was a scraping sound. Like a chisel scraping against wood. It took her only moments to realize that Rodrigo must have fashioned a tool of some kind, and was attempting to scrape a hole in the wood. It was so bold, she felt a chill sweep through her. If he was caught, there would be serious consequences to bear.

The scraping came infrequently over the next weeks. Obviously, he wasn't alone much. Sometimes she'd only hear it for minutes at a time. They developed a code. If the key turned in her lock, she'd quickly rap twice on the wall and Rodrigo would cease his work. When the guard left, she'd tap only once in case his guard had returned. Often, by the time her watchdog had left, it wasn't possible to resume.

It was an excruciatingly slow process. But it consumed her thoughts, waiting for the sound of him on the other side of the wall. Wondering if she'd hear from him that night, or—as she often did—have to wait a week or two at a time.

She had decided to help him. At every meal, she'd looked for an opportunity to purloin a knife, even a spoon. It wasn't easy. She was watched like a hawk as she ate while the guard chatted away. He never told her anything important. He never gave her information about Rodrigo. But she knew everything she had to. He was alive. He was thinking of her. He was coming to her, bit by bit.

Finally, she was able to slip a butter knife into her sleeve when the guard removed his boot to scratch his itching foot. She held it to her, feeling the cold, accusing steel against her feverish skin. As he took the tray, she was certain, from the way it seemed to burn a hole in her sleeve, that he would feel its heat. But he left without ever noticing it was missing.

So she began aiding Rodrigo in their common cause. She was always at the ready, waiting to hear him first before joining in. The first time it happened, she heard him pause. Then, as if understanding, he continued to scrape with renewed vigor. They scraped together in earnest until he tapped to let her know someone was coming. Then she'd settle in to wait again.

Those were her happiest times, when they worked together. The many hours when she waited seemed lonely and intolerable by comparison. But it occupied her mind, kept her thinking of the future. In those months, she could think of nothing else.

Occasionally Hastings came by to taunt her. "I hear your lover suffers," he'd say. "That he pines away. For you or his freedom, it's difficult to say. What say you, Gabby? Is it possible, do you think, for a man to die from wanting you?"

She didn't hear from Rodrigo for several weeks after her half brother's first visit. She worried incessantly, thinking Hastings had spoken the truth. That Rodrigo was ill and dying. Then, one night, she heard the soft scraping and knew it was a lie. It no longer mattered what Hastings said. She knew as long as she heard that faint grating on the other side of the wall that her lover was alive and well.

But it was slow going. The ship had been built to weather any storm. The wood was hard as rock. Gabrielle was barely able to make a dent in it with her blunt knife after weeks of toil.

Eventually, though, she began to make progress. She had to use the rag rug to cover the small groove she was carving in the wood. Claiming boredom with her surroundings, she had the guard move her eating table and chair against the wall, but to avoid suspicion, was careful to have him move other furniture as well.

When they were well into their fourth month at sea, she'd dug a hole the size of a man's fist. Still, she hadn't reached the other side. It was when she was the most discouraged that she heard a sudden crack in the wood one night. She could feel it give way beneath her fingers, hear it splinter within. After that, there was silence. But over the next few days, it came again. Once a night. As if he were pounding his way through the wall one painful blow at a time.

One night, there was a wicked crack and she saw some wood give way. She sat for a moment, staring in amazement. Then, realizing what it meant, she pounced on it and began to fling the fragments aside. She didn't care that splinters pierced her flesh. All she cared about was reaching him on the other side.

As she was thrusting her fingers through the minute hole, she suddenly froze. For where wood had been the moment before, there was now a hand. The touch of him electrified her as if she'd swallowed lightning. She could touch only two fingers to his, but it was enough to bring tears of joy to her eyes. "Rodrigo," she whispered, wishing she could scream out his name. Then his hand convulsed away and she knew the guard had returned.

It was an awful moment. To no longer feel the touch of him after all this time! She rubbed the tips of her fingers along her lips, savoring the feel of him, trying to infuse his touch in her aching heart.

Over the next few days, they were able to enlarge the hole piece by piece so they could reach another finger, and another, through the crack. Soon, she was able to reach in her hand and grasp his. Still, they didn't dare speak. It was more dangerous than ever. If the hole was discovered now, they'd be wrenched away from each other. She just clutched his hand wordlessly, feeling the wonder of his essence for a moment. Then he made a tap and withdrew his hand.

That night, there really was a storm. She couldn't see the lightning, but she could hear the thunder rumbling through the sky. The boat pitched precariously, tossing furniture about the room and crashing books and the lantern to the floor. The guard, recalling her supposed fear of storms, came in to check on her. But as the storm worsened, all hands were needed on deck. He told her he'd return when things were calmer, then left her alone.

Her heart was pounding as she thrust the rug away and stared at the small hole in the wall. The tempest would give them time not just to touch, but to really feel each other for the first time in so long. Momentarily, the hand appeared. She grasped it and a wave of satisfaction and completeness swept over her. As if she'd just come home.

As thunder clashed and the ship rolled and stretched, they held each other. Then, just as a tremendous crash of thunder shook the vessel, something extraordinary happened. She heard his voice. "Gabé. Gabé." The recklessness of it startled her, then sent her heart bursting with joy. She gripped his hand tighter and said, over the thunder, "Rodrigo, my love. I'm with you."

"Are you all right?"

"I'm fine. Oh, Rodrigo!"

"I love you, carícia. I had to reach you."

"Darling, I'm so sorry. This is all my fault. It's because of me that you're chained to the floor, instead of standing on the bridge of your ship. Can you ever forgive me?"

"There's nothing to forgive. I chose this way because I realized you were right. No matter what the outcome, this is the right way."

"Oh, Rodrigo, I love you so."

"Someone is coming. I must go."

Every night for the next few weeks, as the storms continued to rage, they managed to have a brief rendezvous. She would lie on the floor, clutching his hand. Sometimes they spoke of their feelings, and sometimes they used quietly uttered words to make the most passionate of love. While he never touched more than her hand, she could actually feel him making love to her through the long nights. To distract them both from their distress, he wove tender fantasies that she'd never have dreamed up herself. He told her things Shayla had taught him, that he wanted to share with her. Withheld from him, she felt his power more keenly than she ever had. It was a union so total, so exquisite, a level of oneness and intimacy that was rooted in their intense trust of and longing for each other. They were linked together by soft voices in the night. And soon she was saying things to him that she would never say to another living soul.

She began to feel that she would live for these midnight rendezvous the rest of her life. But one morning, just before dawn, as she'd just left his wondrous touch, she heard the distant cry of the officer on watch.

"England!" he called, heralding the beginning of the end.

# Forty-seven

*Gabrielle was in her cell* at Newgate Prison, being prepped by a matron for her first court appearance. The woman was brushing her hair and fastening it into a severe bun, as if preparing her neck for hanging. She'd already been given a frock to wear, sent over by her father, of all people. A forbidding black monstrosity with white cuffs and collar, similar to the attire of a Pilgrim. No doubt Douglas's idea of the sort of modest apparel that would impress a courtroom full of conservative men. Why he'd bothered, she couldn't even guess. She detested the staid outfit, which reminded her of the maid's uniform she'd once been forced to wear. But she couldn't refuse it, as she had no clothing of her own.

She was speaking with Sir Thomas Fowell Buxton, the leader of the campaign in Parliament for the abolition of slavery in British colonies, and thus the official face of the antislavery movement. Sir Thomas was an unimpressive figure, with wavy hair that swirled down a bit over his forehead and round-rimmed glasses perched upon his large nose. His mouth was small but full-lipped and curved like a woman's. He was fashionably attired in black frock coat and lacy white cravat, making her feel frumpy and dowdy in her borrowed clothes.

"Mr. Soro is being held under maximum security," Sir Thomas told her as she irritably wrenched her hair away from the matron's none-too-gentle hands. "They've isolated him completely under the auspices of the Dangerous Criminal Act."

"What does that mean?" Gabrielle asked.

"It's an act that restricts the access of barristers to dangerous criminals. Simply put, it gives them the right to seal him off completely under the certainty that he's too dangerous even to be visited by his legal advisors. Whatever questions his barristers have are put to him in writing by way of the guard and carefully scrutinized by the prosecution. They're taking no chances that his accusations will leak out."

"Then you must do it," she insisted. "You're in a position to get us the publicity we need."

"I dearly wish I could. The vote on the Emancipation Bill is only one week away. Right now, it looks very close. It could turn on a single vote. Now, granted, England has been riding a tide of change since last year's landmark Reform Bill, but I'm sorry to say the antislavery statute is not foremost in the country's mind. Mr. Soro's story might well make the difference for the antislavery forces. But our hands are tied. We've been thoroughly outmaneuvered in this matter.

"Outmaneuvered in what way?"

"The opposition has done everything it can to control the trial so the evidence Mr. Soro has won't come out. They've managed to have their cohort Matson named as presiding judge."

"Judge Matson!" She remembered the ratlike man she'd often seen conferring with her father.

"Surely I don't have to tell you, he's a strong supporter of the proslavery faction. Thick as thieves with your father and the block of votes he controls, which has been preventing my bill from passing. We hadn't counted on his benching this case, and we quite frankly could not have received more devastating news. He's put a ban on any publicity surrounding this trial. Anyone defying this ban will be held in contempt of court. He'll see to it that no word is allowed to be spoken that the proslavery people don't want uttered. So you see, much as I might like to, I can't possibly go to the press. They'd make a mockery of me at a time when I can ill afford such censure."

Gabrielle sighed wearily as the matron left. "What are you telling me, Sir Thomas? Just how dire *is* our situation?"

"I don't like to use words like impossible—"

"But it is."

"It's obvious they're after a speedy trial with the intention of hanging Mr. Soro for piracy before the vote comes up next week, and any whisper of scandal can hurt their cause. I wouldn't be surprised if the trial was over with before the vote had even begun."

"If they're sealing Rodrigo off so effectively, why is it they've allowed me to see you?"

"They didn't invoke the Dangerous Criminal Act on you. I daresay it's because of the influence of your father. As much as he wants to see Rodrigo hang, he also genuinely seems eager to help you. He's overruled his son in allowing me to see you, I understand."

This was a surprise. "Why on earth would he do such a thing?"

"Some late-blooming paternal instinct, perhaps."

"If I have some measure of freedom, perhaps you can arrange for a correspondent to—"

"There's absolutely no possibility a journalist would be allowed in here. Even if he could, what member of the press would risk contempt of court to help you?"

"Then I shall try to get the story out in court."

"They shan't allow you. If you attempt to say anything pertinent on the stand, they'll simply cut you off."

He paused a moment, seeing the hope drain from her face. "I wish to God I had better news."

"So do I, Sir Thomas."

So it appeared she'd been wrong after all. She'd implored Rodrigo to trust her. And he had. He'd blindly walked into a trap to prove his faith in her judgment. And it turned out her judgment was faulty. She must have been mad even to think of putting faith in this society that had done nothing but oppress them both.

"So we've lost before we've begun," she murmured.

"I'm afraid so. I fear your journey here was a fool's errand. They're intent on hanging Mr. Soro and I just don't see any way to prevent it."

The guards came then and told Sir Thomas to leave. Then they manacled her and led her down the long prison corridor. Outside, she could hear the news hawkers calling out details of the trial. The notorious Rodrigo Soro was being tried for piracy, and his lover, being tried as his accomplice, was the actress Gabrielle Ashton-Cross, reported bastard daughter of the duke of Westbury, who'd already scandalized London by playing the pirate on the stage. It was irresistible.

When she was pushed out of the prison door and into the summer day, she was astonished to see thousands of people jamming the square, some picnicking on fare they'd brought from home, some buying fruit and roasted peanuts from hawkers peddling their wares. At the sight of her, the crowd began to jeer. They closed in around her in a sea of gawking faces, so her escort was forced to hold them back with the threat of clubs. "There's that pirate doxy," someone called.

It was like her mother's hanging all over again. With Hastings dragging her to the scene, elbowing his way through the crowd, saying, "Gangway, there, it's the Frenchy whore's daughter." And they'd parted for them, the awful mob, so the daughter could better see her mother hang. Tears welled in her eyes as she remembered it now. The horror of seeing her mother's once-lovely face gasping for a last breath of air.

Gabrielle had had nightmares of hanging like her mother. Now those nightmares were coming true.

As they crossed the street to the courthouse, she glanced up at the Magpie and Pint tavern, where Hastings was likely watching the scene. It was from here that fashionable men witnessed public executions while tipping a pint. No doubt he'd sit just so and watch her hang, with Rodrigo—her beloved Rodrigo—at her side.

She'd betrayed her lover by asking him to believe in her. He'd put himself in bondage to prove he trusted her completely. This, then, was her punishment for her demands. To know she was sending him to his death.

It was slow going through the hostile mob. But finally they made their way up the steps of a large classical building that was the criminal courthouse. As they entered the sealed-off chamber of the main courtroom, the first sight she beheld was Rodrigo in chains. He'd been shaved and bathed, but the months of confinement had paled his golden skin. His hair looked darker than she remembered without the sun to bleach it. But he was so handsome, the sight of him was like a kick to her stomach. In his eyes, she saw his trust of her. But it was so hopeless. Had no one told him? She recalled Sir Thomas's words and felt a chill freeze her soul. *Your journey here was a fool's errand. They're intent on hanging Mr. Soro and I just don't see any way to prevent it.*

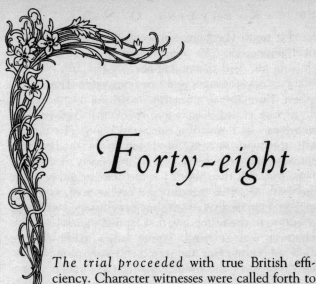

# Forty-eight

The trial proceeded with true British efficiency. Character witnesses were called forth to attest to the inevitability of the defendants joining forces in piracy. Humphrey Hollingstead, Gabrielle's former stage manager, testified to her impulsive rebellion. "She was too rash to ever be a really great actress. She'd go off on tangents, changing lines if she felt like it, walking out in the middle of a performance. I used to say she was more a pirate than the one she was portraying on the stage. Little did I know how apt that prediction would turn out to be—that she'd ally herself with that scoundrel and make a mockery of us all."

When he was dismissed from the stand, he passed her by with a smug smile. She'd refused to grace his bed on numerous occasions. This, then, was her retribution. She despised the hypocrisy of his testimony. If she were still playing Rodrigo onstage and he thought the publicity would help the production, he'd have been the first to capitalize on the news, making her seem the glamorous pirate queen instead of a sea-butcher's whore.

Ranking officers of the British East India Company were called to attest to Rodrigo's behavior at Haileybury before he left for the Indian Ocean.

"He was deucedly secretive. Had us all fooled . . ."

"Pretended to play along, while all the time he was plotting to overthrow one of our ships . . ."

"I've never seen a more devious man. The devil's spawn. I wouldn't put anything past him . . ."

It was crowded to capacity in the dark-paneled courtroom, as hot as the equatorial noon. The air was still, the room smelling of closely packed bodies, hair pomade, and perfume. The best of London society had come to watch the show. They ate oranges and peanuts, the shells of which they dropped on the floor, as if they were at a circus. Even as the audience listened with rapt attention to the testimony, they fanned themselves with whatever was at hand. Proper ladies made delicate shows of putting lacy handkerchiefs to perspiring brows. Yet, in spite of the insufferably stifling quarters, not a soul got up to leave. It was simply too juicy a spectacle to stay away.

Sir Thomas Buxton and several of his allies were there to give Gabrielle moral support on the first day. But with the vote on the bill fast approaching, and a hard fight ahead of them, they were absent on the next.

On this second day, Admiral Fulton appeared in court with several other Royal Navy officers. As the rebellion in Seychelles collapsed with Rodrigo's surrender, he'd returned to England for the trial of the man who was still technically his prisoner.

On the third day, Hastings was called to the stand. He was dressed in conservative black, emphasizing his dark, hawklike features. Glaring at Rodrigo with the impervious stare of a future duke, he ticked off the prisoner's acts of piracy to the breathless spectators.

"The number of men the blackguard has butchered would fill the whole of Kensal Green cemetery. I've seen him run men through with nary a blink. He's a cold-blooded murderer who has used his knowledge of English policies to defy the authority of Britain on the high seas."

"And the other defendant? Miss Ashton-Cross?"

"Miss *Ashton* is as bad as he. I myself was witness to her treachery. It was no accident that she chose to portray this rogue onstage. She took to piracy with a verve I've rarely seen in any man. Her own brother, Cullen, knew what she was doing and brought us evidence. He spent time with the sea-swine's crew after being kidnapped by him. The boy witnessed firsthand the killing by his own sister's sword of at least a dozen men. Innocent citizens who merely got in the way of the treasure she was seeking for her lover and herself. Would that poor Cullen were here to give testimony to just how vile these acts were."

There was a rush of whispering in the courtroom. Gabrielle leaned over to Mr. Ames, the wigged barrister at her side, and said, "The lying pig."

"Don't fret," he soothed. "We've some plans of our own."

"And why would she do such a dastardly thing, my lord?"

"She told me herself, she was in love with the brute."

While she sat stewing, Hastings rattled off a series of lies, each meant to dig another foot of dirt in her grave. It was like being a child again, helpless before her half brother as he told vicious stories to their father to assure that he'd revere Hastings and reject her. When he stepped down, the prosecution requested a brief recess before calling the pirate himself to the stand.

Gabrielle turned to Mr. Ames. "You have to put me on the stand. I'll see what information I can slip in. There has to be a way of getting around this."

But he shook his head. "I can't risk such a thing. You'll forgive my saying so, Miss Ashton-Cross, but you're known far and wide as a creature of impulse. I can't trust what you might say on the stand. I do, after all, have a responsibility to try to acquit you, regardless of Mr. Soro's fate. If you remain silent and leave things to us, we may very well succeed."

"What do you mean, regardless of Mr. Soro's fate?"

But before he could answer, they were surprised when her father joined them at their table. His eyes met Gabrielle's and she saw a softening of his patrician features that she hadn't seen since she was a very young child. Before Hastings had done his dirty work. There was an almost wistful look in his eyes, as if he wished they could begin again.

"You must see to it," he told Mr. Ames, "that the testimony my son has given is counterbalanced. Do what you must to ensure that my—that Gabrielle does not hang."

While Gabrielle was digesting her surprise, Mr. Ames asked, "Will you testify in her behalf? Admit your association with her?"

Douglas glanced at his daughter while she held her breath. For an instant, her heart stopped, thinking he might do it. But he dropped his gaze and said, "I can't."

"Of course not," she said bitterly. "No more than you could stand up for my mother in court. Tell me, *Your Grace*, did you sit just so and watch while they threw my mother to the wolves?"

With a pained look, he left. Mr. Ames patted her hand. "Not to worry. We've a few tricks up our sleeve."

"What do you mean?"

"You'll see in a moment."

She did see when the prosecution called Rodrigo to the stand. He stood and walked proudly to the witness-box, in spite of the fact that he was still bound by chains at his wrists. It was a menacing sight that couldn't help but impress the jury in a negative fashion. As if he were too dangerous to be let in the courtroom without manacles.

With regal dignity, he answered the questions put to him in a clear, honest way.

"Mr. Soro, did you participate in acts of piracy against the Crown?"

"I did. As a way of ensuring—"

"If you please, Mr. Soro, answer only the questions put before you."

"I only wish to explain—"

"No explanations are necessary, Mr. Soro. We understand all too well the heinous crimes you've perpetrated. It runs in the blood, does it not? Now, sir, did you or did you not murder seamen sailing under the British flag?"

He was the epitome of grace under pressure, answering coldly and succinctly. It reminded Gabrielle of his manner in England back in the early days—imperiously silent and distant, yet with an air of one whose enigmatic surface masks hidden depths.

It had to be frustrating. Every time he tried to introduce the issue of slavery, the prosecutor would look to the judge and say, "We will stick to your acts of piracy, Mr. Soro, for which, after all, you *are* on trial." And the rodentlike Judge Matson would say, "Quite so." Rodrigo had to be seething inside. Yet he gave no clue. He was, she decided, not for the first time, a better actor than she.

Still, in spite of his composure, there was about him something elemental that made the stifling air in the courtroom sizzle. As if an untamed lion had been brought in on a chain. When he looked at the jury with those steady, powerful eyes, they flinched as if they'd been burned. Women fanned themselves more vigorously.

When the defense took over the questioning, it was only minutes before Gabrielle understood what they meant to do.

"Mr. Soro, you've heard the testimony of the marquis of Breckenridge as to the willing—nay, *eager*—participation of Miss Ashton-Cross in your escapades. What say you to these foul accusations?"

"I say they're nothing but bilge and blather."

"You deny them?"

"I deny them uncategorically. They're nothing but the fabrications of an oily little jackanapes fit only for the company of baboons."

The courtroom was abuzz.

"Are you insinuating, sir, that the marquis of Breckenridge, while under oath, sought to falsify testimony to this court?"

"I'm saying he lied to this court to make Miss Ashton-Cross appear a flouncy wench. When nothing could be further from the truth."

"What exactly are you saying, sir?"

"That I kidnapped the lady in question and forced her to do my bidding."

Gabrielle leaned across the table with a "No" on her lips, but Mr. Ames pulled her back in her seat.

"You must be silent, I implore you. This is your only chance to escape the hangman."

"By selling Rodrigo down the river?"

"Do as I say! My orders are to get you acquitted at any cost."

"You're saying—" continued the barrister.

"She wasn't a part of it," Rodrigo said, with so much conviction that no one could believe otherwise. "She had nothing to do with any of my acts. I accept responsibility for my own actions, but I won't have the lady so maligned."

*Oh, my God!* Gabrielle thought. *He's decided to sacrifice himself for me. Has he planned this all along?*

"Yet his lordship claims the lady in question was in love with you."

"No doubt his years in the equatorial sun have unhinged his mind. I kidnapped her as a bargaining tool against his lordship. I never cared for her. She never cared for me. In fact, she threatened my life in front of the passengers and crew of one of your own East Indiamen. Believe me, she wouldn't lift a finger to help me if I were stripped and flogged before her."

Gabrielle knew now he was going to hang. So be it, she thought, but she'd damn well swing by his side! No longer afraid, she lunged to her feet. "No!" she cried. "I *did* go along with it. I believe in what you're doing. I'd do it again. I love you, Rodrigo. I don't care about them. I'd do anything for you."

The court was bedlam, with Judge Matson pounding his gavel for a silence that wouldn't come. Rodrigo's eyes, when they flicked to her, were full of fire and fury.

"She doesn't know what she's saying," he roared above the din. "It's the voyage. Being locked up for so long. She's out of her mind."

"I know what I'm saying," she called to him as the judge banged his gavel louder and called for order. "If you're going to hang, I want to hang with you. Do you think I want to be left among these popinjays? Do you think I want to live a moment without you?"

Judge Matson was shouting now. Rodrigo called, "I threatened her to say these things. But you're no longer bound by your promise, my lady. What harm can I do you now?"

"Miss Ashton-Cross," shouted the judge, "if you don't desist, you'll be taken from this courtroom."

She raked her gaze over his furious red face. "Why don't you ask him why he took to piracy? Why don't you see for yourself what an honorable man he is? How he's helped more people than anyone in this court—"

At the judge's orders, the bailiffs came to drag her away. As they did, she cried, "I fought at his side for a noble cause. Coerced, was I?" She freed her arms from the hands of the bailiffs in one strong lunge. Her hands went to the collar of her dress and she tugged hard. Buttons flew in all directions. "How's *this* for coercion?" she flared as she yanked her bodice down. There, for all to see, was the flesh of her right shoulder. And on it, the tattoo of a frigate bird in flight.

It shocked the court so deeply that everything stilled. Even the bailiffs stood rooted where they were, staring at her exposed back.

"Anyone who knows of *Mkombozi* knows he brands only those who willingly request it. I was an eager participant in his cause. Had he the tools in his hands right now, I'd take his mark again, in front of you all."

"Take her away," said the judge, breaking the ensuing silence.

They carried her off. As she looked back, her last sight was that of a pair of golden lion's eyes, staring after her with a profound sorrow mingling with a fierce, proud love.

# Forty-nine

*Anxiety boiled in Gabrielle* as she paced her cell. She couldn't recall ever being so frustrated in all her life. In the two days that had passed since her rash outburst, she hadn't been allowed in the courtroom. She waited restlessly, frantic for news. Today was the last day of testimony. The case was now in the hands of the jury. Tomorrow would likely see a verdict.

That night she heard the carpenters outside her window building the scaffolds from which the prisoners would hang side by side. There was no doubt of the outcome now, she realized, as she watched the instruments of their destruction ascend with frightening speed. Once the verdict was in, they'd be hanged within the hour. Judge Matson would see to it there was no delay in ridding the Crown of this public embarrassment.

Mr. Ames came to her just before ten that evening. "The jury has reached a decision. Your presence will be required in court in the morning for the reading of the verdict. I've been severely warned to keep you reined in. One more such outburst and—"

"What?" she asked defiantly. "What can they do that will be worse than hanging?"

He lowered his head. Clearly, he was annoyed by her suicidal gesture, but he was also enough of a gentleman to sympathize with the veracity of her words. "There can be no other verdict but guilty, for both of you. I anticipate that you will hang together on the morrow. I wish there were something I could do. I wish you hadn't—"

"Jeopardized your case? Mr. Ames, if Rodrigo hangs, I prefer to hang with him. It's as simple as that."

"You'd really want to die with him?" he marveled.

"I really do."

He was silent, musing with a hand at his chin, clearly impressed with her devotion.

"I've an appointment," he said abruptly. "I'll return later if I can."

Sometime later, she was startled by a key turning in the lock. She looked up to see Mr. Ames standing in the doorway. She sensed that a great deal of time had passed, but there was no way to be sure.

"What time is it?" she asked.

"It's late. Hush, you must be very quiet. Come with me."

When she tried to question him, he merely put his finger to his lips and led her down the hall. They walked stealthily through the long corridor. It was quiet and dark, so he used a lantern to light the way. They went down a flight of stairs and then another. Her heart gave a lurch. Were they transferring her to the dungeon?

Finally, they came to a single door. "Solitary confinement," he explained, because it was the only one. "For dangerous criminals only."

"What's going on, Mr. Ames?"

As he opened the door, he said, "See for yourself."

The door swung open with a clang. Gabrielle stood at the threshold. He gestured her inside, but she hesitated. "It's not—"

"Yes," he asserted with a stern voice. "But hurry. There isn't much time."

She entered the cell and found Rodrigo sprawled on a cot, his arms and legs chained to the wall.

He sat up, raising an arm to shield his eyes from the lantern's light. As he did, his chains rattled.

"Gabé," he whispered as his eyes adjusted and he beheld the vision of beauty standing transfixed in his doorway.

She raced across the room and fell into his embrace. In spite of the chains, his arms went round her like a vise. He held her so tightly, she couldn't breathe. The chains bit into her back. Yet it was heaven, being in his powerful arms. She looked up at him, at his dear face. His lips descended on hers in a fiercely passionate kiss.

She felt herself drowning. Nothing mattered but this moment and the feel of his mouth moving on hers. He plundered her with his tongue, demanding, hungry, as if willing her always to remember this one kiss. She was vaguely aware of their barrister's voice warning them that they had only five minutes together. "If I'm found out," he said, "I shall surely be disbarred." She heard but didn't notice the closing of the cell door.

"My foolish, foolish love," Rodrigo whispered feverishly as his lips trailed her skin. "What have you done to yourself?"

She clutched his head in her hands and kissed him desperately, passionately. "I didn't want to live without you," she gasped. "It was unfair of you to ask."

"I wanted you to live for both of us."

"None of that matters now. What matters is the feelings we share. Rodrigo, you made me feel loved for the first time since my mother died. You're the only one who saw the good in me, and helped bring it out. You're my liberator, Rodrigo. You freed me from the tyranny of my past. You believed in me when no one else did. How can I tell you what you've done for me? I'm no longer afraid to die." She took his hands in hers. "Do you remember the love we shared on the ship?"

"Every moment. Every breath. Every stroke of your hand."

"Oh, Rodrigo. In the midst of all the obstacles they put between us, I never felt closer to you in my life. Surely lovers who can transcend such physical barriers can never really die."

"No, never. They can imprison us, they can hang us. But they can't kill this union. It's beyond their power."

They kissed again. Holding each other, they could feel the seeping into their own bodies of the other's soul.

"But I'm still sorry I did this to you," she said. "You shouldn't have trusted me after all. It was a mistake to come here. You were right about that."

"Hush." He put his hand to her mouth. "It *was* the right thing to do. We couldn't have guessed how it would turn out. The only thing I regret is that we were unable to influence that vote, which will be taking place at the same time we hang. It would have been such a victory."

She suppressed a sob.

Nuzzling her, he said, "And you, *carícia?* Have you any regrets?"

"I regret not making love with you on those damned scarlet sheets."

He laughed. He took her hand and stroked the back of it with his thumb. "I wish I'd known. I could have remedied the situation so easily."

The key turned in the lock and the smiles dropped from their faces. She fell onto him as his arms tightened about her. The door swung open. She lifted her face and his mouth descended on hers in a last kiss.

Mr. Ames was holding her shoulders. "Come, Miss Ashton-Cross, we must go."

"I can't," she wept, her tears spilling on the chains that bound her lover's wrists.

Mr. Ames gently pulled her away. "If we're discovered—"

"Go, Gabé," Rodrigo prompted. "You must be brave."

Halfway across the room, she turned back and looked at him through her tears. "How can I bear to be away from you?" she cried.

"We'll be parted for only another day. Think of it as a brief separation before an eternity of being together. That's what paradise really is, isn't it?"

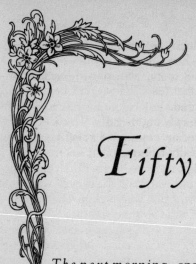

# Fifty

*The next morning*, one of Mr. Ames's clerks came to take her to court. When she asked where the eminent barrister was, she was told he'd been called away on an emergency. She doubted that. Likely he was embarrassed to see her after what he'd done the night before. English men, for all their romantic notions in the dark, were generally ashamed of their deeds come morning—even their good deeds, it seemed.

A detachment of jailers led her out through the crowd. In the afterglow of her tender visit with Rodrigo, the hostility of the crowd came as a shock. The papers had reported the behavior that had exiled her from the courtroom. One even ran a woodcut of her exposed back, the frigate bird clearly visible, if badly interpreted by the artist's hand. Consequently, the crowd yelled a barrage of insults. She could see their lips moving, but, mercifully, couldn't distinguish their words. Only one coarse woman's voice rose above the rest, reflecting the sentiments of the others. "Hang the pirate whore!"

Inside, she saw her father, looking pale. He took an impulsive step toward her, mouthing her name. *"Gabrielle."* How she'd longed for such a look from him all those years of growing up lonely in his forbidding country house. Now, when she was on the verge of the gallows, he finally gazed at her with something akin to compassion in his eyes.

She looked away, crumbling before his pity in a way she'd never bowed before his disregard.

They brought in Rodrigo, manacled as before. She'd been feeling weak and downhearted, but saw a gaze of such love in his eyes that it buoyed her with courage. In a strange way, they'd achieved all she'd ever wanted. They were partners now, equal before God. They would walk together hand in hand to their destiny.

They took their seats. Hastings came in late, looking smug. He stopped by the defense table and glared down his nose at Rodrigo. "You'll be interested to know the vote for the Emancipation Bill is underway. My father has cast his block of votes against. We should win by a comfortable margin. The bill has been defeated, and so have you, Roderick. I just thought you'd like to know before you hang."

Before he left, he glanced at Gabrielle and gave her an evil smile. "Gabby, dear, I always said your impulsiveness would defeat you in the end. You've chosen the wrong camp, dearest."

Gabrielle glanced at Rodrigo, expecting to see fury, but she saw instead a trust so deep that he didn't even blink. Turning to her half brother, she said in a composed tone, "No, Hastings. I've chosen the right camp."

His black eyes hardened like a hawk's. "Then I shall derive the greatest pleasure from watching you hang."

"Is the jury ready to impart its verdict?" asked Judge Matson.

"We are, Your Honor," answered the jury foreman.

"Would the defendants please rise? And I will remind you, I will tolerate no more outbursts in my court. You will behave yourselves with the respect and dignity this bench demands."

On shaking legs, Gabrielle rose to her feet. She felt a

hand and looked down to see Rodrigo clasping her own. To give her strength or take some, she couldn't be sure. It didn't matter. She held his hand tightly, and knew she could bear whatever was to come.

But just as the foreman was standing to read the verdict, the back doors banged open and Mr. Ames came bursting through, out of breath. He rushed up the aisle and stopped by the table to say to Gabrielle, "Pray for a miracle." Then he asked permission to approach the bench.

"My lord, we've new evidence to present. Important evidence. We beg the court's indulgence in allowing us to do so."

The prosecutor objected. "My lord, my opponent knows very well that it's too late for this. The jury has reached its verdict."

"But my lord," argued Mr. Ames, panting heavily, "this witness has the most intimate knowledge of this case. To not hear what he has to say would be the grossest miscarriage of justice."

Hastings rose and went to join the barristers at the bench. "Who is this witness?" he asked, outraged.

Mr. Ames answered softly. Hastings's eyes flashed back to Gabrielle. She could see the shock in them from where she stood.

"Absolutely not!" he cried. "This is a travesty, my lord. It cannot be allowed."

Mr. Ames, breathing easier now, raised his voice so all could hear. "I doubt very much the London *Times* would be happy to hear that the only witness the defense has succeeded in bringing forth in this case has been turned away. If this witness is not allowed to testify, my lord, contempt or no, I intend to take my grievance to the public."

Judge Matson lowered his voice and addressed Hastings, but Gabrielle still heard what he said, "I must let this witness testify."

Hastings hesitated a moment, then stormed back to his seat.

"We'll allow the testimony," said the judge.

Mr. Ames turned and gave Gabrielle an encouraging smile. "Bailiff, if you please."

The bailiff opened the doors and Cullen entered the courtroom.

# Fifty-one

*Cullen walked up* the aisle and took his place in the witness-box high above the court. On his way, Hastings stopped him for a moment, frantically whispering something to him. A threat, no doubt. Gabrielle could hardly contain the emotions that flooded through her—joy, relief, and a staggering stupefaction. How was it that the meek brother who hadn't had the nerve to escape before Rodrigo's sword had somehow made it out of the sultan's palace and across the globe? She could tell nothing about Cullen's state of mind. He looked fit, if a little thin. But he avoided her eyes, as if ashamed to look her in the face.

Hastings went back to the judge, as if to reargue his case, whispering feverishly. Admiral Fulton, who'd sat in the same front-row seat all week long, seemed to note Hastings's unusual influence over the judge and said something to his aide.

As Hastings finally returned to his seat, Judge Matson said, "We'll have dispatch in this matter. I have no intention of indulging this whim with long and protracted testimony. The defendants will be seated until this matter is concluded."

Gabrielle sat beside Rodrigo, but kept her hand anchored in his.

"State your name," said the bailiff.

"Cullen Ashton."

He was sworn in.

Mr. Ames stepped before Cullen. "Mr. Ashton, earlier in this courtroom, the prosecution made reference to your name, saying you'd been kidnapped by the accused, Mr. Soro. Is that correct?"

"Yes, sir."

"He also said you could attest to Mr. Soro's acts of piracy against the Crown."

Hastings edged forward in his seat.

"What I can attest, sir," said Cullen pointedly, "is that Mr. Soro has done more for England than any man since the duke of Wellington."

There was a gasp in the court.

"But he's considered a pirate," Mr. Ames said.

"Only against those Englishmen who have committed the most grievous crimes against humanity. Who have instigated a network of slavery so abominable—"

"Objection, my lord!" shouted the prosecution.

Mr. Ames persisted, "But the slave trade officially ended twenty years ago."

"In the Indian Ocean, sir, it's thriving. Because of men right here in England who profit from it mightily— men like Lord Breckenridge, there, and men like his friend Judge Matson."

The judge thunderously banged his gavel. Hastings stood indignantly. "This perjury has gone on long enough. The brat will say anything to keep his sister from hanging. It's as plain as the nose on his face."

Judge Matson agreed. "This is preposterous. I'm putting a halt to it at once. Mr. Ashton, you will please step down."

As Mr. Ames was protesting vehemently, Admiral Fulton stood and made his way to the bench with an authority that was an island of calm in this sea of turmoil. He held up a hand for silence, and the turmoil subsided instantly.

"My lord, I remind the court that Soro is officially a prisoner of the Royal Navy. So I have some interest here. I think it imperative that this testimony proceed."

The judge wrinkled his nose and, looking for all the world like a rat cornered by a cat, nervously gestured his agreement.

Mr. Ames took a deep breath and resumed his questioning. "Mr. Ashton, you were saying?"

"Hastings—Lord Breckenridge—has been conspiring with the French planters who need slaves, and the sultan of Zanzibar, who provides them. For years, he has allowed the Seychelle Islands to be used as a sanctuary and way station for the African slave trade, which continues to exist, principally supplying the Mohammedans, but also provisioning those islands in the Indian Ocean whose economy is dependent on slave labor."

"How do you know this?"

"I know because I was with them in the palace at Zanzibar as they discussed it."

"And what were you doing in the palace?"

"I was a slave. I was given by Lord Breckenridge to the sultan."

Several of the ladies in the galley swooned. Others fanned themselves and sat straighter in their seats.

"What sort of slaves do you claim these men are profiting by?"

"All manner of slaves. Slaves mostly to feed the plantation economy of that region. Slaves for the fields, slaves for the houses, slaves for the sultan of Zanzibar. The sultan is . . . particularly fond of male slaves. Especially if they're of pale complexion." His implication was clear.

"This is outlandish!" cried Hastings.

"How do you know all this, Mr. Ashton?"

Cullen tilted his chin up and looked the barrister in

the eye. "I have firsthand knowledge. I can't begin to describe the horror of one's life as a slave. In England, it seems a remote concept, easy to ignore. But I'm here to tell you, I was treated as less than human. I was initially kept in chains. I was beaten, starved, forced to obey by all manner of torture. Soon it became easier to comply. I was used—I became the favorite of the sultan. No horror was so unspeakable that it wasn't perpetrated on my person, for the service or entertainment of the brute. And I wasn't alone. There were dozens of us."

"I daresay your experience would break the spirit of most men."

"I've been a slave all my life, sir. I've been a slave to my illegitimacy." He glanced at Douglas, who suddenly stood up with tears in his eyes. "And I've been a slave to my own—and other people's—expectations of me. But never like this. The enslavement of human beings is a curse that must end. We must wipe it from the face of the earth or before God, we're as guilty as those who lock the chains. That is the mission of Rodrigo Soro. To ensure to all human beings the dignity that is our due."

By now, there wasn't a sound in the courtroom. No one seemed to breathe.

"And how did you get here?"

"Lord Breckenridge sent an emissary to the sultan before he left, explaining that he was going to accompany my sister and Rodrigo back to England, and fight the passage of the antislavery bill. I overheard the emissary saying this, and that Hastings intended to see to it my sister and her pirate were hanged without delay. As I said, they began by beating me into submission, but I was a coward. Rather than suffer their torture, I soon began to obey. Once he realized I hadn't the courage to escape, the sultan gave me a great deal of freedom. So I used that freedom to escape, in the hopes that I might arrive in time to explain."

"You escaped, then, and made your way to England to testify at this trial?"

"Yes. I managed to stow away on an American steamship out of Cairo."

"It seems to me, Mr. Ashton, that a man who has braved what you have for the sake of helping others is a man of remarkable courage indeed."

"I had to get here to tell the truth about Rodrigo. I knew Hastings would never allow the true story to come out."

"And what is that truth?"

"That Rodrigo Soro turned pirate only to fight an abomination against humanity. If you will indulge me, I can prove that every ship he attacked was in some way connected to the illegal slave trade."

"You journeyed thousands of miles by yourself to come to this court to give a testimony that must be humiliating at best. There must be some reason beyond the commendable love of your sister."

Cullen looked into the eyes of his father, who now had tears streaming down his face. "Maybe to prove that no man's fate is written in stone."

Cullen and his father exchanged a long look.

"Take courage, Father," Cullen coaxed. "Do what you know to be right."

With a sob, Douglas went running from the room.

Watching this, Gabrielle said to Rodrigo, "Look, he's running away *again*."

"Maybe not," Rodrigo said.

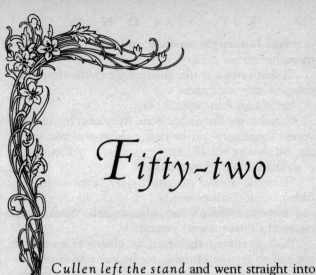

# Fifty-two

*Cullen left the stand* and went straight into the open arms of his sister. Gabrielle hugged him close, then brushed his hair back off his face, the way she'd done when he was a little boy, and looked into his eyes. "I'm so terribly proud of you," she said. Rodrigo just extended his hand and shook Cullen's, silently expressing his gratitude.

Noting Rodrigo's protective arm on her shoulder, Cullen said, "I always thought you two belonged together."

But a more intimate reunion would have to wait, for the jury had been whispering among themselves, and the foreman now stood. "My lord, we wish to hear the witness's full testimony—no matter how long it may take."

Hastings charged the bench. "Matson, you can't let them do that."

The judge looked over at the stern face of the admiral, then, with a lift of his brow, commanded, "Lord Breckenridge, you will kindly take your seat or I will have you forcibly removed from my courtroom."

So Judge Matson was breaking with Hastings. Watching him, Gabrielle saw her half brother take a step back, survey the situation, and bolt from the court-room.

Cullen turned to the admiral. "I think Hastings is going to stop my father."

"Stop him from what?"

"I think my father has gone to release his block of votes. There may still be time to sway the outcome of the antislavery bill. Hastings will try to stop him, even if it means killing his own father."

Gabrielle turned to the judge. "Free him," she called. "Free Rodrigo now!"

"I can't do that," the judge stalled. "Nothing has changed in the prisoner's status."

Rodrigo stood, tugging on his chains in frustration. He had to get out of there. He had to stop Hastings.

Gabrielle turned to the admiral. "Do something! You must want this bill passed as much as we. Let Rodrigo go and do what he can."

"I'll send soldiers," he suggested.

"I can move much faster," Rodrigo countered. "I won't let him escape me."

Grasping the logic of this, the admiral came to a quick decision. Relieving the bailiff of his keys, he said in his most autocratic tone, "As I've stated, this man is a prisoner of the Royal Navy and as such, it is in my power to take him under my personal recognizance for a short time. I trust, Mr. Soro, you will not abuse this privilege. I expect to see you back within the hour." He came forth and inserted the key in the lock.

"I won't betray your trust, Admiral."

As the last chain fell from Rodrigo's wrist, he bounded up on the table, leaped over the chairs, and was out the door. Gabrielle was right behind him. She heard her name and turned. In a bold gesture, Cullen was unbuckling the admiral's sword. He took it in hand and tossed it through the air. Gabrielle caught it, saluted her brother, and ran.

Outside, Rodrigo stood at the corner with his hand

cupped over his eyes, peering down the street. There, in the distance, she saw that Hastings had mounted a horse and was galloping away. Simultaneously, the crowd spotted them. "That's them!" someone called. "The pirate and his whore. Quick! They're escaping!"

Rodrigo grabbed her hand and backed away. "We'll never catch up to him. Think fast, Gabé. We don't need an idea. We need an *inspiration*."

"The river!" she cried.

"Of course."

They turned and ran down the side alley with the crowd of bellowing pursuers following close behind. They had to run swiftly. The crowd called out "Stop them," along the way, and citizens, assuming they were thieves on the run, joined the chase.

They ran past St. Paul's to Puddle Dock. There were a number of boats anchored close about, some barges and a larger vessel or two. Raking her gaze over the waterfront, Gabrielle spotted a steamer just distant.

"That must be the one Cullen came in on," she said.

They looked at each other and had the same idea.

"We'll take it," Gabrielle said for both of them.

They ran up the dock and boarded without permission. Charging their way through the protesting crew, they found the captain on deck. Gabrielle drew the admiral's sword from its sheath and pointed it at the man's throat.

"We're commandeering your vessel, Captain, for a short voyage," Rodrigo said. "Cooperate and neither you nor your crew will be hurt. Choose to resist, and I can't answer for the consequences."

The American looked from Gabrielle's face to Rodrigo's. "Where do you want to go?"

"Palace of Westminster," Rodrigo ordered. "And be quick about it."

Within a few moments the captain had fired the engines and they pulled into the river, executing a wide turn in the direction of the Parliament building.

Once they were underway, they swooped down the Thames with amazing speed.

"You must have brought my brother over from Egypt," Gabrielle told the captain. "For which I thank you." He looked confused. "Oh, you probably didn't know he was aboard. He would have been a stowaway."

"Ah," said the captain. "I see it runs in the family."

She wasn't up to banter. "Hurry," she said. "Make this contraption go as fast as it can."

They sailed under a series of bridges—Blackfriar's, Waterloo—around the large bend in the river. As they were coming upon Westminister Bridge, Rodrigo said with an excited glow on his face, "This ship is fast. We could make it back home in three months at this rate."

"Would you care to book a reservation now?" asked the captain dryly.

Rodrigo ignored this. "Just be quick about this."

He'd no sooner said this than he caught sight of something and raced to the rail. Releasing the sword from the man's throat, Gabrielle joined him. "Tack in," Rodrigo called back to the captain, as if he were now master of this ship.

The American gave the order, but there was nowhere for such a large ship to dock.

"What do you see?" Gabrielle asked.

Rodrigo pointed in the direction of Whitehall, where she spotted Hastings galloping up the street at a breakneck pace. Then, glancing left, she caught sight of her father climbing the steps of the rear entrance to the palace of Westminster—avoiding the crowd that had assembled out front to hear the outcome of the vote. Hastings was barreling down on him.

Rodrigo glanced about. They were too high up to jump into the river. Just then they passed under the bridge. He looked above, jumped onto the rail, and took a flying leap so he grasped the bottom of the bridge just as the ship passed beneath it.

"Rodrigo!" Gabrielle called out. "You've forgotten the sword."

But there was no time for him to turn back. He'd made his way to the top of the bridge, surprising the foot traffic along the way. Shoving them aside, he ran across the bridge even as Hastings dismounted.

As the steamship came to a full stop at the riverbank, Gabrielle heard Hastings shout, "Stop, Father! Don't take another step."

From the top of the stairs, Douglas turned and looked at his son. "You'll not stop me from doing this, Hastings. You no longer have any power over me."

Gabrielle watched Rodrigo stop short as Hastings raised his pistol and cocked the hammer. "Don't I, Father?"

# Fifty-three

As Hastings put his finger to the trigger, Rodrigo was standing perhaps twenty feet away. Without moving, he called out, "Cross, over here."

Hastings kept the pistol trained on his father, but his gaze drifted toward Rodrigo. Now he had a difficult choice to make. Shoot his father and prevent the passage of the bill, or shoot Rodrigo while he was so completely vulnerable.

He considered a moment, then shifted the pistol toward Rodrigo and pulled the trigger. But Rodrigo, sensing the outcome of Hastings's dilemma, dove onto the pavement just as the weapon discharged. The bullet grazed his left shoulder.

As Rodrigo lay dazed on the ground, clutching his bloody arm, Hastings threw the pistol away, drew his sword, and started toward his victim. At the top of the stairs, Douglas saw his chance and entered the building.

Gabrielle looked around and grabbed a huge coil of rope, struggling to drag it to the side of the ship. "You have to help me," she told the captain. She heaved the rope over the side, holding onto the end. "I'm trusting you to hold this while I climb down."

"But my dear lady pirate—"

"There isn't time. Will you help me or not?"

Reluctantly, the captain took the rope in his hands. He wrapped it around the rail and Gabrielle fastened the sword about her hips and took the rope in hand. Carefully, she lowered herself down the side of the ship, threw herself to the ground, and raced up the Westminster stairs to level land.

Rodrigo had managed to rise to his feet before Hastings reached him. But his speed was off, and as Hastings slashed with his sword, the blade nicked Rodrigo's right shoulder, giving him a second wound.

Clearly enjoying his advantage, Hastings smiled and lunged again. This time, his victim quickly darted out of harm's way, but in the process, tripped sideways. In a flash, Hastings was on him, kicking him with his boot so he went sprawling to the ground. Hastings leaped on him, striding his chest, putting the deadly blade of the sword to his throat.

"Farewell, *Roderick*. I almost think I shall miss you. But not enough to—"

Just then Gabrielle came running onto the scene. With her breath burning in her lungs, she called, "Rodrigo!" He turned toward her voice, cutting his throat. His blood beaded like rubies against the skin of his neck.

She didn't pause. Knowing she couldn't make it to him in time, she raised the sword and tossed it through the air. Rodrigo reached out even as the confusion registered on Hastings's face. Rodrigo caught the saber in his fist and angled it up to force the blade from his throat.

In one swift motion, he was on his feet.

"That was a mistake," Hastings gloated. "You'll wish I'd killed you quickly and mercifully, before we're finished."

"When were you ever merciful?" Rodrigo countered.

"When I neglected to murder you in your bed as a boy."

They began to fight in earnest, their swords striking with fierce clashes, the sun glinting off the steel. As Gabrielle watched, the two combatants parried and thrust their way onto the bridge, the foot traffic scrambling out of their path as they slashed their way across. She followed them, wishing she had a sword and could help. But despite his wounds, Rodrigo was holding his own. Both men were streaming with sweat. Both had clothing torn where the blades had slit the flesh. Both were now bleeding on their chests, their arms. This was no polite fencing match. It was a battle to the death.

Hastings pinned Rodrigo back against the stone rail of the bridge. As he was lowering his sword, Rodrigo gave a mighty kick and sent him spinning backward. With lightning speed, Rodrigo dove over the rail and landed below on the river walk, forcing Hastings to leap down in pursuit.

They were both beginning to tire. Even as he fought, Hastings kept up a litany of abuse. "Oh, good parry, *Roderick*," he taunted.

Rodrigo didn't answer. His gunshot wound was obviously troubling him, and he looked dizzy from the loss of blood. They headed for the stairs that led up from the river. There, they lunged and parried back and forth, climbing a few steps, then backing down again. Their blades moved so swiftly, they were difficult to see. It was a graceful, brutal dance by two masters of the game. A crowd gathered, gasping as Hastings slit Rodrigo's upper abdomen and drew more blood.

Seeing her lover's distress, Gabrielle raced to one of the spectators, drew his sword, and rejoined the contestants as they fought their way to the palace stairs. "It's my turn now, Rodrigo."

"No!" he denied over his shoulder. "This is a fight I've needed to have for a long time. I won't be denied because of a little blood."

"Oh, good show, Roderick!" Hastings cried. "How terribly British of you!"

The insult seemed to give Rodrigo a burst of energy. He withstood Hastings's attack, thrust for thrust, and as Hastings tired from what he hoped would be the final onslaught, Rodrigo seized the offensive.

Hastings's confident air turned to a worried look as Rodrigo's energy surged into a bold series of maneuvers that Hastings weakly managed to repulse. As he retreated into the crowd, he stumbled, falling to the ground, and Rodrigo had his opportunity at last. Pouncing, he kicked Hastings's sword out of his hand, sending it clanging down the cobblestones. With a victorious smile, Rodrigo placed the blade of his sword at Hastings's defenseless chest.

"What have you to offer for your life now?" Rodrigo growled.

Gabrielle saw the stark terror in Hastings's eyes as he tried to think.

Suddenly, a roar was heard from the crowd assembled at the front entrance on Parliament Street. The vote was concluded. Then they heard the faint voices of the mob calling out, "The bill is passed. The bill is passed! No more slavery for Britain."

Rodrigo looked down at his victim, sprawled beneath him. Their eyes met. In their shared gaze was a realization that Rodrigo had won at last. After all the bitter struggles through the years, it was over. "I don't suppose it would do me any good to ask for mercy at this point," Hastings said.

"Mercy?" Rodrigo asked, as he pulled back the sword. "Why not?" Then he made a powerful lunge through his enemy's heart.

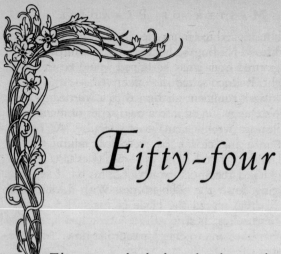

# Fifty-four

*The pirate kicked* in the door and stalked across the lady's cabin. He surveyed the scene of huddled, frightened women, and jerking his head to the ladies-in-waiting, barked out his command. "Out!"

From the front row of the raised theater box, a large figure fidgeted uneasily as the servants on the stage below scrambled out the door, leaving their frightened mistress alone with the infamous brigand—Rodrigo Soro, the scourge of the Indian Ocean.

As the stage pirate ripped the woman's dress, and a gasp of voices was heard all around, the observer sank deep in his seat and shook his head.

Moments later, he leaned forward again as the pirate below struck a melodramatic pose and said, with his hand on his heart, "My name is feared all across the Indian Ocean, from the Horn of Africa to the Celebes Sea. I've looted ships and collected bounty worth a king's ransom. But without the woman I love, I'm only half a man!"

"Enough!" Rising to his feet, the disgruntled spectator put his boot on the rail. "I've never heard such rubbish in all my life!"

Gabrielle tried to ignore the outburst and continued to play the scene. But she became aware of further commotion in the seats. There was a gasp and voices rose all around. Her concentration broken, she turned and looked above the glare of the lights to the royal box. And there, about to leap, was the real Rodrigo Soro.

With a single bound, he landed onstage. "What are you doing?" she cried, as the audience murmured its alarm.

"I've had enough of this libel."

He tossed her hat aside and yanked off the wig and netting, letting her chocolate hair fall free. Then, with a theatrical flourish of his own, he swept her up in his arms and gave her a fiercely passionate kiss. Another gasp swept the aisles, but Gabrielle was drowning in his kiss. Her arms went up to caress his neck as he carried her, like a pirate's captive, off the stage.

After a moment of stunned silence, the audience burst into a thunderous applause.

"Have you gone mad?" a voice cried as they came backstage. Humphrey Hollingstead followed them as Rodrigo swept her in his arms through the wings. "You could at least have waited till the end of the act!" He motioned to the understudy, a slim man standing in the wings, costumed just like Gabrielle. "Take the stage, dear."

Gabrielle had consented to appear in a one-week revival of her infamous play, to benefit Sir Thomas Fowell Buxton's Fund for Freed Slaves. This matinee performance was to be the last, and she'd warned Hollingstead that she'd have to leave at the end of the second act for an important event. But her lover, who hadn't managed to see any of the earlier performances, could bear the ordeal of watching his own portrayal no longer.

"I always said you were too impulsive to be a really great actress!" Hollingstead added.

She lifted her head and listened to the continuing

applause. She'd never had such an ovation in all her life. It had proved to be irresistibly romantic, the spectacle of the real pirate sweeping her offstage.

As they moved swiftly for the door, she suddenly hesitated. "They're still applauding," she said, the actress instincts dying hard. "I'd better go make a curtain call."

But Rodrigo shook his head. "If you want them to *really* remember you, leave them wanting more."

In the alley outside the stage door, a hansom cab was waiting to whisk them away. When they stepped inside, Gabrielle was surprised to find another passenger waiting for them. It was her father, Douglas Cross.

The driver cracked his whip and the cab pulled out onto the Strand. Gabrielle called up, "Make haste, if you would. We have no time to spare."

She sat down and faced her father.

"I've joined you to say my good-byes now," he told her.

"You're not coming to the pier tomorrow?"

"I thought it best not to."

"Does Cullen know this?"

"Yes. I've already spoken to him."

Feeling uneasy, Gabrielle glanced out at the passing scenery as they traversed Charing Cross.

"Daughter," he began, with a tremble in his voice. She looked at him and saw the tears in his eyes. "I want to tell you how very sorry I am."

"You don't have to—"

"But I do. I've wronged you terribly. You and Cullen. I wish I could make it up to you."

Awash with pity mixed with affection, she said, "Maybe it's not too late. Perhaps we can still be a family. Why don't you come with us?"

"I'm afraid I can't do that. I must face some very serious charges here in England regarding my late position with John Company. For the first time in my life, I'm not going to shirk my responsibilities. If I ever get clear, perhaps I shall take you up on that most generous offer."

The cab clattered through an iron gate and a succession of guards to a large structure, walled off from the street. As they reined to a halt, the driver called down, "We're at St. James's, Your Grace."

Impulsively, Gabrielle reached over and took her father's hand. "Why don't you come in with us?"

But he declined with a sorrowful shake of his head. "I don't deserve to be a part of this."

She would have argued, but the bond was still too tentative. "Very well. If that's your wish."

Before he stepped out, Douglas paused awkwardly and said, "I honestly don't know if you're my daughter or not. But I'd be proud to consider you such from now on."

For once in her life, Gabrielle was without words.

Moments later, she and Rodrigo entered St. James's Palace and followed the appointed delegation down the wide hallway to the chamber where the ceremony would take place. Pausing at the entrance, Gabrielle took his hand and whispered, "Are you certain you want to go through with this?"

The former scourge of the Indian Ocean swallowed nervously and said, "If you can live with me, I can live with England."

They entered the august chamber and a sea of faces turned their way. At the end of a red carpet, King William IV awaited them. Beside him was his young niece, Princess Victoria, who'd seen the play three times this past week. In front of them both was a velvet pillow. In a moment, Rodrigo would kneel on that pillow and accept England as his master.

When he rose again, he would be Sir Rodrigo Soro.

# Epilogue

*The small skiff* was lowered from the stern of *El Paraiso Segundo* with Rodrigo and Gabrielle aboard. As they hit the water, Rodrigo took up the oars and left the mother ship. Watching him row them toward the surf, Gabrielle was reminded of those times when they'd meet on the banks of the Ouse River in Bedfordshire and he'd row her to their isle of love.

But that was a decade and a world away. In Mahé, Rodrigo had assumed the office of governor of Seychelles, and the same day, in a starlit ceremony, taken Gabrielle as his bride. The wedding celebration served as a hearty reunion with all their old friends. Wallace, whom Rodrigo had appointed lieutenant governor, was there, proudly wearing the uniform of his old Scots Guard regiment. Higgins was there with the Kikuyu allies he would soon ferry back to their African homeland. And Jonah Fitch was there, as overcome with emotion as any father of the bride. "It's sure good to have you back, ma'am," he said when she hugged him. "Things have been powerful dull around here without you."

After the festivities, the new governor and Lady Soro spent just enough time on the main island to let the French plantation aristocracy know that the anti-slavery laws would be enforced with unusual vigor. Rodrigo had held an assembly in front of State House in which all of the Seychellois planters—the evil trio of Delon, Montand, and DeVille among them—were ordered to bring their slaves and publicly set them free. The abomination of slavery, he told them in no uncertain terms, was a thing of the past in Seychelles and everywhere else in the world where the Union Jack flew.

And now, Gabrielle looked back at the ship that had carried them to Fregate. At the stern, Cullen leaned over the rail and waved with a happy smile. On the voyage, they'd had many long talks about their amazing journey to this point—a new relationship. It had not been a matter of finding fault, these many shipboard conversations, but of celebrating the possibilities of the human spirit, and recognizing the destructive folly of anyone trying to imprison it with the preconceived expectations of class, nationality, or heredity.

He'd insisted on accompanying them this far, but he was anxious to return to Mahé, where he had a new responsibility waiting for him. They'd decided on the long voyage over that Cullen and Gabrielle would form a partnership and set about restoring Beau Vallon—growing copra instead of cotton, and employing many of their old pirate crew as workers.

Rodrigo enthusiastically supported the idea. "Just because you're my wife doesn't mean you must relinquish your dreams," he'd told her. When she reminded him of what he'd said about the emptiness of those dreams, he said, "But those were based on evil. If you can employ men who are now out of employment because our cause has been attained, it benefits us all. You can divide your time between Mahé and Fregate, just as I will."

As he rowed now, he looked at her and smiled. "Are you ready for a honeymoon?"

She noted the seductive gleam in his eyes and said, "I'm ready for anything my governor may desire."

Honeymoon! The entire voyage here had been like one long honeymoon. And yet the prospect of this afternoon's homecoming in paradise seemed so special and so thrilling that it did, indeed, seem like a whole new beginning.

They were surrounded by the orange-and-lavender glow of the sunset. Looking over his shoulder, she saw the brilliant green of their island, Fregate, glistening in the glorious twilight.

As he rowed harder, positioning the boat to catch a good wave, she was once again uncannily reminded of their secret moonlit rendezvous so many years ago in England.

"What are you thinking?" he asked, pausing as he noted the dreamy look in her eyes.

"I was thinking of that night you left me to come here," she said. "You rowed me that night as well. Do you remember?"

"I remember well. I knew then what you didn't—that it would be our last night together. Perhaps forever."

"We've had our share of last nights together," she pouted.

"That's over." He gestured over his shoulder, toward the waiting island. "At last, we're coming home."

"Home," she repeated, and her lips curved up to mirror his smile.

He leaned over then, abruptly, so it rocked the boat, and gave her a withering kiss. She melted against him, falling slightly forward as he pulled away.

Again remembering that night, she playfully echoed her words of long ago. "Rodrigo, don't leave me now."

Raising a brow, he asked, equally playful, "Do you want me to take you right here, in this boat?"

She laughed. "No, darling. I can wait to reach our island of love."

When they'd finally caught a wave and ridden it to shore, Rodrigo stepped from the boat and, knee-deep in water, hoisted her into his arms. She laughed again as he swung her over the tide and up onto the lustrous white beach. The sand took on the hues of sunset, streaked with pink and orange and a touch of gold, shadowed by the swaying palms.

Setting her on her feet, he quickly beached the boat, then picked her up again and kissed her hard. "Let's go to the house," he said.

He carried her to where the beach met a lawn of new-mowed grass. And beyond it, framed in a grove of sheltering trees, was the house of Rodrigo's youth, a house he hadn't been in for over twenty years, except as an intruder, sneaking up the trellis. Now, together, they could walk in the front door and claim it as their own.

Recalling the other time she had been here, Gabrielle suddenly stiffened in hesitation. Feeling it, he asked, "Is something wrong?"

"I'm not sure."

"What is it, *carícia*? Do you fear painful memories?"

She realized she did. The image of Hastings lying in bed with the slave beneath him stuck in her mind. "Perhaps. There is, after all, an ugly association with what's now to be our bedroom."

He gave her an enigmatic smile. "I believe I've taken care of that."

"Have you?" She sprang up in his arms. "How've you done it?"

"You'll just have to wait and see. Do stop squirming, or I'll be forced to drop you on the lawn."

He carried her to the massive banyan tree. Up close, it was spectacular, with its ancient roots climbing the trunk, the split in the middle forming a natural pathway to the house. "That tree has been here for hundreds of years," he told her. "My grandfather built the house around it."

He carried her through. Then up the steps of the open porch. There, Maya and Kaninu waited with smiles brightening the dark ebony of their faces. "Welcome to your new home, *msabu*." Then to Rodrigo, "Everything is in readiness, *Mkombozi*, just as you requested."

Rodrigo and Kaninu began to speak Swahili and, though Gabrielle couldn't understand what they said, she gathered that something special had been prepared for her. From Maya's giggles, she also gathered that the surprise was somewhat scandalous.

"What have you done?" she asked.

"You'll see."

"Then show me now. I can't wait."

He carried her over the threshold like any bride, then up the bamboo stairs. She caught an impression of open rooms built around the spectacular views. But there would be time to explore her new home later. For now, all she could think of was the surprise.

She couldn't imagine what it might be.

At the door of their bedroom, he paused and gave her a decidedly wicked grin. Kaninu and Maya had followed them up the stairs, whispering. He turned then and, in a mockingly stern voice, ordered them away. They left, but it was clear from their smiling faces that they weren't offended. They kept tossing mischievous glances back her way.

"It isn't much," he warned her. "You won't find doubloons strewn about your bed, or any such pirate nonsense."

She laughed. "I'm the wife of a governor now. I don't associate with pirates!"

He joined in her laughter. "Just don't expect too much."

With a dash, he threw open the door. Then he shifted her in his arms and carried her inside.

Even before he set her down, she gasped her delight. For there, against the back wall, beneath his grandfather's pirate swords, was the massive four-poster bed, blatantly dressed in bright scarlet sheets.

"Rodrigo, you remembered!"

She scrambled from his arms and ran to the bed, digging her hands into the silk of the sheets as she'd once buried them in the silken Seychelle sand. "Oh, they're heavenly. I can't wait to—" She looked up to find him smiling his gratification at her delight.

"An unseemly display from the wife of a governor."

"You haven't begun to see my unseemly display. Take your clothes off."

"Aren't we impatient?"

"I always wanted to see you naked against these scarlet sheets."

He obliged her by undressing, but he was too slow for her tastes. She went to him and ripped the studs from his governor's shirt and yanked the fine broadcloth of his magistrate's pants so they fell in a ball at his feet. Finally he was unclothed, standing before her in all his hard-coiled glory, all gilded and godlike, as if his body had been molded from gold for the express purpose of giving pleasure to her eyes. Looking like the pirate once again.

He flopped back on the bed and she let out a heartfelt sigh. The scarlet silk threw his body into beautiful relief. "I could just stare at you all night."

Outside, the orange glow had receded, and deep violet had taken its place.

"I didn't arrange for this so you could look and not touch," he scolded gently. Then, opening his powerful arms, he beckoned her to the bed.

All hesitation vanished, she padded across the room and took a flying leap, landing on him. His breath left his body as she collided, eliciting the gentle roar of a lion. Seizing her in his arms, he rolled her onto her back and pinned her flat. "I wonder," he growled, "how *you* look naked against scarlet sheets?"

As his hands moved on her clothing, she began to giggle.

"Cracking good fun, is it?" he teased.

"Oh, *cracking!*" she squealed.

But as his knees nudged aside her thighs, her laughter died in her throat. She felt her pulse racing beneath the masterful roving of his hands, the hard insistence of his golden arousal. Awash with joy, she kissed him fiercely, then whispered in his ear, *"Now I have my paradise!"*

# Author's Note

One of the bonuses of being a romance writer is the fun of traveling to the romantic places I write about, to research my books. And surely there is no more romantic and exotic place in all the world than the Seychelle Islands—the world's last true unspoiled paradise. It's nearly Christmas, yet I'm sitting on what has to be the most beautiful lagoon beach on earth, with a palm tree shading me from the blaze of the sun, surrounded by an ocean so deliciously and distinctively green, it looks like a Disney animation. My husband and I are almost completely alone. There are no tourists, no intruders of any kind. The calm and quiet lull me, as does the soothing warmth. As I write this, my husband is dribbling heated sand all along my legs—the famous Seychelle granitic sand that's so exquisitely soft and sensual, words can't do it justice. In the distance are crumbling pirate ruins. There are so few reminders of the modern world anywhere on these islands that it's easy to see Gabrielle and Rodrigo frolicking on the beach and cavorting in caves.

Like Gabrielle, I believe in the spirit of places. Place is a more important element in this book than in any I've written before. I was reborn in the savannas of Africa, and nurtured in the gentle tides of the Indian Ocean. I can only hope I've been able to evoke its incomparable magic. I wish each and every one of you may experience this enchantment once in your life. And if you go, take a moment, please, to wish me back there once again.

Thanks to: Beth de Guzman in appreciation for her unflagging support of the book; my incomparable agent, Meg Ruley; Nita Taublib, whip-cracker extraordinaire, which I say with affection and respect; Kathe Robin, for her continuing support of my books; the readers who have sent such wonderful and supportive letters, every one of which I cherish, and which I apologize for taking so long to answer; the regulars: Barbara, Mary, Katie, and Chiara; Michael and Janet Kalm, who became our fellow adventurers in Africa and Seychelles and who can share our safari van anytime; Jill Vanderhoof for the great company and inspiration; Jayne Anne Krentz for all her support and helpful advice; Coral-Mary Namisnak, for her generosity in allowing me to use Gabrielle's name; Susan Kelleher, the world's best travel agent, who suggested Seychelles in the first place and found us the trip of a lifetime; my daughter Janie, who was brave enough to spend a year in France, and whose growth and maturity has made me proud; The One who can't be named, for everything I have and all that I am; and finally Bill, who has shared the experience of this book with me in every way, and without whom I never would have survived it.

Cape Severe
LA DIGUE, SEYCHELLES

## ABOUT THE AUTHOR

KATHERINE O'NEAL is the daughter of a U.S. Air Force pilot and a fiercely British artist who met in India in the fifties. The family traveled extensively and lived for many years in Asia. Katherine is married to William Arnold, a noted film critic and author of the bestselling books *Shadowland* and *China Gate*—a man she feels makes her heroes pale in comparison. It was he who said, "You're a romantic person; why *not* write romantic fiction?" Together, they continue the tradition of travel whenever possible. They also enjoy their dogs, horses, and each other— not necessarily in that order. They have a daughter, Janie, who recently returned to them after a year as an exchange student. They currently live in Seattle, Washington, where Katherine is finishing her fourth novel.

Katherine loves to hear from readers.
Please write to her at:
P.O. Box 2452
Seattle, WA 98111-2452
and enclose a self-addressed stamped envelope for a response and news of forthcoming books.

# DON'T MISS THESE FABULOUS
# BANTAM WOMEN'S FICTION TITLES

# DON'T MISS THESE FABULOUS
# BANTAM WOMEN'S FICTION TITLES

# *Bestselling Historical Women's Fiction*

**AMANDA QUICK**

| | | |
|---|---|---|
| ____28354-5 | SEDUCTION | .....$6.50/$8.99 in Canada |
| ____28932-2 | SCANDAL | .................$5.99/$6.99 |
| ____28594-7 | SURRENDER | ............$6.50/$8.99 |
| ____29325-7 | RENDEZVOUS | ...........$5.99/$6.99 |
| ____29315-X | RECKLESS | .............$6.50/$8.99 |
| ____29316-8 | RAVISHED | ..............$6.50/$8.99 |
| ____29317-6 | DANGEROUS | ...........$6.50/$8.99 |
| ____56506-0 | DECEPTION | ...........$5.99/$7.50 |
| ____56153-7 | DESIRE | .................$6.50/$8.99 |
| ____56940-6 | MISTRESS | .............$5.99/$7.99 |
| ____09698-2 | MYSTIQUE | ............$21.95/$24.95 |

**IRIS JOHANSEN**

| | | |
|---|---|---|
| ____29871-2 | LAST BRIDGE HOME | ......$4.50/$5.50 |
| ____29604-3 | THE GOLDEN BARBARIAN | ...$4.99/$5.99 |
| ____29244-7 | REAP THE WIND | .........$5.99/$7.50 |
| ____29032-0 | STORM WINDS | ...........$4.99/$5.99 |
| ____28855-5 | THE WIND DANCER | .......$5.99/$6.99 |
| ____29968-9 | THE TIGER PRINCE | .......$5.99/$6.99 |
| ____29944-1 | THE MAGNIFICENT ROGUE | .$5.99/$6.99 |
| ____29945-X | BELOVED SCOUNDREL | .....$5.99/$6.99 |
| ____29946-8 | MIDNIGHT WARRIOR | ......$5.99/$6.99 |
| ____29947-6 | DARK RIDER | ............$5.99/$7.99 |

**TERESA MEDEIROS**

| | | |
|---|---|---|
| ____29407-5 | HEATHER AND VELVET | ....$5.99/$7.50 |
| ____29409-1 | ONCE AN ANGEL | ........$5.99/$7.99 |
| ____29408-3 | A WHISPER OF ROSES | .....$5.50/$6.50 |
| ____56332-7 | THIEF OF HEARTS | ........$5.50/$6.99 |
| ____56333-5 | FAIREST OF THEM ALL | ....$5.99/$7.50 |

- - - - - - - - - - - - - - - - - - - - - - - -

**Ask for these books at your local bookstore or use this page to order.**

Please send me the books I have checked above. I am enclosing $_____ (add $2.50 to cover postage and handling). Send check or money order, no cash or C.O.D.'s, please.

Name _____

Address _____

City/State/Zip _____

Send order to: Bantam Books, Dept. FN 16, 2451 S. Wolf Rd., Des Plaines, IL 60018

Allow four to six weeks for delivery.

Prices and availability subject to change without notice.          FN 16 3/96